To all the people who work on the small things which support the **big** things.

We always acknowledge our entertainers. They are contagious, but take us away from the hindrance of our day, which is why it's not easy to become an Icon.

To the loyal troops. Omitting Washington's politics.

You continue to move without hesitation.

You are priceless.

Respect.

WZ
widezike.com

This story was a thrill to write. It's my first and I am already working on the second part of it.

I will have some "Unedited" scenes posted on my website and blog. Be sure to check them out. Feel free to contact me directly, I will try my best to get back to you.

Book Website - www.homesequel.com

Brandon's Web Home - www.imawynna.com

Twitter: www.twitter.com/christianwynn

Facebook: www.facebook.com/imawynna

HOME?

WideZike : WZ Words : 1679 S. Dupont AveDover, De 19901

First Printing, 2013

Ordering Information:Bulk sales. Special discounts are available on quantity purchases by corporations, associations, and others. For details, contact the publisher at the address above.Orders by U.S. trade bookstores and wholesalers. Please contact WZ Words: Tel: (310) 359-8421 or visit www.homesequel.com.

Printed in the United States of America

ISBN-13: 978-0615893587

www.homesequel.com

We've been through pain, struggle, and confusion. Broke to the fullest, but still moved near the richest. In a town where colored people were once not allowed. It gave me the diversity which made me a natural hybrid. It's a gift that can't be bought. A gift which many others had to make our country, yet alone this world a better place.

I wondered...

Why did I title this story HOME?

The last time I visited home, I was with Jamelle and Christina. We made a left turn, and I looked up at our street sign. I then saw the street sign where I grew up.

You sacrificed to make me a better man.

#Weird

Kautious Fred will say;

Momma Wynn

Motivation is a mind feature that arouses an organism to action toward a desired goal and elicits, controls, and sustains certain goal directed behaviors.

- CD

HOME?

Brandon Wynn

WZ

1

ABX-1

Terry Love, one of the fighter pilots for Paragon's AX-1 Fighter Squadron is currently conducting one of his daily duties. Patrolling the airspace at 20,000 feet in the sky. He's trying to let time fly, while listening to Top Forty music hits through his headphones. Since the air patrol rotation varies from 2-4 hours at a time, he's lazily browsing his smart phone. Swiping through photos of his next vacation destination once the Squadron completes a mandatory training mission next week.

It is a partly overcast day just off the coast of Paragon. If a citizen looked up in the sky, they may see Terry circling. At a glance, they would see it and think it is as small and insignificant as an ant. However, if one were next to the aircraft, one would realize it's not that small, nor that quiet. One would understand the aircraft's virility, and why it was chosen to be one of the aircraft to defend the world's newest civilization against money hungry, resource-seeking enemies.

Terry is one of the guardians. The custodians of the sky. The protector of the people who sacrificed much to live in the land of opportunity, happiness, and thrive. Paragon is the land of the go-getters, the ambitious, and respecters of Mother Nature. Well, that describes most people; some people squeeze in the gaps and claim that they love nature during their citizenship interview process.

Looking at his phone, while the fighter jet circles on autopilot, Terry's timer goes off. The alarm signals that his two and half hour rotation is over. He looks out of both sides of the canopy window as if he is looking for something. A few seconds later, he looks again. Waiting on his relief. Terry takes a deep breath, shrugs his shoulders, and begins to look at more photos on his phone. Moments later, Chris, one of the reserve pilots from the BX-1 Squadron, pulls to the right of Terry. Terry doesn't initially see him, so Chris gracefully rolls his plane over the top of him. Terry looks up and recognizes the BX-1 label on the tail of the plane. Chris has his attention.

Chris (with a grin on his face)

"You can stay up here if you want. I've been next to you for about 10 seconds. You didn't see me?"

Terry (calmly without looking at him)

"You're late."

Terry (yawning)

"Anyway. After a few months of circling around this small nation every day, you would understand. I saw you on the radar though."

Chris

"Yo, do you see all those people on the beach? I know it's Friday, but goodness. Don't people have to work? It's just 2 pm."

Chris just moved to Paragon. He isn't too used to the culture just yet. Terry looks out his window, slightly banks the plane so he can get a good eye view of the Seren Beach.

Terry

"Damn, it is thick down there. You're right. They do that once a month. Some group started it. They created a way for corporate executives to approve of their workers to have Friday beach day, once a month. They leave work early. Play volleyball, have food, and the whole nine."

Chris

"Sweet! Looks like I'll be watching it from up here. Unfortunately, the chicks look like bugs."

Terry (laughing)

"Use your eye scope and zoom in. If you see a girl that you like, text me. I'll put a word in for you. But until then, young buck."

Terry presses his radio frequency to speak to the fighter command center

Terry

"Base. X-Rabbit is out. Warmblood has relieved me. 12:06."

Terry makes a swift bank to the right. He is a Cowboy in the sky.

Although Chris might not do it, if he really wanted to, he could zoom in with his eye scope that's in his visor (heads-up display), look for a cutie pie on the beach, then text Terry or one of the guys to try to get her contact for him. Some of the guys like to get corny and say that they are in AX1 Squadron. Then they point out one of the fighter jets that are high up in the sky, and tell the girls that's what they do. Most of the ladies don't believe them initially.

However, when the young pilots show the AX-1 tattoo on their left wrist, the girls change their minds. Some of them even ask if they can get a joyride in one of the aircraft.

Terry zooms off into the sky and heads towards base. He's flies like a young cowboy, always pushing the throttle to the maximum. Terry flies his aircraft very hard, there is never a slight turn with him. Most of it is because he is young, but he is also a speed freak, especially when he drives.
Unfortunately, he doesn't drive much in Paragon, so he gets all of his speed devils out of him when he flies.
Nevertheless, while Terry is heading to the base and Chris takes over the air patrol, the squadron leader Abe is in his own situation.

City Lights

It's night time: Friday: Modern City of Paragon: Traffic Jam

> Abe

"Base, I think the target is down. Any sign of heat on the thermal imagery? He should be just south of where I am now."

Abe is indecisive, not knowing if his missile hit the enemy aircraft. Abe seeks guidance from his radar controller. A middle eastern voice comes over the radio.

> Radar Control (Arab Voice)

"Squid, I believe he is still out there. I can't detect him on our screen, but stay cautious."

In the cockpit of an F-22 fighter jet, Abe is moving swiftly over one of the interstate highways of Paragon. Flying low. No more than 30 feet above ground and at 350 knots (400 miles per hour), the lights and paint stripes on the roads look as if they are one, an amalgam of color and phosphoresces. Inside the cockpit, it's a smooth ride. Outside of the cockpit, is a thundering, squealing engine, and winds stronger than a tornado. The signs on the interstate and water billboards come out of nowhere. It takes a skilled pilot, with advanced training to be able to maneuver a plane low to the ground.

Abe busts one quick turn, dodging a bridge. Scaring drivers on the highway. This isn't normal procedure in your typical country, but since Paragon is fairly new and the roads aren't heavily occupied. The fighter pilots can cruise 15 - 30 feet above the streets almost as if they are cars. It's almost like a super-powered flying sports car. Not safe, but their Captain always tells them,

"If you can't hug an expressway, you can't dodge a missile."

Abe's cockpit display is fully illuminated. It has green and blue lights near the buttons. The small screens are mini computers that have many letters. These are codes that inform Abe how fast he is going, how much fuel he has left, how high he is flying, and how high the oil levels are, the list goes on. The screens also turn into a camera monitor so Abe can see the action from multiple sides of the plane, without having to look out of the window although he prefers to use the window. Relying on too many computers is not good for any pilot. Because when the system has a glitch or fails, they have to know how to handle the situation.

The computerized voice within the plane's system turns on.

Cockpit Voice (Woman Computer Sound)

"Warning, Abe, you're 15 feet above land level. You're 15 feet above land level. Do you copy? If not, I will repe-"

Before the computer voice says that it will "repeat itself", Abe hits a switch on the flight panel that inscribes, "Land Mode". Which cuts the warning system off; therefore Abe can glide as close as he wants to the ground without hearing anything. But it is also a system that has its GPS navigation configured with the plane to assist him in dodging hard objects and buildings. This navigation is giving the pilots more control when flying in the metropolitan area, around the mega skyscrapers and buildings, and sometimes just missing people and cars.

The system is built to help pilots be aware that they are not far from the ground. Traditionally, flying this close down is frowned upon, but this is a practice that the Squadrons' Captain trains them to do. This training is his "Know the Roads" theory. It increases his pilot's awareness simply because there are too many obstructions to dodge in the city, and if all hell ever broke loose, the pilots need to be able to use as many buildings, structures, electrical wires as they can for a defense.

On the other side of the flight panel, are Abe's radars. They give him the ability to track other aircrafts and missiles that are in the sky. They don't play a factor when the other aircraft is a stealth aircraft which can't be detected on the radar. This is the type of aircraft that Abe is going against at the moment, though he doesn't have a sighting on him.

Abe

"Sir, wherever you are and if you can hear me, I am politely advising you to surrender."

Abe plays with his flight controls to see if he can pick up some sort of frequency of the other pilot. A few seconds go by.

Enemy Fighter Pilot (disregarding Abe)

"I hope you know that I am locked on to you. I should be telling you to surrender. The colder the air the slower you…"

Abe (interrupting)

"Fall into my trap."

Abe turns the F-22 fighter jet to the right and swings it under a bridge in the City of Paragon, missing it by inches. He glides the plane 25 feet above Interstate 191, barely clipping the cars that are on the road. The roar from the jet engines sounds like a bomb going off, especially at 800 miles per hour, with a near death maneuver. The enemy fighter pilot roars behind him with the same type of aircraft, which you can see has an unidentifiable flag on the tail as it flies by. The two pilots are fierce with their flying. It's 10 pm, and the streets of Paragon are filled with cars and the untraditional dogfight that is going on. Many cars stop abruptly as the jets pass by. Cars are rear-ending each other. People are frantic, but by the time the people look up, the aircraft has left them nothing but a trail blaze of fire, a little smoke, and a good popping of the ear.

Fires are erupting from a few of the cars that collided. Some passengers die instantly. Other vehicle operators are hopping out of their vehicles to assist with the wounded. Some pull out fire extinguishers, from their trunks - which slow down the buildup of the fires before the cars blow up. Unfortunately, the extinguishers are only large enough to knock out a very small fire, but at this point, anything helps.

Cosmopolitans of Paragon are pressing the red emergency buttons in their vehicles to inform the authorities of what's going on. Others are calling via their mobile phones. Then, there are the people who prefer to take a photo, not thinking of the danger that they are truly in.

Looking into the sky as the two pilots chase each other down, one of them (Abe) is not only dodging the other fighter pilot, but he is also dodging missiles from higher drones which have a lock on him.

It's a dangerously attractive sight. The after - burning fire of the jets and missiles put out a multicolored blue and orange color. It seems like shots of fireworks are horizontally flying around the purplish-hued sky. As people watch the beautiful abstract views of the aircraft fly through the city, there is still much wonder in air.

A husband and wife, sitting in their car look up and see the colored streaks in the sky.

Husband (looking into the sky)

"What the? What is that?"

Wife

"I don't know. Maybe it's a shooting star."

Husband

"No. That's not a shooting star. It looks like those fighter jets are racing again. I forgot to tell you about the night time air and water shows that we have a few times a year. Let's watch."

He pulls the car over, excited to see the aircraft in action. His wife on the other hand is very skeptical because she sees more than the two planes in the sky. She also sees the active missiles.

Wife (worried look)

"Honey, I don't know. This looks serious to me. I don't think they are playing around."

They look out of their window and see a chubby man with his camera out, as he is taking pictures.

Chubby Citizen (taking photos)

"This is the best of the best. Ha-ha! Whew! I never seen them go that fast, must be new aircraft or something."

Wife

"No! That's not training! They are engaging! They are in full thrust!"

As they watch, they realize that they hear silent roars slowly build up. Before they even hear the aircraft, Abe blows right past them. Sixty feet of carbon metal zoomed by so fast, that all one can see are the lights blinking on wings on one of the aircraft from a distance.

Wife

"You see, they are gunning each other down, this is real!"

She looks at him. The husband squints his eyes to get a better look.

Husband (yelling)

"You're right! This isn't a show! Honey! Honey! Press the E-button on your phone!"

His wife presses the emergency button on her phone to notify authorities. Her attempt fails, and then he tries again. The phone is stating: Service is unavailable right now. Find a safe place until notified. In the meantime, the chubby and curious citizen is smiling as he tries to take a photo.

Many people are frantic, more are nervous. The folks that can't get good view of the jets because they are moving too fast are calling 911 to report the crazy sounds. Others, like the curious citizen, are taking photos, so they can sell or save the image for themselves. Police are in the streets telling folks to hide for cover. Although in the back of their minds, the officers know that these aircraft have sufficient arsenals to blow up thousands of feet of land in one-second.

Abe is still being chased down by a pilot of another Air Force. They are squeezing tight turns in the city, rolling around skyscrapers; windows are breaking on many of the floors of the buildings due to the overwhelming noise of the engines. They are stealth also, which means they can't be detected on radar. This makes it hard for Abe's command to give him a location of his follower.

Abe loses the enemy for a few seconds. They are both talking on the radio frequency, which is abnormal for enemy pilots - with huge egos.

Abe (over the radio in his jet)

"Radar, I believe that hawk ran out of fuel."

Radar Controller (Arab Accent)

"Squid, I'm not sure sir. Keep your eyes out. The Amass breach is going in and out; therefore we can't detect any..."

The Amass breaching system helps pilots detect stealth aircraft, which is what the enemy fighter is flying.

The loud noise of a missile comes straight towards Abe's plane.

Radar Controller

"Squid, are you okay?"

Abe

"Affirm, I guess we can't detect his stealth. I'm just going to go manual. I can't depend on this system; it's too unreliable. It's slowing me down."

Abe turns his Amass radar off of his aircraft, and turns the jet only to see a missile hover right over the glass of his cockpit. With sweat rolling down his head and eyes, the heat has turned up for Abe. During this mission, everybody else has been shot down by the enemy bird. Abe is the only hope for the forces' survival at the moment. The majority of this place called home is watching Abe in the sky.

Abe

"Radar, what's the weather at the moment. I'm at sonic speeds, and I don't want to take my eyes off the road."

Radar (Arab accent)

"Moderate, no humidity. No hot pockets detected."

Abe

"How is the wind looking?"

Radar

"350 at 20. Strong gust."

The wind is blowing north at 20 miles per hour.

As he dodges one missile, then another, he sees and smells a trail of smoke, which gives him the idea that his rival has come past him. He thinks to himself.

"Perfect. I'm going to go vertical. He isn't going to fly into the wind because he's low on fuel. I'm going to vert down and light him up with the extra speed."

Abe flies up vertically, straight in the air. Abe levels the plane out and goes straight down, almost like a roller coaster. He eyes the enemy aircraft who thinks that he shot Abe down. As Abe eyes him like a lioness on her prey, he guns the engines at full throttle using his left hand to push the throttle forward. The engines respond to their captain.

Enemy Pilot

"Hmm. Well, it looks…"

Abe (aims his jet directly to the enemy)

"Like you should look up."

Before the enemy pilot can look up, BOOM! All black shows in his eyes, Abe's eyes also! It's an unfortunate ending for both pilots.

Captain James O'Donnell (cutting off the Simulator)

"Okay, ladies, enough fun and games."

Abe and Rory take off their helmets, and crawl out of the simulator (RESNA) to see what just happened to their game of dogfighting in the city.

Abe (pulls his simulator helmet off his head)

"Capt. What the? That was date night money; I had him."

Rory (the enemy pilot in the game)

"Right, that was throw away money."

Abe snaps his neck as he looks back at Rory, one of his wingmen. But in the game he was Abe's enemy.

Abe

"Rory! Seriously? Did you not notice that I cleared you out?"

Rory (scratching his head)

"I don't see a score or a name of the winner on the screen. Do you?"

Abe looks at him, knowing that he had the final strike on him before Captain O'Donnell pulled the plug to the simulator that the whole crew uses to train. Although at times, during down moments they tend to play cops and robbers (fighter jet style) with the high tech program which simulates any combat mode that you set it up for, the system not only gives you an awesome experience but it incorporates real life situations, every possible structure, street, interstate, car, and even how people will react. The RESNA has air pressure and temperature setting so you can get the full effect as if you were flying a fighter jet. If you make a turn too steep and you haven't squeezed your legs tight enough, the system will declare you dead. In reality, if you're making heavy G maneuvers in a fighter jet, you need to be able to control how much blood flows from your head. One way to manage that blood flow is by squeezing your legs. If you don't control it, there is a good chance that you will pass out. This is good practice for the pilots, but the only difference is that in real life, you don't get many second chances once you pass out in a fighter jet.

The guys like to use the RESNA for fun when they aren't training. Mostly because it helps them practice maneuvers for when they horse around in the streets every now and then. O'Donnell doesn't like it by any means, but he has to accept it because it's part of the ABX Squadron's training. In case there is an invasion, they will have a core advantage of knowing the ins and outs of the city, in the aircraft.

When the pilots fly in the streets in real life, it frightens the hell out of most people; many people do love to witness fighter jets with their blazing afterburners at night doing twist and turns in the city. It is amazing to watch them fly swiftly 30 feet above the streets. But as the old saying goes, "Many things are fun, until somebody gets hurt." In this case, hundreds could get hurt, but the guys do it anyway.

Capt. O'Donnell

"We have our Scramble runs this week. I know you want to have fun, and I'm sure it can get boring here on base all day with the small number of missions that we have taken. BUT, I am going to need you guys to be focused as this is the real deal. You guys did amazing last month, but we need to better our times. Over west, they have been really on my butt. They are trying to degrade our aircraft. We can't miss any steps. No close calls, no aborts, nothing."

In the room of about 30, the squadron are all attentive. They are wearing their traditional fighter pilot / military pilot jumpsuits blue with light blue trimming. There are about 7 women in the unit, and the rest are 40 males. Most of them are young, but there are few men that are growing in some grey. Terry Love walks in right when Captain starts to speak.

Capt. O

"I don't want any hogging around this week."

Captain pauses and looks at Abe, then over to Terry Love.

Capt O

"We need to stay focused, and treat these missions as if they are real attacks, otherwise we all will be going back home wherever you are from. Is that clear?"

The squadron says "Sir" at the same time.

Capt. O

"I'm not trying to go home, not anytime soon, at least. You know how they look at you guys, so you need to be way above par. We aren't birdies, eagles, or double eagles."

Captain O'Donnell pushes his finger on a blackboard and begins to write words with his finger tip on the board. The words illuminate in a greenish glow on the dark color. He inscribes on the digital chalkboard.

We are a WHOLE in ONE. Not a hole in one. A Whole In ONE.

Capt O

"Are there any questions?"

Terry Love (whispering)

"What if we are timed out?"

Capt. O

"Timed out? Love - you better get some protons in your system."

Capt O

"Any real questions?"

Nobody responds.

Capt O

"Goodnight ladies and gentlemen. Rest up. Love, welcome to the real squad. If you want to think about time-outs, then you're in the wrong league. We go; we go, and we go. So always be ready. Grow some chest hair, son; you're with the big leagues now."

The captain walks out of the room.

Rory

"Terry. Some questions need to go unsaid. It shows weakness."

Terry Love

"Who are you to tell me what to do?"

Younger than Rory, Love is getting his second chance at flying as in training, he crashed two aircraft. His abilities are amazing, but he'll only be an amazing pilot if he can get through his stubbornness. He is in the best physical shape of the squadron, but his attitude and immature personality are what gets him into trouble.

Rory (walking into Terry's face)

"Look, kid. I don't know who you think you are. But you need to recognize deference, humility, and respect in this squad. We don't roll like that. This is no joke!"

Abe cuts in between the two, looks at Rory and walks Terry Love away.

Abe

"Love, Love, Love, Love, Lovvvveeee. Terry Love you can't do that, bro. It's only week five since you been here. Just week five."

Terry

"But still, no man should talk to me like that."

Terry looks over Abe's shoulder and eyes Rory down. Rory notices but ignores and begins to take his shirt off.

Abe

"Terry, trust me, I understand. But you're taking it the wrong way. Rory is just like you; he's a hothead. He is right, though. Some things need to go unsaid. You don't ask about timing-out during a scramble mission or briefing. You don't get tired. In this squadron, we fly until we can't keep your eyes open. But even then, you pop a Go pill, and you add some pounds to the plane and go."

Adding pounds to the plane merely means fuel up. A Go pill is simply a pill which gives pilots the energy to fly longer missions without getting sleepy.

Abe

"Just be easy. Trust me; if he didn't like you he wouldn't say anything. There are only a few slots available in this squadron, and you can be replaced. You already know that we are at a slight disadvantage anyway. There aren't too many guys fond of having a diverse Air squadron - pilot wise, especially on the Olympia side. Maybe ramp guys, but..... not pilots. So lead as an example, a good example. Don't be an example of what not to do or be. Be a benchmark, young T!"

Abe hits Terry's chest softly. Terry takes a deep breath and looks to the side. His young mind makes him very stubborn, but a part of that was being raised in a hostile neighborhood.

Abe

"The only enemy we have is, well, the enemy. I'm not your enemy; I'm not your friend. I'm your battalion brother. Rory's also. You need to say something to him before you leave. Not to kiss his ass, but to squash the baloney. We have too much on our hands to worry about this. We have call ball approaches next week, vertigo tests. Trust me; you will have a headache from that, so try to enjoy the cool mind right now. After the scramble we should go up and work on some Thrust Vectoring and Precision Approaches. It's a bit different from the 18 to the 22."

As Abe walks away, Terry's mind is saying "Fight Rory - Fight Rory" especially because Rory is the only one who bothers him. Rory is also the only one who tries to defend him when things aren't in his favor. Mostly because Terry reminds Rory of himself when he was 23. Terry takes it in a way where it's an attack, but if anything it is Rory looking out for him, not having it out for him.

Ext. Hangar. Abe sitting next to F-22 jet. Dawn

A few hours pass by as the sun slowly sets. Abe is sitting next to his fighter jet, wiping her down clean. On the side it says in bold Arial letters: Squid 2013 AD: Leah. Squid for his call sign, 2013 Leah because that's the year that his mother passed away in a bombing in Paragon. Leah is the name he knows her by.

Captain O'Donnell (from behind the plane)

"You know somebody can file a grievance for that."

Abe (folding a grey rag in his hand)

"I wouldn't be surprised. But you know this is my baby."

Capt. O

"Yeah, I remember when I used to wipe my first one down all the time. I mean, all the time. Then, she went down. Eventually, they just become another machine. There's still nothing like your first bird."

Abe is still wiping the plane down, getting small bug marks off of the nose.

Capt. O'Donnell

"You know there's going to be a million bugs on there the next time you go up."

Abe

"Yes. Captain. Yes, I know."

Abe looks at him.

Abe

"Can I have this panel painted? I need your approval."

Capt. O

"We need to check with engineering. I doubt they will allow it. These things are so sensitive to weight, since they are stealth. Even a strip of paint can affect the whole engineering of the plane. Anyway, son, get some rest. You got a big day tomorrow."

O'Donnell pats Abe on his back then walks away, holding his laptop bag.

While Abe is cleaning off the small bugs from his aircraft, he hears the roar of a fighter taxiing towards the hanger. He looks and squints his eyes, so he can see the logo of the tail. He sees the BX-1 logo on it, as it pulls closer to him.

The plane makes a quick 360 degree turn, which blows Abe's bucket and towels an easy 30 feet away from him.

Abe (speaking to himself)

"Dammit."

It's not a good feeling, although the other jet is under very low power. The engine can still produce enough wind to blow many things over.

Abe feels the heat on his face.

The Air Support personnel guide the plane into its appropriate part of the hangar and the plane is turned off. The canopy lifts up and the pilot takes his helmet off. Abe looks up and sees Chris saluting the air support group that makes sure the plane is secure and a post mission inspection is complete. He grabs a bottle of water and walks over to Abe.

He's wearing his full flight suit, a black base with green tint to it. Chris folds his mission papers up, and puts them in the front slot of his pants. He stands next to Abe.

Abe (wiping the bottom of the plane)

"I can see you still working on handling that nose wheel."

Chris

"Yeah, it's a headache. Why did I get you?"

Abe looks at the other side of the hangar, hinting to Chris that he blew all of his items away from him when he made the turn.

Chris

"Oh...Sorry, man."

Abe

"It's all good. It's not like you blazed me. Plus, it's nothing like feeling the heat of a little jet blast every now and then."

Chris

"I'm not a big fan of the heat, but the fumes aren't replicable though."

Abe

"How's your first week going?"

Chris

"It's cool. Although it can get pretty boring doing slow circles up there,   I enjoy it. This is a cool unit. I'm happy to be in the reserves, my brother."

Abe shakes his head while he continues to wipe off his plane.

Chris

"Any reason why you're scrubbing the plane down? Don't they have people for that?"

Abe

"Yep, but she is my bird. I take care of her, she takes care of me. You know? Kinda like a woman. Well, the right woman."

With a rag in Abe's right hand, he looks up at Chris.

Chris

"I hear you. What time you getting out of here?"

Abe

"I'm about to finish up now. I got some studying to do tonight, for Red Ice. Where are you staying? Sector A?"

Chris

"Yeah, with all the newbie's."

Abe

"Hey man, that's where all the chicks are. It's just like the first day of college, isn't it? Every quarter, there is a new wave of chicks from 20's and up. Trust me, sir, you're in the right place."

Chris is new, and all new citizens of Paragon stay in Sector A for their first year in the country. This decision was made so new residents can get acclimated with living in a new country. Plus it gives others the chance to meet people with like minds, most of them being the type who made the sacrifice to move across the Earth for the unique opportunity.

Sector A has everything that the pilots needed to live. It's not necessarily like a college dorm room, but it works because people don't have to travel far for shopping malls, grocery stores, or electronics. It is near the heart of the downtown capital of Paragon, Devon. All of the guys like to hang out there because they know that there is going to be new fish in town. Mostly, the town is full of people who have accepted a job role, and most of the job roles are advanced in the country from Architecture, Engineering, and Computing. Most of the people that move to Paragon are single, so it makes it a perfect place for Singleville.

Abe

"As a matter a fact, you can ride with me."

He looks at his phone.

Abe

"Meet me at the Pod Station in about 15?"

The pods are a way of getting around town in Paragon. It's an alternate way of driving. A lot faster, and in its own way – a lot better.

Chris

"Sure, I may need a few more minutes. I need to shower. It was hot up there today."

Abe

"Oh yeah, I forgot you did patrol. I remember those days. Okay, cool; 20 minutes or so."

Patrol is usually for newer guys in the squadron. The only time Abe or any of the AX-1 members have to do it is if somebody calls out, or is ill. Patrol is used for building flight hours, along with protecting Paragon. It helps the pilots learn more about the airways of the country. By flying most of the day, that's Captain O'Donnell's recipe for defense "know where you are. Knowing your land will save you from life and death. Not just for yourself. But for all the people who are relying on you guys for safety and protection for the sacrifice that they made to move here."

Once Chris is done washing up, Abe is waiting for him outside of the ABX Locker room. He is watching television and the World Basketball Finals. Chris signals to him that he is ready. Abe looks at his phone, presses a button and they begin to walk towards the exit of the base area. Channing, another member of the BX-1, walks past. She handles many of the communication systems and radars for all the aircraft.

Abe

"Hey, Chan."

She walks passed both of them without saying a word. Once she leaves the room, Chris speaks up.

Chris

"I don't think she likes me."

Abe (chuckles)

"Why?"

Chris

"I don't know. The other day my weight and balance system kept going out in my aircraft; I think she thought I was the one messing it up."

Abe

"Yeah, she can get bossy like that. She will open up. Just talk to her a bit, she will open up. You trying to tap that?"

24

Chris (laughs)

"No, man. She's cute and all. Not my type though. I just think she doesn't like me."

Abe

"You're good. Plus you have to earn some respect. You're a newbie. Once you show 'em what you are made of, you will be another warrior in the sky. Which you are already."

Abe has an ego that frustrates many, but he is still a team player. He is humble, just like his father when it comes down to real life things.

As they enter a new room, the room lights up and something directs, "Private Pod - Paragon Officials - Next Left." The dark rooms light up as the two walk through the room. A pod pulls up insisting on entering a code. Abe puts his phone next to it. They get inside. It then responds. "Hi Abe, where can I take you? Home? Baba? Are you in the mood for a salad?"

Abe

"Sure, a salad will be swell."

Computerized Pod Voice

"I see you have a guest. Chris is who I detect."

Abe

"Yup, that's him. Let's get rolling though."

CPU Pod Voice

"Sure. One mile before most restaurants, the logo will appear on the window. Let me know if you need me to stop. Until then, as you are government approved, we will be going 25% faster than normal on special track 5."

Special Track 5 is the track where only government officials or high ranking officers can travel on. Most of this is because there could be an emergency, but it is also a perk because they can go faster than other pods, though the pods already go fast enough.

Abe hits the mute button on the pod. He looks at Chris

Abe

"It's cool at first. But after hearing that voice she gets annoying."

They laugh.

The pod begins to move. Chris is looking around, still being new to the land. He looks out of the tinted windows and checks out the bioluminescent trees of Paragon; he's amazed how they light the edges of the streets. Some are purple, some are green. The trees are significant in Paragon; they are one of the first things that people talk about when they visit, and the last thing that's forgotten.

The pod is very comfortable. The seats are plush and made with strong fiber. It is clean. It doesn't have gum on the floors like typical public transportation. The monitor that is built-in on the windows feature different types of music that you can listen to, and since Abe has a travel account with the Pod service, the system already knows what genres he prefers. They have movies also. The pod goes about 60 miles per hour, and is smooth. It isn't rare for a person to wake up with saliva on their cheek once they arrive at their destination.

Though there are cars on the street in Paragon, the pods make traveling smoother, efficient, and in a way more convenient. Although people love their independence of their personal vehicles, the pod still gives the same effect. It virtually goes anywhere in town, with tracks above the streets to underground. Most restaurants and stores have a track that accepts the pods. It's simple; they pull over and allow a person to stop and get something to eat or tools to fix something in their house. It's still a fairly new system. It has its kinks and glitches every now and then. But the citizens are satisfied. The pilots also love it because they can stretch their legs out without worrying about pushing pedals and weaving through traffic after being stuck in a cockpit for hours at a time.

Chris

"So, how you like it over here?"

Abe

"It's cool. It works. Been here most of my life. I guess you can say it's cool to watch everything grow."

Chris

"All of your life? They just started accepting people a few years ago."

Abe

"I split much my youth in between here, Olympia, and Europa. I moved back permanently about 4 years ago. But my dad has been here forever, so in a way I feel like I never left. Even when I was in Olympia, I kept up with everything that was occurring over here. I would have never imagined this, though."

Chris

"Wait, your dad is? Your dad is? Ha. Knock, knock."

(He softly knocks on his own head).

Chris

"Dalton. Charles Dalton. That's your last name. I would have never known for him to be your dad. So that's how you got the -."

Abe looks at him, as he knows what Chris is going to say.

ABE

"Ha, everybody thinks that. Don't go there. He didn't even want me to be a pilot. I started flying in Olympia, bro."

Chris

"Oh, okay. Then you moved back here?"

Abe

"Long story, but I'm thankful though. Glad we got the F-22s. They are dope, aren't they?"

Chris

"Man. Tell me about it. I would have never gotten a slot back at home. I can't even believe that I got this one."

Abe

"Well, believe it. When we reviewed the applicants for the position, we considered everything. You definitely had highest test scores. You were in the top 2 percent of the 100 who applied. Even then, what made you really stand out was that you went through some trials growing up. I don't want to bring it up but, you were raised in the 'hood, with a single mom, a sister who was murdered, and yet you still strived for it all and made it. You deserved it. Not taking anything away from anybody else, but you went through a little more than somebody who had a silver spoon, like me. Although I went through my own trials, I had access to planes all my life. It wasn't an issue for me to pay for flight time. I never had to deal with gangbangers, nor did I have to worry if I turned the wrong corner or said the wrong thing to somebody and my life would be taken. We wanted you. You deserved the opportunity. If you went through that, you can go through anything."

Chris looks at Abe. You can see the memory of pain in his eyes, but also see the joy of being where he is.

Chris

"Silver spoon or plastic spoon. Pain is pain. Hard times are hard times. I hear you. Thanks. Whatever I can do to show my appreciation for being over here, I'll do. I just hope my work shows that."

They shake hands.

As they pull up, the pod CPU voice speaks. Chris looks out the window.

CPU Pod Voice

"Pulling up to Nate's in 1.8 miles."

Abe looks at Chris.

Abe

"Care for a Falafel?"

Chris

"I'm starving. The only thing I had today was a darn kiwi. I'm buying."

Abe presses the CPU reply button

Abe (pressing CPU reply button)

"Yes, take us there."

CPU Pod Voice

"Roger that. Estimated time is 90 seconds. Be prepared to exit, as this is a busy time in the POD Stop. The pod will park once you exit."

As they pull up to Nate's Falafels, they get out of the Pod. Inscribed on the external side of the Pod is "Special Unit," so the people who see the Pod pulling up know that a special unit is inside. Only the fighter pilots and high ranking officials have access to these pods. They are noticeable and display power.

The pod door slides open and the hot air hits their face, reminding them of Paragon's warm climate.

Abe

"Even if it were possible for this land to be perfect, this heat immediately eliminates it from that list."

Chris

"Damn right. I learned the hard way by not putting sunblock on the other day."

Chris softly touches the left side of his forehead, where his skin is chafing from sunburn.

Abe

"Dude, that's a necessity over here. No matter how dark or how light your complexion is."

As the two air warriors step out of the Pod, the door closes and a red light begins to flash, alerting bystanders that it is about to move. It then pulls away.

Chris

"I haven't been to one of these yet."

Abe

"Really?"

Chris

"I didn't know how to work that system. I just wanted to make sure I made it to my apartment."

Watching the pod back up, the two are standing, wearing shirts that have the AX - 1 logo on the left chest. Chris's shirt is green and Abe's shirt is orange. They both have dark pants and high top basketball shoes on. A person will think that they are members of a basketball team, especially because the two are lean and fit. Abe has an Egyptian gold necklace on, tucked under his shirt. It's a cool accent that most women immediately notice. It's simple but very unique.

Chris (looking at the pod)

"Is it going to wait for us?"

Abe

"Yeah. If you look over to the shed, the Pod will pull into one of those spots. Then when you walk out, you press your button on your Pod card and it comes out. It's like having a Valet without the guy running back and forth."

Abe points over to the group of Pods that await the other riders. Chris looks and is dazzled, not regretting moving to the other side of the world. As he looks at the pod parking itself, four women in their mid-twenties, dressed for a night out, walk pass him. They have light sundresses with thin material on. Chris is now even more dazzled. He starts to tap Abe as he looks.

Chris (energetically under his breath)

"Yo! Yo! Yo! Yo! Abe. Abe. Look…"

Abe finally looks after Chris's many attempts. Abe looks and laughs at Chris being new to Paragon.

Abe

"Get used to it. Welcome to Paragon. You still have no idea. You've seen nothing, Warmblood."

Chris stands there with complete awe. His jaw is dropped and mouth almost open. He now knows for sure that he didn't make a mistake by moving. He is flying the airplane of his dreams; the country has corporate beach events on Fridays, the pod service is better than any vehicle and public train made, and then there are the women. He is in a dreamworld that he never dreamed of. Chris is still standing in the same spot dazed, as Abe looks at him and laughs. Then, two more sets of women walk by. Chris snaps his neck at Abe, and shares his viewpoint of one of the women that walked by him.

Chris (mutely)

"Did you see that?"

Abe shakes his head yes.

Chris's night is made. He is standing stuck. Not realizing what he is in for. It's an experience of a lifetime.

Chris's jaw dropped, as the women are running through his mind. The women: the shapes, the sizes, the different complexions, from white to chocolate, thin, chunky, and even the perfect bottle-shape ones. He wants to go out tonight, but he needs to make sure he gets rest as the scramble mission is tomorrow. He also has plenty of studying to do because he has to get a hang on some different maneuvers.

The two walk into Nate's. Once they get in line, Abe offers his recommendations on what Chris has to choose from the menu. Chris gazes at the monitor that displays the food. As he looks at his options, he feels someone gazing at him. He quickly looks to the right, and he does one of his favorite maneuvers with women. He catches one that he thinks is attracted to him. Once their eyes meet, she looks away, then looks back as she notices his light brown eyes and he scopes in hers also. Even if the two don't speak and this eye connection ends at "just that", Chris has his internal confirmation about the better aspects of Paragon, and this is only the beginning. All anxiety of being in a new territory is gone.

PAUSE:
ABE : JOURNAL ENTRY

I try to respect all of humanity. I'm a strong lover, but I am a fighter. I'm also a pilot. With one move of my finger. I can kill one hundred, or even thousands of people at one time, and that's a small strike. I hope that the day never comes, but if I have to, and it's for the sake of humanity, I won't hesitate to do so.

I'm Abe Dalton; First name is spelled "alpha bravo echo", last name "delta alpha lima tango oscar november". That's aviation lingo.

I was born in the year 2005; I'm 26 years old. But who knows? I don't even know what to believe in, after all the crap I've just been through. These days somebody can tell you that you were born in a particular year. But how do you know if you can't remember the year?

I heard that something called DMT prevents us from knowing anything before we are a certain age. The other day, I looked DMT up on the internet. To my surprise there is no advanced evidence of it. Personally, I think it is true. How else will we just not remember a live action like birth? We also forget what we dreamed about, as soon as we wake up.

Through all of that, I am confident that my dad can probably remember what he ate on his first birthday. That guy is smart. People like to label him as a genius. A Mecca. Sometimes a prophet. I can't lie; that man has done some amazing things.

Only a few things in life can truly be done alone. Breathing being one of the few. But I can literally say that I watched my father create a country, and civilization out of nothing. From what I remember at least. I think I saw the easy part. You know, the groundbreaking ceremonies for all the initial construction of the towers that now stand in Paragon. The place I call home. I was only about five or six at the time when all of it began to grow.

I remember when my dad would hold my hand firmly as I walked through the buildings with him. Every time that I let his hand go, he would only allow me go so far. Now, when it came time to hold his hand again, he would hold it tightly. Damn, it hurt too. That guy is strong. He is around six foot three, and has a strong frame. I learned that the hard way.

I didn't learn by getting ass whippings left and right. I learned when we played basketball, in the airplane hangar in the backyard of our home. When I was young, playing sports against him was fun. But as I grew up, that all changed. He showed me what being Charles Dalton was really about. The lion came out of both of us.

Heck, one of my first strings of stitches came from a five on five game that we used to have, and guess WHO fouled me? He did! The shit hurt!

Come to think of it. We had some darn good moments playing ball. I remember his pilots and mechanics began to trash talk about who was better. We all would walk to the court and the games would begin. Mechanics were oiled up with black stuff on their arms; nobody cared, though. Sometimes the games ended at three in the morning. Many times it would be after a long haul when they used to have to touch four countries in three days. I don't know where they got that energy from. You would think that they would be tired, or even play just for fun. The games got really heated. Pilots were pissed. Ramp men played dirty. They became ball warriors during those moments. Heck, they even fought every now and then. If my dad ever sensed a loss coming, his competitive spirit would rise. You'd know it because you will hear his proper European accent come out, and he will say, "Play me in a real sport." Those being soccer, polo, and water polo.

Pops is untraditional.

My dad is black. I mean ninja black. Not purple black. Just black. He is strong, muscular, with a six pack, and sometimes, with a shadow beard. When I ask him why hasn't he shaved, he claims that he's busy. Honestly I think he just loves the beard. It gives him that rugged but sharp look. I know that because I do it every now and then. Obviously the women like it also. He is more clean-cut than me. I'm the type that wears sweats the majority of the time. Unlike me, my dad enjoys the tailored button down, with the sport jacket that is made to grip his body. His shoes are never scuffed; his collars on his shirts are always crisp. His pants are crisp too.

Before Paragon (the country, which he created) became this phenomenon; we would go to Olympia. Olympia is a 13 hour flight, sometimes faster. It all depended on what aircraft we used, and how the weather was looking. If we flew eastbound from Paragon, the tail wind would push us a bit faster, and we could be on Olympia's west coast in ten hours. Either way the trip was long.

When we arrived there, he made sure that he spent one solid day with me, his mom, and his younger sister, Charlotte. Although he lived in Olympia for a good part of his life, he didn't like staying there for long. Mostly because when we got to particular parts of Olympia, he was judged and stereotyped.

Not to be superficial, but this is a cool example. If we walked into an expensive restaurant for dinner, especially if we had casual clothes on, we would step up to the host. Before my dad said anything, the host would immediately tell us, "We only take reservations, and we are full at the moment". Then they will walk away or look down at the computer as we stood there, waiting for service. I loved this moment.

Pops used to raise his eyebrows a bit, give the host a head nod, and softly bite his top lip. THEN PUNCH HIM!

I'm kidding; he wouldn't do that.

Noticing that the waitress is being a jerk, Pops would take a few steps back. Pull out his cell phone. Less than a minute later the general manager of the restaurant would be out with a security guard, and 2 waiters. Then they would escort us towards the back of the restaurant. My dad would then give the host the look of gold, and just walk past him or her. Always saying, "Thank you." Most of the time his European voice would throw them off. Although I am humble, it's a good feeling when a person stereotypes you, then a minute later they realize that they made a big mistake. That's why all should not judge a book by its cover. I deal with it all the time.

When I go to flight training in Olympia, wearing my traditional street clothing (a basketball jumpsuit with basketball shoes) they always assume that I am a ramp service man. It dazzles them when they realize that I have my type-ratings to fly 3 different fighter jets, and even one of the world's largest cargo planes. The look on their face is priceless.

When I was six years old, life was normal; it was cool. My dad and I used to have a blast, traveling the world. But that suddenly stopped. I still have all that I want. But life was never the same. Our world changed. When I was attending school in Olympia, my dad suddenly became world renown. Millions of people wanted to get in contact with him. People began to flock over to

Paragon, just to have "conversations" with him. Most of them were dealing with money. I didn't really know what was going on. But I became Charles Dalton's son. Not Abe.

I tried to stay distant from the subject of my dad. I would visit him every now and then. Oh, I enjoyed it, but it became overwhelming. Even when I would go back to Olympia for school. Some kids liked me, but other kids began to secretly call me the "son of a devil." Initially, I couldn't grasp it, but as I started to grow up, I figured it out.

As Paragon expanded, the hatred for my father grew. It hurt. I transferred to a few different schools within Olympia. Moving around didn't help.

When I turned 16, I enrolled in a school in Europa, where the politics were far less hostile. It was weird though. Many adults respected my dad. Especially some of my science teachers.

They would always try to find a way for my dad to donate funds so our class could take an amazing field trip. I'd ask, and he'd never hesitate, and when he did it, he wouldn't just do it for my entire class. He would do it for the entire school. It was cool, but it was hard on me. I didn't know who was "cool" with me per se; I didn't know who liked Abe for Abe. Not Abe for his dad's money and the cool things Abe had access too. Everybody and their "momma" found some way to bring money into the conversation.

After finishing high school in Europa, I moved back to Olympia. Although hatred for my dad was growing in some areas, I had the opportunity to join the Air Force to became a pilot. I couldn't resist. My prior move to Europa lowered my profile as "Dalton's son", and I went in as a regular cadet. People knew me as Abe and Squid (my pilot call sign). I loved it; I was just like everybody else. No perks. I went through various ranks, and passed plenty of tests. I made it through flight school, and eventually became one of the youngest cargo pilots in the service at 22. Then the issues began.

I had a senior captain named Captain Title, who just couldn't accept me for who I was. Out of all the pilots, I was the only black in my whole squadron. He gave me so much trouble. He was obviously racist, and poorly represented his own race. I will tell you one story. I won't elaborate too much on the racism that I have dealt with. If I did, I wouldn't stop venting about the prejudice I've had directed my way.

When I flew in the Olympian Air Force (Captain Title was my commander), I came in on a very hard approach (landing) during bad weather. Technically, the plane was not supposed to land in that weather but my fuel tanks were below reserve, and I wouldn't have been able to land at another airport. I declared emergency to my base air traffic control so I could land. They cleared me. It was a rough landing but the plane was built to land in bad conditions, including a desert full of sand. I'm sure other guys in my squadron could have pulled the landing off. But I'm equally sure many couldn't. The visibility in the sky was low and the runway visual range was less than none. The runway was semi-flooded, but I had no choice.

I landed and didn't even do any damage to the aircraft.

In fact, many on my base were stunned. Title wasn't. It gave him yet another reason to chew me out. Only because, technically, I had the option to divert to another airport. But if I had; I would have died. I have no doubts in my mind. I am not going to go too far into detail about what he said, but he called me every word that you could imagine a confederate-minded person could say behind closed doors. And all in front of my squadron.

I didn't cry. But that night, I did. The tears flooded my eyes. The rain saved my ego. Nobody was able to see those tears climbing down my face.

I wasn't crying because of Captain Title's slurs. I was crying because I was 22 years old, and this was my first mayday emergency landing. It was in the rain, a storm, with lightning, and 50 mile per hour shear winds crossing the tail of my plane. If I had let go of the yoke just a tiny bit, my plane would have spun around like a figure skater on clean ice. I would have had to bring the plane in sideways, and turn it in the last 3 seconds to land it. As it was, I had to keep my speed up to fight the winds so I didn't get turned around. Then I reversed every bit of thrust in the plane that I could, and it landed right on the centerline of the runway. Just like it would have been on a 75 degree day with no wind.

If anything he should have been there for me. Not castigating me.

The military fire fighters were out by the runway with the red lights flickering. They had been braced for a crazy impact. All they could do was check on me, and shake my hand. They were worried if I was okay. Especially Ty, the new pilot that I was training that day. Ty. He was in shock. He couldn't even move after we landed. I looked at him and told him that he was fine, and since he got thorough that, he should never have a fear of flying again. Then came Title.

His only worry was to make me melt in the rain. Not my life, not even if there was any damage to the three hundred million dollar aircraft parked behind me.

I requested an honorable discharge.

After numerous hearings, I was granted my full pilot rights to fly in other countries. As long as I didn't release any confidential Olympian details.

Without looking back, I headed home. I didn't feel welcome in Olympia anymore. I felt like an extra issue to too many people, especially the tea-sipping conservatives. I got tired of the negative energy. I got tired of the scandals, the politics, and the life that wasn't life. Not to get on my dad's high horse, but Paragon was the shit.

Before moving back, I had to let go of that fear of being the son of the founder of the country. That's who I am, who I was, who I always will be. It's one of the best decisions I have ever made. Although I keep a low profile and focus on my flying, I love Paragon. It's my home. The women are gorgeous. The air tastes good. The people are awesome. Heck, I don't even have to pay for gas. Nobody does.

Why? Because my dad found a way so his people don't need to use fuel anymore. It's a life-changing mineral, found in the Paragon Mountains. It's called A28, and many would die to get their hands on it. Literally.

2

Cuddy Buddy

In her bedroom, Abe opens his eyes, gazes over, and looks at his old school clock radio. The radio with the red numbers and the black, almost brown, background with the big snooze button on the top of it. The music on his phone follows, then Gil's rings also. The peace has turned into a frenzy. Sounds of an alarm clock can be a nightmare for people who don't enjoy the morning. It can also end that perfect dream.

The light of the moon is peeking through the window as Gil looks over at Abe, who is half asleep, trying to press the snooze buttons on the three gadgets.

Once he is awake, he begins to inch out of the bed and puts his back on the headboard. Gil (short for Gillia) can almost see herself as she looks at him and his dark coarse hair and light eyes. Both of their complexions are like fine sand, but have a light tan from the sun, which can't be avoided in Paragon.

Abe (taking a deep breath,)

"Goodness, that felt like 10 minutes."

Gil chuckles, referring to an earlier moment

"Because it was."

Abe (yawning)

"No, you purvy. I'm not talking about that. Time just flies by when your sleep."

Gil

"Purvy? Whatever. It must have been a good dream then. Because the night lasts forever when the dream isn't going your way."

They both chuckle as Gil grabs Abe's dog tags, which are hanging from his neck while Abe scrolls through the messages on his phone and clicks "Telda". He sees nothing new and puts the phone back on the nightstand. Gil rubs the engraving his dog tags.

"ABRAHAM DALTON: Squid: 02901: PAX-1"

Abe is an Ace; in fact he is a triple Ace in the Paragon's Air Force Command. In aviation terms, "Ace" refers to a fighter pilot who has had 3 or more successful air strikes. Abe has 9. He is one of the youngest to ever do it, which occurred at the age of 25. He is now 26, and though, he's had a slight advantage to handling the yokes of an aircraft since he was 14, he thanks his father. It is also rare for a fighter pilot to have that many air strikes these days, since dog fighting isn't as common as it was back in the day. Most of Abe's strikes came from hostiles trying to invade Paragon's territory, while hunting for A28.

Gil and Abe relate well to each other. They both have lived in Olympia and Paragon throughout their lives. From what Abe knows, both of Gil's parents died in the same bombing that took Abe's mother, Leah. Neither one of them know what exactly happened besides where it occurred, which was in the downtown area of Paragon.

Unlike Gil, Abe has full support from his father, Charles - the creator of Paragon. The perks of being the son of the creator of a civilization are good, but there are still many pros and cons of his status. Not only is he a target for ransom, politics, and secrets, he is expected to follow the similar footsteps of his father, which is a business magnate. This didn't sit well with Abe, or Charles. Charles wanted Abe to be courageous enough to make his own choices in life. But the last thing Charles expected him to do was for him to join the military when he turned 17.

It was bittersweet, but Charles had to respect Abe's choices. Abe could have been virtually anything he wanted, but he chose to be a fighter pilot, as he has always had that need for speed. It is a living nightmare for Charles, but he'd rather Abe be doing something productive instead of running around the world spending dollar after dollar, up to no good. Abe likes it also because it gets him away from his dad and people, since he works in a secure area, and when he flies nobody can reach him. It gives him daily peace.

Abe lives a very private life. Due to his light skin tone, many don't know that his father is Charles and he wants to keep it that way. He blends right in, as most people in Paragon speak strong English and are competitive. In some ways, it has become a hub for many military pilots, which also works in his favor.

The Gulf of Paragon holds a joint base for Paragon and Olympia's Air Force and Naval Command and many training missions occur there. Life in Paragon is challenging, not necessarily because it's the poor vs. rich, but because it is the land of the go-getter. Everybody contributes, no exceptions. Once Paragon was a vast land where many military units were positioned during the revolt between Olympia and other Middle Eastern countries. Therefore, Olympia and other allied countries sent the best of the best to Paragon for fieldwork and to support the war, but it also became a nesting place for many companies to support the militia, as the war lasted for fifteen years. Paragon is pretty small compared to other civilizations. It only has a total radius of no more than 500 miles. It has 5 military bases, and the rest of Paragon is mostly community development, but Paragon also has significant corporate development from all the companies who moved their headquarters there.

Not only did companies have access to hundreds and thousands of troops who lived there, Paragon is also a tax haven. Since the landholder was Charles's father, he enjoyed the fact that companies came to his land, which in turn gave him the ability to provide more for his citizens and natives of the surrounding territory. In exchange, companies just had to pay utility fees and they had an agreement to share a portion of their profits to further develop the territory.

Over time, Paragon became more relevant in different economies of the world as more Olympian citizens began to migrate there. Soon after, the Europeans, Chinese, and other cultures and races followed. Many of these people created companies and offered temporary tax-free jobs and contracts, which supported the troops and the development of the war hub. But once many realized that the war (a thousand miles away) was going to continue for a few more years, many companies stayed and expanded their headquarters, and the corporate profits continued to rise (as jobs were vanishing daily in Olympia and other places due to the economic recession).

Opportunity isn't the only advantage to move to Paragon. The weather is breathtaking, as it is never too cold, although at times the heat can be a little extreme. Certain parts of Paragon have some of the world's most amazing waterfalls. The beaches that surround the eastern part of the country are lined with soft and graceful ivory-speckled sand, with 30 foot palm trees that line the shore. The turquoise blue water offsets the heat waves that occur in the summer.

These aspects are a surprise to migrants because most people only expect to see the desert and safari land, which are beautiful also. Most of this is because the media in Olympia limits the amount of beauty that Paragon offers and focuses more on the training of the war, which isn't as appealing. More so, they want to keep it a secret, so more people don't move there. That has become tough though, now that social networking plays a heavy role in everyday life. People can see and know more things than they ever would have known prior to the internet boom.

As businesses started to grow, more people migrated to Paragon, which resulted in more development. In the early 2000's, once troops and migrants found a way to keep their families in Paragon, temporary housing sites slowly began to turn into smaller short term apartment complexes, which then turned into single family homes, then communities began to appear over the course of 10 years. It was an accident that needed to happen.

Paragon

In 2007, cars from Olympia, Europa, and other countries were being shipped via airplane and sea vessels. Exactly how prescription medicine rolls off a cargo plane during an outbreak. At times there were 30 vehicles a day. That may not seem like many, but adding over 200 new cars a month equated to an average of 3 people per vehicle. This was interesting because there were no car dealerships in Paragon. Eventually the manufacturers recognized the demand, only because they had to pay visits to keep the vehicle fleet contracts up for the military. It was quite a transformation. Back in 1990 there were no more than 50 vehicles (mostly safari trucks) in the entire nation, and now there are 30,000 and still counting. Charles's father loved it. But Charles didn't, as he is an environmental critic.

Even so, Paragon is different. The roads are unique and even glow in the dark. They are laid out with illuminated markings which are solar powered and the markings turn colors when it's dark. When it rains, the roads show rain drops. Though it will never have icy conditions, the roads can even show that there is ice on the roadway, or even alert a driver that traffic is ahead. The roads are consistently paved for smooth driving as they are routinely inspected and holes are fixed quarterly. The streetlights are also solar powered, and a day's worth of sun can supply batteries with a charge up to four months at a time. Since most citizens have electric cars, they can drive on the shoulder and their vehicle will get charged as the shoulder has charging stations on specific points on the road. This led to the world's first fully solar powered territory. Not to mention the hydroelectric developments that have been made, along with the water collection systems that are streetside.

The people who live there live to make a difference.

Though there are still certain citizens who don't contribute much to Paragon, the people who chose to come to the land were those with a tremendous amount of courage. Other factors contributed since most of the companies paid for relocation, but taxes were notably lower than other countries, and the country was also simply something new. It still took plenty of faith to make the jump and leave that place called home. These migrants were the best of the best in all of their industries, and if they weren't the best they had the drive to want to be the best. Most of them were workers who were stuck in a company which offered very little pay, and even if the pay was good, the room for growth was low. College graduates who wanted a challenge and to use their degree, masters, and PhDs were offered internships for many different fields ranging from marine biology to understanding space.

All of this worked out because Paragon had to be able to support its growth, not only for the military bases but for the land overall. This was foresaw by Charles's father as he chose to bring in specialists for large and small structures, planning, schools, agriculture, but he also eliminated many costly unnecessary expenses and ventures which opened the way for better jobs like working in the world's first mega vertical farm where plants and food are harvested in the middle of the city, inside a sky scraper. This worked well because it saved much energy, especially since everything was in walking distance. Delivery didn't even require much energy. Companies were able to place orders and the food would be delivered by a pod or one of the wind pipelines that sent goods to specific checkpoints in Paragon. Companies didn't have to waste money on fuel, which also wasn't a factor in Paragon. Though Emirate is a neighbor, and they are known for their fuel, Paragon has their own solution, which saves the country billions of dollars a year.

With the mass global friendly developments, many highly motivated individuals were attracted to Paragon and wanted to be a part of it. This being said, this led to the creation of small school systems where the students received nothing less than a great education experience, not just a class. These migrants took education for their children very seriously.

Some of the main questions that parents had when they received were (and still are):

"Are there schools in Paragon? "Where will our children go to school?" "I don't have any kids yet, but where will they learn if I choose to have some in a few years or so?"

In a fear of the unknown, many parents initially chose to put their children in private schools back in their homelands (Olympia, Europa, and etc.,) before they moved to the Paragon. This all changed once they saw the schooling plans, safety, and the structure of Paragon. The fear that accompanies the move to a new territory decreased. As a team, the migrants came together and thoroughly planned all aspects important to a quality life. With little argument, but much debate, they hired qualified teachers, and implemented effective school strategies and systems so their children would get the best learning possible. In many ways, this was a benefit, simply because most school systems are very bureaucratic, especially in Olympia. Paragon was new and open to change and improvement, new strategies and revolutions. But the transitions weren't always smooth.

Because of the high migration rate, there was a shortage of teachers. Therefore, students were limited to only 5 hours of schooling per day. With this personnel limitation, parents were forced to make a decision to mandate all students to get involved with an accredited company in Paragon. These leaders of the future were required work or shadow a company of their choice, after school at a minimum of 10 hours a week to move to the next grade level. This wasn't the original plan, but it worked. Adults were annoyed by the fact that they had to deal with the young ones certain days of the work week, but it gave the children a different perspective of their future. It allowed them to work in various professions from top design firms, law, technology, to the local water / hydroelectric plant (which effectively produces much of the Paragon's electricity as it saves money spent on power for the country and individuals). As many children grew in age, they eliminated careers that they had initially thought they had wanted to do, and focused on jobs that they would love to be a part of. The days of working at jobs they were forced to do, simply to get paid, were over.

The closest country to Paragon is Golia, which is 150 miles west. Golia is occupied by over a hundred million of people, but it is still crippled. The government only allows its lower class citizens to do so much, ranging from education to having access to medical utilities. The last time Charles visited a hospital at an impoverished town there, he cut his finger and they didn't even have a band-aid on site. He had to have one of his assistants to run to his personal SUV and get one out of the first aid kit. This disgusted him, and since then, he has pledged to himself that he and his colleagues would send an unlimited amount of band-aids to Golia and other third world countries. He feels that no kid should be denied the small privilege of receiving a band-aid, especially in a country where they still have a gross domestic product.

Although there were still some wealthy people in Golia, many of them traveled to other lands, pursuing the finer things in life, only to return home to check on businesses and their mega mansions which are closed off to the general population. This is why so many Golian's come to Paragon in search of jobs; an opportunity to make a better living.

This created a stir. Now, Golian natives would do anything to enter the new world of Paragon. Although Paragon is open to anybody, there is still an application process to become a prospective citizen. Many Golian natives didn't understand this. Not because they didn't want to apply, but because they didn't have the resources to apply to get into Paragon, and get a visa.

Not that Paragon discriminated against any one type of person. The issue was mixing well-seasoned professionals coming from a free will country with Golian natives who barely knew how to use a cell phone, and may even have issues with supplying their own water. Many people who made the jump to move to Paragon came for a better life, and they felt as if they worked hard to create a moderately safe world in the new nation and if the Golians indiscriminately came in, citizens knew they would slowly destroy the land and its equable culture. Barring these people from entry caused a good amount of cultural segregation and unrest until Paragon offered to unilaterally help all of those who wanted the opportunity to live a better life, not just the people from already privileged nations. To support this movement, jobs were created not only in Paragon, but small companies like bottling and recycling plants were created in Golia, as they needed the recycling plants for both territories anyway. This foreign policy system allowed people to establish the initial skills and resources needed to earn their way into Paragon.

At the end of the day, no matter what, this was all necessary as Paragon became a powerful neighbor. Heck, this has even caused some small battles that were quickly managed before they had a chance to escalate. The natives felt as they were being left out for people from the richer and western worlds. Most of it was Charles Senior's choice. As he morally felt it, it was right. Some of his older colleagues weren't too happy about it, but they eventually got over it.

With a friendly and invisible electric fence separating Golia and Paragon, the neighbors slowly integrated. Some of the Golian natives received education and training, and others who were older were able to obtain blue collar jobs. There were also some sharp Golians who already made many educational achievements and they brought much value to the community, especially their ability to use Paragon's resources. Golia lacked these assets, mostly because of their corrupt government which continued to cause friction. Although there was much development being done in the new territory, there were only so many jobs to could be created and offered. It was a very hard thing to watch when the natives traveled all the way to Paragon's border just to apply for a job. Many of them arrived in tattered clothing, blistered palms, and their bodies showed a lifetime of hard labor.

As mentioned before, Paragon is gorgeous, and less than 150 miles away from Golia. Just like certain Olympians were ready to leave Olympia for the chance to make a better living, Golians were ready also. The only difference is, it wasn't for money or "more opportunity," it was for the simple things like medical care and adequate shelter. Though Paragon only had few hospitals, they had awesome programs. However, when the natives started to come for assistance, that also created friction.

Golia's corruption gathered momentum and started to make its way to Paragon. The leaders of Golia wanted a piece of the pie. They were after the funding, but they also wanted use the nation's entertainment, food, and enjoy the Paragon quality of life. They even wanted the distilled water that the nation produced (although they could have done the same thing, but they didn't). Initially, it started off with the Golian leaders wanting to be a part of the booming economy of Paragon. Charles was fine with assisting any way that he could. Then Golian leaders learned about something that was bigger than water and small profits. They found out what was in the soil and mountains of Paragon, and the reason Charles's father only allowed the military forces on one side of Paragon and the citizens on the other. A28.

They knew this mineral could change many power factions in the world. Very few knew about it and where it truly exists. The researchers and scientists are just a few years away from putting it into production, and the price tag on it is big and the moral tag on it is even bigger.

Back to Gil and Abe: Bedroom

Though they both love the intense moments of being together, Gil is a bit more balanced than Abe. She knows how to sit back, observe, and wait. However, Abe makes instant decisions depending on the moment or the situation that he's in. Gil gets the credit for her patience; Abe won't allow his self to get credit for being patient. Most of the time, he has no room for patience in the role that he serves with AX1. He can't have too much patience; otherwise he wouldn't be the fighter pilot that he is. In Abe's mind, when it is time to make a decision on launching a missile, he can't be a double-minded man; otherwise the mission wouldn't get completed. The target that he has a lock on will put a lock on him, which in turn, means doomsday for him, and the $100 million dollar aircraft that he's flying.

After feeling the indentations of his name on the Egyptia gold dog tags for a few moments, Gil begins to caress his chest. She gets her final kisses in and holds on to him for their last moments of the early morning. The feeling is mutual amongst both of them. They have a strange, but kinetic bond. She is laying on him - kissing his neck.

Gil

"Sweetie, I don't want you to leave yet."

Abe (chuckles and softly pushes her off of him and gets out of bed)

"Well, if I don't go, you won't be enjoying any of me later tonight."

Gil

"Whatever, I still probably won't get to see you. What is this mission about anyway?"

Abe takes a deep breath as he ignores her; he knows that there is a significant possibility that he may not come home. Though he never really knows what type of mission that he has to look forward to, having a job where you could possibly be in another country overnight for a day or so is the perfect excuse to give a woman, especially if he meets and spends a night with another girl while he's out with his wingman. Gil has caught him in that lie a few times, so that bridge has been burned.

Abe walks to the bathroom, still in her eye view, and splashes some water on his face, adjusting to the early morning. He looks at his shadowed beard in the mirror and notices Gil looking at him in the reflection, but he pays her no mind. He lifts his lips checking, to see if his teeth have any tartar build up. He notices a little plaque so wipes them with the inside of his shirt for a few seconds, licks his teeth with his tongue, and looks into the mirror verifying they are clean. He then blows his nose, walks out of the bedroom and picks up his grey sweatpants which are lying on the floor, next to the bed, and puts them on.

Gil (looking at Abe as he gets dressed)

"Really? You're not gonna to brush your teeth?"

Abe gives her a look, and continues to get dressed. She squints her eye, just as many women do when men do "men things."

Gil

"Abe, you're disgusting.... At least gargle."

Abe lifts his eyebrows and gives her a disrespectful look. His ego fuels her. Gil locks in on his eyes, gets out of the bed, and walks towards him.

She is wearing a white tank top and gym shorts. She pushes him toward the wall, causing him lose his balance, displaying her strength. Standing five foot six, she looks up at him, rubs her finger down his right cheek, then grabs his neck.

Gil (seductively)

"Then again, I appreciate the fact that you don't want to forget the taste of my lip....stick, Mr. Mach One."

Abe is flattered but more enamored with her correct use of Aviation language. As for every Mach, it's about 600 miles per hour.

Abe (leaning back)

"Two Gil, it's Mach two. Well, now it's really three. I think you're still stuck in the twentieth century. One is for practice."

Gil

"You're such a geek. What time are you done today?"

As she speaks, she begins to hold onto him tightly. She grabs his back, massaging it, not wanting to let go.

Abe

"I have no clue. It depends."

Gil (holding him tightly)

"Depends on?"

Abe (closing his eyes)

"On whatever time I get done. I can't call it. I really got to run. You got me in trouble with this last time."

Abe can't be late for his post. Though he is one of the leaders in his squadron, if he is late it will hold up his copilot, deck hands, and other aircraft that are scheduled for takeoff. It's a ripple effect. Also, today is a possible big day for him, the scramble test. In other words, he'll be doing a practice run for when a fighter pilot needs to be 5,000 feet in the airspace in 3 minutes in case of an attack or hostage situation.

Abe (as he begins to walk away)

"I'll be sure you will be looking for me though."

Gil

"Babe, I'll always be watching out for you."

Abe (walking away and winks at her)

"I'll shoot you an email later."

As she enjoys his wink, she dislikes it highly. The door closes behind him and she jumps on the bed, back first. Puts the back of her hands on her eyes, and tries to control her thoughts. There's so many 'what if's' in this situation. She likes him, she can't like him, she gets closer, and he gets further. What confuses her is that when he gets further, she gets closer. It's a situation that she has to accept as their relationship has no particular agenda or title.

She's wondering. Why did she put herself in this situation? A friend whom she knows has girls for days. His career involves life or death at times. He can be so warm, yet turn so cold? Why spend his last moments with her knowing that he doesn't want to take her seriously.

The bigger issue is that she won't get to see him. She knows that every time he goes up, there is a good chance of him not coming back down, no matter if it's a mission or a simple training day.

Gil works with the front office of the government. She is aware of all the hostility going on with the politics of Paragon, especially since they are only a few documents away from being one of the newest recognized countries by the United Nations since Sierra Lenora back in 2009. Once that happens, the United Nations will protect Paragon and tie them with powerful allies from around the world. This means that many countries won't be able to legally nor immorally intrude, or call any shots upon Paragon unless approved otherwise. Initially, it wasn't a big deal, but as world leaders began to recognize that Paragon was becoming a very powerful force, they want their hands on it.

Paragon is like a new car. It comes with a cost but is more efficient. It costs a bit less to maintain and needs less maintenance.

Locker Room: AX1 Base

It's early morning, but it seems like it could be 7 pm. The sun has yet to set, and the locker room is alive. Jokes are being made, lockers are clanking, towels and shirts are all over the place; it is a typical men's locker room. It always has a weird smell, no matter how clean or state of the art it is. There is something about the aroma in the men's locker room. It still has that has that gym smell to it. It could be some of the flight suits that haven't been washed yet, and some smell like urine. The fact that it's always hot in Paragon doesn't make it any better, because sweat is standard.

There are about 20 men in the locker room. Most of them are flight load masters (guys who calculate the weight of the plane), missile coordinators, as every department has their own section. Some of the men are reading through notes, some have headphones on with an array of music playing on the surround sound at a low level. It's more like your regular football team locker room, not a locker room for airmen.

One unique feature in the locker room is that the lockers have a visual video of each member in the unit. Meet the unit is on the Marquee:

Tex Atlantis, Dusty Rhodes, and Willard Douglas, flight team squad members / support. These guys support the missions as far as making sure the aircraft are all maintained and the systems are properly operating. They communicate with all the pilots, navigators, and command center to assure communication is always proper, before during, and after mission.

Fighter Pilots are Terry Love, Rory Edward, Mason Stewart, Carter Finfrock, and Abe. With Abe, Rory, and Terry being the youngest, they usually take many words of wisdom from Mason as he is the one who trained them all, since he was a pilot in the Olympia Air Force for 20 years now.

Jason Danders, Kirus Vandal, Timber Gray are the Navigators. Kirus and Timber are both young, in their 20's. They are both number crunchers and can pinpoint coordinates on a map with their eyes closed. Jason is the lead navigator and is in his 40's. He was also a Navigator in Olympia for most of his adult life.

The women have a separate locker room, though some of the guys beg to differ. Just like brothers and sisters, pranks occur monthly between the two sexes. Since they are an elite unit they always have to stay serious about their duties, but there are moments when the women have cut all the hot water off for the men's showers. Leaving nothing but cold water for them to shower in. Then the men have gotten them back by soaking all the women's dry towels in water. Leaving them nothing to dry themselves off with, and those are the low level pranks. The sex wars have gotten serious many times.

The women in AX1 are Telda Blanchard, Roxanne Bruda, Channing Bolts, Lex Luser, and Kelsey Gre. Telda is the youngest, and the sole female fighter pilot. Roxanne and Kelsey are in their middle thirties. They handle systems on the aircraft, making sure the avionics and communication systems are properly working. Lex and Channing are in their mid-twenties, and they are both war battle coordinators strictly for AX1 unit. Their main role is to communicate, facilitate, orchestrate everything with the pilots when a conflict occurs.

Back to the locker room

Tex, irritated, is digging through his items because he can't find his underwear. He's moving everything in his locker, tossing items around, and pacing the floor. All while a few of the other guys are laughing at him. This is when the pranks happen.

Tex

C'mon, guys, seriously, I got 10 minutes; this shit is not cool! Not now! I got shit to focus on! Where are my Jockers?

While Tex is turning red out of frustration, two other guys look at each other, silently laughing at Tex because they are the ones who hid his underwear while he was showering.

Tex

It's too early for this shit. Really, guys?

Tex is right. There is no room for hesitation or error, especially today since he may get a last minute test mission. To make it worse, there is nothing fun about flying with no underwear on, especially at 30,000 feet. Sometimes the temps can get below 20 degrees, although the planes are heated, cold air still finds a way to creep in when you are flying at a minimum of 400 MPH. Not a good feeling for most men, nor the thought that he wants to have on his mind before he puts his flight suit on.

Tex

"Not today, not today!"

He continues to search for his underwear, wearing his gym shorts. He realizes that there are only 8 more minutes until he has to report. There is no fun in wearing no underwear flying high in the sky. Tex has done it before, and it wasn't comfortable.

Meanwhile, Abe is running late, as usual. He walks into the locker room, enters his digital code (Number: 02004) to open his locker and takes a seat on a bench. He looks over at the drama of the pranksters, and as a leader, he tosses a pair of his underwear to Tex. The black jockers unexpectedly hit his chest, and he grabs them before they fall to the floor.

Tex

"Thanks, man."

Abe gives him a nod, and glares down the two fellows who were part of the prank. They immediately stop laughing. Sitting next to Abe is Carter Finfrock. He and Abe have known each other since college. They both take everything that they do seriously, they have like minds, but they have different approaches to how they think and act.

Carter (From across the locker room)

What's going, lover boy? Still sneaking out before game day, huh?

The guys always give Abe a hard time about his nights out with his women. But with the way he performs, they can't knock him for much of anything.

Abe (closing his eyes briefly while he putting his socks on)

"Here, we go. Mr. Carter. How's your ummm? How's your mom doing?"

Carter

"She's not doing you, Buddy."

Abe

"You sure about that?"

Carter's mom, Miss Finfrock, is loved by the entire squadron due to her playboy modeling younger days. Carter used to get jealous about it. To the point where he would fight anybody that ever mentioned it, but as he matured, the jokes became amusing.

Carter (looking at Abe in the eye)

"Am I going to have to back you up again today?"

Abe

"Dude, you never had to back me up. I really don't know HOW and WHY that continues to register in your mind. By the way, remind me. Who did better on PFQT?"

PFQT (Paragon Fighter Questionnaire Test) is a written and practical test in which each airman has to take every year. It is very difficult to pass, and Abe had the third highest score in the squadron. Carter was fourth. Timber and Kirus tied for the highest.

Carter

"Blah, Blah. Please don't justify your skills because you tend to beat me in points from a freaking piece of paper. Points don't matter when you have stupid moments, smart guy. Like yesterday, if I didn't cut that SAM off, your ass would have been toast."

A SAM is a missile that is shot from the ground that forces use to shoot down enemy aircraft.

Abe

"Carter, you didn't save me. You can't save me. The SAM wouldn't have gotten me. I don't understand why you always think that you can protect me. Thanks for your generosity though, sir."

This is when Captain Ego comes out of both of them. They are like two young bulls. They both stare each other down for a few seconds; Carter closes his locker, shakes his head, and then walks away. Abe and Carter joke around with each other, they both have a competitive spirit. Other than that, Carter won't be making jokes to Abe, as he doesn't display humor to many. His philosophy is that leaders don't display humor, although Abe does. They are the leaders of their squad, and most of the team look up to them from Point A to Point B. Carter feels like he should always set an example. Abe, on the other hand, feels like he needs to lead when he needs to, which is usually during battle scenarios or when he feels like the squadron is losing focus.

Carter follows the books, and rarely makes a mistake. Abe is the opposite. He still follows the routine, but he always has to test the limits. Abe has proven some manufacturers that their products can do things they didn't even consider when designing and manufacturing their aircraft. Even when he's told not to make a specific maneuver, he does it anyway. He's the type who enjoys a bloody nose after a flight and even some near death experiences. It doesn't sit well with many, particularly his father. But his willingness to perform them and risk-taking has also given everyone a better understanding of difficult maneuvers.

As Abe gets his flight suit on, he grabs his cheat sheet out of his locker and puts inside a pocket on top of his right thigh. He closes the locker and walks out of the locker room, leading to the airfield. As soon as he opens the door, the heat of Paragon smacks him in the face, along with the sounds of the jets. It's loud, sunny, and windy. Airmen are all over the airstrip along with 20 fighter jets, helicopters, rover SUVs, and other essential tools which any airforce has.

A few jets are taking off one by one. It's mission day. It happens twice a week where all the airmen have a scramble analysis.

A scramble is when there is a security threat within a nation. It can be an invasion, a hijacked commercial airliner, and many other situations. Today is a flight run, which means Abe has to be ready to fly at any minute, while he's on his duty. Last year, he was in the middle of getting lunch, and then the horn went off.

There are two squadrons in Paragon: AX1 and BX1. They both handle similar missions but the AX1 squadron has a bit more flight experience than the BX1. The AX squadron has transitioned to the new F-22 aircraft from the older F-18 (which a few of the BX squadron flies). Though they have two different focuses, they both know on either base that once the big horn goes off, it's time to drop everything and get inside the aircraft within a few minutes. Some guys even sit in the plane for several hours, so they can beat the minimum time required to be in the air.

The assignments for the 2 squadrons are random; therefore they all need to be over par when it comes to their response time and performance.

The same thing will happen this year, sometime within the next 8 - 16 hours. Captain O'Donnell likes to keep his airmen on their toes, as all real life scrambles are unexpected. No matter what time of day it is, when a scramble alert goes off, it means that there is serious business to handle somewhere in the country or in a surrounding territory. The pilots, loadmasters, airmen, and the guys who guide the aircraft out, all have to be able to hop right into an airplane, or be near it. The desired time is less than 3 minutes to get the engines rolling.

Though the engines are already warmed up, because they are heated 24 hours a day, the pilot has to run one quick check within a matter of minutes and the plane should be taxiing towards the runway at any moment. Normally this checklist takes about 15 minutes, but not in a scramble situation. The plane needs to be fueled and ready to go.

As the pilot takes off, he gets his orders from his command center of what's going on. These orders range from directions (headings), speed, how high he should fly, etc. Scenarios that require a scramble range from a commercial airplane that has possibly been hijacked and is non-responsive, a missile launched, battleships impounds, and any other unknown activity. Once the pilot receives the orders, he investigates and upon his discretion, he will engage if he believes it's necessary which typically means that something is going to get blown up. Most of the time it is a pilot or an aircraft that has a communication problem, or a disruptive passenger who is making threats onboard an aircraft.

Today is a brief test run, to ensure that the squadron make it to their post at a certain time, and make it to their target at a specific time. They don't know where they are going. Their focus is to make sure that they take off in due time, then they are told where to go once they are in the air. It's a mission. All the way from the communications of the initial reporting of the matter to the radar control room to the dispatcher who tells Abe where he is going and what the problem is. The squadron also test the airborne re-fuelers. Though in Paragon, refueling in the sky is not as necessary as it used to be in the early 2000s since A28 has been integrated into many of the planes.

Again, test day is non-predictable. Although you know you're going to have a scramble, you never know when. The command can dispatch you at 6 am or 11 pm, or any time in between. You can be eating a pop tart, or even your favorite Sunday night dinner. Some of the guys are caught in between video games. It's like being a firefighter, but instead you're flying fighter jets.

Abe is now suited up. He doesn't know what time he will be dispatched so he figures that he will grab a bite to eat early, in case he has an early scramble. Just like athletes, military pilots don't eat too heavy while they are on duty. Especially fighter pilots, as most cargo pilots and even typical airline pilots have bathrooms behind the cockpit, fighter pilots don't have the luxury of a toilet since most missions are short. Every now and then, a long mission is possible. They have to do a good amount of refueling in the sky since the aircraft only hold a few hours' worth of fuel. In those cases they need to pull the piddle packs out, which is what they urinate in. So it's a good idea for them to lay off the ague de mineral before flying.

All women eat tomatoes...
Abe walks down the hallway to the squadron's cafeteria. He notices that some guys are active in the RESNA. More than likely they are pilots, who were just accepted into the squadron for training. Next in the hallway is the centrifuge room. This is where guys do G force Training which is full also. A heavy amount of training is occurring because the "Acceptance of the United Worlds" is coming up. This means Paragon will have to beef up their military command in all areas.

Abe enters the cafeteria, which features many different types of food. He makes a wise decision and grabs a handful of pineapples and fresh banana slices. The fruit is delicious, all organic and nothing sits for more than a day on the base. The extras are sent to Golia through one of the wind tunnels. So the people who live in poverty can enjoy free food that is still fresh. Abe's craving orange juice, but looks away because for some strange reason, it makes him sleepy.

The smell of eggs and the tofu bacon cooking is making him gravitate to the omelet bar, which he is really in the mood for. Then the thought that he might be going up sometime soon makes him hold off on anything heavy. After settling for his light breakfast, he bites the delicious banana slice. As he begins to walk out of the food area, and feels a small but firm tap on his back. He turns around, and it's a sight that he prefers over the sunset.

Telda

"Toga, what's up?"

Telda calls Abe toga, because that's what he called her during training, since he could never get her name right.

Abe

"You're never gonna let that go, are you?"

Telda

"Nope, I won't because you have everybody calling me that bullshit."

Abe (as he eats his fruit)

"Telda, it's really a cool name. You know, Toga, Yoda, the Greek god thing. It, ummm, kinda puts you in line with the greats."

Telda (looking on the wall)

"Ummm. I'm already in line with the greats."

They both look at the LCD screen along the wall in the cafeteria, which shows the lineup of squadron pilots. Telda is the only female fighter pilot shown. They both chuckle and Abe just realizes that he is waiting in the omelet line with Telda.

Chef

"How may I help you, colonel?"

Telda (sounding fatigued)

"Just an omelet. Whites only. All the veggies, except for tomatoes."

The chef nods his head and begins to mix up the egg whites and veggies in the spatula.

Abe

"I thought all women ate tomatoes?"

Telda

"See, there you go, stereotyping. Didn't you learn the hard way? Don't be jealous because you can't eat what you want right now - Abraham."

Abe takes a closer look at her hair. He notices that a few pieces of her hair are sticking out. He rubs them so they lay back down. Also getting a good feel of her head.

Abe (as he rubs her hair)

"You sound tired."

Telda (trying to ignore Abe rubbing her hair)

"I am. They had me doing holding patterns for 4 hours over Omalia. Wasn't cool. Had to refuel twice, and circle around again and look at a boat most of the time, until the Navy arrived to declare the "hostages" free."

She takes a deep breath.

Abe (Still looking at her)

"Well, it looks like you got a tan. At least you got something from it."

She chuckles, but she looks away modestly.

Telda is comfortable on the eyes; she's Asiana with a bit of Olympian in her. She is 5'5 with a 6'6" mindset along with a soft but tough voice. She is known for her long dark braid which extends down to her back, and every now and then she braids her hair, in a circle, just above her hair to keep it in order, so it is comfortable when she flies. She's a strong young woman, and has toned arms which showcase her steady workout routine. She's made Abe melt since the day he met her in training. He was so into her that his leg shivered a bit when they were sitting next to each other. The two seem like a match made from heaven. They love aircraft; they both favor and enjoy each other. It was a good memory, but it was also an embarrassing one.

Flashback to a few years ago: AX1 Training Room
Captain Smitten, a tall, dark and loud instructor is standing in front of a group of 10 ABX pilots and navigators, lecturing them on formation training (when 2 or more planes fly in a group).

As usual, Smitten is hyped up. Not because he is happy, but at the fact that he asked Abe three simple questions and Abe wasn't paying attention, therefore getting them wrong.

Captain Smitten

"Dammit, Dalton! You just blew up another $100 million dollar aircraft. That's your third one today! You also blew your wingman up also! So that's a few more bucks for Paragon to expense! Wake up!"

That's Captain Smitten. He gives the squadron tough love when required. Unlike Captain O'Donnell, Smitten gets in the skin of his pilots when they are wrong. He is very prideful in his flying as his roots extend to aviation.

Abe

"Sorry Capt. Just got to clear my mind."

Captain Smitten looks away from Abe and looks at Telda, who just joined the Squadron. Then he looks back at Abe as if there aren't ten others in the room. He looks down at Abe's feet and notices that his right foot is shaking. Then he looks back up at Abe and back at Telda.

Abe

"Sir."

Captain Smitten

"Don't sir me. Call me dumb ass!"

Abe

"Sir. I'm not going to call you that."

Captain Smitten (cutting Abe off)

"No! I'm not your sir. Call me dumb ass. That's an order, Dalton!"

Abe

"Sir..dumb ass."

Captain Smitten

"That's it, Abraham! Say it again!"

Abe

"Dumb ass."

Captain Smitten

"That's my name don't wear it out! Now say it again anyway! Say my name. Say my name, baby!"

Abe

"Dumb ass."

Everybody in the room raises their eyebrows, but this is nothing new to them, besides Telda. Telda speaks up and nobody expects it. She's short, petite, and hasn't said a word to anybody in the squadron since she was first introduced.

Telda

"Dumb ass. Slowdown otherwise you overshoot. It's simple, we learned this shit in sixth grade. Pay attention. Otherwise, you're gonna be the one overshooting."

The entire room is quiet, and Abe hasn't taken his eyes off of Captain Smitten yet. A few seconds later, Smitten gives Abe a nod of approval. Abe looks to the right and sees Telda glaring at him. He is just now realizing that she was talking to him. This got Telda on Captain Smitten's good side. Though he still gives her a hard time like everybody else.

Captain Smitten (calmly)

"Wake up, Squid. You're the leader of this whole platoon. Although everybody is behind you during drills, in real battle you never know who you will need to be behind."

The Captain walks out of the door. Abe's leg is still shaking. He just got chewed up by Smitten, and it doesn't feel good but it's nothing new. Since the first day he took flight for AX1, he has been getting eaten up by him. Abe looks at Telda again. She winks at him. It's a sight that he will never forget. A glamourous girl with a sexy braid telling him what to do in an aircraft that many people don't know much about.

Back in the Cafeteria.

There are a few problems that play a factor in Abe and Telda's relationship. One, Telda has a boyfriend, who ironically works in the financial district of Paragon, and two, she believes Abe loves Gil. Not to mention that she knows of Abe's playboy ways along with his big captain ego, which most of the pilots have anyway, and Telda won't put up with it. Therefore she prefers her guys who are just a bit less egomaniacal. Like her boyfriend Colin. He's there for her; he has a great job, and takes care of home, he calls her, the basics.

60

Telda is a 'tough son of a gun'. Though she can't beat the guys in physical stunts, her mind beats matter. She can be intimidating. She is known to laser in on folk's eyes when she talks to them, especially if she feels if they are a threat. Most people use common respect and look away every now and then, but it kind of freaks them out that she hasn't looked away once. You would think that you would get relief when she blinks, but the blink makes it worse. It's quite evil, but to most men it's deceiving. To Abe, it's seductive.

Abe

"Don't think that slipped. I eat what I want. When I want, and where I want, Ms. Blanchard."

This comment catches Telda off guard

Telda blinks a few times.

"Whew. Well, the last time you did that, somebody sounded very uncomfortable on the radio frequency. Did it make your seat warmer? Did it offer more of a cushion? I bet Jason thanked God for the invention of the air mask that day."

Abe

"Ahh. So you want to go there? Low blows. Low blows."

Telda

"Next time try to assume, that it ISN'T gas, Mr. Dalton."

Telda is referring to a time when Abe had a very good meal before one of his flights. The flight ended up being a bit longer than he expected because he had to refuel. He had only expected the mission to be an hour, but it turned into three because Abe was having trouble landing on a water carrier, and he kept missing the catapult line which stops the plane. As a result, that day Abe had a moment that he will never forget. He thought it was gas. But it wasn't, and he did the number two in the plane - with his suit on. It was even worse on Jason, his navigator because air inside the jet circulates, and unfortunately you can't open a window at 40,000 feet.

Abe (humorously throws his hands up)

"Why can't we just take some things to the grave?"

The chef hands Telda the omelet that she ordered.

Telda

"Thanks, sir."

Abe

"Well.....Looks like I have to-"

Telda (interrupting)

"What? Are you about to go?"

Abe

'Yeah, wanna be close, don't want to have to make a run for it when that horn goes off."

Telda

"Did you ask for permission?"

Abe

"Permission for?"

Telda gives Abe the stare.He gets the picture. When it comes to Abe, Telda is spoiled. She gets what she wants, when she wants, with him at least. She can care less about controlling other men in the unit. She just makes sure she controls Abe. Though she won't give into Abe's playboy game, she still enjoys "her" time with him.

The eyes almost make Abe give in....

Abe

"Uhmmm, I think it will be best if I..."

Telda quietly gives him another squint.

Abe

"O....kay. Captain, Lead the way."

She gives him an innocent but devious smile as he agrees. She knows how much he likes her, but she also knows of his ego and rockstar status that comes with being a fighter pilot in Paragon. She won't allow herself to give into it. This is why she has held back from Abe since their first week of training. Her boyfriend Colin is mainly her excuse for the past 3 years. She tells Abe no, because it's 'not professional.'

The two sit down at a small table in the contemporary cafeteria. Every table has a television, with very few TV shows, but you can search for videos on a video site called WideZike. Command figured that they would rather have their crew watching videos to advance their knowledge of life, even if it's a video of lions hunting or a crazy prank video that was recorded in Olympia. It's a bit better than just watching a TV show just to fill time. You can hear the "whoas!" from the other side of the room, from some other airmen reacting to a crazy video they are watching. Abe is not a big Television watcher, nor is Telda therefore Abe cuts their monitor off.

Telda (covers her mouth, chewing her food)

"So... mister. How is your girlfriend?"

Abe

"Zelda........ I don't know who you're referring to..."

He calls her Zelda partially because of her demeanor, and she reminds him of Zelda from the old school video game.

Telda

"You know...."

Abe cuts his eyes at her with a blank expression. Knowing that she is doing what she does best, bothering him. She likes to ask for answers that she doesn't want to hear, but she still wants to know.

Telda

"Intel girl...I forgot her name..Gills..FishGills. Thrilla."

Abe

"She is NOT my girlfriend, and..."

Telda (interrupts and chuckling)

"Just admit it."

Abe

"She's not my..."

Telda (interrupts again)

"Jockstrap. I'm sorry. I forgot. She's just one of your jockeys? Duh. Why would even I say you have a girlfriend? I forgot that I'm talking to honest Abe here."

Abe leans back in his chair and takes a deep breath.

Abe

"Okay. Is this what you wanted me to stay here for? Because I got to go."

He begins to ball up his napkins and puts it inside his half-eaten fruit cup.

Telda (grabbing his hand)

"No, No, No. I'm just kidding. Don't go."

Abe lets out the frustration he rarely shows. A few seconds go by and Telda puts her foot along his leg under the table. Playing footsie, flirting with him. The table in between them gives makes her comfortable, but it also gives her the leverage she needs so she doesn't fuel any further actions.

Abe

"Gil, - Gillia is fine by the way, and she's not my girlfriend, and for the record, she's not a whore, or a jockey, as you call it. In fact, I was just with her a few hours ago. She had this perfume on last night. ---- I didn't shower this morning just so you can still smell it."

Abe reaches his hand across the table for Telda to smell his wrist. She strikes her eyes at him as she chews her food.

Abe

"What's the problem?"

She doesn't respond.

Abe

"Figured so."

Telda

"For the record, don't do what you did again."

Abe

"You asked. I was just trying to tell you how she smelled."

Telda

"No, I'm referring to your crappy ass mission with Carter last week."

Abe

"It wasn't."

Telda (Interrupting)

"Abe.....Don't do it again... I don't care how many Aces, diamonds, whores, whatever. DON'T do it again. You have 20, and soon to be 45 guys that look up to you. Leaders make mistakes but not dumb ones. You're gonna jack something up one day."

Abe (frustrated)

"First it's Finfrock, now it's you. Anything else?"

Knowing not to further the conversation, Abe sits back and looks around the cafeteria to avoid an argument. He starts to think about the discipline that his wing mates have been giving him, and if he should accept it or not. Telda presses her leg against his again, this time with more pressure.

Abe (looking under the table)

"Do you have an itch on your leg or something?"

Abe reaches under the table and softly grabs her right leg. She quickly pulls it back after feeling his fingers dig into her calf muscle.

Abe

"Speaking of girlfriends and my female jockeys? How is your lover man doing?"

Telda (face tightens)

"I'm not discussing my personal life with you...."

Abe (Puzzled)

"But you just…"

Telda gives him the same stare and squint. Abe knows what this means. Now instead of her rubbing her leg against his, she gives him a kick in the shin.

Abe's gives her a confused squint and a deep breath follows.

Abe

"Zelda, Zelda, Zelda, Zelda, Zelda, Zelda."

Before Abe can finish what he has to say. A large alarm goes off in the cafeteria and strobe lights are flashing.

The monitors turn red and the PA Speakers are blasting out.

"3 Thirty 3! 3 Thirty 3! Squid 1 Emergency Scramble"

Abe looks at Telda, she gives him another glance. The alerts are still blasting over the speakers.

Abe (getting up)

"Gotta go. Gotta go."

Abe has to sprint to the corridor where the rest of his crew is sitting. Though it is unexpected, the team has drilled for this many times. Abe's flight gear is awaiting him on a ladder set right next to the front of the airplane. He hops in the plane, and as he gets in, his wingman, Dell, hands him his mask, helmet, air hose, and even tosses some handgun ammo into Abe's lap as he closes the cockpit window.

Abe (intensely talking with his mask on)

"I need some more forced air! I'm taking too many quick breaths. F-1, throw me more three packs of A28's. Dell, I'm loaded up with 300 pounds of reserve A28. I need coordinates."

Abe is now in battle mode. He is looking at his flight control panels, checking his flaps, rudder controls, and making sure his systems are functioning properly. In a matter of seconds, he needs to review the weight and balance of his airplane, check the amount of fuel that is loaded up, and check all of his backup systems with his navigator, Jason.

Abe (looking over his systems, pressing buttons)

"I see the winds are at 180 at 9. I have no heavy ammo! Why isn't this armed!"

Talking fast, Abe talks to his Navigator, Jason, who is sitting behind him.

Abe

"Flaps."

Jason (Abe's Navigator behind him)

"Check."

Abe

"System."

Jason

"Check."

Abe

"Cowboys and Cows."

Jason

"Yup."

Abe

"We don't have much time, Jay; we got to roll."

Jason

"Leggo. If we don't get a heading in 10 seconds we're rolling vertical."

The jet engines are turned up, squealing with treble. The Paragon flag at the back of the hangar is whirling with the powerful winds from the engines.

Abe

"Lex, Base is taking too long. Upon emergency scramble approval. This is Squid and Flipper, and we're rolling out on Runway 22 Left heading straight up. Clear any aircraft within Class B. Airspace. I have no ammo, except this small thing - in - my - lap. Again, no missiles on hand, and we are heavy on the tanks for a long ride."

In other words, Abe has no time to waste, so he made his own clearance as it is an emergency, and he is going to Runway 22 left. He has advised mission support to clear any inbound aircraft, as he will take off no matter what's in his way. The Argon military support fixes Abe's air pressure mask and the Air Marshals with the orange sticks wave Abe out of the sheltered hangar.

Over the radio.

Radio Voice (Arab)

"Joint Force 5827, are you ready sir?"

Abe (pumped; checking his flight panels)

"Dude, you're late, I'm already headed out. Again We have no missiles so if a target needs to come down, nine times out of ten this plane is not coming back and nor are we."

This is a deep moment, as the mission control room gets quiet. They all look at Captain O'Donnell whose face is still, as he knows Abe is relentless. Captain Smitten is quiet, scratching his bald head while he watches the action on a monitor in a separate room. No matter what either one of them tell Abe, if an aircraft is to be intruding and Abe has no missiles, there's a good chance that he will Kamikaze it down. Abe's job is to first find out what's going on, but since he has no weapons, his only weapon are his flares, the 9 mm that him and his navigator carry, and the fighter jet which has pounds of fuel loaded up on it. In other words, this could be a suicide mission. Although it's a practice scramble, O'Donnell knows that Abe will still react in the same way in a live situation. He's too prideful, not only for flying, but for his father's land.

Radio Voice (rapidly)

"Joint Squid 5827, you are clear for takeoff. Catapult Runway 22R."

Abe

"No. We're going 22 Left there is no time to taxi all the way to the right side. I don't see any aircraft on final. We're out."

Abe cranks the plane up at full speed, and the engines and afterburners are at full tilt. He takes off and goes vertically into the air. The mission room is surprised and a few guys are rather pissed because Abe has made them look bad in a way, as he beat them to most punches. Commander O'Donnell loves it only because he knows how he trains his men, and they need to be in the sky 30 seconds before the minimum take-off time.

Jason (grunting)

"Radar, what's my coordinates?"

Radar

"250 for now."

Abe turns the plane slightly, banking it just enough to see the city and the coast of the Argon Nations.

Abe

"Nothing better than that feeling say, huh, Jason?"

Jason is Abe's Navigator, right behind him in the aircraft.

Jason (still grunting)

"Nope. Especially not with a driver like you. Bank 252, no delay."

Jason is probably the only person who can fly with Abe. He understands him, but he's the complete opposite. He's comfortable when Abe flies. He knows how to ignore Abe's ignorant sounding judgment, because he knows he means well, plus he trusts his skill. Jason used to be a solo fighter pilot but he surrendered that to be Abe's Navigator. Captain Smitten wouldn't let Abe go up alone, only because he knows the way he flies, he can and will lose consciousness at times. Instead of taking chances on losing their top gun, they put another top gun with their best. If Abe ever loses consciousness (it has happened before), Jason will take the sticks.

Abe banks again after taking Jason's orders. He starts out making a soft turn, but to save some time, he turns the plane upside down.

Jason didn't expect this.

Jason (grabbing his neck)

"You fuck! I said bank, not roll."

Abe (grunting also disregarding Jason uneasiness)

"We don't have time for that! What's next? What's our story?"

Jason

"Well, I'm not trying to pass out back here."

Jason gets a bit light-headed because without being notified about the roll, he snaps his neck. As for Abe, he expected it to happen, because he knew the roll was coming. This the bad part of flying with Abraham.

A moment goes by as they both take in the view of the beautiful landscape of the downtown area, the sandy mountains and the sea. At 20,000 feet, it looks like a Lego world. They have only been flying for 25 seconds and the aircraft is going about 800 MPH (620 knots) at 20,000 feet in the sky.

Abe

"My bad about your neck, BUT as far as tonight goes, after this mission, we will be scrambling for some of those fine mamasitas. I won't mind being stuck in Emirate."

Emirate is the country across the gulf. It's also a very modern nation similar to Paragon. But it is well recognized, has a large population, and a good amount of tourists. Abe likes it because many Olympian and European women travel there to shop.

Abe points to the city outside his window. He begins to rhyme musically. Something he likes to do when he flies.

Abe (rapping and singing)

"I got my missile... I'm ready for them, well, at least one of them, well maybe, two of them. You know what I mean. Yeah, you what I mean, yeah you know what I mean."

This is another crazy trait of Abe. It's a habit that started when he did his first cross country when he was 17. He doesn't handle the slow periods very well.

Jason

"Roger that...But let's knock the mission out first. We are at 32,000..."

A voice comes over the radio, cutting Jason off.

Radio Dispatch (Arab)

"Squid Flipper, there has been a diversion. This is live. I repeat this is live 0209. There's been a report of missiles of the coast of Paragon and our ships can't get an eye view of them. Can you confirm your ammo load?"

Abe

"The coast of what?"

Jason (Interrupting Abe)

"Paragon.... Hey radio, we are holding nothing but a plane and flares. What's the location? We need fuel though. Coordinates of the nearest 135?"

This is a significant reason why Jason is Abe's wingman because he doesn't back down or hesitate. No matter if he has plenty of ammo. Or if he is flying with none.

Radio

"Sir, we cannot send you out unarmed."

Jason

"Then what are you telling us for? You're wasting time! Where is the nearest re-fueler at?"

Radio (Arab)

"200 Miles. Heading 310 degrees."

Jason

"At least, it's kinda close by. How many heads are we going against? Anybody rolling with us?"

Captain O'Donnell gets on the radio. You can tell the difference in the voice change, as his is very strong.

Capt O'Donnell (Serious)

"Jason, you're the only aircraft with stealth capability. It is a sensitive zone, so we need you to check it out. Only fire if fired upon. Just be careful, you know we are under heavy scrutiny, Abraham. Hold your horses if you have to! There's no aircraft on the radar, but there is much unexpected ground activity and one of our ships may be in danger. You and Squid are the only ABX fighters in the sky."

O'Donnell has a deep moment when he realizes that they are flying empty and he knows that Abe and Jason will fly into the eye of the missile or a cockpit of an airplane, and a ship if they have to. All these will complete the mission. But the last thing that any Captain wants; to lose a man.

The engines rev up.

Abe (speeding the aircraft up)

"What's the problem sir?"

Radio (Captain O'Donnell)

"Squid, you need to put everything to the side right now. Luna 2 we need imagery. No engaging unless you're engaged. Get in and get out of there. Throttle up if you have to. We will have two Emirate 135s 50 miles out at 40,000 feet."

Jason

"Roger. Heading 310, we will be loading up for some water in a few and one A28 pack to follow. Question, can we take a quick dip instead of doing it airborne?"

Radio (Captain O'Donnell)

"No, we haven't practiced that enough. Just stay on course."

There's a brief moment of silence in the aircraft. Abe has a deep look on his face, butterflies in his stomach. Jason begins to put numbers in the cockpits system.

Jason (as he enters numbers on the CPU)

"Squid, are you all right up there?"

Abe gives no response. Stay's silent. Seconds go by.

Abe

"Just wasn't expecting a true mission today."

Jason (country)

"Is that really why? Usually you're ready to press that red button."

Abe

"I hope that it's nothing. Maybe it's a false alarm."

Silence continues. The aircraft continues into the sky en route to their new mission. They get refueled in the sky. En route to the south coast of Paragon, which is only about 15 more minutes away.

3

A Deep Breath

In an orange-colored desert, two black Range Rover convertibles are rolling through the desert leaving a trail of dust.

Charles Dalton, age 44, a handsome and well groomed black man with an Europa accent, is in a Black SUV with 3 other men. Tommy, the driver, is 25, Jim is a 47-year-old experienced military admiral, and Charles's Africana born cousin, Joro Lateru. They are all dressed in brown military camouflage, except for Joro who is in his traditional west Africana military uniform that has an arrangement of colors, mostly green and blue. The desert terrain is rumbling from under the truck. The men have the windows down, enjoying the heat, wind and the driver, Tommy, is a silly and young cadet, fresh to the land. He also has a trigger-happy mouth.

Tommy (Young Driver)

"Yo, I believe we are about to run out of fuel soon. The meter says 15 miles left until empty, and we are in the middle of nowhere."

Jim (relaxed, looking out of the window)

"Tommy, we will be fine. Just follow the gravel road, and relax."

In the back seats, Charles and Joro look at each other as they laugh at the rookie who has never been to Paragon's testing terrain before.

Tommy (nervous, but amused)

"All right... All right. Well, don't act like I didn't say so. We're in the middle of nowhere. Is there a fueling station out here? Shit, if it was it would probably be blown up, it's so dang hot. I'm not gonna be the one filling it up."

Jim

"Tommy.... Just keep driving."

Tommy looks at Jim as if he is crazy. He continues to drive. He sees a group of windmills, desert mountains, and other SUVS in the area just like any other military base. He just landed in Paragon, and has never even seen the place.

Tommy

"Where are we going anyway?"

Jim

"Tommy. Just drive."

Tommy hushes his mouth as he takes a big gulp. He continues to drive. Then a loud missile soars across the sky.

The bang from the missile forces Tommy to slam the brakes of the SUV. All the men jolt forward, inside the vehicle and hang on for dear life. Jim spills water all over his military clothing. He begins to wipe it off, frustrated at his young cadet.

Tommy

"What the-!!!"

Jim (interrupts calmly, hand on the dashboard)

"Tommy, keep going... It's just defense testing. Get used to it, son."

Jim (disregards the drama)

"By the way, Tommy, everything that you are about to see is classified. Everything."

Charles puts his head outside the window, looks at the sky and his whereabouts, and puts his head back in the vehicle. He realizes that a test missile was just launched but nothing was hit.

He looks at Joro with seriousness.

Charles (looking at Joro, with frustration)

"That goes for you, too. Everything is classified, Joro. I don't even know WHY I brought your corrupt ass out here."

Joro laughs, grabs Charles's shoulder, and smiles. Highlighting his dark, coarse goatee, and pearl white teeth. He has more of a "joker" smile than a friendly one. Charles can't stand it.

Joro (Golian accent, looking in Charles eyes)

"Don't worry, cousin. Blood is always thicker than water."

Another missile is launched, but this time it is in plain sight of the front window of the vehicle. It shoots across a blue sky for about 8 seconds and hits a large radio controlled test aircraft. Tommy looks at Jim in surprise.

Tommy slams the brakes of the SUV, again.

Tommy

"What the....!"

Jim

"It's a just piece of paper son, defense testing. Welcome to the future. By the way, everything that you are about to see is classified."

Again, Charles reaches his head outside the window, looks at the sky, his whereabouts, and puts his head back in. He looks at Joro with seriousness.

Charles

"That goes for you too. (Shaking his head) I don't even know WHY I brought your corrupt ass out here."

Joro laughs and looks at Charles with a big smile on his face, and grabs his shoulder in excitement again. Joro has one of those weird smiles. He is the type who would smile at you and shoot you at the same time. He is really not the guy to not have on your bad side. Fortunately, he's Charles's cousin on his grandfather's side of the family. If that weren't the case, they would despise each other even more.

Joro (replying to Charles' comment)

"Don't worry, cousin. Blood is always thicker than water."

Another missile is launched, in plain sight from the front window of the SUV. It shoots across a blue sky with smoke trailing behind it. It comes from a Windmill looking device, as if it were a decoy. It's meant to be unexpected, more so a short range defense for the civilization. If a person were to look at it, you would think that it is a windmill farm.

Another missile is launched from one of the windmills.

A slot inside the post of a windmill opens. The missile ignites and begins to PROPEL to the sky. It travels into the air where one can see the skyline of a downtown area on the horizon (miles away), mountains, and other desert terrain of Paragon. As it travels at 400 miles per hour, it hits a few bugs just like they hit the windshield of a car. Now at a speed of 600 miles per hour, the MISSILE is inches away from the jet, in plain sight of the pilot. The pilot looks to the right and comes eye to eye with the missile before it collides with the aircraft. The pilot, Abe, blinks once as the missile gets closer to his face. He is eye-to-eye with the nose of the 7 foot bomb. Everything turns into slow motion and he slowly closes his eyes for his last moments of life. Jason won't feel it coming because he's looking at the navigation radar. Captain O'Donnell won't even see it coming back at the ABX base, because it happened so fast.

All the wonders of not being prepared, not sleeping enough… Why didn't his commander inform him of multiple missile activity? Did he take the scramble too lightly? Was it a setup? Why now? At home? How will Captain Smitten feel about it?

Back in the SUV, Joro grabs Charles' shoulder with the same joker smile

Joro

"Don't worry cousin, blood is always thicker than water."

Abe (in the cockpit)

"Jason! Jason!"

Abe prepares for his final breath.

The explosion occurs. By the time Charles looks up, he sees the fire and composite parts flooding the sky. There are other sounds of aircraft jets passing by but that can be the aftereffect that planes make when they are going at high levels of speed. In the back of his mind he also knows that today was Abe's Scramble mission. Joro is stunned, Jim is already out of the truck running towards the scene, and Tommy is shaken wondering what he has himself gotten into by taking the assignment to move to Paragon.

Two weeks later

Charles wakes up from one of his recurring nightmares while he is in the bathtub. His phone begins to vibrate, alerting him of a message. He is in a bubble bath within a luxurious yellow-toned bathroom with marble features. He takes a few deep breaths and puts some water on his face.

It's tough.

The idea of losing a child for any parent can be devastating. The situation is made worse as the incident replays in his mind over and over. The fact that the system that he had created to defend his territory had, in a way, come back to haunt him. Unfortunately, defense is the double standard of war; in this case, it was a double standard to prevent a war.

He dries his right hand and grabs his blackberry from the side of the bathtub. On the screen of the phone, it reads.

Email from Lisa -
I'm still deciding what to wear for the Gala tomorrow. Then again, I'm not sure if I want to go. Any Suggestions?
- LISA M. GASQUEW

Charles Replies
I'm sure you can manage a decision of that magnitude, BUT, then again.... I don't know, BOSS.... :-)
-CD"

If there is any woman that Charles has respect for (besides his mother), it would be Lisa. They have known each other since they were children. Although they came from two completely different worlds and demographics, they both stayed connected during and after college, and even studied abroad while in school. Both of them are ridiculously ambitious people. Lisa took a more executive role, whereas Charles was always the risk taker. They have a very different, but sarcastic type of a relationship.

After a few moments, Charles gets out of the bathtub. He looks at himself in the mirror as he begins to dry himself off with his towel. Since he quickly snapped out of his nightmare, he still has a few suds on his strong and broad shoulder. He wipes them off. He wraps his towel around his waist then starts to brush his teeth. His phone begins to vibrate again. He glances at it and picks it up with his free hand and reads the next message from Lisa.

SCREEN OF MOBILE PHONE. AS CHARLES READS:
 "Funny guy, I guess I will 'See' you tomorrow, sir"
He chuckles. He replies back and types with his left hand using his thumb.

"Ditto, :-)"
Once he's done with his bathroom process, he goes to his living room. Just like Paragon, his penthouse is immaculate, large but still cozy and intimate. Everything is solar powered, and when he is not in a particular room, the power automatically goes off. In the mood for music, he turns on his iPod which wirelessly connects to his surround sound system. He sits down on the couch, and shuffles through songs for about a minute. He cuts on some rap music, but realizes he can't take such words at the moment. So he turns on some Beck, leans back, closes his eyes.

As he listens to the melody, a male begins to speak over the song. Charles looks at his iPod wondering what happened, not expecting the voice. On the iPod he notices that in the subtitle it says, 'L. Gasquew' and a note under it which says, 'Earl Never Fails'. L. Gasquew is Lisa's online profile name. The male that's speaking over the tune is Earl Nightingale (A motivational speaker). Charles is somewhat surprised as he remembers Lisa sent this to him a few months ago, but he's never had the opportunity to sit down and listen to it. Lisa has always motivated Charles and she knows how much Earl Nightingale touches him. Nightingale's words keep Charles going and his ambitions high. This is what makes their friendship (business and personal) unique.

Charles needs all the motivation that he can get. No matter how successful he is, his endeavors seem to be ever-cycling and never-ending.

Since the passing of his father, he has taken the reins of keeping Paragon afloat. It's been a mission, not only operationally, but politically. Many people and countries want the land of Paragon, which is unofficially in Charles's hands. It has slowly become a place where if you visit, it can be very hard to return home. Simply because Paragon has a tremendous amount of opportunity and joy instilled in the territory. Citizens of Paragon who stay out of trouble receive awards every five years, just for being a good

Sumatran. Since the government monetarily self-sustains itself, a portion of the leftover profits go to the residents of Paragon, based on contribution. This, in a way, is an incentive for their sacrifice to keep the country running ever since the majority of the militia has left.

Charles also has a target on his head simply because he is the holder of the A28 mineral, a resource which will replace fuel one day. It is multipurpose as its main purpose is not only for combustible fuel but it is also a powerful defense tool that every leader in the world wants to get their hands on. It's about money and power, and even the people who don't want to do business with Charles have to stay close simply because if he releases A28 'inappropriately', it can tank all the fuel companies, the people who make money from fuel, and the government(s) will also lose out on billions of dollars that the fuel industry generates. A28 can change the world in many ways, on both ends of the spectrum. It's like a soda. People think they need it because it's marketed to them, but in actual fact they don't need it. They just think they do, because that's how the product is marketed to the masses. A28 will allow fuel to burn slower; it uses water so therefore irrigation plants can be used to make it. It's an awesome remedy that will not only save people money, it saves the world money.

As Earl speaks, Charles falls asleep on his couch. His balcony door is propped open while the warm air of the night creeps in. The skyscrapers of Paragon illuminate the skyline. A view that one wouldn't want to fall asleep to; it looks more like a painting than a balcony view.

A few hours pass by, and he wakes up. He's cold. Mostly because the air conditioning is pumping and he still has nothing on but a towel. The sun reminds him that he accidentally left his balcony window open. Not that anybody can walk in, since his downtown condo is 35 stories in the sky. It's simply not a good habit. There is nothing worse than a falcon flying in, or any annoying flies buzzing around which happens often in Paragon. Even so, if something or somebody were to intrude on Charles' penthouse, his security detail would be on it immediately, from armed men to helicopters.

The door knocks. Then opens. It's Bill, Charles's lead security guard.

Bill (Southern Olympian Accent0

"Dalton, its Argon 22 coming in."

Charles's eyes squint as the sun is peeking in.

Charles (grunted morning voice)

"Billy Bob. What's going on?"

Bill

"Hah, Nothing much. How ya holding up? It is eight hundred hours, man, get up."

Bill walks in. He's a big country guy. He is white, with a bald head, and always wears sunglasses. Even when it's raining. He has a personality like a favorite uncle. He is quiet when you don't know him, but is loud when you do get to know him. Bill mostly wears a jumpsuit which says Argon Unit 7. At 45-years-old, he is in incredible shape. He has tattoos that cover his whole right arm.

Bill (accent)

"We're running late, Chuck D! Optimus just got back in town. You owe the hay dog a visit for that high placement that she had. Shit, that purse was worth about 2 million dollars. Let's not talk about endorsements. Although first would have been betta, second don't hurt especially for a young rehab like her."

Charles

"Oh. So she did win, huh? I forgot she was competing this   weekend."

Bill

"Oh, yeah. She almost beat Wiz Bear. But I heard it was some other bullshit that happened there too. So wipe that drool off of your cheek and let's get moving, boss."

Optimus is Charles's thoroughbred horse. She was rescued from an owner who left her for nothing because she wouldn't run for him. Charles heard about her, and took her in, and it turned out to be a blessing.

Charles

"I don't know. She's usually hotheaded when she is done with a long haul. How long until they arrive?"

Bill

"Any minute now. So we gotta go. You know she will be calm and happy once she sees you! Come on."

Bill's country accent hasn't left him. Although he is from the southern states in Olympia, and moved to Paragon 6 years ago, he still carries that twang and that lingo. The only thing that he misses and still craves is a cold soda every now and then, since Paragon doesn't sell soda, which has helped him with his diet. He used to be a flabby 290 pounds, and now he is a 220 pound rock, with less than 8 percent body fat on him.

Charles gets up, still groggy from the night before. He hasn't rested the same since Abe had his fighter jet incident. It haunts him many nights of the week. He never thought that creating defense mechanisms for his nation would possibly backfire on him with his only son. It changed his perspective on defense. Initially, it was easy because one doesn't think of somebody that they knew meeting the end of a missile. It haunts him every day. Despite his grief, Charles still has to continue to implement the missiles to protect the people, this new world that he has created. Along with the rich and natural assets that Paragon holds.

Bill looks at the television.

Bill

"TV. What's goin' on?"

The television that is mounted inside of the wall turns on, and speaks out.

TV (CPU voice)

"Hi, Charles and I think I heard Bill. If so, hi, Bill. Today, there is breaking news going on 28 networks worldwide. In central Olympia networks are talking about politics. There are also 5 soccer matches in place, and I have the recording of Optimus's race. Do you care to watch?"

Bill

"No, show me what's breaking."

TV (Woman Voice)

"Sure, sir. I'm turning to Foxwire networks."

Bill

"Ha. You know better than that... "

TV

"I'm just kidding sir. How dare I? Turning into WNN."

The TV automatically turns to WNN (World News Network) networks, which is based in Washington, Olympia. Once the screen changes, one can immediately see chaos at a protest in front of the Presidential Lawn.

Signs are reading. BRING OUR PEOPLE BACK. BRING OUR WORKERS BACK. SEND HIS HORSE BACK.

Bill

"Oh, shit. Hey, Chuck. Chuck, get ya ass out here."

Bill turns his head looking for him. Charles is in his bedroom throwing some clothes on. He comes out a few seconds later in the hallway, tucking his pinkish colored button down into his black slacks and looks at the TV.

Charles (hooking his belt up)

"What?"

Bill (small smirk)

"Hell. They even brought Optimus into this shit."

Charles

"Into what shit?"

Bill

"I dunno, I think it's those Coffee Party folks. The ones who are always mad."

On the screen, you can see angered Olympians outside the President of Olympia's home, as they are outraged at the state of their union. Most of the crowd is white, although there are a few blacks in the group as well. You can see some are arguing with another small group. Some have signs, and others are rooting their hands in the sky with the same chants.

Protestors

"They are thieves! They are thieves! They used us! Send that   horse back! Send that horse back! Send that horse back!"

Bill

"Idiots, he's coming back anyway. He ain't tryna live over there, he like breathing in this good air over here. Get with it, baby."

Bill and his country humor, he can make light of any dark situation. As they watch the protest, the voice of the news reporter begins to speak over the broadcast. He has a traditional anchor suit and is very clean-cut.

Reporter (Older Male)

"As you can see, many Olympians are protesting and outraged. President Grover has yet to address them and is not likely to. Now, this is nothing new. But next to this clip is a new one, and is probably what triggered yet another Coffee Party rally."

The network changes to another clip.

Reporter

"So I guess this is a new place for a political protest; a Horse Race. Yes, I said it. At a Horse Race, and these are not animal rights activists. At around 3 am this morning, gatherers flooded outside the stable of Charles Dalton's racehorse, Optimus, who was runner-up in the Olympia Derby last night. Somehow many found a way to access the private areas of the racetrack and began to throw things at Optimus, mostly hitting her stable. By the looks of things, they were protesting and were upset about Dalton's tactics and the rise of Paragon. Optimus's placement must have rubbed it in a bit. As you can see, many people are upset about her being runner-up, especially on ground in Olympia. This is the second time this month that this has happened to Dalton's horse."

Charles loudly tells the television to turn off, but Bill overrides him, and tells the TV to stay on.

He looks at Chuck.

Bill (crossing his arms)

"Not yet, Chuck, Not yet. I heard Optimus showed them up. You have to learn how to handle these situations anyway. Everybody ain't gonna love ya, Chuck, especially when you're winning on their track and on their soil."

The voice-activated television stays on and the crowd is still visibly upset. The police are trying to escort Optimus out, but people won't move from her stall exit. Her trainer tries to get her out and into the transport trailer which then will take her to a helicopter that's made exclusively for her and other large animals.

As police and racetrack personnel try to move people out of the way, others who support Optimus and Charles begin to step in to make way for her to be transported. Once room is created, Optimus is slowly brought out. She is bold, shiny, and bay-colored. She looks bolder on the TV screen. She has her black throw wrapped around her, a mask to protect her face from insects, and her hair is braided tightly along her strong neck. One can see the bay-coloring on her as if she was dipped brown ink. Optimus's eyes are relaxed, and she is gentle, that is until she becomes rattled.

Reporter

"Now, we all know Optimus Prime as a competitor. But she is also known for her charismatic antics on camera as she likes to show off her teeth and nibble on male reporters' hair and ears, sometimes licking them. But last night, this was a different Optimus. As the protestors began to beat on her stable and harass her, the mare's qualities and capabilities that make her stand out at the racetrack emerged."

As the video continues to play, Optimus stands still. She looks at the 30 - 40 upset people around her, and then you have to add the 20 personnel who are trying to restrain the crowd from her. She begins to neigh loudly. Her trainer, Marco, is leading her out and he stays calm as he takes hits from variations of paper and small pebbles of stone. Then the moment came when one of the protestors pushed Marco to the ground. This ignites Optimus. As Marco lies on the ground and the protestors begin to kick at him, Optimus neighs louder; her eyes get big and the borders turn red. One can see the breaths come out of the side of her as she breathes. Her veins begin to emerge and anybody close to her can see every muscle tense up in her body. She grunts and moves in fast circles, moving all the protestors out of the way of Marco, who is still on the ground. One person tries to go for Marco, and Optimus brings her spirit out.

She goes next to the person who is attacking Marco. She eyes him down and drops her nose into the dirt. She sniffs some up, and blows the dirt out of her nose as if she were a bull. Optimus begins to paw her hoof as if he were a bear, then she rears up on her hind legs. Another trainer tries to grab her reins, but she snatches them away. People are still taunting Marco and the horse. She then rises and is about 13 feet in the air standing on two legs. The protesters now begin to scatter. The one who continues to kick Marco gets the worst of it. Since he is so busy trying to beat on Marco, Optimus eyes him, knocks him over, and pins him to the ground with her hoof putting some of her 1,000 pounds on him. Others begin to step back as they realize she isn't going to let her captive move. Folks are frantic and crying for help. Next, Optimus goes for the person's neck and shakes it endlessly. It looks fatal, but if one looked closer it seems like Optimus was trying to send a message more than hurt the male. This also made people step back.

Crowd Person

"See, he's evil! He's attacking him!"

Now they can see why her name is Optimus. Optimus looks meaner with her mask on her face which only shows her eyes, ears, and nose. She continues to pin the man to the ground by holding his neck. Reality has hit, and the man is not moving. Charles is watching and is nervous, because he doesn't want anybody hurt at the cost of him or his horse, as it is pointless. Life is bigger than all of this.

As the man lay still and Optimus has him pinned by the neck, it's a sight that will never be forgotten. Marco slowly gets up, and once he rolls away, Optimus shakes the protester a bit, and finally releases her grip on him. It's a weird moment. Folks are watching a horse that is 17 hands tall pinning a man as if to keep him motionless for the police to arrest. The man is still motionless, and one more bite Optimus can kill him. As Optimus releases him, folks are expecting blood, hoping the guy isn't paralyzed. Was he innocent or did he provoke her is the question. This question can make a big difference on how all this plays out.

Once Optimus pulls up, she looks at her trainer Marco and bends her neck down numerous times. This is what she does when she is about to compete before a race. She is breathing hard, and it looks like she is trying to say something to him; almost as if it were an apology. She rubs her face next to his, demonstrating her loyalty towards Marco. Most horses would have run off. But Optimus backs down from very little, besides small critters (she doesn't like mice). However, when a horses' pyramidal world is distorted, they will protect those that matter to them. Usually for their own protection.

The man lies down motionless. Charles and Bill are watching. Hoping that the guy didn't die or suffer a horrific injury.

Reporter (Voice over the Video Footage)

"After all the turmoil, the man did not suffer from any injuries although he was rushed to the hospital. His treatment was limited to a Tetanus B. Shot, and he was quarantined as Optimus lives across the world in Paragon. Authorities don't want any international diseases to contaminate across borders."

Charles (watching the screen)

"Looks like we will be hearing from a lawyer soon."

Bill looks at him, drinking a bottle of water.

Bill

"Three have called me already. Representing that guy."

Charles shakes his head as he continues to watch the clip.

As the man is attended to, he eventually gets up on his own power. He is sitting down and is holding his sign saying, 'Paragon is Hell and they are Thieves.'

Charles's lead environmentalist, Andy, who travels with Optimus, tends to the protestor. He tells him to sit still until he is examined, as he could have some sort of spinal injury. Despite his display of anger towards the horse and Andy's home, Andy instructs him not to move. He lays him down and puts a sheet under the man's head. Most of the other Coffee Party members walk away in disgust, not tending to their fellow protester. It's a not unsurprising act of selfishness.

Once Optimus is completely calm, she is loaded into a small trailer which is just outside of a cargo hold of a large black helicopter. It has a tail number of P-H2, meaning Paragon - Helicopter 2. Three men, wearing green vests and helmets, guide her into the trailer with ease as the cameras get the last pictures of her hind end going into the trailer. The trailer is then pulled into the helicopter by a cable. The rear door slowly closes. While Andy makes sure everything is secure, a person walks up to him, and they speak for a few seconds. Andy reaches in his pocket to give him something like a business card. They wave each other off. The copilot of the helicopter does one more walk around. Makes sure all straps are removed. One more guy does another walk around and scans the whole helicopter to make sure that it is in balance, since there is a thousand pound animal on board. The lights turn on near the tail and the red beacon light begins to flash, meaning it is about to be operational. The blades begin to move as the officers tell people to step back so they don't get hit or killed by a blade turn. The cameras are all shining on the helicopter as if Optimus was a superstar, which she is. The bulbs from 15 cameras, the lights from the helicopter, the horse show grounds and the horizon along the dark colored sky illuminate the area beautifully.

The helicopter begins to lift, and soon it leans forward and goes off into the night. Leaving the protesters, camera men, and fans of Optimus behind with a night that none of them will ever forget. All they can see is them head to the nearest airport which Optimus will then be transferred to an airplane laid out with a stable and hay, so she can head back to Paragon. As the helicopter's red and white lights blink, fade into the distance; the sound of the chopper blades diminishes. Optimus and the Paragon team are gone. Safe and sound. The protesters are leaving though some are still unhappy. Some have second thoughts of what they did after they saw Andy, who had a Paragon shirt on while helping the guy who tried to harm the horse that Andy cares for. Though some won't admit it, many believe they saw something amazing tonight and frightening as well.

Reporter (looking at the other anchor)

"Well, that is something that we never want to see. Good thing that the person is okay, and Optimus too. Right, Susie?"

Susie Reporter

"Right. In other news, GELT Industries has announced..."

Charles (interrupts and talks to the TV)

"Turn to FOXWIRE. Live Breaking News."

As the TV changes the station FOXWIRE turns on. Not surprisingly, they are covering the same incident. But this network changed and produced the incident entirely different. They are playing a video of Optimus holding the man by his neck. Then they freeze it, which is a frightening image because it is zoomed in on Optimus's eyes, mask, and his human-like teeth gripping on the man's neck. Foxwire supports the Coffee Party, and aren't the best advocates of blacks.

FOXWIRE Reporter

"Optimus Prime, the horse owned by Leader of Paragon, Charles Dalton, is the Pit Bull of Horse Racing."

Bill (interrupt)

"Damn, this shit is all over the damn place. You know FOXWIRES gonna twist this ish..."

FOXWIRE Reporter

"Watch this frightening clip as Dalton's horse attacks an innocent fan after winning runner-up today at the Olympia Derby. It was a terrifying scene. I mean, she just erupted into Chaos out of the blue. Maybe it was because she knew she had a beating awaiting her due to her loss. Her owners have been contacted, but failed to respond. As for the poor fan, a source says he is in critical condition. This is why people like Dalton shouldn't be allowed to have pets of this size; if any pets at all."

As the reporter continues with the story, they show an interview of a protester.

Coffee Party Protestor (East Coast accent)

"He just attacked him. We were all out here discussing things, and he just attacked. That horse and its owner should be put to sleep. No exceptions. I've never seen anything like it. Dalton has done no good for Olympians. He's a liar. He is the Antichrist. This horse is the devil. I wish it broke its leg or had a heart attack!"

The reporter hands the microphone to another person.

Protester (Young black male)

"He's a thief. He should not be allowed to perform with our organizations."

Foxwire Reporter

"Sir, you are similar race to Dalton? Well, at least in skin color. No disrespect, but being a person of color, why are you protesting against him? Why chose to be one of the few blacks out here with the majority whites, protesting against Dalton and his horse. Umm, his horse that goes by the name of…"

He can't remember the horse. However, the Protester remembers.

Black Protester (Black Male)

"Optimus. That is the horse's name."

The protester looks into the reporter's eye, and puts his lips close to the microphone. A little too close.

Black Protester

"As far as being black, I am out here for principally for my Olympian pride, as I am a patriot of this nation. Dalton has done NOTHING for me and he NEVER will. He's turned my friends against me along with my parents. They all have left Olympia for Paragon, and I no longer have any one here. It's not about color! It's the principle of the thing. He is the devil! He is a liar and he is going to send our world to pieces. He should be poisoned, and after tonight so should his Fighting Horse Beast. This is senseless. He needs to stay home and that horse needs to also."

As the protester finishes speaking, the FOXWIRE reporter pulls the microphone back, realizing that the guy has spit all over it from his aggressive talking. The reporter looks at the small white spit balls on the black microphone cover and tries to ignore it.

Foxwire Reporter

"Thanks, sir."

The protester reaches for the microphone again.

Black Protester (grabbing the microphone)

"Wait, I'm not done…President Grover. You need to get a handle on this situation. You suck at being a leader! As for you, Dalton, you and your whole country deserve to be…"

Before he can finish, Charles speaks loudly to the television.

Charles (European Accent)

"TV OFF....."

The TV turns off...

As Charles and Bill watch what's going on the news networks, they have a mixture of feelings. Part of it is amusing, but the other part of it makes them realize that they are in the unenviable position of receiving a high level of animosity from the citizens in Olympia even though they are on the other side of the world. The good thing is that nobody was injured, and there was a good chance that Charles, or anybody from Optimus's team, weren't at fault. It is still bad publicity, and if it had gotten worse, it could land a fat settlement, just to keep the case low profile. A lawsuit still may occur, but thanks to video footage and proof that the horse was attacked, Charles should be fine.

FOXWIRE has Charles on their red radar. Just like they switched the story around by only showing parts of the clip, they do anything that they can, to diminish Charles's reputation, just as they did the first Black President about 20 years ago. Their whole goal is to make Paragon look bad, and if that involves using a horse that is linked to Paragon, they will use it. It is funny, but it also shows how the media can have total influence on many.

WNN is a bit different from FOXWIRE. They tend to stay neutral on many affairs, and they aren't as negative or biased towards any sides. FOXWIRE looks at many things one way; they are very insensitive when it comes to equality, unity, and diversity. Most of their anchors and host are members of the Coffee Party, which is mainly a group of people who can be very prejudiced, racist, and one-sided when discussing equality and balance amongst all. If they see another race suffering, most of them, if not all, wouldn't piss on a burning body to extinguish it. Instead they would watch and laugh, or possibly cook s'mores or kabobs around the burning bodies.

When Charles thinks of the remarks from the people referring him to the devil, evil, and the Antichrist, it hurts his heart. This typification is far from who he is. Charles cares for many, almost to the point that he cares too much. He receives hate because he was the founding father of a place for opportunity for all. Not necessarily a revolution, but a new way of life. Something different, unique, and intriguing enough for millions to move to a vision that he had. There are many rewards that come with it, but there are also many thorns in the roses.

Charles

"My own skin color dislikes me now. Wow. He really thinks I took his family away. I mean, it was their choice. Right?"

Bill

"Didn't I tell you that I'm going to stop reassuring you of things you already know –"

"No son, you're not wrong. You've made an amazing place. It is life, and people make decisions. It's unfortunate that the boy's people left him. Hell, he coulda' came too. You can't be perfect son. You know this..."

Helping all is one of Charles' flaws, and that is one of the thoughts he has had to accept when people began to migrate. Paragon was a settlement when people weren't there. Nevertheless, as the people began to move there, many were professional and awesome people. Citizens died, got sick, and people got fired from their jobs. Some were forced to deport due to crime. Seeing this and making this world has its awesome pros, but it has the con of all cons.

It makes Charles hurt even more when people of his same race despise him; initially he thought they would support him more. He was wrong. It's equal. All colors support. He has gotten more support from whites and other races than he ever expected, although he still deals with a tremendous amount of racism. Many love Charles because of his diversity, kindness to many people, and openness for various conversations. They teach him lessons and he teaches them lessons, it equates to an amazing experience.

Charles (shaking his head)

"Wow. They are sick. My goodness. You know, Bill, I really don't get them. I mean, I like some of their TV shows. But where the heck do they get lost with their politics and views on particular people?   As long as Opt is okay. Then we're okay. You say he just touched down?"

(Opt is short for Optimus)

Bill

"They weren't always like that. But now, its nuts! Yup, he's here; you ready to roll out? I think they have him unloaded by now. He's at the SafeHaven."

Charles

"Let's roll."

4

Hi Mr. Juntow

Preparing for the day is Bin Juntow, a twenty-nine year-old Asiana - Olympian business man, with a hidden, but very upbeat personality. He's the type who is very reserved with people that he doesn't know, but after a few years of getting to know him, or even after a few cocktails, the real Bin emerges.

At the moment, Bin is putting the finishing touches on his necktie as he prepares for his dream job interview for a company called GELT industries, who are the global leader for producing energy, structures, and large machinery. Bin is really into fashion. He is very particular with how his collars look and is equally picky about ties, which he prefers tied in the Windsor knot.

Bin looks in the mirror as he puts his black rimmed eyeglasses on. He straightens them out and speaks to his self, in reflection.

> Bin

You are the man, I don't care what they say, Hyinngunngg!

(Mocking his Asian culture) It is this exercise that he does, to boost his confidence.

Bin has lived majority of his life in Olympia. He has also lived in Japa for a few years, which is where his family resides. Japa is an Asiana country, on the opposite side of the world. He has an accent of a traditional Olympian. He can also speak his native language, though he really tries not to. That's why he makes fun of it; he was picked on at school a lot because of it, so joking about it in a way made him more accepted. Bin is a chameleon. He knows how to blend himself in almost any situation. It's a trait that he learned from his father in early years. Thus these traits have been carried over to Bin while he was raised.

Bin, still getting dressed, puts his watch on with excitement as he walks to his bedroom, and realizes what time it is.

BIN (talking to himself)

"Shit! You're not going to be the man today at the pace you are going."

One of his other bad habits, he talks to himself, out loud.

Moving swiftly, but not efficiently. Bin puts on his steel-colored sports coat, and the side effects of running late begin. Pens are falling out of his coat, his collar is stuck under the blazer, and he's struggling to put his cufflinks on. It's a running late marathon; a frenzy.

Bin: (under his breath / irritated)

"Fuck 'em."

He tosses the cufflinks onto the counter. Bin, frustrated, rolls up his sleeves to his dress shirt. He looks at the mirror on his wall for a final 360 degree check. He grabs a piece of tissue and wipes off the accumulated sweat that's on his forehead and neck. Once he is dry, he looks in the mirror, then approves by giving himself a thumbs-up.

Bin walks into his living room. It's a futuristic apartment, not too big, not too small. He double checks his briefcase, and sorts through the documents which are sitting on his breakfast bar.

Bin

"Resume, documents, tablet, umm, that's everything."

Bin heads towards the door, checks for his keys in his pocket. Opens the door and as he walks out, he grabs his pockets and realizes that he forgets his cell phone.

Bin

"Shit!"

He walks back into his room and comes out holding his cell phone, checking for new messages. Bin looks at his phone and notices that he has one new message. Looks at the time (9:45 am), and walks out of his apartment towards the elevator in his complex.

As the elevator door closes as Bin presses LL (LOWER LOBBY). He is sweating as the elevator goes down and he hopes that it doesn't stop on another floor. It doesn't. The doors split open to the lower lobby. He walks out, into the lobby which looks glassy and clean. He sees the Door Attendant / Receptionist Eddie.

Meet Eddie Edward. He's 34, slim, well-groomed male of the building. He takes his job seriously. But most people think that he believes his hair is more important than anything else. Eddie is humorous, and very flamboyant. He can brighten up any room, any person, and change the mood in many situations. That can be for the good and the bad.

As Bin walks off the elevator Eddie looks over his shoulder and eyes Bin. His flamboyant voice comes out, and he snaps his finger.

Eddie (winks at Bin)

"Mr. Bin. You're looking Binntasstic, as usual..."

Bin walks past Eddie, grabs another napkin as he passes the front desk. He wipes his forehead, again.

Bin

"Thanks Ed. In a rush, bud, but have a good one."

Eddie

"Oh, I know you will."

Bin paces out of the door. Puts two fingers up, saying peace, with the napkin in his right hand. Eddie continues to be nosy.

Eddie

"You must be late for that coffee date."

Bin

"Nahh, bud. Interview."

Eddie

"All right, big timerrrrr! Good luck!"

Eddie turns away, starts to walk towards his desk; he then speaks under his breath.

Eddie

"It's not like the bastard needs a damn job anyway."

As Bin walks out the building, there is moderate traffic, the sun is shining, but it is quite chilly out. Most of the morning crowd is on their way to work wearing business attire, gossiping, and sipping coffee. There are also a few homeless people sitting on the sidewalk.

Bin is walking down the street looking for his taxi. He locates it, grabs the door, looks inside and there's a woman sitting in the back seat. She looks up, startled by somebody opening the cab door. Bin looks at the driver, and the driver turns around to look at Bin.

Bin

"Stahl, really?"

Stahl (Taxi Driver)

"My friend, you were late. You know I love you but I got to make my money. The, guy behind me. He takes care of you...... He is a good guy."

Bin takes a deep breath, closes the door, and begins to walk to the next taxi. He opens the door and gets in the back. Bin and Stahl ride together many times, in a way they have developed some kind of friendship. Bin looks at the driver's reflection through the rear view mirror of the taxi.

Bin

"Larga and 28th, please."

Taxi Driver

"Okay. That will be 14 dollars, sir..."

Bin

"That's fine. Please expedite... Safely."

Taxi Driver

"Yes, my friend. Me best in whatever I do. No worry."

Bin

"Sorry, just have a big interview in a few. Want to get there early."

Taxi Driver (humor)

"Good man, Good man. Early bird always gets the worm......."

That is, if he doesn't let another bird steal it from him. Seconds go by. Horns are in background.

Taxi Driver

"From the looks, my friend, you look like the Boss man. Good luck anyway."

Bin

"I wish, man, I wish. Thanks but it's more about the prepping and the going for the opportunity than the luck. I don't believe in luck."

Seconds pass and it is silent. Bin is looking through his phone, going through emails from his other job, which he is on a small break after handling a project which had him traveling around the world. In Columbus, the traffic during the morning can be harsh; there are plenty of taxis who are taking folks to work, but not as many as it used to be. Everywhere you go you see an advertisement as companies will almost do anything to get your business. Bin takes a look at the video monitor that is mounted in the taxi, on the back of the driver's seat. He clicks the weather icon. A woman's voice pops up from the screens audio.

"Today's weather is 72 degrees, with moderate skies, no chance of rain. Anything else."

Taxi Driver

"So where are you from, my friend?"

Bin (Looking at him awkwardly)

"The West Coast, Chicaga"

Taxi Driver

(small chuckle)

"Chicaga very nice city. I really meant what nationality are you? If you don't mind?"

Bin looks back with a weird look. He doesn't like to talk about his race. It is a sensitive topic for him.

Bin (with confidence)

"Asiana. Island of Japa."

Taxi Driver

"I've been there a few times for convention. While I was in School. Me. I'm from Tanzana. In Afra."

Tanzana is in the same continent as Paragon. Afra.

Bin (relaxed voice as he looks at his phone)

"How long have you lived here for?"

Taxi Driver

"15 years too long. Came here for an internship, I was in school to be an engineer. Couldn't afford school no longer. Two kids. So this is what I have to do to pay the bills."

Silence sits, as Bin looks back at him with surprised look.

Bin:

"I understand your boat. Stay positive, my friend."

Taxi Driver

"Yeah, it's okay though. Saving money, then I go back home. Learned enough over here to be an assistant at a company. I will work my way up then. It's about faith my friend, faith."

Suddenly the sounds of tires skidding are coming from all over the place. A few cars hit each other, nearly hitting Bin's taxi. Madness and loud honks are all you can hear for a few seconds, and then things calm back down. Two taxi drivers jump out of the car, making strong hand and arm gestures at each other. Bin is holding on to the door, as he is startled. He and the driver remain in stasis. Then he slowly drives away.

Taxi Driver (in sarcastic response to accident)

"Yeah, faith."

In the background, the taxi's automated woman comes back on and repeats:

"You are approaching your destination. How will you like to pay?"

Ben is getting ready to get out the taxi, looks at his watch. He gives the driver a $20 bill, and his business card.

Bin

"I wish you the best. Call me if you need anything. You seem like a good guy. I got a few buddies in that field."

Taxi Driver (Taxi Driver looks back and is surprised)

"Wait, sir, your change!"

Bin (as he walks out)

"Dude, I hate it when you guys do that. Just keep it."

Taxi Driver (with a BIG smile, his teeth from ear to ear)

"Thanks, my friend."

Bin puts up two fingers as he walks away.

Meanwhile, in back of the taxi cab, the automated voice still going off, annoying the taxi driver:

"Thanks for your business, how will you like to pay"

The taxi driver continues to smile as Bin leaves. Once Bin walks away, he reaches in back of the taxi, begins to press and hit the button with frustration, numerous of times.

Taxi Driver (talking to the machine as it's driving him crazy)

"Shut up! Shut up!"

GELT TOWERS

Bin walks towards the skyscraper where it has a large company sign that says "GELT and Corps". Many executives are walking in and out of the building.

Bin walks in, looks to the left and right, and sees a sign that says "VISITORS". He walks to the desk where a suited male is standing behind it.

Suited Security

"Good day, sir, how may I assist you?"

Bin

"I am here for a 10:30 interview with Ms. Lisa Gasquew."

Suited Security

"Okay, sir, photo identification please."

Bin pulls his ID out of a slim wallet from the inside of his suit jacket, and hands security his ID. Security takes a deep look at Bin, enters his name into the computer. A few seconds go by, and he prints out a Visitors Pass for Bin and hands it to him. Bin sticks it on his suit.

Suited Security

"Okay, Mr. Ito, once you pass security, take your first right and go to floor 33. It will take you right where you need to go."

Bin

"Thank you."

Bin moves towards the security checkpoint to get searched. He takes off his blazer, sets his briefcase down to go through the metal detector. He is then checked in by suited security for the tower. Once he is searched, he looks at his watch, and begins to walk down the hallway towards the elevators.

There are many people in the building talking to each other, each in their own worlds. As Bin stops at the elevator he presses the UP button, although it is already lit due to a few other employees who are also waiting for a lift.

The green light to Elevator # 4 turns on and a chime follows. Bin begins to walk on, but before he gets on he realizes that a woman is next to him. He stops and politely lets her on, and then a redheaded woman rushes in, rudely squeezing past Bin. He raises his eyebrows and continues on.

The two women are on the elevator gossiping, both standing right next the buttons to all the floors which are 4 - 47. They both have on elegant clothing, sunglasses, and top name brand shoes on their feet. The red-haired woman is holding a cup of coffee, and she presses floor number 17. She looks at Bin, notices his Visitor pass and rolls her eyes, then gets to gossiping under her breath to the other woman who is wearing a grey suit. The elevator silently begins to move up.

Red-Haired Woman (under her breath to her co worker)

"I bet it's a new guy."

Bin is waiting for the women to offer to press the button. They don't.

Grey Suited Woman

"So did you hear about DSP shoe house closing down? I can't believe it."

Red-Haired Woman

"I just get most of my stuff off the internet these days anyway. It seems as if the malls are getting smaller and smaller. Maybe not smaller, but stores aren't how they used to be. Online is okay. But you can't try the shoes on. I bought some pink Christians last month. They were one size to small, but they were so cute. Unfortunately, this was the outcome. Look."

The redheaded woman slides her foot outside of her heel and shows her toe, which has a blistering corn on it. The conversation has distracted Bin from pressing the button to his floor.

Grey Suited Woman

"Ewwwah, Janet. That's disgusting."

Red-Haired Woman

"I know. I have to learn the hard way."

Grey Suited Woman

"That thing needs surgery. Yuck."

Red-Haired Woman

"Stop, I didn't ask for all of that. I was just showing you why buying shoes online sucks. We need these stores back. But I will be honest, girl. I'll wear those shoes again in a heartbeat."

Bin snaps out of watching the two women talk about shoes, corns, and blisters, as he is amazed what women go through for their shoes.

Realizing that he hasn't pressed his elevator button yet, he takes a step and reaches for the button.

Bin (as he reaches for the button)

"Excuse me, ma'am."

As Bin reaches to press the button for floor 33, the red-haired woman notices Bin's Rolex as his sleeve rises when he tries to press the elevator button. She gives him a peculiar look, then looks at the other woman with a surprised look on her face. Once Bin presses floor 33, the women get even more quiet and stiff. They then begin to give Bin quick but surreptitious glances that he barely notices. The elevator arrives at floor 17. The two women exit, they wait for the elevator to close, and begin to gossip.

Both are women talking as they walk in the hall.

Red-Haired Woman

"He had a chunk on his wrist didn't he?"

Grey Suited Woman (with serious humor)

"You see every man's wrist, don't you? Nothing... New."

The red-haired woman bumps her softly with her elbow.

Red-Haired Woman (smacks lips)

"Whatever, if I knew he was going to 33, I would have held his hand and offered to walk him there. Mmhmm."

Grey Suited Woman

"You little poindigger, you."

Both women give each other high fives as they walk into their department with a giggle.

Bin, alone in the elevator, is thinking about his every move as the elevator counts down (beeps) from Floor 7 - Floor 33. Within the next 20 seconds he thinks to himself.

Relax, Know, Relax, Know, Listen, Know, Hear, Know.

He has learned from his father that relaxing is one of the key things for a leader to have during an interview, meeting, or negotiation.

The elevator arrives at floor 33. He walks out and moves towards a receptionist's desk. The floor is very quiet, and nothing can be seen but visitor chairs and the reception desk.

Bin walks in and can finally see the receptionist. He also sees her name 'Cat', which on a nameplate on the desk. She is browsing on a dating website as Bin walks up to the desk. She just completed a status saying "Had one TWO many drinks last night. Shhh..."

As she sees BIN approaching, she exits the screen really fast.

Cat (looking at his visitor tag)

"Hello, sir, how may I help you?"

Bin

"Hi. Yes, I am here for an interview with Ms. Lisa Gasquew."

Cat

"Okay. Have a seat. I think Lisa is on a conference call right now. I will give her a call. I'm sure she'll be out soon."

Bin

"Okay. Thanks."

Bin walks to the chair, looks around the lobby, and notices the glass doors with the gold trim. The GELT logo and paintings surround the office. He sees a picture of Lisa with many leaders of different nations. He is impressed. Bin picks up a magazine - Business Week with a cover story of "Why so many are leaving? He begins to read it. His phone vibrates. He quickly turns it on silent but reads the message which is the same one that he disregarded earlier.

The message states (in Japa)

Email from Dad:

"息子、インタビューが両方の方法を行くことを忘れては

いけない。また、彼らにインタビュー。あなたは素晴らし

いです。あなたを愛しています..

- 勝伊藤 "

Bin looks at the message, and mumbles.

BIN (looking at phone)

Son...Son... Let... Umm... Umm... Yeah...

Bin opens his internet browser on his phone and opens an instant translator. He copy and pastes his dad's message, translating it from Japanese to English. The message states.

"Son, don't forget that the interview goes both ways. You interview them also. You are great!
- Masaru Ito"*

Bin shakes his head at his father's message. He has forgotten most of his Japanese language because he hasn't studied it, nor has he been home since he was 15. He is close to his dad, but his dad prefers to speak to him in Japanese, although his father speaks broken English as well.

Cat

"Bin, she is tied up in a meeting. It may be a few more minutes."

Bin

"Okay. Thanks."

Cat gets up and walks down the hallway towards Lisa's office. As she walks she instantly remembers that Lisa is in a meeting with many members from the executive board of the company. She hears them talking in one of the conference rooms. She peeks in through a corner of the window and she sees what she thinks is a heated exchange. Inside it is chaos.

Lisa is sitting in a chair at a roundtable.

"You wonder why we are in recession! You wonder why we are in shambles! You guys act as idiots and hand out shit burgers, and expect folks to eat it! Then when they eat it and shit it out, you don't give them a toilet to use. Now you're going to try to clean it up. Shitburger City. That's what this is called. Shitburger City."

Lisa can be one of the sweetest things. But when somebody really ticks her off, she is ticked off. The bigwig of the company, Gordon Sams, isn't making it any better. He is sitting back in his chair, glasses below his eyes resting on the middle of his nose, and his legs crossed. He has a head full of white hair, and his skin is wrinkly. He loves Lisa, but has grown apart from her ever since she started expressing her opinions about the company.

Gordon Sams

"Lisa, we have to do what we have to do. We can claim production of our subsidiaries and over production is a good write-off. War is probably going to be coming up some time soon. So this will eventually wipe itself off after the government requests more contract fulfillments. As well, this will give us room to give us some bonus funds. We can all use an extra bonus, after the bonus, right?"

He grabs his tie, grimacing, waiting for her response.

Lisa

"Gordon, you can't depend on warfare to wash out unnecessary over-expenditure. That's a scam! Maybe not technically, but it's a Ponzi. You are pushing out money that we don't have. You're promising money that we don't have. We might as well make a money printing machine and pay everybody cash. Have you considered that?"

The room is quiet, after her sarcastic money counter punch line.

There are 8 people in the room, all on the executive board of GELT industries. They are at a point of making particular decisions to bring the company back to a profit status. Most of the men in the room are against Lisa, except for one Joe Maklin. But he is still quiet with his responses because he is fairly new to the company and if he truly voices his opinions it can affect his job and bonuses.

Gordon Ramsey

"Lisa, what you are proposing doesn't make sense. I don't know where your viewpoints are coming from. The funding is backed up by hedge after hedge and bank after bank. We will be fine. If a problem arises, we will deal with it when we get to it."

Lisa (serious)

"Hedge fund after hedge fund? Are you kidding me? Half of the hedge funds in this world are not real, and two, this is stupid! Flat out stupid! Why are we having this conversation? I know where my viewpoints are coming from. We cannot continue some of these practices. Eventually the shit is going to get blown up, and who is going to be the one of the news stations? Me! Then what? You're going to leave me on Capitol Hill to request bailouts because of my relationships? You're going to embarrass me in front of this world because of the mistakes you made! The lives you have are messed up. I've bailed us out once! I don't want to go through that again."

The majority of the men in the room are giving Lisa a cold glare. Because many of them know that most of the company is corrupt. Though Lisa has been aware of it, it hasn't been as bad as it has been since the bailouts in the early 2000s. It was worse on Lisa because she was the public face of the company when she had to testify under oath. It really made life tough on her. She also came to many different realizations about herself and how Olympia operates.

Gordon

"Lisa...we are going to do it. Like it or not."

Lisa

"This is why this country is messed up now. This is why. And you can care less on how to make it better. You just want to look good on paper."

The men are quiet, giving her a nastystares.

Gordon

"Lisa, you're always welcome to leave."

Lisa (packing up her materials, notebooks)

"Don't threaten me!

I got to go. I'm wasting 15 minutes of my life, and I have an interview to do. This is baloney; you are in the wrong world."

They continue to speak as Lisa walks out of the room. She closes the door behind her and leans her back on it. She takes a deep breath and looks at her watch.

Lisa (realizing what time it is)

"Oh, goodness."

She begins to walk down the hallway. She shakes her head in disbelief what the executive board is considering. In the meantime, she has to zone out and act like all is going well because she has to interview Bin.

After 15 additional minutes of waiting, Bin is reading an article on his phone. He looks up at the glass doors across from him and sees Lisa's reflection as she stands over his left shoulder.

Lisa

"Benjamin?"

Bin (turns around)

"Yep, it's me. It's really just Bin, with an "I". But Benjamin with an "I" will work. You're the boss."

Lisa catches Bin off guard. Not only because she is stunning, but how well put together she is. She doesn't look too girly, but she looks like a seasoned executive. Her long brown hair touches past her shoulders; she has a simple and elegant shape. She has short sleeves on, so you can see the slight tone of the muscles in her arms. Then, Bin looks at her shoes, which are reminiscent of the women in the elevator. Bin is now wondering if Lisa shops online or in the store. Knowing a woman like Lisa, however, she may have an assistant who aids her with her shopping.

Lisa (in a cocky manner, as she walks away)

"Boss? First you got to get the job, and then you can call me boss... You ready?"

Bin shakes his head yes and stands up. He taps the reception desk, thanking Cat for being polite.

Bin follows Lisa down the hallway, walking past the offices. He sees a few workers typing, on the phones, and some looking to see who is walking in. Bin also notices that many of the offices are vacant with lights off.

As they are walking Lisa asks.

"So did you drive or take the metro in?"

Bin

"I cabbed it. I didn't want to deal with parking."

Lisa

"You too good for the metro, huh?"

Bin (Looking away like, WTF)

"Umm.... No. Just felt like taking the cab. I'm guessing that you ride the metro here?"

Lisa

"Nope. Never had and hopefully never will."

Her response confuses Bin.

As they walk down the hallway. A man comes out of an office to the right. It's Gabe Hawkins, Lisa's Boss. He is the Chief Operating Officer of GELT. He has a suede sport jacket on, and has dirty blonde hair.

Lisa

"Oh, I guess it's your day, Bin. This is Gabe, my boss."

Bin looks at him and extends his hand out towards Gabe. Gabe looks at him, raises his eyebrows, and walks passed him. Bin is stunned.

Lisa

"Don't mind him. He must have a lot on his mind."

Bin didn't like this one bit. He comes into the office of a company, and although one of the top executives is busy, he didn't like the fact that he didn't treat Bin like a person. Let alone a person of interest.

Lisa (looking at Gabe as he walks away)

"Let's keep going. All the offices that you are passing are our global support teams, from logistics to product development and integration. Everybody is fluent, except for me. Most of these guys manage teams globally, right from their desk. Thanks to technology, they don't have to fly too much. Sometimes, I keep them sharp and keep their frequent flyer miles up. Can't go easy on them...."

They make a right, enter Lisa's office where she has her own executive assistant just outside of her oak wood office. There is a large picture of the Dalla Cowboys Troy Airman team. She has a large flat screen in the lobby which has WNN live on; and all of this surprises BIN. He looks at it, but doesn't say anything.

Lisa's assistant looks up over her desk and stands up.

Lisa

"Binjamin, here's Gwen."

Gwen

"Hi Binjamin, good to meet you."

Bin

"Likewise. Good to meet you also. Thanks for everything."

Gwen (whispers)

"Good luck."

Bin loathes the word luck. Bin and Lisa continue to her office which has a view of the whole city. She has a library full of books, binders, and small model buildings. Bin notices a picture of her when she was young, posing in what it looks like a city in the middle east.

Lisa

"So, Mr. Ito. Let's get this started. Wait, do you need any water or anything?"

Bin

"No, ma'am, I am fine."

Lisa (aorting through papers on her desk)

"So to be upfront, I am impressed with our first two verbal interviews. You handled them well, especially the last one with Gabe. I just have to print a few things out quickly, give----me---- a----- second."

Lisa turns halfway and logs in to her CPU. Once the screen comes on, she gets an email from Charles:

Subject - Paragon Openings

She disregards the email, clicks "send to trash" and continues to print out documents for Bin.

Lisa

"If your team has hit a dead end on a project, and they have no clue what to do next, in other words, they are lost, how will you paint direction for them? How will you get them back on track?"

A few seconds go by.

Bin

"First, I want them to find out why we got lost. What happened? When was the last time that we were on schedule? Once that is figured out, I will then tell them to look up the word lost, and its meaning. We will then talk about the word and make sure we don't get lost again, well, anytime soon. Depending on the size of my team, I would want to them to each come up with a new path, this may be tough, but hey, they are seasoned execs. I would then share my path, my boss's path, but more so lead them down the path that leads to success, and not to a dead end."

Lisa

"How do you know your path isn't a dead end?"

Bin

"That question is not relevant, because I wouldn't have made it to this interview if I had anything about dead end written on me. Am I perfect? No. Can I predict everything? No. Am I going to lie to you and paint a perfect picture before I even know what colors or tools that I have to use? No. Do I have a record of making solid decisions, effective solutions, and logical approaches to global demand? Yes, I have been the foreign defense advisor to the Republic of Asiana for the past 3 years. I know a bit about making solid decisions, and steering people along the right path."

Asiana is a global leader in manufacturing defense systems and parts.

Lisa nods her head and looks at her CPU as another email comes in. On the screen:

Email from Gabriel: Subject - Ari Shonzki
Lisa disregards the email and continues to interview and talk to Bin. They go through many questions, but Bin

decides to take his father's advice and interview Lisa a bit, so he can have a better understanding of working with GELT.

Bin

"I have the most utmost respect for you. I have done my due diligence, and before that, your name has always crossed the smart briefs within the defense industry as a solid decision maker. I do have to ask you a few questions myself."

Lisa nods her head in a confident manner. She is surprised at the fact that an interviewee is asking her questions. Normally once she is done the interview is typically concluded.

Lisa (eyebrows come together in consternation)

"Go ahead."

Bin pulls his iPad tablet out of his briefcase. He loads it up. This takes a few moments. Once he is ready he points towards Lisa's computer with his stylus.

Her nervousness begins to show. Her leg begins twitching under her desk in nervousness, and her black Christian heels make a slight tapping noise on the floor.

Bin

"Make sure you're logged in. ----You should receive a file in a few seconds. Accept it and open it in the Dobe software once you see it pop up."

Lisa's leg continues to shake, and she is trying to hide it as she opens her desktop screen again. She sees the file and accepts it. Bin is her top recruit. She knows he has been the top of his class for years while he was in his master's program. She has also heard many good things about him throughout the world, due to his ability to find new technology and the best way to incorporate them into a company's business model or structure. He is a walking computer and can detect a goldmine without trying.

Lisa looks at her computer, waiting to see what Bin is transferring. A pink folder pops up on her screen, and it is labeled "Discrepancies". She crinkles her eyebrows and double-clicks her mouse to open it. Bin is somewhat nervous, but is pulling out his confidence because he needs to be strong if he wants to land this position.

Bin

"Now, Ms. Gasquew, again, I respect you. After our conversations, I have a good amount of trust in you. This information isn't necessarily privileged as GELT is a public company. I have been doing my homework for the past few weeks and I created this report. Can I be in trouble for having it? Yes. But I don't think that will be the question if a person finds out that I have it. I think the question will be "How did you get it?" In this world, somebody might kill me, knowing how these crooks are."

Lisa looks at the report and it opens with a graph of one green dotted line that goes up, and many red lines that are going down.

Lisa

"Okay, explain what you are showing me. I won't share it. Just show me."

Bin

"GELT has been lowering production with companies that serve under their umbrella. Over the past 10 years, you guys have had mass layoffs. It is perceived that these jobs have been positioned overseas. Now, -----looking at the subcontractors of your contracted companies; you guys have concluded contracts with them also. That means no service is being conducted or rendered.

I am not sure of what exactly is going on. GELT has been showing the SEC that they have been making billions over the years even when our population in Olympia has dropped almost 1% every year for the past 12 years. GELT has obtained numerous bailout allocations, grants, and tax breaks. The company hasn't created jobs, nor have they produced the services that they claim to be doing. Let's not mention how high profile executives, you being the exception, are getting multimillion dollar bonuses. Now, remember I have been studying this for a while. So it hasn't turned me away from the opportunity, but if I am walking into a major position within this corporation, I would like to know what is going on. This makes me a liability, along with my name, and my legacy."

Lisa looks at the documents in disbelief although she has known that something fishy has been going on with her executives, she is still shocked.

Bin

"One of my major turnoffs is that executives are getting multimillion dollar bonuses. Cry broke to workers who work hard in the field every day, and complain that they received a bonus which was basically eaten up by taxes. But that's a personal issue that I have. So you can disregard that, let's get back to the business."

Lisa looks at Bin, speechless.

Lisa

"Mr. Ito. As a worker of this company and vouching my service to my workers and my directors, I can't go off of any speculation. My job right now is to see if you are the right candidate for helping me get my department get back on the right track. As you know, we have had a few people leave."

Bin

"And some have been incarcerated..."

Lisa bites her tongue. Leans towards Bin as he is bringing to light of how some of the people from the GELT executive board have been jailed over pseudo schemes and laundering internal information and revenue for the company.

Lisa (Stern)

"I like your upfront ways, but this is still an interview for a job in which you applied for. If you came here to scrutinize me or the company, then you can take it to the media. I like you - if you haven't noticed. As far as anything in the past, it's the past. I want MY global department to do well. My question for you now is, "Are you here for the job? Or do you just want to know ins and outs?" If that's the case, I can schedule an appointment with communications while you are here. They are right down the hallway."

Bin

"I definitely want the job. I just had a few questions."

Lisa looking at Bin, but also thinking about what is going on within the company.

Lisa

"Would you mind if I keep this document?"

Bin

"It's already off of your computer. I had it set for a 10 minute viewing. After that last second, it is deleted as if it was never on your desktop. We can talk about it another day if you like."

Lisa is looking for the document in her trash bin of her CPU. On the screen she can see that the trash bin is holding 3 files, which are "Lisa Gasquew - Resume" "Charles Letter" and "Abe as a Baby"

Lisa

"Okay, Mr. Ito. Well, you should be hearing from me very soon."

She takes a deep breath.

Lisa

"I appreciate you being up front."

Bin

"Likewise, and like I said, I am very interested in being a part of this company. At the same time, I just want to know what I am walking into."

Lisa

"You've been well groomed, Bin."

Lisa begins to walk Bin out the door. She gives Gwen a look.

Lisa

"Okay. Down the hallway, make a right. Press ML and that will take you to where you entered. - 14th street, correct?"

Bin

"Yep. Okay. Thanks again, it was a pleasure."

Door closes as Bin leaves. Lisa looks at Gwen.

LISA (as she walks past the Gwen's desk)

"That kid has guts!"

Lisa walks into her office, sits down at her desk. She opens her email from Gabe. It reads:

Email from Gabriel - Ari Shonzki
"Lisa, I have a candidate whom I have already personally interviewed for the global lead position. I want you to check him

out. As your lead, I want him working with you. No questions asked. By the way, are you coming to the champagne toast tonight? Grover will be there.
- Gabe

Lisa's eyes squint as she thinks for a second. She begins to type a response and realizes it's not worth the energy. She responds

Email from Lisa - RE: Ari Shonzki
"I will discuss this with you later"

Lisa closes her computer down for the day. She looks stressed out. Looks out of her window and thinks. She is looking at the streets. At all the executives, brokers, and other people walking on the streets. How they are all on their cell phones. It's empty. She reminisces about the days when Olympia was a place for joy. Now, it has turned into a place of freedom, but it's overshadowed by corruption, lies, scandal, and pain and suffering. Which is causing it to fall.

Lisa packs her laptop bag, walks out of her office, and closes her door. She looks at Gwen.

Gwen

"So how did it go?"

Lisa

"I felt like I got interviewed. Goodness. It went well. Smart guy, I want him."

Gwen

"Whew, usually you have them walking out of there sweating. He seemed like he was leaving a business meeting, not an interview."

Lisa

"No, he's a smart kid. He doesn't know but I know some of his professors from his graduate school. I mean, an amazing kid." [Gwen nods.]

Lisa

"So are you coming to the Champagne toast tonight? You can just walk in with me. I cleared your name on the security list. President Grover is going to be there."

Gwen

"Lisa, you know I would love to, but I have no babysitter for   CJ. I'm going to have to pass it up."

Lisa, whines a bit

"Gwen, you never come out. Come on... You're just using that as an excuse..."

Gwen

"You know I want to, but I have no choice. Unfortunately I'm not you. I got this hyper kid at home. It's okay. Take a glass back for me."

Lisa blanks out for a few seconds.

Gwen

"Hello, anybody there?"

Lisa

"Yeah sorry, had a brain freeze."

Gwen

"Well, like I said. Take a glass back for me and an extra for yourself."

Lisa

"After what I just went through I will need it. Then I have to deal with Gabe once I get there.... The day just never stops."

Gwen

"Well, try to enjoy yourself. You're always working hard."

Lisa

"I guess, I guess...... Do I have any meetings tomorrow?"

Gwen checks the computer

Gwen

"Not until 2pm."

Lisa

"Whew, I'm going shopping. Need some mall therapy..."

Lisa begins to walk out and winks at Gwen.

Gwen (Laughing)

"Well, I wear a size 8!"

Lisa

"Adios."

Gwen

"Amigos."

Lisa exits her office...

5

Mr. President

President Jacob Grover is in his black Cadillac limousine along with his 5 car motorcade trailing behind him. Sitting next to him is Gary Dusette, his lead Advisor. On the opposite end of the limo is his Secretary of Defense Rob Polan, and one secret service agent. Most of the time, Jacob only rides with Gary, but since there are issues going on in the world, Grover and Rob Polan decided to hold their briefing on the way to the reception. The President's schedule is swamped.

Rob Polan

Sir, Paragon. They are having movement again within their mountain areas. We can't get a pinpoint on what it is though. We have intelligence officers on ground over there. They are getting closer to the nucleus. But they are being limited on access.

President Grover (speaks while changing his tie)

"Hey Gary, I think I'm going to go with the blue instead."

A moment of silence goes back, as Rob Polan is awaiting a response. He doesn't get one. Meaning the President isn't interested in the issue.

Rob Polan

"Asiana is closing ties with Paragon, and it's looking like they are building a strong relationship. Which means Paragon might have their vote, when it is time for the United Worlds to recognize Paragon as an official nation. Which will possibly allow mandates, meaning we will have to play self-defense at all times with them. We won't ever be able to intrude without penalty."

President Grover

"Okay. So what's the problem, Rob?"

Rob Polan

"Sir, they haven't come to a deal for A28, and I am not comfortable with Charles Dalton."

President Grover

"Okay. What does that have to do with us?"

Gary

"If they put this mineral out on the market, then the prices for fuel will tank. Intelligence is saying that they have found away to use a water type substance, but it burns just like fuel. It's also more efficient."

President Grover

"Okay, so what? You guys want to send jobs over there? What?"

Rob Polan

"No, sir, we need A28. I also failed to mention that over the past 15 years, a part of our population has left for Paragon; 88 percent of them being middle and low class."

President Grover

"That's what happens when you smart guys take them for granted."

Rob Polan

"Sir, we are failing as a nation. If we take one more financial blow, or even attack, we would be controlled by Dalton or the Asiana's. We can't cover this up too long. We need to strike."

President Grover

"Charles Dalton is not trying to control anybody and we aren't striking at anybody."

Rob Polan

"What's happened to you, Jacob? You've become brainwashed! You used to be on our side."

President Grover stops tying his tie and gives Rob Polan a small grin. Rob looks at Gary, and Gary nods his head back to Rob

Gary (looking at Rob)

"Tell him."

Rob Polan

"We believe that an F-22 has been struck off the coast of Paragon. An Olympian F-22. It was struck by a missile in a dust field just off the coast. They have been silent about it. We were only informed because of an inventory inspection was completed last week, and that aircraft was missing. But we never received the reports of it being in a crash."

President Grover

"Did they find the pilot? Any recordings?"

Rob Polan

"No, sir, and their authorities are playing dumb. Sir, we have a serious issue and we need to do some planning."

President Grover

"That is not the solution. We aren't planning anything. The last thing we need in this country is to be a part of a war. Or any war talks. We have lost many people in wars; we have alienated people. Our money system sucks. We have many people out of jobs, and guess where they are going? To Paragon. Trust me, war is not a solution, plus we don't want to kill any original Olympian citizens."

Rob Polan

"Sir, they are not Olympian anymore! They left! They are Ex-Pats. They can rot in soil for all I care!"

President Grover

"Why, because they made a choice? Because they want a life that's a bit different? Heck, I don't blame them, especially after President Royce left this mess for me to clean up. We have to figure out a good plan, not a bombing. I'll call Dalton soon."

Rob Polan hands Gary a report. He begins to read it.

Gary's job is to be the President's second brain although he is almost an assistant to him. His major purpose it to play dumb around folks, as if he doesn't know much. But he is really there to analyze critical decisions, conversations, and moments, then give the President proper advice on what to do. Gary is very important; although many look at him as the short chunky guy with the glasses. He still can influence the President on major decisions that can affect the world.

Gary is reading a report as they are en route to the GELT's champagne toast.

Jacob

"On another note. I hope this greeting doesn't last long. Not in the mood for any late night correspondence tonight. Want everything done by the time we land in Dalla."

Gary

"Housta sir."

Jacob

"Ooops..."

Gary

"At least it's not a long flight to Housta from Dalla. Unlike the time we thought we were going to go straight to Hawa, only to find out that we had a quick stop in Los Angela."

Jacob looks back in humor, all while Rob Polan sits tight-lipped on the other side of the limo.

Gary

"Jake, tonight's engagement will be a five minute speech. It's a formal, but "informal" event. Therefore, there will be no prompters. Keep it simple, let it flow. Senator Teitenbrus will be in attendance."

Jacob

"Really. Sharon will be there?"

Gary

"Yes, Sharon Teitenbrus."

Jacob (chuckles)

"At least somebody that's on our side will be in attendance."

Jacob takes a quick look at Rob Polan.   Gary

"Ahhhh, stop it, Jake... Mayor Tomkin will also be in attendance. They claimed that it will only be 200 guests, but by the photos it seems like a few more are in attendance as usual."

Gary hands Jacob a tablet with actual photos of the event and the podium view of which Jacob will be speaking on. The pictures show a well illuminated ballroom, few dinner tables, and many tuxedo and dress wearing guests in attendance.

Jacob

"I like the coloring. The lights... Is that fuchsia?"

Gary looks at Jacob and scratches his nose in response to his "fuchsia" comment.

Gary

"I think it is purple, sir."

Jacob

"No, it is fuchsia."

Gary

"Okay. It's fuchsia. It's purple. It's lavender. Whatever you want it to be."

Jacob

"How long are we staying?"

Gary

"A 5 minute speech and 4 minutes for handshakes, or a 5 minute speech with 10 minutes of handshakes?"

Knowing that he isn't going to go by their schedule, President Grover shakes his head as he is still browsing through the tablet. He clicks on a live camera view of the audience. It shows people in the gathering preparing for the President's arrival. Cameras are out. The CEO of GELT is speaking.

Within tablet video

CEO of GELT (Speaking on podium in ballroom)

"President Grover will be joining us in a few minutes."

Jacob stops the video immediately, and softly tosses the tablet to Gary since he doesn't care for the CEO that much.

Jacob

"Something isn't right about that guy."

Gary

"I agree. A few college grads are in attendance. Communications already has them in a transition for a meet and greet. Let's make sure we touch on them also, so we can keep them here."

Jacob

"All in 5 minutes?"

Gary

"Yes."

Jacob

"I may be longer. It depends. If I stay. I want to see the kids who don't expect to meet me. Not just the kids whose parents got them in here. That's what this event is really about."

Rob Polan is disgusted by the President's Comments. Rob knows he is directing them towards him. In the meantime Gary receives phone call from secret service informing him that they will be approaching the destination in 40 seconds.

Gary (hanging up the phone)

"Okay. We will be there shortly. Take a sip."

Gary hands Jacob a bottle of a clear-colored drink called Oldman Classic Chapbev with a Presidential Seal on it. Jacob takes it, sips it, and looks at the bottle.

Jacob

"This is new. Just for me, huh? Tastes like Cherry. Although it's clear."

Gary

"Well, the last time we gave you a colored flavor. You had red teeth on live television, from the red coloring in the drink. So, here's the solution. It was the first lady's idea."

The limo driver knocks on the aisle window signaling that they have arrived at the venue. The destination is a Ritz Hotel ballroom. Jacob exits the vehicle along with his secret service agents, team, and his assistants. He sees pillars of the hotel, along with a crowd and paparazzi taking photos of him as he walks up. Gary continues to walk next to him as he walks into the venue, and straight to the back green room where another two agents await him.

Once inside, Jacob sits down and sees a tray full of Sushi Rolls. While he bites on one, he is greeted by a few young workers of the event. They are the two young chefs who made the dining tray, both females. The secret service tries to kick them out of the room and Jacob interrupts and speaks to the two young cooks.

Jacob

"Hey! Did you guys make this dish?"

First cook,

"Yes, Mr. President, well, we both did."

Jacob begins to munch on a chip and spinach, cheese type of dip. His assistant tries to get him to stop in case of any poisoning. Jacob gives him the hand to back off, and looks at him. Then he looks back at the young chefs as he munches.

Jacob (eating)

"Well, I was hoping that I didn't have to lie, and say that it's good. Goodness, it is superb! You two work at this restaurant?"

Second Cook

"Well, we are just interning here, we are still in school, sir. That's why we were limited to the dish and not the whole meal."

Jacob pulls out two $20 bills to tip the young cooks.

Jacob

"Here take this, keep at it. Thanks."

The young chefs look up in surprise and accept the cash. They shake the President's hand in awe and go on about their day. Gary hates it when Jacob is too down-to-earth. Since he is Jacobs's advisor, he's the person who looks out for him. Jacob's food has been poisoned before, but it doesn't prevent him from being normal. Oddly enough, he still likes to keep that communication with the real world that he misses out by being the President of Olympia.

Jacob (in response to Gary's frustration)

"What?"

Gary

"Nothing, wipe your face. It's show time."

Jake wipes the dip off of his face and puts his serious look on. His assistant walks up to him and fixes his tie. Another two women come into play and begin to put foundation makeup on his face for the cameras. They dust his suit off. Just when he thinks he's ready, one of the women grabs his head and wipes the corner of his lip off.

Appearance Assistant One

"Sir, can you smile for me?"

Jake looks at her, smiles widely in a sarcastic manner as she checks to make sure that he doesn't have anything on his teeth. His appearance crew can't afford a mistake as the last time a bad photo and video clip went worldwide. It looked bad on him during campaign time. Some people called him a bloodsucker.

Once the assistant approves she moves to the side and gives Gary the green light for Jacob to move forward.

Jacob walks through a hallway with his protective agents and Gary. As he gets closer to the ballroom, the music and the crowd get louder with every step. Once he gets to his door he takes a deep breath.

A song named "We Take Care Of Ours" is playing. The speaker is the CEO of GELT Industries; the same company that Bin interviewed with Lisa. Jacob doesn't have the best feeling about the company but they have a large following and they donate a lot to his campaign. It still makes his stomach sick when he hears the voice of the CEO, the one who cuts pay for the lower class, but gives his friends and rich colleges millions in incentives.

CEO (Standing on the podium in the ballroom)

GELT and friends. Please applaud for the President of Olympia, Jacob Grover!

Door opens the music waves into Jacob's ears, the cameras are flashing as if a strobe light is going off.

Jacob walks to the podium and gives the Presidential Wave to about 500 guests whose ages range from 18 years to 80 who can barely stand up. It's a very elegant ball, and Jacob receives an ovation for over two minutes. He is saying, "Thank you" looking at each direction and noticing the non-diversified audience. Jacob's fast moment begins to turn slow, he begins to sweat more, and his stomach turns as he sees nothing but gold jewelry, pearls, high cost suits, and crystal cut glasses.

This is supposed to be a fundraiser, an event for new jobs that GELT is opening up for future college graduates. Jacob is looking for college students, but the only ones that he sees in the audience are all current employees of GELT. Father next to son, and daughter next to father. In his mind, Jacob wonders, where are all the students? The only ones that he would think are in college are the cooks, and a few other young folks working during the event.

Once the crowd begins to quiet down Jacob begins to speak.

Jacob (enthusiastically)

"What a night, rain or shine!"

(Crowd cheers)

"Well, I am delighted to be here amongst all of you. GELT has been an amazing company for this country for decades, and it is a honor to see it still continuing. Although our country has been plagued by natural issues, we always find a way to achieve greatness of human endeavors; from our university systems to internships - and speaking of interns. - The cooks who prepared my pre-speech snack did one heck of a job. Salute them, please. They are interns as well."

The crowd cheers in his response, as Jacob beams his eyes at the GELT CEO, showing him that he doesn't appreciate the fact that the true students are the ones working the event and not enjoying the speech.

Jacob

"As a matter of fact, bring them out here. You know what? Bring everybody that is able to leave their post into this room. We are all one. If they built this stage they deserve to be in here also."

The crowd goes silent. Jacob points to his agents, hinting to tell them to find those who set this event up. The agents leave the stage and one by one; the attendance at the stage slowly grows. You can see the difference in attire, between the event goers and workers. Seconds go by, as the few who are working the event slowly come into the room.

Jacob

"Now, today is about our future. Today is about serving as role models for our successors. This means our current successors need to continue to show our predecessors how to succeed. Even though, our younger generation are the ones who show us how to use all these gadgets that confuse us old folks. I think, in a way, they are taking over the world slowly."

The crowd chuckles. Jacob looks at Gary on his right, Gary nods back.

During the President's speech, Lisa walks in late, as usual. She spots Gabe, her boss, and stands next to him. She looks gorgeous. She has a blue dress on, hair down to her back and gold shoes with a burnt orange bottom.

Gabe (whispers)

"I am guessing that you are just leaving the office."

Lisa

"No. I fell asleep. Does this look like something I would wear to work?"

Gabe

"Yes."

Lisa (quickly whispering)

"Whatever. Cut to the chase, Gabe. What's going on about this Ari guy? I told you I had a candidate in mind."

Gabe (Whispers)

"Ari knows our system. His father knows me, therefore he knows us. I said that the decision was final, and I am not discussing it again."

Lisa (strong whispers, as others begin to notice the two talking)

"Bullshit, GABE!"

Gabe

"Please, I am enjoying this night. I think you should too."

Gabe rudely hands his champagne glass to Lisa, spills a little bit on the front of her dress, and walks away. Lisa looking disgusted tries to hide it with a fake smile as a few bystanders notice the mini argument, and the small wet spot on the chest of her dress.

Jacob

"We have to continue to lead. GELT has done a great job on the forefront with being one of the world's top infrastructure, defense, transportation, and capital leaders. It has been an honor to have them headquartered here, in Columbus.

"I look forward to a stronger year from your CEO Herb Kinzel, as I have known him for many years. For now, I want to simply toast to a great evening, people, staff, and an even better future. Thanks, guys."

Jacob waves his hands. Music plays as Jacob exits the stage. He is met by his agents and Gary.

The "We Take Care of Ours" plays again on the speakers.

As Jacob walks off, the song begins to register in his head.

Jacob to Gary.

"Was that short enough?"

Gary gives Jacob a look.

Gary

"I got a note that the rain has severely increased. I suggest you use an umbrella."

Jacob ignores him. He stops to take pictures with some guest. Jacob hates umbrellas. It's his way of showing that he is a man. Even in the worst weather Jacob would rather be seen with raindrops over his wet and soggy salt- and pepper-colored hair. The only problem is that when he has on a bit of makeup that he is forced to wear, the water leaves the residue on his suit. Not good for tabloids. Sometimes it can look like he's melting.

Jacob

"Hello. Hello." (Hello to all of them that he meets and greets.)

In between photos Gary whispers to Jacob.

Gary

"Don't you want to get going? So you can finish up this call with Kosimov, the Russian President?"

Jacob (enjoying the pictures being taken)

"He will be fine, he is in Asiana. It is morning over there."

Gary gives up. Takes a few steps away and lets the President be. Jacob likes it when he is interacting with people.

Jacob

"Okay guys, I have to go. It was a pleasure."

One woman walks up and asks Jacob for one more. Jacob stops. Puts his arm over her shoulder, smiles, and pats her on the back. These are the moments he loves. One thing that the agents won't interrupt with Jacob are his moments with the people. He embraces them. Though he is a tough President, the people voted him in because they feel that they can relate to him. There have been times when he would personally invite a person on his plane if he was flying from Columbus, as long as the person passes the background check. It became a serious stipulation when Jacob invited a "nice person" on the plane once, and he happened to be on trial for a murder and rape charge. Talk about judging a book by its cover.

Jacob and his team walk down the hallway. The song is still playing in Jacob's head, even though he is out of the ballroom. "We take care of ours."

They walk outside of the Ritz Hotel, as his motorcade awaits him. Although it is raining, Jacob still refuses to take an umbrella from Gary and his assistant. He looks up to the left as he is halfway down the stairs and sees his double just behind him with an umbrella, and they catch eyes. Looking just like each other. The all black 6 car lineup awaits him and his staff. Normally it is 12, but since it is an inner city detail, the size of the motorcade is lowered.

As they get into the Jacob's limo. Gary folds the umbrella and sets it in a compartment made specifically for the umbrella. Alongside it sits a shotgun for the President's protection.

Gary

"I don't know how you do it. Then again, I know the background of how you don't do things."

Gary is pissed because he is wet and his tuxedo is soggy. He can't hold an umbrella next to Jacob because it will be bad for publicity. If one man goes without an umbrella the next man can't have one. It's a visual symbol of power. The news makes a story out of anything.

Jacob

"I guess Rob wanted another way home, huh?"

Gary ignores Jacob's smart comment and hands him his cell phone. Jacob chuckles and presses *982732 and it dials a number reaching the Russian President directly. They have an incredible relationship. The Russian President has never had an American burger from a burger establishment. So Jacob made it his business to cancel their 5 star dinner to buy burgers and fries from a Shack in the Capital. The President liked it because he never ate a burger around a group of strangers before especially in a small restaurant.

Jacob (on phone with Russiana president)

"Vlad! I'm sorry. I had an event that ran a little longer than expected. Can I call you once I get home?"

Pause as he listens to Russiana President.

Jacob (responding to the Russiana President)

"Okay. Will do."

Jacob hangs up the phone. Looks at Gary.

Jacob

"Pushed the call back to midnight, that should work."

Gary

"Good. Surprised he picked up."

Jacob

"Yeah, that guy is…"

A huge boom occurs outside the limo, Jacob and Gary are startled. The strike from the ceiling makes Jacob dizzy;

Gary falls to the other side of the Limo as the vehicle comes to a stop. He notices that he has blood pouring from his lip. Jacob can barely see.

Limo Driver on intercom

"Are you okay? Mr. President, sir are you okay?"

Both guys are shocked, but are fine. Gary looks at Jacob to make sure he is okay, as blood is dripping down Gary's lips. Jacob gives him the thumbs-up. Then tosses him his handkerchief.

Gary

"Yes, we are fine. What's going on up there, Tom?"

Limo Driver on intercom

"I had to avoid a big piece of debris in the road. Everything is okay, correct? Do you need the med?"

Gary

"No, just keep going."

Jacob and Gary look startled, and look at each other as if they thought they got bombed. Then they laugh. Normally, if anything happens to the President, the medic needs to tend to him. But in this situation, since the President had to speak to the Russian President, the doctor who normally rides with him is in the vehicle behind him. Gary tells the driver to continue again, so the press doesn't get wind of it.

Jacob (holding his head)

"By the way. Now that Rob isn't in here. What is the status on Operation 28?"

Gary

"Jake, we just talked about it."

Jacob

"I don't trust him, but I trust you. So tell me some more fine line."

As the two speak on the operation, Gary pulls up the operation on the monitor in the vehicle. Special effects show the Satellite begin to hover over the mountain terrain of Paragon.

Operation 28 is an investigation that Intelligence is working on. They are trying to build intelligence on Paragon, since it is building rapidly and has a great deal of activity. They have many military orders, drilling, travel, and ties with many nations, including allies of Olympia working with them. This can have a major impact on Olympia and it's been weighing in on the stock market. People are also begging to give up their citizenship to move to Paragon and work. If the trend continues, Olympia is braced to go to war and strike this land because they pose as a threat, not necessarily offensively, but monetarily.

Gary

"Intelligence is having a tough time gathering data. The last report showed that the retrieved satellite communications are not accurate with our findings. Every time they get a feed, the images come back unclear. Engineering and IT are working on it as we speak."

Jacob

"Our future is counting on that image."

They lock eyes...

Jacob (serious voice)

"Keep me updated. I need that information, or I will be en route to Paragon. I'm trying to control this before it gets out of hand."

Gary (may be used as a VO also)

ASAP, sir. Though I do need to share one thing with you as Rob mentioned.

Jacob gives Gary a go ahead nod.

Gary

"As far as the aircraft that went down."

Jacob (cuts Gary off)

"Why was one of our guys over there? And why, am I just finding out about this?"

Gary

"I didn't want to say this in front of Rob. But that pilot was an ex-pat, and technically he isn't ours anymore. The plane isn't either. Paragon has a training contract with us and they purchased the planes on their own with Rob's approval although I think he got his cut out of the deal. But Dalton never gave him a "personal" option to receive any A28, which I believe he wanted."

Jacob gives Gary the stare. Wondering why he wasn't informed of this earlier. But lets it slip his mind because it's not his aircraft, he's not his man. At the same time, two Olympian products down doesn't sit well with him. Along with his Secretary of Defense making side deals.

Jacob

"Find out what happened."

Gary nods.

Jacob

"With Rob, I will handle the aircraft, A28 and Dalton. Something is fishy going on with him, so you focus on that. That imagery also."

This catches Gary off guard. Even so. He accepts the duty.

Jacob

"I won't be forced into a pointless profit war, Gary."

Gary nods again, looks down and notes it in his notebook.

6

With Regrets

The next morning, Lisa prepares to go to work. She calls Bin on the phone to regretfully inform him that he is not getting the job. It's hard because she wanted him, but Gabe wasn't going to allow it. Lisa gets Bin's voicemail.

"HI, you've reached Bin Ito, I can't come to the phone right now, so leave a detailed, but short message and I will be back to you shortly."

> Lisa (on phone)

Hi, Bin. Lisa Gasquew with GELT. I just wanted to give you a call in regards to the position. Give me a call at 811 533 2211. Thanks.

As Lisa was leaving the message her other line was ringing. She clicks over. It's Gwen.

> Gwen

> "Hi Lisa, I have Mr. Bin on the phone. Are you busy?"

> Lisa

> "No, send it over."

Bin is sitting on his couch, in regular clothes with an uneaten full bowl of cereal in front of him.

Lisa (picks up her office phone)

"Good day, Bin, this is Lisa."

Bin

"Hi Lisa, just saw your phone call. Sorry, I was just caught up in something. How are you?"

Lisa

"I'm well. You?"

Bin

"Hah, couldn't be better."

Lisa

"I was just calling you concerning the position."

Bin

"O..kay...."

She takes a deep breath.

Lisa

"Bin, I think that you are an excellent candidate. We have..... Well, management has decided to go with another individual. If anything else comes up, I will be sure to keep your information on hand.

Bin (surprised)

"I appreciate your follow up. It's better than an email. Although I don't know how much better it can get than an "Excellent Candidate". All is understood."

Lisa

"Bin, I really DO appreciate your time."

Bin

"I do too."

Lisa

"Bin. I also wanted to ask."

Lisa hears an empty tone as Bin hangs up.

Lisa

"Bin, Bin..."

Lisa puts the phone down, hurt, and in disbelief. Bin is the candidate whom she wanted to hire. But Gabe, her boss, wanted another candidate whom she doesn't even know, all

she knows is that Gabe has a relationship with the new
hire's family. Somebody is his uncle. She also has researched
what the company has been covering up and wants to know
what is really going on.

Lisa picks up the phone and calls Gabe.

Gabe's phone begins to ring while he is inside a private jet
with 4 Asiana men and 1 Asiana woman

Gabe

"Gasquew, we're taking off in Asiana, please make it
quick."

Lisa (with a strong tone)

"Why would you put me in a situation like this? You know
we had a great - I mean, a great candidate! He can help us
become strong again, and get us out of this mess."

Gabe is speaking low so others won't hear

"Ari's father has helped me in many ways. He knows
everything about our company. So it's a good fit. I'm not
losing control on what we are doing and we want to do, and
he won't object to any of our future dealings. I didn't like
your kid anyway."

Lisa

"You didn't even try to shake his hand when you walked
past us in the office! There are other measures that you
could have taken, Gabe!"

Gabe

"Lisa. Like it or leave!"

Lisa

"Don't....threaten..... me!"

Silence is on both ends of the line.

Lisa

"And can you please tell me what is really going on? I
have been looking at some docs and I notice that there's lots
of laundering going on!"

Phone call goes into pause.

Lisa

"Oh, so now you get quiet."

GABE

"You shut up! I don't have time for this. I have a very important client with me...I will see you later. Goodbye."

Lisa slams the phone down and Gina can hear it from outside the office. Gina cautiously walks in.

Gwen

"Li, are you okay?"

Lisa

"Yes, Gina. People...Just... Ahhhhhhh!"

Lisa, frustrated, takes her shoes off from under her desk. Kicks them, and puts her head down on her desk.

While Lisa is venting, Gabe is in the sky working on closing one of the largest investments in the GELT portfolio.

Gabe

"Sorry, Mr. Ito. Just had some things to handle back in the..."

He pauses and thinks to himself of the last name that he just mentioned. Gabe then looks into the eyes of Mr. Ito, Bin's father. Gabe glances at his phone, which is sitting on the table in between them. Mr. Ito looks at him and Gabe realizes that Mr. Ito has the same last name as Bin.

Mr. Ito

"My investment has nothing to do with my son. But it doesn't feel good when you train your son to be a business warrior in this world, and a cheater cheats him out of a possible path that he could have taken. Just as he followed mine, I'm going to follow him. Now where will you prefer to land, it's on me. It's all business, nothing personal."

Mr. Ito turns around to one of his assistants.

Mr. Ito

"Tell the captain that we need to turn around. Our deal is done. No point of flying."

He looks at Gabe. Gabe responds with a deep breath.

Back in Lisa's office.

Lisa gets an email alert. She doesn't respond to it for a few seconds. She tells her self.

"30 seconds Lisa, 30 seconds."

136

She gets up, grabs her stress ball and looks out the window for 30 seconds. As she looks, she oversees much of the city and realizes how many fewer cars are outside than 5 years ago.

She thinks back to when she got her first promotion, and moved into her office.

Gabe

"Here's your office. You will have your own receptionist, and new keys will be made for you by the morning. So don't lock anything important in here because I am the only one who will be able to help you, and I'm not getting out of bed for that."

Lisa is looking at her office. Sitting in her chair for the first time. She looks at the view, amazed by how many cars are on the street, pedestrians, and happy messengers.

Lisa stares out the window

"This view is amazing."

The scene goes back to what Lisa was looking at initially. She looks at her office. Luxurious, wooden walls, television monitors. She takes a look at Gina. Who is helping a custodian pull trash out of the trash can. Lisa turns around in her posh leather chair, and looks out the window. Leans forward and connects her wrist on her chin. Taking in the view that she once thought was amazing, years ago.

Her mind goes deeper. She compares her view to that of 5 years ago. She looks at the streets, and realizes that there are fewer cars outside, fewer cars parked, fewer buses operating. She remembers when people used to walk on the streets, and now the streets aren't as busy. With the mass amount of layoffs, there are not as many people coming to work anymore. Robberies have increased. Stores are slowly starting to get boarded up leaving the thieves with less to steal.

It comes deep to her, that all of these years of living an amazing life, from state to state, meeting to meeting, country to country, shopping mall to shopping mall, that she hasn't even noticed that the economy has taken a major hit. She was just given a $5.5 million dollar bonus, even when other workers salary decreased and the economy decreased. Another incentive came in for her when many people lost their jobs, due to "downsizing". Though these are good distractions, her reality was a fantasy to many others. She bought three homes in the past two years, while Gwen just lost her home to foreclosure.

Gwen (still standing at Lisa's door)

"Everything okay, hon?"

Lisa snaps out of her zone, and turns around in her chair.

Lisa

"Yes... All is good. Just another day."

Gwen

"You sure? Girl, I been working with you for the past thousand something days. I'm no fool, missy."

Gina hands Lisa some papers and walks away.

Lisa's computer chimes and she looks at her computer screen:

Email from CHARLES
"UMMM. You've been quiet, you o.k?"

Lisa responds

"NO. Call you tomorrow..."

Thoughts about meetings with her higher execs, thoughts and images come into her mind about the board meetings in conference rooms, Executives talking about moving jobs overseas, and new accounting contracts. They are all in a blur.

She thinks about how the CEO of GELT talks about President Grover behind his back, but smiles in his face.

GELT CEO

"Grover, that idiot... All we have to do is "show" him that we are for the people. Those people he's mentioning don't need a good bonus. What do they need one for? We work harder. This is our country. Our money."

Flashing back, Lisa thinks about Gabe at the Champagne Toast

GELT CEO

"We now present to you OUR President whom we adore so much. President Grover!"

Lisa's having more flashbacks. The thoughts are shuttering through her mind.

Gabe

"He knows our system"

Gwen

"I can't go to the toast, Lisa, I got to watch CJ. No babysitter. Or should I say, I can't afford a babysitter?"

Lisa comes back from her flashbacks. She drinks some water, takes a deep breath as she realizes everything that she has been overlooking during the past years. She thinks about her multimillion dollar bonuses, and how Gwen can't even afford a babysitter. She thinks about the things that the company has been covering up. How her father was a part of the scandal, and how her connections have done her well. But her connections are the ones running this country into nothing, simply because they aren't supporting the base and foundation, who are really the low and middle class.

LISA begins to type on her computer

> *Email to Gabe:*
> *I will finish up your reports, I will let Gwen know about "Ari", and I will be taking a personal leave starting in 48 hours. NO Questions. Thanks... By the way, I hope your meeting with Mr. Ito is going well." :-)*

Lisa walks out of the office and looks at Gwen.

Lisa

"Gwen, has your banking info changed?"

Gwen

"No, why?"

Lisa

"Just asking, HR sent me an email about direct deposit updates. Nothing big."

Lisa walks out of the office.

Lisa walks into the bathroom down the hallway. Inside the stall, she puts her head on her knees and begins to take in everything that has been going on. Two women walk into the bathroom to wash their hands. Lisa looks at their heels while they speak.

BATHROOM WOMAN 1

"Did you apply for that job yet?"

BATHROOM WOMAN 2

"Yeah, I actually got it. I don't know, if I'm going to take it though."

BATHROOM WOMAN 1

"Why not?"

BATHROOM WOMAN 2 (O.S)

"It's too far away, too many what ifs. But I have to do something, I feel like I am stuck. I've been processing the same documents for the past fifteen years ..."

The women walk out of the bathroom as their conversation continues but fades away as the door closes.

Lisa comes out of the bathroom wondering who could have been talking. She washes her hands, deep in thought, then hurries out of the bathroom.

7

Payback

Lisa walks to the bank, which is down the street from GELT Tower, and takes her sunglasses off. There is a line and she patiently waits as she is examining the bank, looking at the marketing signs, bankers in the back and different movements.

Bank Teller

"Ma'am, you can step up."

Lisa looks to her right and walks to the teller.

Lisa

"Yes, is there any way that you can give me your, I mean, my balance…"

Both women laugh

Bank Teller

"Trust me. You don't want my balance… (laughs) Just hand me your driver's license or another form of ID…"

Lisa reaches in her brown leather purse. The teller scans Lisa, noticing her high-end purse, watch, and jewelry. Lisa continues to dig in her purse, looking through her wallet. She can't find her ID.

Lisa

"I know I have it somewhere."

Bank Teller

"Well, if you can step to the side. I'll help you after…"

Lisa

"Up, I found it…You know how these purses get."

Lisa hands her ID to the teller. They both smile, like it's a girl thing.

Bank Teller

"Okay. Please enter your social number in the key pad to your left."

Lisa enters her social security number, but it takes her a few seconds to think of the last digits since her brain is fried.

Bank Teller

"Which account do you want the balance on?"

Lisa

"Both of them, please."

The bank teller begins to type on her computer. After a few clicks with the mouse, she notices Lisa's balances. She takes a small gulp and looks frozen. She writes them both on a sheet of paper and hands them to Lisa.

Bank Teller

"Here you go… I wrote your third one out also."

Lisa looks at her balances as if it is an everyday thing.

Balance for Account #8429: $3,569,320.00

Balance for Account #4321: $12,129.292.76

Balance for Account: #82118: $25,932.99

She looks back up at the Teller.

Lisa

"If I want to make a series of Cashier's Checks what will I need to do?"

Bank Teller

"Well, all of them will need to be made payable to you, a business, or an individual."

Lisa

"What about a Money Order?"

Bank Teller

"Money Orders go up to $1,000 dollars max. But you can leave it blank, just like a blank check. Just don't drop it. Or else it will be somebody else's."

Lisa chuckles.

Lisa

"Hmmm, so if I make them payable to myself. I can endorse them over so another person can use it right?"

Bank Teller

"Yes."

Lisa is indecisive.

Lisa

"Okay, what time do you guys close today?"

Bank Teller

"Five pm ... Wait, I'm sorry. We close at 7 pm. It's Friday."

Lisa

"Okay. What's the earliest I can come in tomorrow morning?"

Bank Teller

"Yes, we open at 7 am. On the dot."

Lisa

"Gotcha.... Will you be here?"

Bank Teller

"I sure will, so that means I won't be going out tonight... Well, I can, but I'll be half sleep. My manager wouldn't like that."

Lisa

"I hear you. Well, I will try to come back today, at worst, tomorrow."

Bank Teller

"No problem, anything else I can do?"

Lisa

"Mmmm… no, that's about it."

Lisa grabs her keys and wallet off of the counter.

Bank Teller

"Okay. You have a wonderful day. Thanks for stopping in."

Lisa

"Thanks for your help."

As Lisa walks away, the teller tells her coworkers to come by her station and to take a look at her screen. She whispers to them,

Bank Teller

"Look at all of this."

The coworkers look. They are all stunned. Eyes wide open. The second teller voices her opinion.

Bank Teller 2

"I need to change my major. What does she do? She an actor?"

Bank Teller

"Nope. She works for GELT."

Bank Teller 2

"My mom does also, but she doesn't even make what she makes in one month."

A few hours pass.

With a full moon flashing in Lisa's bedroom, she looks at it while in bed. Under her eyes is a greenish spa-type cream to keep her skin tight, a satin camisole, and half a dozen pillows on her bed. She is as comfortable as she can be. The bedroom has a blue haze as it is being illuminated by the moon. Making a beautiful color, but makes her feel so alone. Fighting sleep and thoughts, she reaches over, grabs her phone and dials a phone number. The phone rings and Charles picks up the phone as usual…

Charles

"Dalton speaking."

Lisa

"Hi..."

Charles

"Oh, wow, a phone call. Didn't think you could afford an international plan."

Lisa

"Shut up..."

Charles

"What's wrong? You never call."

Lisa

"Just going through a lot... Work, life, and thoughts. I'm just a mess right now."

Charles

"What's the problem?"

Lisa

"My bosses are overruling decisions that I make...They are corrupt and nothing has changed since the bailouts. I have this new hire that I have recruited for years in my office for an interview, he's amazing. He damn near schooled me. In fact, he did school me. I wanted him, and Gabe wanted to hire his nephew, who has no clue what we do. There are too many fishy things going on within this company. Let alone in this country?"

Charles

"I told you that a long time ago, but this isn't the time for that."

Lisa

"I just... I think I just need to get away...I love Olympia, but this country has really lost itself."

Charles

"Let me guess some, uhhhh. Some London therapy?"

Lisa

"I think I have had enough shopping therapy. Actually I think I may take you up on your offer and come that way. Is it still on the table?"

Charles

"How do you know that it's still on the table? Have you even looked at any of the emails I have sent you?"

Lisa

"I took a peek a while ago."

Charles

"Sure, when do you want to come?"

Lisa

"Give me a week or so."

Charles

"Okay."

Lisa

"Thanks, I'll give you a date soon. On another note, how is Abe doing?"

Charles (hesitation)

"He's ummm. He's good. Why you ask?"

Lisa

"I just deserve to know, Charles."

Charles

"He is okay. We had a scare not too long ago. But he is okay. Back to you, though. You stay strong. I will get your trip coordinated. We just have the get the dates right, and I guess we will talk once you get here."

Lisa

"Thanks, Chuck."

Charles

"It's Charles... I have one more request."

Lisa listens.

Charles

"I need you to bring a few people with you. I need as many new faces here as possible. Plus you will need some company for when I am away. I do have a country to run. I will be back and forth to Europa, and I may even have a stop in Asiana."

Lisa

"Charles, you know I don't have any friends."

Charles

"You've got some people, and don't bring anybody who can't contribute. Bring me some "braniacs". I need help over here. Maybe they can consult for me on some things. There is a lot to get done."

LISA   (chuckles)

"Gotcha, I'll try. Good morning."

Charles

"That's my girl. Good night, madam."

Charles's voice vibrates through Lisa. Not just his accent and his tone. It comforts her. He is always relaxed, but he's just simply there for her. Even though he is on the other side of the world. It is very rare that he doesn't respond up for Lisa when she calls or emails.

In Paragon it is morning time and in Olympia it is evening. The worlds are opposite. Not only dealing with the time, but the status levels on both countries. In Paragon, people are happy; they are striving for greatness with building the country to be the next recognized place in the world. In Olympia, they are struggling. Though the poor and middle class already know how it feels to struggle, the rich are starting to feel it. Many of them never knew the true meaning of sacrifice. Many didn't understand the meaning "can't afford it" and "can't do it". Although many still have enough money in their reserve bank accounts, the economy is getting worse. People are leaving, slowly, but surely. Though life is somewhat the same, things have changed over the past 25 years after the big financial deficit.

Life was overpriced, people were underpaid, the conservatives complained about the world being fair on both sides. Therefore, people listened to their ramblings over radio stations about how they felt colored people are nothing but thieves. How the first black President, Brock Woden, was a failure, although he brought the country out of shambles and back on track. How life should be the Coffee Party way, or no way.

It turned many Olympians away, and it wasn't only the colored Olympians who chose to leave. It was many. With 100,000 jobs opening in Paragon, and 10,000 jobs in Asiana to support Paragon were created, many people jumped on the opportunity. Many of them were college students, but then families followed, even if it meant that one person wasn't going to work in the household, they realized that they can live a better life off of one semi-taxed income in Paragon than 2 or even 3 incomes in Olympia. In Paragon, they could save money. All of their funds weren't taxed. Fuel was cheaper. There was no true electric bill. The school systems were awesome, and the country had amazing ventures going on with other countries, which meant that their children could get education from around the world, at little to no cost.

Life began to be fun. It wasn't a trap. The question of living was not a question anymore. The question became more so of, what is next? What else is out there?

Paragon became the place for opportunity. But it still wasn't a handout. There was criteria that had to be met to obtain residency to live there. People had to have a job lined up. Letters of recommendation were required. All people under the age of 25 must choose an education program, which were very flexible. People couldn't have a true criminal record - but if they did, they needed particular waivers, and they were granted temporary visas to live in Paragon and prove that they would be an awesome citizen. Paragon became the place for opportunity.

Charles gets off of the phone with Lisa. It's a surprising moment, as Charles has been trying to get Lisa to visit him in Paragon for years. But she resisted. It wasn't appealing to her. She saw Paragon as just another place in Africana. She thought of vast lands, corruption. Nothing of what it is. Even when she sees it on the news all she sees is the Olympia fighter jets taking off after a joint exercise. No more than that. Charles has been trying to get more media influence in Olympia. However, since he hasn't handed over A28, the media has not featured him as a prime country. Simply because the people who control the networks want a part of the money that A28 brings. As a result, the media is trying their hardest to keep Paragon as a viable country on low radar. Nevertheless, when tourists really start to come to Paragon, most people will realize the effect that it will have on the world. The only way the media and many world leaders will allow that to happen, is if they get a piece of the pie.

Charles gets out of his bed. He heads to his kitchen and makes a bowl of cereal. A person comes from behind him in his kitchen. Charles continues to eat his cereal and suddenly...

George

"Now, Mr. Charles, you know you pay me well to prepare meals."

George is Charles's 57-year-old chef who pops up from behind him. He's wearing a white chef outfit, glasses, with his hands behind his back.

Charles responds with a mouth full of cereal.

"George, you know I just try to stay down to Earth......sometimes. Smells good though, so give it to me for lunch! How are you?"

George

"Honestly sir, I couldn't be better. Do you have any request for lunch and dinner today? What I prepared for this morning is strictly breakfast."

Charles

"Don't make me feel bad, George. Pack it up for me and I'll take it to the office."

Charles walks past him and pats him on the back. George loves Charles's humbleness, but it makes his job hard because he always has to make sure that Charles is satisfied. Charles sits down on the couch and George turns on the television for him with the remote control. The screen goes directly to WNN. Charles looks up at the screen and sees that Olympia's Stock Market is going down, and they feature a list of companies that are going under. This is causing the economy to drop. He looks for a few moments, puts his food down and grabs his mobile phone and dials a phone number.

Charles

"Mother...You okay?"

Ms. Dalton, a feisty 65-year-old Olympian, is wearing a white housegown and is braiding Charles' 16-year-old sister's hair. His mother is in the living room of her apartment. She is surrounded by numerous cats, old newspapers, and antique dolls. Her southern accent is highly noticeable.

Ms. Dalton

"Son, I'm always okay. Why are you calling this late at night, boy?"

Charles

"It's early over here. I just cut the TV on and saw that things are crazy out there. Checking on you. How is Charlotte?"

Ms. Dalton

"She's okay. I'm braiding her hair now, so she can go to bed and get up early for school. They stopped the bus service, so now the kids either carpool or they have to walk."

Charles

"Really? Why?"

Ms. Dalton

"The Parent Teacher Association claims that they can't afford the contract although the school officials are still getting their fat pay checks. - Don't make sense."

Charles

"Does Charlotte have a ride?"

Ms. Dalton

"Yeah, the neighbors are always good to me. But I don't know, they are talking about moving when the next semester comes. There are so many people talking about moving. I remember these units were hard to get in, now folks are rushing out."

Charles

"Does that group of people moving include you? The offers still on the table to come here, mom…"

Ms. Dalton

"Boy, I - told - you. I'm not flying over all of that water. Momma is just fine. I'm just fine, baby….Jus' fine."

Charles

"Jus' fine huh? You said that one too many times."

Ms. Dalton continues to braid Charlotte's hair and has no response. This is hard on Charles. No matter what he does. He feels as if his mom doesn't have faith or support what he does. She never asks about the country that he pretty much created, or about any other major projects that he has worked on.

Charles

"Mom, you need to come over here. It's not that bad."

Ms. Dalton

"Charles, boy, you just like your father and his brother, always predicting something. Although they were good at it, them boys just wouldn't stop. Whew, those British scouts, they were something. I'm okay, baby… I'll let you know when I need you."

Charles

"You need any money?"

Ms. Dalton

"No, Chuck. You sent me more than enough last time."

Charles

"I'm going to check your bank account. Because I know you…"

Ms. Dalton

"Well, son, all I can say is this. Worry about you. We will be okay. If I need you I will call you. How is Joro?"

Charles

"He's good, he's over in Golia but same as always.. always conning me or somebody out of something. Haven't spoken to him in a few days though."

Ms. Dalton

"Abe?"

A few seconds go by.

Charles

"He is well too. You need to see him. He is a grown boy now. You're coming to visit soon. In fact, I think he will be over there for some fighter pilot competition. I'm not sure if he will be able to leave base. But I will let him know."

Ms. Dalton

"I love you, but Abe is the only one that's gonna get me on a plane. Oh. I'm so proud of him. You two have come a long way. Don't know how you did it over there.

"So, have you had that talk with him yet?"

This is the question that Charles tries to avoid with anybody that is close to him.

Charles

"About what?"

Ms. Dalton

"Don't what me. You know what, Charles."

Charles closes his eyes.

Charles

"No, I haven't. I want him to stay focused. Telling him that will tear him apart, and when he is down he shuts down."

Ms. Dalton

"Charles, he deserves to know. He is a man now. You can't fill a void with an unnecessary lie for too long. Especially with your one and only son."

Charles (deep breath)

"Yes, I know.....

"Look. Make sure you stay next to your phone. A lot is going on. You stay in the house and tell Charlotte I love her."

Ms. Dalton hands the phone to Charlotte, who is sitting in between Ms. Dalton's legs as she gets her hair braided.

Ms. Dalton

"Here, tell Charles you love him."

Charlotte

"I love you, Uncle Charles."

Ms. Dalton

"No, baby, that's your brother."

Charlotte

"I love you, brother."

Charles

"I love you too. You going to be a big girl for me? Gonna watch out for mommy."

Charlotte

"Yes... Unless she starts to get mean."

Charles (laughs)

"Well, you're the big girl now. I want you to come here soon, okay?"

Charlotte

"Okay. Love you."

Charles

"Love you too."

Charles hangs up the phone. Looks at the TV as President Grover has just completed his press conference at the White House.

Jacob

"Thank you."

He walks from the podium, out the door and out of sight of all press and cameras. He and his team go on to his office after a tough series of questions by the media.

Jacob

"I don't know who to blame. Myself? Corporate America? Or is it Dalton?.. Dammit!"

Gary

"Jake, calm down."

Jacob (loudly)

"Calm Down? Calm Down? This shit is getting thrown in my face and I am the face of this country! I knew I shouldn't have run for office! I'm here cleaning up the world's bullshit! I walked into it! Just walked in....to...it!"

As Jacob slams his hands down on his desk, Gary watches as his colleague vents. Gary excuses the secret service from the room and other staff, and pours Jacob a glass of water. Jake picks it up and sits down.

Jacob

"Gary, you're probably the only guy I trust. My VP is only around when he needs to be or when he needs me. What do I do?"

Gary

"We just have to take it back to the basics... Which means think and not do, nor speak... Honestly, your whole team

153

wants to set war on Dalton especially before he gets fully recognized as a sovereign state. That's something that we don't want to do. However, I believe that's what they are trying to bind us into doing."

Jacob shakes his head and takes another sip of water. The phone rings. Jake looks at it and ignores it. It rings again. Jacob picks up. It's his Vice President, William "Billy" Thomas

Jacob

"'Sup Billy?"

Vice President Thomas

"Just calling to check in with my old pal."

Jacob

"Old pal. You've got that right. What do you want? Thanks for ditching another conference that you were supposed to handle!"

Vice President Thomas

"Let's keep this thing civil."

Billy and Jacob don't get along.

Jacob

"Billy. I'm done. If I wasn't your friend you would be relieved of your duties. I'm trying to salvage our friendship of many years and I don't want to embarrass you, but I will. What do you want?"

Billy

"I just wanted to inform you that I won't be making the Europa trip for the United Worlds. Marilyn is pregnant and I can't miss out on this."

Marilyn is Billy's wife.

Billy

"So, I will be here, in Californa."

Jacob

"Figures, Billy. You have any more bullshit to tell me? Last time you gave me this nonsense, your wife was never pregnant or had any signs of pregnancy."

Billy

"You need to watch your tone. Remember I am the VP. I am less watched than you, and come in line right after you. Do you really think the public will over look it if they found out that you set up the death of your wife, the First Lady? Wait, I mean the former First Lady? It won't be a good look, would it?"

The betrayal digs deeper into Jacob

Jacob (slams the phone)

"You freakin' monster!"

Jacob slams the phone. He is both horrified and astounded at the comments that his Vice President has just made, especially since it is a low blow towards his wife, Cindy, who was poisoned during her birthday dinner two years ago. Jake has never been the same. He and Billy have been best of friends since they both entered politics. The two have traveled the world together, done fund raising trips, and been big time golf buddies throughout the years. Ever since Jake has changed for the better and not remained greedy like his party, Billy has turned for the worse. He uses Jake's small secrets against him, threatening his impeachment. He makes Jacob sign off of documents that he doesn't support, but he has to because Billy says he will exploit him and make him look untrustworthy to the world. He goes to the extreme to make him look like he killed his own spouse, when it was a setup. What makes matters worse is that the world knows, well, thinks, that Billy and Jacob are close. But, in reality they aren't anymore.

The two only go to events that are mandatory for the President and Vice President to attend together, such as showing up to high profile meetings. For the most part, Jacob has to let Billy get his way because Billy is holding Jake's nuts by the threshold and to the max. There are moments when Jacob wonders if Billy had something to do with his wife's death. He doesn't think he did it, but he knows he had some role in it. When Cindy was poisoned, most of the party turned against him. They didn't support him in any way and they started blaming him because he immediately received sympathy from the people of Olympia. Many people on the blue side of the voting pool gave Jacob the support that he didn't ask for, while the red side continued to try to get as much money and Presidential support as possible. It was at this point that everybody Changed. They all began throwing out conspiracy theories of Jacob poisoning Cindy on the table. They threatened to tell the media if he doesn't sign off on a particular bill. It hasn't been pleasant. So, Jacob is playing the easy boy roll so he can get out of it safely. Although Olympia loves him, they have grown to dislike him because they feel that he is wasting the country's money. That, however, is not the case. He is simply getting blackmailed and is making decisions that are against his will. This means saving his presidency, and at times maybe even his life. It's tough.

Jacob changes the topic.

> Jacob

"Gary, do you have a bulletin on you?"

> Gary (wiping his eyeglasses)

"Not a physical one, but I will email it to you."

Jake puts his hand up displaying NO.

> Jacob

"Just let me see it. At this point I don't know who is looking at what."

Gary looks Jake in the eyes. He slides his tablet across the table towards Jacob. When he looks at the file, he sees a full scale digital map of Paragon.

> Jacob

"What is this?"

> Gary

"Dalton has something going on. It's unreadable; I don't think it's nuclear though. Something is giving his land the leverage that no land has right now. He has built relationships with several governments and corporations over the past year. He has done much good, but at the same time our country has taken severe hits. We have lost 5 percent of our working class over the past two years. It is crippling us. Next, one of our pilots goes down in his territory? An aircraft made here! This "civilization" called "Paragon" also has a less air and heat imagery than the entire world. But it is warmer than many other places. Something isn't adding up."

> Jacob

"He started green and he's gonna end with all the green. I don't blame him either, but I have a job to do. We can't dissect the guy because his country as a whole is producing less heat than a single city over here."

Jacob gets up, and opens one of his books from college called, "The Negotiator". Opens it up, looks at it and peers out the window of his office.

Jacob

"Do you know where Bob Polan is?"

Gary

"He's in California, with Billy."

Jacob

"Figures. Let him stay there. We need to take a trip. On the small bird though."

Jacob is speaking about a smaller version of the typical Presidential plane. It only seats about 15 people. It's very low profile, as he is ready to head to Paragon.

Gary

"Why the small one?"

Jacob

"When the public sees Sky Force One moving, they know I'm moving. We are going to Paragon, and I'm going unmarked."

Gary looks at Jacob in the eyes.

Gary

"I love your determination, Boss."

A few hours later, Jacob, Gary, his technical assistant Tom Ford, and six secret service agents are in the sky.

Flight Attendant

"Mr. President, at your choice."

The flight attendant offers an assortment of different juices with small alcoholic containers.

Jacob
"I think I need all of them."

Flight Attendant (winks)

"Sir, even I wouldn't allow you to do that. Even with further approval, I'm not going to be the one responsible."

Jacob smiles at the flight attendant and takes a small bottle of alcohol and a ginger ale.

Jacob

"Can you bring me a hot towel?"

Flight Attendant

"Of course, sir. Anything else?"

He shakes his head no. Jacob looks at Gary and a few of his members within his advisory circle.

Tom Ford speaks up

"Now, for the most part, we are the only ones who know that we are over here. This is a serious risk, though we have coordinated with authorities and they prefer it this way. They still don't believe us. Dalton isn't available at the moment due to an emergency. But his team said they will be ready for us when we land."

Gary

"This is a risk, Jake... The protection isn't."

Jacob (interrupts)

"If I were to die, it would have happened already. Let's just go. It's a "vacation"."

Gary

"Yes, but it's going to hit the media. Everybody will know about it, if they don't know already."

Jacob

"It can do more good than the shit they have me in now."

Gary (quickly)

"It can also do more bad than good. You're going to be with him next week. The house is going to want to know why you are visiting him again. We need to turn this around, Jake. This isn't the right time to go over there. Take my word for it."

Jacob

"This meeting needs to happen."

8

Pennies

Back in Paragon.

Charles opens the door to his office with a magnetic key swipe which turns from red to green. He hits a switch to provide lighting in his office. The twenty-foot windows in the room turn from a very dark and black tint to a clear window from which you can see the city and ocean, while providing light to the room. This design makes Paragon unique. Though Charles loves beautiful aesthetics, he is more interested in efficiency. Even the landfills are solar powered; it saves billions of dollars in electricity. It is also good for the environment. These ideas were passed down from his father who was the best of the best in environmental energy. His dad was the first person to show people how air looked.

Charles is meeting today with Anthony Billow (28), a twenty-eight-year-old Olympian athlete. Anthony is a freak of nature. He is 6'8" tall, 250 pounds and is, hands down, one of the best athletes in the sports world. He wanted to reach out to Charles after he noticed that Charles was consistently with NBA Team owners and other leaders in the world. But, everybody else looked at Charles as if he is a regular guy. As he stands behind Charles, he is surprised with what just happened. They both are wearing casual business attire.

Anthony

"Wow. Now that was impressive. They instantly tint like that?"

Charles

"Yeah, I got it from an idea that was used in an aircraft fuselage years ago. It's not as impressive as that winning 3 pointer you had last month to seal the Finals."

As he explains it to Anthony, he picks up a model-sized aircraft. It is like a miniature airliner but it is all glass. Charles holds it, and presses a button. The whole plane turns from clear to a dark color as if it were painted blue. It's the same idea he used for his windows.

Charles

It cost a good amount but it saves money in the long run. When we tested it on a plane, it was outstanding. It is a hijacker's or terrorist's worst nightmare. With a touch of a button, you can see everything within the plane from the outside. On the inside, you wouldn't have an idea that you're being watched. It's just like tinting your car windows, just reversed, and I guess just digitally. As far as the lights are concerned, around here they are run on solar, windmill, and hydro electric. Saves me billions with A28. Rain will turn into money for the first time, well, since irrigation.

Anthony

"Well, send that contractor to my house when you can."

Charles (changes the subject)

"So, you wanted to speak with me about some things that you want to do? My ears are open."

Anthony

"I like what you have going on over here. Not to step on any toes, but you seem to be changing the world every day. Simply, because of your model and how you offer opportunity too many, not alone with what you haven't released. I just wanted to see if there were any business opportunities or investment opportunities for me. I mean I have made a fortune while playing basketball, and I want to make good use of it for when I retire....Leave a stronger legacy for my kids, you know?"

Charles sits back and chuckles. He begins to reminisce about his days at almost becoming a pro soccer (football) player; until he tore his ACL. When he was a kid, he never understood the type of money his dad dealt with. But his dad never sold anything. He focused most of his time on developing his land and preserving the environment.

Charles

"Yes, I understand. First, I like the fact that you even considered flying all the way over here to speak to me. It also feels good to know that there are some athletes out here who see more than the glitz and glamour and are willing to make solid investments outside of the norm. Anthony, I can tell you this type of business is no guarantee. Much money can be made, but even more money can get lost."

Anthony shakes his head, listening to Charles.

Charles

"Anthony, I want you to keep your money. You have more than enough of it. Many people dream to be in your victories (as he looks at Anthony's basketball shoes). Frankly, your millions will make such a small difference within this development. Not that it's pennies, but your money alone is…"

Anthony looks in disbelief and feels disrespected. His right eye squints.

Charles (leaning forward, forearms on desk)

"Don't take that personally. You will understand one day.

"Look, if there is anything that I need, I need you. Now I will look over my books, and see if there is anything that will fit you. I need you right now, way more than your money."

Anthony

"Charles, I understand. But everyone has always needed me. From endorsements to playing…"

Charles (interrupts)

"Playing ball… Pardon my interruption. You need to understand that is your gift. You have another gift as well.

Yes, you're talented. But you are still YOU. Do you see that over there?"

Charles points to what he shows Anthony, then his secretary Orchid knocks on the door.

Charles

"Come in."

Orchid walks in. She immediately catches Anthony's eyes as he examines her. She looks part Middle Eastern with long black hair. When she turns her head to see Anthony, one can see that the other side is half-braided. Her lips are full and from Anthony's perspective, her body looks amazing. He is looking at her like he has an x-ray machine is embedded in his brain. She is wearing a sundress down to her ankles. She has a tattoo on her whole left arm that is a light orange color, it's some sort of design, but Anthony can't make anything of it. She has a nude lipstick on her lips, no more than a bit of foundation of make-up on her face, and she looks as if she works out daily. She looks at Anthony.

Orchid

"Hi…"

As Anthony replies she pays him no mind and looks at Charles.

Orchid

"Your guests have arrived. Lisa, Bin, and a guy named....."

She looks at the palm of her hand.

Orchid

"Yes - Lisa, Bin and Eddie are here."

Charles is surprised and looks at his calendar. Not realizing what day it is.

Charles

"Wow. It is the fourth. Ummm…where are they?"

Orchid

"They cleared our customs a few hours ago. Bill said that they are on their way here now, Tommy is driving them. I believe they just were outside of Sector B."

Sector B is 20 miles away from Charles's office, which sits in Sector A of Paragon.

Charles

"Okay. Thanks much."

Anthony is still looking at Orchid. Though she acts like she pays him no mind, her face begins to turn red, even redder, and she is still as a stone. Charles expects her to leave, Anthony does too. However, she still hasn't yet. Still sitting down, Charles looks at her again and chuckles.

Charles (raises his eyebrows)

"You okay?"

Anthony finds his way into the conversation.

Anthony

"Yeah, everything okay?"

It's now clear that she is averting her eyes from Anthony. Now she's blushing even more. Orchid then says "Yes". She then turns her head the opposite way from Anthony, and gives Charles a small wave with her left hand as she swiftly walks out of the office.

Anthony (looking at Charles)

"Now, who .... is?"

Before he can get the last word out she comes back to close the door. She still manages to sneak another sneak peak of Anthony. He couldn't see her face but he noticed piece of that tangerine colored sundress that she had on.

Anthony

"That? Yes, who is that?"

Charles

"Ha. Everybody loves her. That's Orchid."

Anthony begins to inquire about her with Charles. Before he can get a word out, Charles cuts him off.

Charles

"Uhhhh. She's off limits, buddy. She's like a daughter to me.   Don't - even - try it."

Anthony

"But..."

Charles

"Nope, and you don't need any women anyway. Stay focused."

Anthony.

"Chuck, c'mon. But damn! I didn't know they were looking like THAT over here."

Charles

"What do you expect? We have people from all over the world here. They eventually made babies and many of them came out looking rather different I should say. You got a mix of Asiana, Middle Eastern, Olympia, Golia, Austia, the whole nine."

He looks at Anthony

Charles

"It is a sighting. But any who - Do you see that over there?"

Charles points at a LEGO board that is in the corner of the room.

It's a Lego town that he built. This is why Anthony respects Charles. He has seen Charles come to sports games very quietly, usually with the owners, who were always showing Charles around as if he was the new #1 draft pick or trade. This was different to Anthony. Charles stood out. He always wondered why the people at the top respected Charles.

Charles

"While you practiced every day, day and night, you had the choice to do other things. But you had a gift, a calling, and you went for it. To do something and be amazing at it isn't easy. Not saying that you don't have another gift, but you responded to your gift as an athlete; just as I am responding to mine. Now, I don't just take money from anybody. I didn't just build this place off of money.

"It's about support, alliances, and mutual benefit. All that outweighs money, but you will be an asset to me, and I promise that I will make use of your investment desires. But now, I need you to help me with a challenge. It will also help you as well. It's a challenge though. You have to be down if I show it to you. Then maybe I'll let Orchid take you out on a date. Yes, she will take you out. You don't know your way around here. But you've got to roll with me first."

Anthony

"And what's that?"

Charles looks at Anthony, grins and leans back.

Charles

"Let's roll."

The men walk out of the office and head down the hallway towards the elevator. Orchid is sitting at her desk as Anthony and Charles walk by. She sees them, but turns away so Anthony can't see her. As he walks away he turns his head again, only to catch her in the act of looking at him. Then she looks back down. He knows she's feeling him. Well, he thinks so. It doesn't matter because it's Charles's call. Then it would be up to her if she likes him or not. However, it's a hard task for some women not to like a decent looking athlete, especially the best basketball player in the world.

Charles and Anthony get into the elevator

Charles

"I didn't expect guests today, so that's my fault. You okay with that? They will be in a separate vehicle."

Anthony

"Yeah, I'm okay with that."

Charles

"Well, they are from Olympia, so they may get a bit starstruck. But, these folks don't watch too many sports so it should be fine."

Anthony nods his head.

Charles

"We're going to drive around a few parts of the downtown area, and then we are going to head into the project that I want you to help me with. It shouldn't be long. It's going to be a bit different. Also, this is between us because it is still in development, and I don't want many to see it until it is media ready. How many guys are with you?"

Anthony

"Two. My manager and my good friend."

Anthony is rather excited, but still nervous. He is on the other side of the world, has never been to Paragon before, and he knows nobody who lives in the area besides Charles.

In no time they reach the bottom level of the skyscraper, the elevator door opens, surprising Anthony. When they walk out, they can see three black SUV's lined up and about six people mingling around them. Charles sees Lisa, and doesn't recognize anybody else. The group looks as if they are talking and getting acquainted with each other. Some of them are drinking bottled water. It may be easy for them to get acquainted with each other, as they are all from Olympia. As they get closer Charles gets a better sight of the group.

They are all standing there, sun beaming in their faces. As the two step outside, there stands Anthony's manager Dallas and his close friend Walter. Then to the right of them stands Bin, Lisa, and Eddie - the happy doorman from Bin's apartment.

In a heartbeat, Lisa runs to Charles and jumps on him as if she hasn't seen in him in decades. He hugs on her, although he wasn't expecting so much excitement. Everybody is looking at the two, as Charles looks at Lisa in the eyes. He freezes. Moments from when they were kids; battling to see who is going to get to before the other. Going on a study abroad trip in Emirate. Being there for one another during many difficult times. He thinks about their first romantic moment, which was also their last. He wants to kiss her but he can't, there are too many people who he doesn't know around them. He also doesn't know how she will react to him kissing her lips. Her hug clamps his body, her dark blue fingernails dig into his back. One of her hands lands on his upper back, and the other on his lower back almost as if they were slow dancing. The sun is meeting her eyes, so she has to squint to get a good look at him. He still looks like young Charles, but she can see how he has matured. She also sees much worry in his eyes.

Charles

"You still have those rich brown eyes, I see. They are still scary."

Lisa

"I know. I see them every day when I look in the mirror."

Lisa slowly pulls away from Charles, as it looks like her energy level took a plunge.

Lisa (looking at Anthony)

"So, you got the Player of the Year in the land of Paragon, huh? What you're trying to have him as first president over here? Barkley style?"

Narles Barkley is a Hall of Fame basketball player who was considering running for office a few times after his career over. He is well liked in Olympia, since the television networks enjoy poking fun at him during the commentary of highlight reels. Anthony looks over at Lisa, and is surprised at her confidence to speak to him as if he was a regular person. He loves it. The only person who he receives that casualness from are his close friends and family.

Anthony

"Dalton won't even hook me up with his gorgeous secretary. I'm sure he won't let me be the President."

Everybody chuckles at the semi-low blow that Anthony gives off.

Charles

"Anthony, this is Lisa. We've been colleagues ever since college. I've been trying to get her over here for years, because she's someone that can really make this place boom, but she's been scared, and sorry this is my first time meeting..."

He turns to Bin and Eddie.

Lisa

"Oh, I'm sorry, guys. Meet Bin."

Bin (reaches out his hand to Anthony and Charles)

"Bin Juntow, nice to meet you. I heard many good things about you and Paragon, very impressive so far. I liked the mall area that we drove by."

Charles

"Thanks. Thanks for coming."

Lisa (points Charles toward Eddie)

"And Charles this is Eddie. He is Bin's assistant."

Charles reaches to shake Eddie's hand. Their heads nod, and Eddie stays quiet. Dallas and Walter also shake Charles hand. Everybody gets acquainted.

Charles

"It's up to you guys, I was planning to take Anthony out into the woodlands. You guys can come or??"

Lisa

"We're pretty lagged. So I think we will take it in for now."

Charles

"You sure? I don't want to be rude."

Lisa

"Oh no, that was a long flight. We had to make a stop too because weather was bad."

Charles

"You must have flown private, because the charter flights only come on the weekends."

Lisa

"Yup. Why not?"

Charles

"Well, you could have saved half the money. I do have a few aircraft that is used exclusively for special travel arrangements. Regardless, I'm going to roll with Anthony. Orchid should have the hospitality waiting for you. If you need anything let one of the guys know, or just call me."

Lisa

"Wait. Ummm… How far are we staying from here?"

Charles

"Oh. It's only about a 45 minute drive."

Lisa raises her eyebrows, tilts her head, and looks at Charles. Bin and Eddie look at him also, being appreciative but also concerned. They are tired.

Charles

"Ahhhhh … Relax. You will be staying right up there."

He points to the skyscraper that towers above them.

Charles

"It has everything you need. Literally."

Eddie (waving his fingers)

"Really, like a pedicure!"

Everybody pauses for a moment and looks at each other. Realizing but respecting Eddie's aura.

Charles

"Yeah, it has all of that. Pedicure, Manicure....Wax." (as he looks at Lisa)

Eddie

"Look, I got to do what I got to do. Cause I don't want my feet looking like his."

Eddie looks at the driver Tommy's feet, everybody else does also. His toes are hanging out of his sandals and you can see that the dirt has accumulated, along with fungus and toe jam. When Tommy looks down he realizes how nasty his feet are, then he looks up at everybody as they are holding their laughs in, while they stare at his feet. He is more so surprised that Eddie called him out like that. Tommy is speechless. He squeezes his face and looks at Charles, then Anthony, then Lisa. He looks back down at his feet; there is nothing that he can say.

Lisa

"I think we will be fine. You boys go ahead."

Tommy (looking at Lisa)

"If you need something, let me know...Okay, baby..."

She looks back at him, totally not attracted to him, but recognizes his humor. She smirks, and then looks at his feet as she walks away. It's another Tommy Moment.

As Lisa, Bin, and Eddie and the rest of the group head into the skyscraper. Charles and Anthony get into the Rover SUVs which are waiting on them. Bill is already inside the vehicle, and Tommy gets in once Charles and Anthony are settled in their seats.

The Black Rover SUVs which are polished to the dime. Anthony notices that Tommy and Bill have an athletic looking jumpsuit on which says "Paragon: Special Unit 1".

They are usually the ones who are on Charles's detail and make sure that he is transported safely. Though Charles does not want to be looked at as the President of the new nation, he still has to be protected because there have been people who have moved to Paragon just to assassinate him. Most of it has to do with A28, but some of it is because some just hate the fact that he is creating a new nation. He doesn't allow certain businesses to operate in Paragon, and he is a dark-skinned leader in a diverse territory. It's frowned upon by many racist and inflexible conservatives. Many can't accept that fact. Although he is primarily European, now he needs special skilled men to protect him at all times, and they go through similar clearances that Olympia's government does with the President's secret service officers. In fact, they are trained by Olympia through the agreement that they made years ago which was the use of some of Paragon's land for a war hub.

As Tommy begins to drive, they begin going around the town of Paragon's sector A. The group sees that everything is new. Anthony's colleagues Dallas and Walter and one of Charles's special units are in a vehicle behind them.

Driving around Paragon is amazing. They are sweeping through the streets and the strobe lights on, so the vehicles move to the side. The restaurants on the streets are gorgeous; people are eating and enjoying the sun. All the streets have grass and if they don't, they have artificial grass because it gets too hot over there to grow the real thing. The palm trees in the middle of the roads aren't average palm trees. They have different colors to them. Some have dark brown base trunks and others are lighter. Some have different colored leaves, ranging from purple to orange, though the majority of them are still green in order to keep the natural tree look. The roads are unique. It is hard to tell during the day, but they illuminate the road at night. Lines are visible on the paint, which is where they get charged with Paragon's beaming sunlight during the daytime hours.

The detail is driving through the streets, and people are watching as they know that it is Dalton coming through. Though he has a lot of power, most of them are really worried about who he is with, because most people have met Charles personally as Paragon is not too big and it has grown slowly. As the Black Rovers drive through the streets, they turn towards Sector B, where most residential communities are.

Charles

"Tommy, can you turn the remote speaker phone on, tune in the vehicle behind us."

Tommy presses a button in the center console of the Rover. The computer in the vehicle speaks.

"You are linked to vehicle 022, you may begin speaking. Drive safe."

Charles

"Hi, gents. This area that we are in is almost developed. As you can see they are beautiful homes, and most of them have already been purchased. Not many of them are occupied at the moment. We are working on that, but many people have been using them as vacation homes or they rent them out to contractors who are here on temporary assignments. Now, as you can see to the left one of our first schools. This one is one of our Agriculture institutions. It focuses on Agriculture for the young ones, and old folks come in to advance their knowledge. Parents here have decided not to do use the traditional "grades" for schools, and work with what the kids are most interested in. Instead of them being forced to learn something that they don't care for, they learn something that they enjoy, but it still challenges them."

It's an amazing sight for Anthony and his friends, as many people have no idea of what type of place that Paragon has become. All they have seen is what is shown on television. Which is mostly protests, maybe a hotel every now and then, but nothing more.

They continue to take the brief tour of Paragon. Seeing most of the inland and the inner city (Section A) took about 45 minutes. Though it's not the full country, a lot was still seen. They make a quick stop in Sector B and taste some of the fruit and veggies from the Vertical Farms in the middle of the city, which are almost shaped as pyramids which save space of farming, money, and provides citizens with a more controlled harvest. The fruit is amazing and it is even more amazing because everything was in one place which saved many miles of natural land, and made it easier for the farmers to harvest crops.

They tour the beautiful skyscrapers which use solar powered glass which in turn generates power for most of the Inner City. The multicolored windows are so stunning that they don't even look like they generate power, they look as if they are made to resemble a magnificent structure, or an architect's dream. The buildings on the east side of Paragon reflect the turquoise view of the water. With the coast of Paragon and the Seren beach nested right next to many of the buildings, it is a beautiful panorama.

As they drive, Anthony notices the people that walking around are different races, cultures, but all seem to have an inner spirit, which is to want more and most seem happy. Some people are dressed in a very sophisticated manner, but there were also the very casually dressed person, some afro-centric, all the way to your traditional skateboarder. There is no predominant race in Paragon as every race is balanced. It's a land of diversity. People look happy. The police are cool with most citizens, as some of them hover around in their vehicles which can float up to 40 feet in the sky, which gives them the ability to get to places faster. The same goes with ambulances. Anthony gets an immediate feeling of home. He even saw men who had less clothing on and were holding hands. He figured that Eddie would appreciate that, after hearing his pedicure comments and his gestures.

As the day fades into the evening, Charles instructs Tommy to drive towards the woodland.

9

Face-to-face

The two matte green Rovers are now riding into the forest area of Paragon. It is very hilly, and in the distance, Anthony can see how the fog borders the peaks of the cliffs, like the dew point in the morning. As they are driving, Anthony can see some concrete trucks laying pavement down to create a road, which makes the two SUVs veer off to the right and drive on an unpaved road.

Charles begins to talk to Anthony while they are in the backseat. Tommy and Bill are in the front seats; Tommy is driving, and Bill is the passenger. Anthony's colleagues Dallas and Walter are in the other SUV with Charles's other casually dressed security officers. Andy, who was in the other vehicle, hopped in their vehicle so he could ride with Charles through the woodlands, which could be said to be Andy's office as he leads the biology sector of Paragon.

Charles is talking to Anthony over the music in the vehicle, and has to raise his voice in order for Anthony to hear him. Charles is leaning in, while Anthony is looking out of the window at the magnificent views. They have to hold onto the rail on the car because there are still some bumps in the terrain, as it is still being constructed.

The land is green; most of the road is smoothly paved. Trees are growing, and there are grasslands, and ponds that stretch for miles. There are small huts that seem to be properly placed every other mile or so, as if people live in them. It's a beautiful and natural vast land. Wild animals are spread out, as are flocks of birds. There are aerial hovercraft which are solar powered, and they are sprinkling a powdery material onto the land. There's another one that is spraying a mist-type substance right behind it. The animals in the land look relaxed, happy, and calm. It looks like a zoo, but it's not. It's a piece of paradise that Charles's father preserved. As one of the few lands that the world was not able to conquer, it belongs to nature, and the Daltons preserved it.

Charles (loudly)

"Now, what we are doing is creating a safe path through our Forest Reserve development. This project is going to create recreational use of nature and preserves, but at the same time allow people to enjoy watching nature in its natural habitat versus a cage. We will have no public zoos in Paragon, only natural habitats."

The road is bumpy and is putting the Range Rovers to the test. The wind flowing through the vehicles freshens the experience, almost making Anthony forget about the bumpy ride. The SUVs come to a complete stop.

Tommy is at a halt to allow a lioness and her two cubs to cross the road. Then, for some odd reason, the lioness stops in her tracks. She boldly turns her head, and looks at the vehicle. The gravel cracks and crunches as she walks towards the idle vehicle. Anthony's stomach begins to twist a bit. He isn't used to this.

The sounds of her steps symbolize how her worn paws support the 300 pounds that she weighs. She first comes toward the front of the vehicle and makes her way towards Anthony's door. Anthony is quite afraid, as he can now hear every breath the beast makes. Anthony pushes his finger towards the up function of the window, to raise it up. Charles grabs his wrist and stops him.

Charles whispers

"No. No quick movements. She's more worried than you are. By the looks of her stomach, she's eaten anyway. You are fine."

Anthony looks freaked out, but still amazed.

Less than two feet away from her, looking down from inside the Rover, Anthony is eye-to-nose with a wild lion for the first time in his life. It's an incredible experience. He has seen many in the Zoo, but this one is different. He is looking at her hazel eyes, as she nudges the door with her nose and ears. The small scars from living in the wild are apparent, even with a fresh gash that she received from her last hunt. Her beautiful golden hair is bright, but still has a dirty overlay. He's listening to the strong breaths that she makes, and then she takes one final one which turns into a large snort; the residue of which lands on Anthony. She then slowly walks away into the woodland area as her cubs watch for her to come back towards them.

Anthony is disgusted and speechless as Charles laughs. Anthony's hands are raised and he doesn't even want to move as the lioness's saliva is on his black T-shirt. Charles and Andy continue to chuckle and they begin to drive off.

Andy (handing Anthony a small towel)

"You can handle it, bud."

Anthony takes the towel in disbelief, shaking his head, and then wipes himself off.

Charles

"I have already increased Paragon's tourism just by saving over 100 lions from losing their lives. Now I have to put up proper fencing to prevent them from entering town. Electric fencing. The females like to come in every now and then, and it's never an inviting sight, especially in a metropolitan area. We've had to shoot a few. The public always makes an outcry when it happens because they think we kill them, but we don't."

Anthony

"How do you shoot them without hurting them?"

Charles

"We shoot with a special gun. Exactly like the one Bill has, if you have noticed. But instead of bullets it is aligned

175

with small injection pellets that knock the lion out within seconds by immediately attacking the bloodstream. Only problem is when it hits their eyes. It can blind them. However, it's better than losing a life, on both ends."

Anthony

"So you have a bit of Mike Tyson in you, huh?"

Charles gives him a laugh and hits him in his arm.

Charles

"Well, Tyson had tigers. I met one of them when I visited his house. That was my boy."

Anthony

"Really? Wasn't that in the 1990's? That was like 50 years ago."

Charles freezes for a moment. He and Anthony catch eyes.

Charles

"I was a baby, young."

Anthony (scratching his forehead)

"Oh. Okay. I was wondering, because that was a long time ago."

Anthony has learned a whole other side of Charles than what has been portrayed. Most people only know Charles because of his strong business acumen and the civilization that he inherited from his father. Many like him, but the media puts him in a sometimes unfavorable light; partly because corporations and politicians don't always agree with Charles's values. As it happens, because he controls A28, Charles controls the world. Many countries, corporations, and even the stock market have been anticipating Charles's every move because he has the power to change not only business, but the world governments and populations with A28.

A28 is the source of Charles's power. If he wanted to sell the mineral off, he would put many of the fuel companies out of business, simply because they can't compete with it. Therefore, the government, taxes, and support companies would all be affected. The mineral has brought many allies to Paragon simply because everybody wants to have first dibs at the product, so they can sell it and save money on rising fuel costs. This gives Charles the ability to receive trade, and the force and technology that he needs to run the civilization. Charles's contact list is enormous, from politicians, aerospace companies, and engineers. For one, he is respected by many, and two, he has something that they all want. Nevertheless, this mineral has also made Paragon a target.

There have been times in the past where his grandfather was invaded and many lives were spared through Charles's allies. Though Paragon isn't registered with the U.W yet, they still had much moral and physical support. This support prevented invasions from other countries because their allies had some sort of relationship with Charles, and they didn't want to jeopardize their position on the next phenomenon of commodity. They also didn't know where exactly to find the mountains where the mineral sits. Also, the mineral must be processed a particular way otherwise it won't be effective.

Many business men despise Charles because he won't share the processing secret, but they don't want to start war with their own allies. It's a difficult situation. But since the year 2013, and the rise of fuel costs, pressure has been on Charles not only to release this product for distribution, but to do so correctly. He wants to be a part of the U.W so it can be revenue for his country, so he can build and have an awesome civilization. He will be the first person to start his own country in years. He doesn't just want to sell his precious commodity then get bombed due to the greed and thirst for power that runs the world.

The only problem with that this is, once Charles is aligned with the U.W., other countries will have to buy the product, but they won't own the rights to it. Hence the reason that Charles has to be on the alert constantly because threats of "war" have been sparked a few times. Olympia has been the last to truly be ready to threaten war on Paragon, especially since their citizens have been emigrating due to the lower cost of balanced living and significantly lower taxes. Additionally, the quality of life is more productive than the lifeless work mentality of the Olympia. In Paragon, everybody contributes; working around the world is a must. Though everybody is taxed, the government has its own revenue, and offers extensive jobs; everything is for the most part solar or hydraulically powered. Though crime is everywhere, life is better in Paragon, as there is more opportunity for all. Over in Olympia, Charles is portrayed in a different light. He is scrutinized by the media because of the way he conducts his business. Some of that comes from politics of companies and politicians because he doesn't share all of his secrets with everybody. Charles and Anthony are beginning to bond like brothers. Unlike Joro, who corrupts Charles's every chance, he needs an extra dollar or two.

The vehicles begin to head in the direction of more construction vehicles. The workers are drilling in pipes, moving dirt. There is a worker monitoring a huge water hose which is putting water into a hole. The workers are of different races.

Charles continues his lion conversation

"I made sure that I contracted workers from all over. It builds relationships with governments and corporations. The stronger the relationship, the more they have my back although I think a few of them are in it just for the money, which I can't control. So I just stick to my instincts."

Anthony

"So what are you building? A zoo?"

Charles

"Come on man, now if you really want to start to invest your money into something, you got to think deeper than that."

A few seconds go by.....

Charles

"Ever heard of the Tuff Mother?"

Anthony

"Yup. What; you're challenging me to it?"

Charles

"Not only that. I want you to help me get some participants. I'm having the first one in three months. I need your sports counterparts. I need it all. Soccer, baseball, hockey, tennis, musicians. They will bring the people, as they influence. I want this one to be the largest ever and the best ever. I have dedicated land and a plan to be able to accommodate 50,000 people. Business-wise, it will attract more people to Paragon,. It will expose what I-----, I mean what we have created. So we be more socially recognized by the United Worlds.

"We are RIGHT there, I MEAN RIGHT THERE! We just need a few more people, a few more tourists."

Anthony

"So, what do I have to do?"

Charles

"Just be you... Just help me make this a success."
Anthony looks at Charles and notices that a tear has rolled down his eye as Charles turns his head and looks out the window at the beautiful nature that has been preserved. The trees are moist, as the aircraft that flew over previously has misted them all down. The flowers are blooming, as it is late July. A baboon is sitting on a tree struggling to open a coconut.

Charles (wipes his eye)

"I have gotten clearance from the International Aviation Admin and other governments to Approve Large Aircraft to land at our airfield. It took me 5 years to get that approval. I have arranged to Charter aircraft from States in all directions. I need those seats filled. Let's start from there. You've got trustworthy buddies who are looked up to. Let's get them here, let's show them what has been built and the opportunity that is being offered. I just want people to see a better life."

Anthony

"So if I do it. Will you be on my team?"

Charles

"Well, I don't know if I will let you participate. I don't need any lawsuits; and your career is more important. Help me on the business end of it."

Anthony

"Okay. Let's make it happen."
Tommy intervenes from the driver seat. His eyes on the rearview mirror, looking at Anthony.

Tommy

"Yo, Charles, you mind if I can help him? I mean, I've been watching Anthony play for years, I remember the time."

Charles interrupts Tommy

Charles

"Tommy, just drive."

Tommy has been holding his breath for the past 30 minutes waiting to say something to Anthony. He was one of his favorite players. As a military person, the last person that Tommy would have expected to see on foreign soil was the star basketball player from the country that he grew up in.

Tommy looks back in the rearview mirror with his usual scowl that he gets when he is denied something.

He doesn't like it, but in a way he's privileged over many of his cadets. Although he's missing out on fun, nobody gets access to see the arenas that Tommy has seen. Though he doesn't know it, he is liked by many. Tommy is bright and humorous, but when it is time to handle his business, he has an amazing shooting capability. He is an even better driver. He has been heavily trained in vehicle maneuvers and driving in any type of terrain. This means he can flee other vehicles in time of a threat. But his bubbly personality does not reflect it.

Charles

"And yes, Tommy. I will find something that you can do. But for now. Just drive."

Everybody in the vehicle laughs.

They pull up to the land where the Tuff Mother competition will take place. The men get out of their vehicles, along with the SUV behind them. The security is all on alert. They all have handguns on their thigh and one on their waist, with enough ammo to have a long shoot-out. One guard has an M16.

Charles gets out of the vehicle, closes the door, and walks with Anthony for about 10 steps. Charles's guards follow, and he raises his hand to halt them. Charles bends down to the ground and picks up a piece of soft mud. He then looks at Anthony.

Charles

"My father had rights to all of this land, where my developments are, everything. But he didn't know what to do with it. So he just took care of it."

Charles drops the mud. He thinks of sharing the mineral with him, but he's not ready to yet.

Charles

"He handed all the rights to over to me. Everything. Years ago, there were a few people here, over these millions of acres. When I was a kid, all I wanted to do was create, but I didn't know how or what. I always wondered why he handed the land to me. But now I know. I know exactly why. I just wonder if he knew it would turn into this."

A few moments pass.

Charles

"You take care of Mother Nature; Mother Nature takes care of you. Well, depending on what mood she's in. Fire means she's on her period, so leave her alone. Water, well, water can be a few different things."

The men chuckle.

Charles is happy, but tears slowly begin to fill his eyes. He still looks strong and bold. They don't roll down. These are the moments when he gets so passionate about what he has completed, been through, and what's ahead of him.

Charles

"The diversity that my mom gave to me as a child became adversity. I'd like to go home, back to Olympia, but I don't."

Charles begins to have a flashback to when he was a kid. He was sitting on the ground playing with a Lego board, in deep thought as if he was playing chess. Other kids are playing around in the background, some basketball, and others are playing tag. Most of the kids are white, no blacks. Young Charles is staying to himself, building his miniature town. He sets Lego by Lego, color by color. It normally took him days to finish his creations as he was very particular.

As he is putting the finishing touch to the small Lego city a Teenager's shoe comes from out of sight and kicks over Charles's Lego city. Then another follows and kicks Charles to the ground. His vision becomes blurry and it takes a few moments for his sight to come back. He overhears…

"You nerd…. Find something better to do."

All of the other kids begin to laugh and tease Charles as they walk away. As his focus gets better, he can see how the kids are all African-Olympian, and mostly his same complexion.

Charles sits up and begins to pick the Legos off the ground, one by one. He looks up to his left and there is a short brunette girl who has bent down next to Charles. She glows in a plaid blue and yellow school uniform. Her voice is light and soft.

Lisa bends down to help Charles pick up his Legos.

"Those kids are jerks. Ignore them. My nanny always says be the bigger man…"

Charles is brought back to the present by the sounds of Anthony's voice.

Anthony

"Chuck, you there?"

Charles

"Sorry, just had a few things cross my mind. But yeah, this is where the competition will be."

Anthony looks at Charles, giving him an even deeper look.

Charles

"If my dad could to see this, I really wonder what he would say."

Grabbing his hand, Anthony helps Charles up as if he was a basketball teammate who was on the ground. The walk back to the Rovers and get back in.

As they continue the tour, Anthony notices that there are many gated facilities in the confines of the forest with armed men around all of them. Almost as if they are work camps. Anthony begins to wonder where he is. He trusts Charles's judgment, but wonders if this is too good to be true. For every great businessman, there's also a mind over matter. The camps are lined with fences and signs on them stating, "High Voltage, Authorized Access Only". Before Anthony can think any deeper, the men begin to notice something running in the woods. They stop the vehicle, but then whatever was moving stops also. There are many animals in the forest so being careful is wise.

From out of nowhere, they hear more sounds of rustling bushes. They slow the vehicle down, so they don't accidentally hit whatever is moving. The men begin to notice that the animal stops every time they do. The trees and bushes seem to scramble every time the vehicle moves, but all movement stops when they stop.

Andy looks out his window.

Andy comes over the radio,

"Bill, do you notice that? Three o'clock."

Bill

"I thought I was the only one. Don't know what that shit is. It may be a bird or something?"

The men continue to drive slowly. However, the rustles continue, and they can clearly see that it's a large animal, almost as if it's hunting them. But this creature is big and strange-looking.

Bill

"Stop the vehicle. Let's see what this is."

Bill gets out of the vehicle. He's not worried as he is armed with two handguns. One is for protection, the other is to tranquilize any animals or other things that are being replicated at the facility.

As he gets out he notices the brushing. He can see a creature that is greenish and blends in with the forest. It is slumped over and sitting still. It's not a lion; it seems as if it's standing on its hind legs. Bill draws his weapon. He slowly points the tip of his gun to the men insisting that they raise the windows in the vehicle up. They do.

As he approaches the creature, which is green, brown, hairy, with mud blotches on it, it jumps from out the bushes and onto Bill. It begins to grapple with Bill. But the creature isn't trying to bite Bill, instead it is fighting him. They are both scrambling for each other's hands as both of Bill's weapons are on the ground now due to him falling suddenly. Bill begins to fight for his life. Gunshots ring out.

Both Bill and the creature are on the ground motionless. Charles and Anthony can't believe what they are witnessing. It's a Goliath man-sized creature that is made of a mud-like substance, with abnormal hands, and it is motionless on top of Bill. Both of them have been shot.

Charles jumps out of the vehicle screaming at his security guards.

> Charles

"Why did you shoot? Why!"

> The guard responds

"Sir,"

> Charles (interrupts)

"You shot him!"

> Guard

"Sir, we shot tranquilizers."

Anthony is in disbelief. Charles and his Environmental lead, and Andy get out of the vehicle and cautiously walk towards Bill, who's on the ground with the beast that nearly killed him. The men are nervous; all they hear are the sounds in the woods, the birds chirping as they are flocking away because the gunshots frightened them. The ground is murky from the last mist of rain. They take a few more steps, and then the beast jumps up in a last attempt to attack Charles. It falls back down as the sedative settles in.

Charles is now next to the creature, looks over at Bill as the other guards are checking on him.

> Charles

"Is he okay?"

> Guard

"Yes. Pupils are in full reaction."

As Charles receives the okay, he kneels next to the animal with Andy.

Andy is examining the creature as it is covered with strands that seem like moss and mud as if it was created in the forest. It's struggling to breathe, still alive, just sedated. Andy wants to tend to it, not knowing what it is. With the woodlands being his office, he lives for moments like this. He wants to know what the thing is and where it came from.

Anthony and Tommy wait in the background. Over the past few years, Tommy has adapted to these types of experiences. He seems to be always with Charles when emergencies occur. As for Anthony, this experience is a first, especially being in the middle of nowhere, 8,000 miles away from home.

Tommy

"Is it one of the Neo'?"

Charles and Andy look at him

Charles

"I'm not sure. Just stay back."

Andy is examining the body, as Charles kneels next to him. Anthony is still in shock as he has no understanding of what he has walked into, or what to do. He's a rich, famous professional basketball player. Why is he in the woods, on the other side of the world, wondering what a Neo beast is? Is this a place where he really wants to invest in? Invite people to?

Anthony

"What the heck is a Neo?"

Tommy

"A Neo, one of Chuck's projects. A Nedirtthal."

Anthony, at 6'8", looks down at Tommy who is only 5'5", as he is surprised at how bad he mispronounced the word Neanderthal. What gets to Anthony is how confident Tommy was with his reply, as he is obviously getting the name wrong.

Anthony (squinting his eyes)

"A what?"

Tommy (confidently, as he hits Anthony's chest)

"A neo man. A Nedirthal."

Anthony

"A what?"

Tommy

"Dude, a Ne-Dir-Thal. Tarzan. The old humans from back in time."

Anthony

"You mean a NE - AN - DER – THAL."

Tommy

"Yup, however you wanna to say it. Shit."

Tommy looks up at Anthony

Anthony glances down at Tommy, wondering what's going on in his mind. Tommy looks back up Anthony and you can clearly tell the difference in their height levels. But Tommy's personality and height complex interferes with him knowing when he is wrong. So in his mind he's always right, even when he pronounces words wrongly.

Tommy

"What?"

Anthony shakes his head.

Tommy

"Now seriously, you see all these little buildings we've been driving by? They are all for testing. These folks are trying to bring extinct creatures back - Jurassic Park-style. However, there are no dinosaurs yet. Well, at least no big ones. I've seen some of the little ones. Shit, one bit me right here."

Tommy shows Anthony a very small cut on the tip of his finger. It's hard to Anthony to see so he looks closer and realizes it that it's no bigger than a paper-cut, more so a scratch. Anthony looks back at him, as he realized why the guys tell him to just drive.

Tommy

"Charles's scientists have used DNA to regenerate them back to the world. I met one or two. They were woman. Pretty stacked too. I should have them make one for me."

Anthony is in shock. What has he gotten into? What kind of man is Charles? What kind of freaky situation is this? Why is he standing next to a guy talking about sexy Neanderthals that have been genetically engineered?

A few moments go by as Anthony has to process what he is hearing and witnessing. Andy and Charles continue to intensively examine the creature.

Andy (over his radio frequency)

"I need a vac, I'm at maker 18 in the woodlands."

Andy

"No. It's not a Neo? I need some gloves!"

186

The men are looking at the motionless creature. It's barely noticeable. If it had been lying down in grassy terrain, the men would probably have walked over it. A guard brings the gloves to Andy, and hands some to Charles. He then braces with his gun, in case of any more movements or attacks from the beast.

Andy puts the gloves on, moves his hands through the creature's mossy skin. He notices that it is loose and gooey. Andy is somewhat of a nature freak, so he doesn't hesitate to dig deeper. He begins to pull on the mush. It begins to come off; its, strong, dark green and brown, like it came from a jungle. It has an awful smell, almost rotten. The creature is about 6 feet long; it has a body shaped like an ape.

As the men dig through its exterior, the icky mush begins to come off. The creature begins to make noises, deep moans and groans. Andy and Charles begin to dig deeper. As they begin to pull more substance off, they realize that the creature also has teeth, gums, nostrils, and it's under skin has a pale pigment.

Andy

"It has eyes! What the? Pull this crap off! Get me a tube, a stick! Any oxygen kits in the vehicle? Something!"

Andy realizes that he needs to get some oxygen into it immediately. Initially, everybody is wondering why he is trying to save it, but after hearing his tone change, they begin assist him.

After pulling the gushy substance off the creature, its breathing becomes more apparent as the breaths get deeper. The throat begins to make noises, its eyes are squinting.

Andy

"Fuck, this is a…It's a.."

Andy realizes that it's not a morphed creature, nor a Neo. Most, if not all, of Paragon's Neanderthals are ape-ish in appearance, have a hunch in their back, and many aren't tall. Many of them don't have the strength fight a human because most of them are still in development stages. Unless it's one that has morphed.

The creature's chest begins to heave.

Guard

"Sir, we don't have any Oxygen kits. I'll have to have one hovered!"

Andy

"We don't have time for that!"

Second Guard

"You're nuts. Let it be!"

Andy

"SHUT THE FUCK UP AND STEP BACK!!"

There is a moment of silence as everybody is surprised. Eyebrows rise at Andy's response to the 6'3 240 pound body guard. The guard takes a few steps back. He doesn't like that a nerd just cursed him out. He then looks at Charles, who respectfully tells him to back off.

It's risky to do CPR on a wild creature, but Andy has no choice. There's a possibility that it can have diseases, and it can bite at any moment. Giving CPR in the wild is just as good as going mouth-to-mouth with a stray dog that has rabies. None of this is Andy's concern.

With his index and middle finger, he pulls more of the gooey substance out of the creature's mouth. These are the type of enthusiasts that Charles hires. He hires the ones that devote their lives to their craft. Some, like Andy, will even risk their lives in the process of doing their jobs, as they defend what they love.

Andy begins to perform CPR.

Andy

"Charles! Press his chest, right here!"

Andy points his finger to a center area of the creature and looks at Charles.

Andy

"Let's go, we're losing time!"

Charles wipes his hands off, not expecting this situation. He begins to push on the chest of the creature. In his mind, he is saying:

"1, 2, 3,4, Push 1, 2, 3, 4, Push."

After several seconds of compression, Andy returns his mouth to the slimy lips of the creature.

Its lips contain goo, blood, slobber, and mud on its lips. Its face is still unrecognizable. Andy can't afford for it to die, because he prefers to find out where it came from, and how it came to the woodland. If it dies, Andy will have the mystery of its original whereabouts. Its breathing is getting intense, and its upper body begins to jump.

Andy

"Great, the chest is rising. Keep pushing, on that exact spot."

Charles continues to push down on its chest. It's been nearly two minutes now and it's beginning to feel like a workout for him. He is starting to perspire and his arms are getting tired. The moss on the creature is making it difficult for Charles to pump its chest.

After another series of CPR compressions, Andy dives in for another round of mouth-to-mouth. The creature coughs, followed by a cracking sound. Mucus comes out of its mouth and it smacks Andy in his face, onto his eyeglasses. He immediately throws them off and begins to wipe the creature's face off and cleaning more slime out of its mouth.

Charles leans back and looks at the creature in the face, as the residue is wiped off. He steps back, but looks closer. All the men freeze. It's a surprising moment.

Charles

"No, no, this can't be right."

It's not a beast, nor is it an alien. Under the moss, the camouflage, and the make-up underlies a human, a person one whom Charles closely recognizes.

1 0

Your baby boy

In his traditional attire which includes a pressed colored shirt, tailored slacks, and sleek shoes, Charles walks into the lab area that is typically used for the Neanderthal study. It's located in the middle of the woods, close to where they found the human that they found and sedated a few days ago. Charles has his coffee in his hands, and Andy walks up to him, holding a manila folder full of papers. He somewhat looks like a doctor since he has his lab coat on, a stethoscope, and brown-rimmed eyeglasses on. He gestures Charles to follow him, and they head down the hallway of the lab.

    Charles

"Any updates?"

    Andy

"Heck. I don't know where to start. We have some issues on our hands. Good thing is that he is alert. It's only been

---

36 hours since we found him, and he is already talking to us."

Andy stops walking, prompting Charles to stop. They look at each other.

Charles

"What?"

Before Andy can tell him, a brown-haired Neanderthal and a female scientist begin to walk past the two. The Neo takes a long look at Andy, and it stops walking. It can't do much as it is harnessed, for safety reasons. Andy looks at it, towards the scientist, then back at the Neo. It's short, no more than five feet tall with brown hair, smooth skin, and light brown eyes.

Andy

"Good. She's getting total recall. But Donna, I am kind of busy right now. I will see you later."

Andy looks at the female Neo. She won't move. She reaches her hand out to Andy, then grabs his stethoscope. Andy takes the stethoscope off his neck and puts it around the Neanderthal's neck.

Andy

"Okay, Leigh, here, keep going. I will come by later; I know I haven't been around for a while. But just not right now."

The Neo gives Andy a small smirk and grabs the stethoscope with its right hand. The scientist gives her a small pull, and they begin to walk away. As they walk down the hospital-like hallway, the Neo turns its head and looks at Andy. Andy looks at it as he feels her eyes on him; Charles looks also.

Andy

"I'll tell you one thing. I'm going to wear a mask the next time I have to interact with one of those things during the first year of their life. They all think I'm daddy."

Charles

"Hey, it's what you signed up for."

Andy

"Back to the issue."

Andy pulls a metal necklace out of the manila folder. They are military dog tags. Charles reads them.

"Capt. Finfrock, Carter

18th Fighter Squadron

Olympia Air Force Reserve."

Charles

"Wow. That's one of Abe'swingmen. How long did it take to clean him off?"

Andy

"That's the small problem."

Andy pulls Charles to the side of the hallway; they stop walking.

Andy

"We have an Olympian Airman on our soil. This can mean war, and you know they want a reason to take this land away, along with…"

Charles

"No, I know him. He's an Olympian ex-pat. He flies with Abe in AX-1. Nothing more than that."

Andy

"Charles, I may love science and weird stuff, but I know better. Open your eyes. He is an Olympian Airman. One who was disguised, in ultra camouflage. What if we never found him? Who knows what he would have done or what he was looking for."

Charles

"Where is he?"

Andy looks at his clipboard,

"Room Y-0292. I'll take you there. He's guarded, and he isn't too happy about being restricted to that room."

Charles,

"Why is he limited to the room? I mean I understand but…"

Andy (interrupts)

"Since we have Neos, and other DNA programs going on, we have to make sure he's detoxified. But outside of all the bullshit, we don't know if this fucker is a spy, and you know they are running around out here."

Charles

"Who's in the room with him?"

Andy

"I don't know. At least he's not acting crazy. He asked about you a few times."

Charles pats Andy on the back they begin to walk down the hallway. As Charles nears Carter's room, one of the security agents quickly steps up to meet him.

Agent

"Sir, your badge, please."

Charles disregards him, and tries to walk around him.

Agent

"Sir, only authorized personnel are allowed in this area."

Charles

"Really? I think I am authorized, please let me by."

Charles tries to walk past the Agent, and the Agent puts his hand firmly on Charles' chest.

Agent

"Sir, please stop."

Charles

"If you don't move, you will be made. You sure you want to do that?"

Agent (steps closer to Charles)

"You better get your..."

Another agent walks out of the room abruptly.

Agent 2

"Tim, Tim, Tim. Stop... Stop."

Agent 2 puts his hand on Agent 1 and gets in between him and Charles. He then turns towards Charles.

Agent

"Senior Dalton, I thoroughly apologize. Tim is new. This is his first day since getting out of training."

Charles

"I need to see the pilot. Is he responsive?"

Agent 2

"Yes, sir. He's hooked on to the IV by the docs. He's been in and out."

Charles

"Have you gotten anything from him yet?"

Agent

"No, all he is saying is that he was lost and didn't know where he was."

Charles

"Excuse me."

The agent steps aside so Charles can walk up to Carter. Charles walks into the room and looks at him. He's lying on a medical bed, with gauze wrapped around his head. As Charles sits over him, he can see the abrasions on Carter's hands. He is very thin, and his skin is pale. As Charles sits down, a person knocks on the door, and Andy walks in.

Charles looks down at Carter

"What was the point of knocking?"

Andy looks at him and shrugs as he walks in.

Andy

"Isn't that what doctors do anyway?"

Charles pays his humor no mind at the moment.

Andy

"The docs said he's very malnourished. He has been living in that reserve for over a month. We think he's the pilot that was hit in the accident where we thought we lost Abe. He ejected and must have wrapped himself in multiple items of terrain and mud and other elements. The preservative spray that we put down really got into his system, which he wasn't immune to. He'd probably be dead within the next week or so."

Charles

"I wonder how he even survived that long."

Andy

"Well, the food he ate was, let's say it was very nourishing. Which is probably what kept him alive out there." Andy gives Charles a deep look.

Charles

"What?"

Andy

"All I can say is that he definitely had his...... vegetables, and it wasn't the way that we eat our vegetables."

Charles

"Andy, you're creeping me out... It's just veggie-"

Andy (cutting Charles off)

"Phylo...."

Charles's face sinks, he looks at Andy not believing his response.

Charles

"You are telling me that he ate Phylo?"

Andy

"Yup, and that's why his tusks weren't removed when we found him. He wasn't poached. He was eaten. By him."

Charles

"How do you eat an elephant? How do you even kill an elephant?"

Andy

"A trained military man can do anything with a weapon."

It's an awkward situation. Charles is a broad, robust businessman and a leader of a thriving territory, and is sensitive about a particular wild elephant. Phylo was different; he grew on Charles as he was one of the first elephants to interact with humans in Paragon. Charles not only witnessed it; he was a part of Phylo's life.

When Phylo was born, his mother was already dead as the natives poached her for her tusks, not knowing that she was pregnant. It was about 15 years ago, and Charles and Andy were in virtually the same place as they were when they found Carter. They were hiking, and they noticed the dead matriarch. As usual Andy went to examine her. Though she was dead and faceless, they usually tried to get the large animals hauled back to the lab to test for diseases and act as a research resource for students.

This time was different. As they were waiting for the tow truck to come, they noticed that the elephant was still breathing, but these weren't normal breaths. They were like kicks. Andy, being the ultra animal lover started to investigate as he normally does, and just like how he was when he realized that Carter wasn't a beast, he realized that Phylos' mom was pregnant, and a had a live calf inside her body.

The scene was gruesome. It wasn't as bad as Andy giving CPR to an unknown creature. But in this case he had no need to give any breaths; he had to pull his knife out. After a few attempts to cut the skin, he realized that it wouldn't get deep enough. Therefore, he had to resort to using a small power saw.

After about fifteen minutes of careful sawing, Andy managed to get the calf out without harming it. Since the calf's mother was dead, they had no choice but to take it back to the Zoology office, and nurse it back to health since it couldn't get any milk from his mother.

The bond started when Charles had to clean Phylo's trunk out since it was stuffed with mucus. While he was laying down, the baby elephant looked right at Charles, and Charles felt it. He knew that the baby knew that they saved its life. Charles felt horrible having witnessed how the calf's mom was killed. He felt Phylo's pain and after that experience, Charles took initiative to make the environment safer for animals.

Phylo became a big attraction to the growing world of Paragon. Many of the visiting military men got to play with the baby elephant, since he was being nursed for two years near the base. So, to find Phylo dead was not only a burden on Charles, but for many in the area. It will be weird once word gets around that he was eaten by a hungry pilot.

Charles

"Phylo was something else. He used to feed people the best fruit. He will reach up and grab it from a high tree and bring it down. Folks love him - I mean, loved him."

It hurt to know he died, but it was weird to hear that was eaten. By a person.

Andy's

"Elephants are some of the most nutritional animals on the planet as they eat many of veggies throughout their life, and once they die or are eaten, they provide a multitude of nutrients to other animals, well in this case it was to....him."

Deep inside Charles wants to strangle the ill airman.

Charles

"I think he saved Abe."

Andy

"What?"

Charles

"He was the airman who went down. He cut in front of Abe just before the missile hit. It looks like he ejected before he cut him off. Then he fled to the forest, as he didn't want to be caught as a detainee."

Andy

"But he wouldn't have been detained. Right?"

Charles

"Nothing is formalized, he didn't know. But like you say. He is still wearing Olympia dog tags. So who knows why he didn't call or seek help."

A moment goes by.

Charles

"I don't know why he would eat an elephant though. Must be trained fairly well because he didn't even use a gun."

The two look at Carter as he is passed out. He has an IV running through his system, a heart monitor, he's in recouping stage.

Andy

"It is to be hoped that we can talk to him in a few days. Have you talked with Abe?"

Charles

"Just a bit, he usually gets quiet around this time. It's Mother's day in Olympia."

Andy

"Does he know everything yet?"

Charles looks back at him and takes a deep breath. Then a voice with low energy joins the conversation.

Carter

"I hope she's hotter than my mom."

Charles and Andy are stunned by the unexpected words.

Carter

"It would get me off this hook. Abe talks about my mom all the time. If I find out she's hot, he's in for one."

Andy

"I think you have a lot more to worry about than his mom. How you feeling?"

Carter

"I feel like shit but I wonder if this comfy bed is making me feel worse. I didn't feel this bad behind the lines."

Andy

"I'm sure you were operating on adrenaline. I don't think you were a human for a few days."

Charles

"Weeks, not days."

Carter

"Can you pass me that?"

He points to a juice box on the table. Charles grabs it and hands it to him. Carter slurps it, painfully.

Carter

"So what am I, POW?"

Andy

"No, but we don't know what the hell you are and who the hell your with. Olympia, Paragon? All I know is that you're are an ex -pat who is on the loose with Olympian dog tags. Not Paragon."

Carter

"Has my command come?"

Charles and Andy look at each other

Charles

"I don't know all the details, but they were assuming that you were lights out."

Carter

"Abe? Did I intercept it? - Or did it hit him too?"

Charles

"He's good. You're the only one."

Carter reaches his hand out to grab Charles's hand. They lock eyes as Charles grasps his hand.

Carter

"He doesn't listen, but I love him like a brother."

Charles shakes his head in response, as words can't describe the moment that Carter risked his life for Abe. Carter's handshake and comment make him feel like another son to Charles.

Carter (as he falls back to sleep)

"Mr. Dalton. We got some talking to..."

He falls back asleep. There's a lot that's going through Charles's mind. Not only the fact that Carter saved his son's life, but he also needs to know Carter's mission assignment, and who he is with. Technically, if Carter is still with the Olympia Forces, then this situation has to be reported to them, and if he isn't, it can be considered as a hostage situation. This means there are no rules for a breach of entry. Until Charles becomes a part of the UN, Paragon is open territory for whomever to intrude upon. The only thing that is holding Olympia from entering Paragon is the moral ethics of the people, a few allies, and that President Grover is a leader of value.

Andy and Charles leave the room. They inform the guard that they will be back soon and that nobody is to enter or speak to Carter.

Andy

"That went well."

Charles

"Yeah, but that's only the beginning. Like you said, once Olympia finds out we have him here, or even that an aircraft crashed, hell will ignite."

Andy

"Well, let hell break loose. You're prepared. I'm tired of living amongst these threats anyway."

This was a deep moment for Charles. His brave ecologist has more balls and brains than some troops in various military units. He gives Charles the confidence that he needs. Not just to go to war, but just the fact that an empire has been built. Even though Paragon is small, it could defend itself. Charles's relationships with different nation leaders will also go a long way if Paragon were to be attacked.

The next day, Charles walks back into the hallway. This time, with his advisors. A few of them used to be heads of many governments from around the world. They were a part of the building process of Paragon, but they haven't chosen to leave, as they find life there unique. They didn't want to go back to a place where greed and politics run everything. Most of them wanted to be a part of building something historical; something that can be documented for centuries to come.

Charles's group walks in and Carter seems to be a bit more alert than he was yesterday. As they close the door, Charles's phone rings. It's Lisa. He ignores it.

Charles

"Carter, meet John Patel, Judy Ruiz, and Deen Hollis. They are a part of my team, they just want to talk to you. I will be back, guys, I just have to make one quick call."

Once Charles steps out, he dials Lisa back. She picks up after the second ring.

Lisa

"Hey, Mister. Just wondering when we are going to link up. Are we all rested up after a day of sleeping?"

Charles

"I'm sorry Lisa, I just had some unexpected events occur. Will you guys be free later tonight?"

While on the phone, Charles looks into the door window of Carter's room. He is talking to the group, gesturing his hands as if he is explaining something.

Lisa

"I really want some me and you time."

Charles (looking through the window)

"Trust me, I do too. I'm just swamped."

Lisa

"Charles, sometimes you just need to take a break."

Charles

"I could if I would. Sorry, I mean I - would if I - could.

"- Don't mean to be rude. But I really have to go, Lisa, I have a situation on my hands. I will have Orchid arrange something for you."

Lisa

"Charles, I flew across the world to see you. I would also like to see Abe."

Charles

"Okay, we can arrange that. How about this. We will meet at the Aqua lab first thing in the morning. I want to show you some cool things also. It may also help with your job. Then we can have breakfast. Plan?"

Lisa

"Okay. I will tell the fellows.

- Wait. Are they invited also?"

Charles

"Yes. Whatever you like. I have to go."

Lisa

"Okay. One more thing."

She waits for Charles to respond. He doesn't

Lisa

"Charles, you there?"

She looks at her phone and realizes that he has hung up. She shakes her head, and gives Orchid a call. In the meantime, Charles walks back into the room, where elevated voices are coming from Carter and one of the Officials of Paragon.

Carter

"I didn't sign up for all this. All I did was save a boy's life."

He pauses.

Carter

"All right! I also killed the freaking elephant. But he tried to kill me first."

John Patel

"This is the case. Respectfully, you're wearing Olympia dog tags. In that case, you are in a foreign territory and a few weeks ago, a hundred million dollar plane went down. Olympia will have questions and we have to be prepared for them."

Carter

"Understood. What's your name again? I forgot."

John Patel

"John Patel."

Patel looks at Charles

John Patel

"Is he okay memory wise?"

Charles shakes his head up and down.

John Patel

"Okay. First, are you still in the Olympia Armed Forces? If so, are you in any kind of intelligence unit?"

Carter

"Kinda… In a way. I am."

Patel

"Are you? Or are you not? You have to trust us, otherwise this whole country will be in turmoil."

The heart monitor begins to beep faster, Carter's heart rate suddenly increases.

The group gets quiet, as this is a critical answer. If Carter is still the Service for Olympia, this warrants an investigation, even if there was no wrongdoing. The bigger issue is if he is a part of the Intelligence Agency. If yes, then there is a spy organization in Paragon.

Carter

"Obviously, your machine answered for me."

John nods his head and puts his hand up to his ear.

Carter

"Dude, you are an idiot. Yes, I am. Only for Aviation Auditing though."

Charles takes a big gulp and his stomach drops

Charles

"What do you mean yes? I thought you were an ex-pat?"

Carter

"Don't do that... There are only a few of us, I'm not the only one. We're auditors... Nothing more than that though, we're just here to make sure no bad activity is going on with any American-made engineering. At least from what I understand. That's all I know. I was just doing my job. The Secretary of Defense, Bob Polan, is my boss."

The group looks at each other. Speechless. Judy Ruiz speaks up as she is the Defense lead for Paragon

Judy Ruiz

"So they've got eyes and pawns. I knew I felt some kind of way when I met you at the base."

Carter looks at Charles

"Look. Dalton, I have nothing to do with anything deeper than that. I just make sure aircraft are being used correctly and aren't illegally being modified. Ever since the War on Terror ended different Air Forces began to be audited because some regimes were modifying their planes to use chemical weapons."

Charles,

"It's not that! I just knew it!"

Dean Hollis, Charles's intelligence director, speaks up. He has a country voice, similar to Bill's.

Dean Hollis

"They know everything that we are doing. We got eyes on us guys. Up the crack of our ass and the tip of our..."

Judy Ruiz cuts Hollis off. She has her phone in her hand, with a startled look on her face. She'll assist Charles with Defense and Security of Paragon.

Judy Ruiz

"Grover just landed."

Charles

"Who?"

Judy Ruiz

"President Grover. Jacob Grover just landed on Migs Field."

The abrupt visit is unexpected. It all runs through Charles's mind. The President of the Olympia has landed in Paragon without any notice. Though there are proper personnel to handle this situation, Charles is more startled at the last minute visit without any notice. This has been the first time that a President has visited Paragon since the end of the war. Now the second has come, without a notice which is rare in any country, state, or city.

Charles takes one look at Carter. Carter looks back

Carter

"Don't look at me."

Charles

"If you're setting this up, you're in for one!"

Carter

"Fuck you! If I set you up, your baby boy wouldn't be- "

11

Eye of the moon

While Charles and his colleagues are haranguing Carter with questions, Abe and Gil are hanging out for the night at one of the nightclubs in Sector A. There is an assortment of people in the venue, mostly women dancing to hip-hop and pop songs. The colors and sound in the establishment is a paradise for a dancer or club goer.

It's almost been a month since Abe has had a good time ever since the crash situation, and he's finally letting loose. He has been quietly dealing with the fact that he almost died, but little does he know that Carter saved his life. He assumes that Carter ran into the missile, accidentally. But it's still been hard on him because he hasn't talked to Carter since that morning. The base has been tightlipped about Carter being dead because they know that somebody ejected, but they are not sure that it was Carter because he wasn't even supposed to be in the air that day.

Either way, it's still a scuttle feeling for Abe, as this is when he gets down because he mourns the death of his mother whom he never really met. All he knows about her is that she was from Olympia, and she died in a bombing while traveling.

Distancing himself from negative thoughts, Abe and Gil are on the dance floor, dancing and drinking shots of tequila. Abe, who rarely clubs, only has a few days before Operation Red Ice, the annual training expedition. So he is trying to enjoy his last few days in Paragon until he goes to Olympia for ten days.

Gil (dancing in front of Abe)

"I'm in the mood to go to a few different spots tonight."

Abe

"Let's do it."

Abe leads the two out of the venue, Abe shows up two fingers to his wing-mates, Terry Love, Chris, and Rory who arrived in the club with him. Just before Abe turns his head, Rory sticks his hand out and gives him a thumbs-up as it is never a bad idea to leave the bar with a good looking woman. However, Abe and Gil have been seen out plenty of times, so she is a familiar face to the fellows.

Some ask if they are boyfriend and girl friend, and Abe politely tell the guys that she is just a close friend. Abe is the type who likes to explore all types of women. As for Gil, again, she is much more reserved than Abe and prefers to deal with just one man; even so she still prefers not to be in a relationship. Although she wants Abe to be hers, and she loathes him being with other women.

After the walk out of the doors, they head in search of the next venue for the night. They are in an area of Paragon that's developed into something similar to a Chinatown. It is like a mini Beijinga, with illuminated lights and street side stores. Just undeniably more modern. In Paragon, there are many towns that resemble different cultures as when it was built, it was made to make life just a bit more unique for those who live there.

Walking down the street and passing by a multiple amount of people, Gil latches onto Abe's hand.

Gil

"You know you're fun when you let loose."

Abe

"Am I? I thought I was always loose."

Gil

"You're loose like a bullet. You shoot, but you can be so, so, so stiff."

As she squeezes his hand a bit, she avoids making it a deeper conversation because she knows this is when he thinks of his mom.

Abe

"You think you know me, don't you?"

Gil

"More than any other chick in this world..."

This gives Abe pause.

Abe

"What makes you believe that?"

Gil

"Let's see. I've known you since we were 10 years old. Um, know what every type of plane that you've flown."

Abe

"And what type of planes are those?"

Gil

"Let see, a C-17, a B-1, F-18, and F-22."

Abe

"Well, you just received a C. I give you a 75 percent. I've only flown three out of four of those aircraft."

Gil pauses.

Gil

"That's right. I don't even know how that slipped out. Anyway, I gave you your first scar, unfortunately that's the only first that I have with you..."

Abe

"Oh here we go...Virginity Time."

Gil (

"Hey man, as long as you're proud of it..."

Abe

"Look, I did not lose my virginity to Valerie Osborne."

Gil

"Hmmm. Well, you guys came out of the bathroom looking very suspicious."

Abe

"Blah Blah..."

Abe

"Maybe you should have walked in..."

Gil (laughing)

"Nope, you wanted Big Bad Valerie."

She pushes him, almost making him trip. The alcohol is finally starting to settle in and the shell that Gilly usually has is finally setting upon her.

Abe looks at his watch

Abe

"So, I have to run to the base tonight."

Gil

"For what?"

Abe

"I just have some last minute things to do before Red Ice."

Red Ice is the annual military exercise involving fighter pilots from around the world. It is combat to combat and simulates real war-like scenarios.

Gil

"Abe. Not tonight? Where did this come from?"

Abe

"I just have to."

Gil is internally furious, and Abe can see it. She tries to put her poker face on to shadow it.

Abe

"Look, we leave in a few days. I just want to be on track. I can hang with you tomorrow."

Gil

"Dude, you're drunk. Your whole crew is back at the club. There is no way that you're going up."

Abe

"Just because you were drinking doesn't mean I was. I'm perfectly sober. Smell my breath."

She smells it and there is no trace of alcohol.

Abe

"Told the bartender to give me apple juice instead of Tequila. You know I don't drink that much. I can't, unless I am out of town or on leave. I always have to expect to go up until they expand the unit."

She looks at Abe

Abe

"When you toast the shot with everybody, knowing that you don't have tequila in the shot glass. The best part is faking that face folks make when taking one. It's priceless."

Abe looks at Gil in the eye, hugs her and kisses her on the cheek. This is an immediate indicator to her that he is still holding back. As he walks her home, it's quiet. It's a quick walk since she only lives a block away from the strip where they are. Once he arrives at her building, he opens the door for her. He then wishes her a goodnight and gives her another hug. Gil is mute.

Intentions

Abe closes Gil's door and walks halfway down the block, he calls Telda. As the phone rings, he looks back to make sure Gil didn't walk back out of the complex. After a few rings, Telda's voicemail answers. He hangs up and tries calling her again, same result. This frustrates him, because whenever he tries to contact her, she never picks up.

Tonight she doesn't answer because she is having dinner with her boyfriend, Colin. In the waterfront restaurant, Telda, sitting across from Colin, looks down at her phone, wondering why Abe has called twice, something that he never does. She decides to text him back. Colin looks at her, noticing her fingers sliding across the keyboard.

Colin takes a sip of his wine)

"What are you doing?"

Telda

"Nothing. Somebody from my Squadron is calling me."

Colin

"Who?"

Telda looks up at Colin, who has the look of a model with sea blue eyes, and a suit that he had made specifically for tonight. It is all black, to match with Telda's all black Dress. He doesn't like Telda on her phone when she is around him, as he feels ignored.

Telda puts down her phone and digs into her salad.

"Sorry hon, it just came out of the blue. I didn't mean to do it. How is your Merlot?"

Her tough exterior is completely different around Colin. She isn't as hard as she is around Abe and the guys from the Squadron. She is very sweet to him.

Colin

"Don't answer my question with a question."

Telda pauses midway into her salad and looks at him, not believing what an asshole he's being. Especially on her birthday.

Colin

"Who is it? What's wrong?"

Telda answers sarcastically.

Telda

"I don't know. I'm about to find out."

She is clearly agitated, but is trying to avoid an argument with Colin as he is easily quick to temper and highly jealous of any move she makes. As he stares at her, she pulls her phone back out of her purse and texts Abe.

They begin to rapidly go back and forth.

Telda : What do you want?
Abe : I need you to meet me at AX-1 base.
Telda - Why?
Abe - O'Donnell and Smitten said that we have to run a mandatory AWACS test before Operation Red Ice.
Telda - Why the hell do you need me? I never even ran or even tried to use the AWACS
Abe - Meet me there in 30 minutes. I'm on my way now.

Telda - Abe. It's my birthday. Not today! I'm with Colin. Do I have to be there?

Telda - Did he say that it's mandatory?

Telda waits for a few minutes, as Colin watches. Abe hasn't responded. After a few more minutes the waiter brings their entrée to the table, but she doesn't want to start to eat until she receives Abe's message. However, Abe hasn't responded.

She follows with a few more messages.

Telda -?

Telda -?? I don't want to ruin the night he planned. We're out at dinner!

Telda - Squid, pick up. Is this mandatory??????

Abe still hasn't responded. She begins to text other members of the base and nobody is responding. She looks at Colin and realizes that she has to tell him what's going on, so she isn't the only one left out. The last time she missed a last minute briefing without excuse, Captain Smitten had her take a pod back and forth to the base for the whole day. He is very mental when it comes to disciplining the squadron.

Telda

"Don't be mad, but I have to go to base. Something came up."

Colin

"What? What do you mean?"

Telda

"Captain called us in for a mandatory system test before we go to Olympia in a few days for the Red Ice. It shouldn't be long."

Colin

"So I planned all of this for nothing."

Telda

"Colin, it's not like that. Plus, how many times have we been here? This place is nothing new. This is your spot. I'm guessing that it won't be long, and then we can do something later. But I really have to go."

Colin

"Why didn't your work phone go off? Why are you using your personal phone?"

This catches Telda off guard, as she realizes that it was her personal phone. Usually her work phone is the one that rings or receives text for work matters.

Telda

"Colin, I know. It's jacked up. I don't want to be there on my birthday, but nobody is responding. I really have to go, sweetie. Are you going to walk me out and I take a pod?"

Colin doesn't respond. He looks away. She softly grabs his hand.

Telda

"Or will you rather drop me off? I really want to ride with you at the least. Even though it takes longer to get there."

He pushes her hand away and picks up his wine glass. He drinks all of it ignoring her response.

Colin (ignoring her)

"Fly safe."

Telda

"Really?"

He continues to ignore her. Telda reaches under the table and puts her high heels back on.

Telda

"Okay, and for your comfort, I'll walk myself out and take a pod."

She picks up her purse; gets up, kisses him on the forehead and walks away. She wanted him to take her, but this is the way he gets. Most of the time he is an asshole to her, which is partially the reason why she decides to leave without much hesitation. She texts Abe one more time, telling him that she is on her way. She also puts a request in for an immediate pod to meet her at the front of the restaurant.

Once she arrives at a pod station near the entry of the restaurant, there are a number of people waiting for their pods, and some are waiting for the valet to bring their vehicles to the front. Expecting to wait a few minutes, she sees that a pod which says "Private - Paragon Official."

A few other people look at the pod waiting to see who gets in. Some are single and a few are with their wives. Once Telda begins to walk towards it, a few men are surprised. She pulls her ID out, flashes it at the door, and the door opens. She looks very formal, but ridiculously sexy. Her hair is bouncing, and she has two small braids holstering the side of her head. One of the men's wife's eyes Telda down and gives her snobby look. She then loudly whispers to her husband; who is delightfully looking at Telda's figured body and how her dress hugs every curve that she has.

Wife

"Probably one of the heads sluts"

Telda hears her. She puts her heel in between the Pod door before it closes. The door opens back up. She bites her bottom lip, knowing that she can't get in trouble, especially over somebody calling her a name. She looks at the women for a few seconds, digs in her purse and flicks a rectangular shaped card to the woman's direction. It falls on the floor and her husband picks it up. It has Telda's full color picture and it reads.

Paragon AX1 Unit
Telda Blanchard : Call Sign ZELDA
Pilot: F-22 Single Seat

To contact, press the edge of this card and Telda will receive notification

The spouse is intrigued by the card, and hands it to his wife. She looks at it and she is surprised. She flips the card over to see if it is authentic, and when she does a video begins to play inside of it and it is of Telda taking her mask off in the cockpit. These cards are normally used to give to kids who stop by the base.

Wife

"I don't care what she does. Who gives a damn?"

Husband

"No babe. You just got served. You shouldn't have said that. I've told you about your mouth with other women."

She disgustingly looks at him as he watches Telda's pod pull off, with the tinted windows all they can see is the glare coming from the lights of the restaurant.

Husband

"Female fighter pilot, huh? Maybe we should tell out daughter to check that out."

The wife is pissed off even more. She gives him a cold look. He was still fascinated by Telda, his eyes are glued to the video on the card.

Husband

"Hmm.. Hmm Hmm."

After a ten minute pod ride, Telda arrives to base. She sees Abe and two ramp service men loading up the plane getting it ready for a launch. She sees no vehicles but only a few pods. She also doesn't see O'Donnell's, or Captain Smitten's cars. Which makes her wonder if everybody left, since Abe texted her 45 minutes ago. She walks over to Abe in anger.

In her black dress, and eye shadow that she just added while in the pod. Abe hears her high heels clicking towards him.

Abe wearing his flight suit, looks up.

"Whoa! Look who it is. Awww, the supermodel is so gorgeous."

Telda

"Shut up, what is this entire ruckus? Why is nobody here?"

Abe

"We have a test to run on the Airborne Warning Control System, and nobody else is to know about it. Lex and Channing are here in the radar room. You need to change. We are about to crank up."

Lex is the air battle coordinator. She and her team usually sleep at the base, as her job is to always be ready in case anything occurs and Paragon needs to respond with Airborne Support. There are also always 3 pilots on duty at all times. Overnight it is usually the BX1 guys.

Telda

"This is horseshit. It's my birthday."

Abe

"Have you been drinking?"

Telda

"I was about to begin."

216

Abe

"Cool, so you won't pass out to early. You know, when you drink and you fly very high, it takes your alcohol level very high. We don't need any of that, madam."

Telda

"Ummm, I learned that when I was 16, first flight class. I hope you did also. Get Smitten on your ass."

Telda always refers to when Captain Smitten drills Abe on the basics of flying. Most of the time it is stuff that is learned during basic lessons.

Abe

"Go suit up. We got to roll.... Please."

Pissed off, she abruptly turns and walks to the female locker room. Dell, one of AX-1's flight technicians looks at him, shakes his head and laughs.

Dell

"She will be all right in a few."

Abe scratches his head)

"Yeah, I know. Did you put that recording into the system."

Dell

"Yup, just press B-Day on the Flight Information System and it will come through the headphones. I threw some other tunes in for you as well."

Dell always comes through for Abe. If Dell didn't work so much, they would hang out more often. The two have worked together since they were young and have an incredible friendship and bond. Dell is one of the few men that Abe really trusts, as he has been there since day one.

They shake hands. Abe climbs the ladder and gets into the cockpit of the aircraft, and Telda comes out 10 minutes later looking gorgeous as ever.

Abe

"Birthday girl, let's roll. We got a confidant 1,000 miles out and he's going subsonic."

Telda

"Don't rush me."

She wraps her pony tail around her neck and climbs into the back of the dual seat F-22 aircraft right behind Abe. Once she sits down Dell climbs the ladder and hands both of them their air masks and helmets.

Abe

"You're not doing any flying today. You are just here in case something happens to me. I didn't trust anybody else. I'm so sorry that it happened on your birthday."

She doesn't respond as she enters her weight into the system to make sure the plane is balanced.

Dell gets off of the ladder, and puts his headphones on.

"You guys ready?"

They both give him the thumbs-up and salute. Abe cranks the engines up and the canopy to the aircraft comes down showing the orangish tint that glows on them both. Dell then grabs the two orange lead sticks to marshal them out on to the taxiway. As Abe nears the runway he gets his final clearances from the radar and tower control.

Abe

"Tower, this is Squid one ready for Runway 22 Left."

Traffic Controller

"Squid One. You have one arrival for runway 22 left coming in. Hold short."

Abe

"Roger, holding short 22 Left. Squid One."

Abe holds short of the runway as one of Paragon's Cargo Aircraft are on final approach to land. As they wait, the clear sky presents a full moon, and the stars surround it. The waves from the coast are seen, along with palm trees waving with the wind. Telda is in the back of the aircraft, with her visor up with her palm on her cheek, and she is also biting her bottom lip as she thinks about her situation with Colin. She is frustrated, she isn't flying, and her mind is floating all over the place. Her mind bounces from pure exhaustion from being on call, the constant arguing with Colin, who is a person whom she settles with. She is also annoyed at the fact that it is also her birthday, and she is doing unexpected work. However, deep inside, she has a hidden joy because she is with Abe. It's a beautiful night, she is about to go into the sky, doing something she loves. There's no pressure.

She is not too upset because she enjoys being in the sky with Abe. This is the first time that she has been inside of an actual aircraft with him, and he is in pure control. She feels weird, because she doesn't feel bad about being away from Colin, especially on her special day. She begins to look at all the computer systems in the aircraft, the radar, her throttle lever, the joystick with the small knobs that have the power knock down threats of all sizes. She looks to the right, watching Abe test the flaps on the wings. She looks to the left and she sees the other set of flaps go up and down. The small machine noises that they make turn her on.

She looks at display in front of her which features the weapons that the aircraft has loaded. She looks at the navigation radar, the guidance systems, engine power, and fuel load. It's very rare that she gets in the backseat of the aircraft, especially since she isn't doing any flying. She is really just there to analyze the systems while Abe runs a test on the systems with Lex.

Abe turns on the left engine of the aircraft as he sees the red and green wing lights of the Cargo Aircraft get closer as they land.

He only had one engine on, because it saves the amount of fuel burned while they are idling on the taxiway. Hearing the second engine turn on, Telda instinctively pulls down her visor and straps her air mask to prepare for takeoff. Abe does the same. As the Cargo Aircraft lands, the reverse thrusters turn on, which slow the large plane down. The traffic controller gets on the radio.

Tower

"Heavy 260, you can exit the runway at Zulu, straight to Juliet, make a right and to Spot 3 at the West Apron."

Cargo Pilot

"Roger, Zulu, Juliet, and Spot Three. See ya!"

Now that the other aircraft is clear of the runway, Abe and Telda are clear to go.

Tower

"Squid one. Are you going for an immediate 5,000?"

Abe

"That's affirmative. We want to go 5,000 then to clearance."

Immediate 5,000 means that Abe is going to take off then power the engines at full power and go straight vertical in the sky.

Tower

"Okay, Squid One. Runway 22 Left, immediate 5,000. You're clear for takeoff."

Abe reads back the instructions, and powers the fighter jet into the sky. He and Telda brace themselves for the high G's and the soon to be grunts and deep breaths as they roar into the air. After a few seconds of speeding down the runway, Abe and Telda lift. A few seconds later, Abe pulls back, and they are straight into the sky.

Abe soon goes into contact with Lex. She will be the one in communication with him while he is in the sky to make sure that he is clear of any aircraft, and to alert him if any aircraft come within his battle zone. As they fly into the cloudless sky, they both take in the moment. Telda senses something, as Abe isn't accurate about a system.

Abe is plugging in numbers into the complicated flight system, Telda keeps her eyes below, looking at the illuminated city. She can also see the lights on the border of Emirate. Since it is Friday night, all the lights are on the coast, which looks like a small world from 20,000 feet up. Since Paragon is nestled in between Golia and the Emirates, the airspace is tight. However, since they have good relationships with both countries, all they have to do is call for clearance and they will be cleared with proper reasoning. They can see both countries, and the water on the coast has a slight reflection of the moon.

Telda

"Any reason why we are going so high? There's no reason to be at 25,000 Abe."

Abe

"Because this is what I wanted to do. I'm sorry if I interrupted your plans."

Telda

"What do you mean what you wanted to do?"

Abe

"You wouldn't have responded if it wasn't work related."

Telda

"So you you're telling me you had me mess up my birthday evening with Colin for something that YOU wanted to do?"

Abe

"Well, it still is testing, isn't it?"

He contacts Lex on the Radio.

Abe

"Lex, are you on? I think we are ready. We are at 30,000. I'm about to turn to 170, are you going to put the autopilot in a holding pattern?"

Abe banks the plane to the right, turns the autopilot on, and pulls something out of a small compartment of the plane. As the plane slowly turns, Lex comes on the radio. Her soothing but technical voice guides Abe.

Lex

"I'm linked in with you Squid. I've got control of the aircraft. Be advised that you have 1 Emirate patrol fighter in the sky. No threat; he has been notified of your whereabouts."

Abe

"You got me on the other favor?"

Lex

"Yup."

As the airplane slowly circles, all Abe and Telda can see are the lights below. She then looks over to right and she sees the full glow of the moon. As this occurs, Abe opens up a package that he has pulled from the compartment near his foot. Telda has no clue what is going on. As the plane sets closer to the moon, it begins to slowly rise and get closer. She has been quiet for most of the flight, partially because she is enjoying the view, but also confused as where she should be. She looks at Abe as he is maneuvering in the front of the plane. She assumes that he needs to use the washroom.

Telda

"You need a piddle pack?"

A piddle pack is a small bag that fighter pilots use when they need to use the washroom.

Abe

"Nope. But do you need one of these?"

Using a flexible stick, Abe maneuvers it around his seat and over his head rest, handing her an interesting sculpture of her favorite fruit. It's a pineapple that is shaped as a rectangular birthday cake, but it fits in her hand. She looks at it, and holds it up to the center of her heads up display in her visor. As it enhances the very small letters, she sees that it reads:

Happy B-Day T

I gotcha, didn't I? - Abraham

This makes Telda warm. It is completely unexpected and she leans back as far as the seat allows, only to see the moon. Not just the moon but they are 40,000 feet closer to it. With the huge presence that it holds, it is beautiful. The cockpit is illuminated with lights and it is being controlled by Lex, who is all the way at the base.

Telda is happily melting. She is speechless as she looks at the pineapple with surprise. Abe begins to recite a poem to her.

Abe

"From the moment I saw you

The sky was no longer...

Before he can finish off the poem she reaches over his headrest and grabs the shoulders of his suit and pulls him back. Since the cockpit is so small, she can't reach him. So she settles to talk to him, it frustrates her because she can't do what she wants to do to him.

Telda takes a deep breath.

"Why are you doing this?"

Abe

"Doing what? I'm just giving you some birthday wishes. Can't lie, the poem was kinda corny though."

She is thinking about kissing him, something that she has been wanting to do for a while.

Telda

"You know I try to stay away from you."

Telda continues to play the moment in her mind. She closes her eyes and she feels herself biting on Abe; rubbing her hands on his cheeks, shoulders, chest, trying to reach for his thighs. She imagines a plane that has more room in the cockpit, so she can have room to do what she wants to do. Her back is on the window and she knows that she will need to be careful so she doesn't accidentally hit the ejection or throttle lever. Although he won't mind that, either.

Her and Abe, pretty much skydiving in the sky, kissing each other, then releasing the parachute as they near the ground.

Telda opens her eyes and attempts to reach over the seat and grab Abe, which she fails again. Since the plane is so lightweight you can see that it is slowly rocking from her moving. Lex, who is controlling it and can see it's every moment, and she has an idea of what is going on.

Lex cuts in from the radar room

"Okay guys, we are just testing this thing. Not too much rocking."

She is smiling while other officers who have been secretly been assigned to this project, are looking in wonder, two of them include Gil and Telda's boyfriend, Colin. Both of them are still wearing the same attire that they had on an hour or so ago.

Gil and Colin analyze the muffling that they hear on the radio. Though they don't know what is going on. They know that Abe and Telda are in the sky, on Telda's birthday. Colin is frantic, although Telda told him the truth. Gil is furious on the inside, holding everything in. She can't allow Lex to know that she is spying on Abe. Same goes with Colin, who is an intelligence officer not only for AX-1, but also Charles. He and Gil know each other well. They are playing it off, as if they don't hear anything nor, know what's going on.

Lex (looking at Gil)

"She didn't know that he was planning to surprise her for about a month now. This isn't the safest thing though. But hey, it's Abe. Why not? Life's short."

Gil soaks it all in.

Gil

"So this system you guys are creating. Is it done yet?"

Lex (unaware of Gil being a spy)

"No, not by any means. We have operated it a few times. It shuts down whenever we take it full throttle. The aircraft's mobility system doesn't respond. Well, at least in intense situations. In this case, it's fine because there aren't any crazy maneuvers during this "exercise". Once it's complete we will be able to remotely control any aircraft that comes into our airspace. We hope that it's soon, because we have a very small air unit. We can use all the help that we can get."

Gil

"How long have these two been going up like this?"

Lex

"No clue. Abe just asked me to do this one favor for him. I think it's cute."

Gil taps Colin, telling him to come meet her in the hallway. When they meet, Gil is pissed because Abe played her, when he said he had actual work to conduct. She realizes this is more so a mission to take Telda in the sky for her birthday.

Gil

"What is this? What?"

Colin

"What is what? Let them do what they do."

Gil

"Your girlfriend is with Abe."

Colin, with a small grin

"So, what's the problem? You shouldn't have fallen in love with him."

She looks at Colin as he chuckles at her being in love with Abe, but she also knows that Colin is correct. She shouldn't have fallen in love with Abe. However, being a spy on Abe has put her in a vulnerable position.

Telda and Colin have been assigned to an Olympian Intelligence Unit assigned by Bob Polan and other officials for the Olympian Department of Defense. Their objective is to accumulate as much information about Paragon, Dalton, and Paragon's inner defense systems. They don't directly work with Carter (Abe's Wingman), but they do gather as much information as they can for Bob Polan and his administration.

Back in the plane, Telda is talking to Abe

Telda

"You know how much I care for you. But I don't want to mess the squadron up. We have a good friendship too. I don't want to push this."

Abe remains quiet. He grabs his joystick and rocks the plane softly side to side, which tells Telda that he acknowledges her reasoning.

Telda

"Abe, we need to land."

Abe

"But I'm not ready to yet. I'm enjoying this."

Telda feels it internally, she feels Abe internally.

Telda repeats

"So you hunt me down for the past few years, and the moment I want to kiss on you all night - you back out?"

Abe's eyes get big. Not expecting her response to the birthday flight, he immediately turns the plane over to head back to base. Telda gets knocked back to her seat. Abe gets back on the radar and speaks to Lex.

Abe

"Lex, this is Squid. We got all that we need. We're homeward bound."

Lex

"Roger. The skies are clear, along with the winds. Stay with me."

As Abe and Telda land the aircraft, they taxi it towards where Dell is waiting to pull the ladder out. Abe informs him that he is going to do a self engine run up at one of the far taxiways of the airfield, and to come back later. As Abe takes the plane over, Telda immediately takes off her helmet. She tells Abe to lift up the cockpit window, and she jumps out on the side of the cockpit into his lap. She realizes she can't fit because it is small, so she sits at the lip of the plane and looks at Abe.

Telda

"This isn't going to work. We almost broke something a few times. Plus, we're out in the open Abe."

Abe

"So."

Telda

"You're such a guy. Stop it. Somebody may be watching us."

They both chuckle and look to the left at a parked C-17 cargo aircraft. They see that the door to the aircraft is open. Abe and Telda meet eyes. They look at each other like they haven't seen each other before.

Abe

"I think the maintenance guys are on break right now. Let go."

They walk towards the plane, holding hands. Realizing that this creates much attention, Telda lets Abe's hand go. It's one of the best walks ever, especially for a man because he knows that he is definitely going to get some.

Abe and Telda slowly get into the cargo plane and Abe presses a button which closes and locks the door. The only way somebody can now get in is if they know the code or have the key. Once they walk into the gigantic aircraft they can see that the plane hasn't been completely cleaned since the last trip that it was on. It probably shipped some troops around the world for training exercises, or maybe even humanitarian efforts. However, there are a few air mattresses on the floor, which are used when a crew is on a long haul.

Abe grabs Telda and pushes her onto the mattress. He looks at her in her eyes and locks in on her lips.

He unlaces her boots, begins to rub her legs, starting with her calves. He feels her soft skin through her thin layered

226

Brandon Wynn

fighter suit. As he touches her he can tell that she is awaiting him. She is shivering, even though it is hot inside the plane. They both have been waiting for this moment for years, but Abe never saw it coming. Telda's legs are shivering. He begins to kiss her, locking lips for the first time. He rubs her back and massages it. She digs her fingers into his back. They continue to lock lips, he bites her lower lip. He grabs her neck and infects her with his love for her. She pulls her legs up and around him to bring him closer.

Telda

"You really think you're going inside?"

Abe (chuckles and leans over her shoulder)

"You know you want me..."

Telda

"Doesn't mean you're coming inside of Ms. Blanchard, buddy."

Telda's last name is Blanchard.

She grabs Abe's wrist, and rubs her body with his hand . Telda closes her eyes, thinking about all the possibilities that the two have. She wants to experience Abe, but she knows that it's not the time and she wants to do it when it is right.

Abe studies her. Looking at how her skin is bright and smooth. How her hair flows even as the braid begins to loosen up. She has a devious look in her eyes. He never thought he would have this moment with her, even though many women in Paragon and even other countries will drop whatever that they are doing to be with him. Even so, Telda is different. This is why he likes her, because even though she can let him inside at the moment she doesn't. She carries that substance about her as she knows it isn't the right time to rumble in the jungle.

Abe is relishing the taste of her lips.

"Pineapples, huh?"

She's got him hot. It's been years since Telda has done anything, as Colin acts weird and avoids sex with her.

Telda

"Imagine if I only ate tomatoes."

Abe

"That probably won't be the best taste for me."

227

The duo laugh. Abe gazes into her eyes while she studies his. She sees warrior, respect, fun, engaging, intelligence, egotistic, and love. She rubs his head, feeling his soft hair, his trimmed beard, and touches the edges of his ears. She savors the moment, wishing it can be frozen. She expects Abe to go further, so she braces herself for his next move, but he hasn't made one yet. He just goes in for soft kisses, and the only part of her body that he touches is her hair. To finish it all off, he twists her braid, one of the only cosmetic things that she pays daily attention to.

Telda

"We better get out of here before somebody walks in."

Abe gets up and puts his hand out for Telda to grab so he can help her up. As he pulls her up, just like a teammate would. He pulls her into him, only to lock lips again. He brings her closer so her leg can feel all of him. Her breaths are gasping, and sweat is accumulating on her forehead.

Telda

"Abe, come on, sweetie, we need to go."

That's the first time she has called him that. Abe notices but acts like he pays it no mind. She doesn't notice. She grabs his hand again as he opens the door to the aircraft. They walk out the plane only to see Dell standing there, acting like he hasn't seen or heard anything.

Meanwhile, Gil and Colin are back in the radar room on the other side of the base, discussing how they are going to handle the situation.

Colin

"You need to learn how to control yourself. We are still on a mission."

Gil

"Colin, I freaking love him! I didn't expect this. I didn't!"

Colin

"Look, after Red Ice, this whole mission will be over, and you need to let it be, because there's a good chance that your sweetie will be dead. So cut the crap!"

Gil gives Colin a deep but confused look.

Colin

"This mission will make your career. You're going to throw all the hard work that you spent your entire adult life on; for a damn flyboy who doesn't even give himself to you!"

Gil

"He does care for me. If you were screwing her good enough, he wouldn't be doing this!"

Colin

"You're funny, you know. She's cute, but I don't give a damn about her, you, or Paragon. All I care about is this paycheck that we will receive once we can get GELT to produce that A28 and so we can operate Paragon as ours. That's my goal. Now get it right. We have work to do. Let her have him. They can die together for all I care. Set the graves up!"

Colin's phone rings, he picks it up.

Colin

"Gabe, did you secure the deal with Mr. Ito?"

As Colin talks to Gabe, Lisa's boss, Gil walks away. She thinks how stuck she is because her life is about her career. She has put her all into what she has done, but she has also fallen into deep feelings for Abe. She knows that Abe will be departing for Operation Red Ice in the next few days. With the moment that he had with Telda, she knows that their relationship is going to do nothing but get stronger. She also knows that she can't have him also. Not only because his heart may be with Telda, but because her job, as a spy, makes a false relationship with Abe.

Special Guest

The next morning, Charles, Bin, Lisa, and Eddie are in the lab where A28 is produced.

Lisa

"So, President Grover is really going to be with us today?"

Charles

"Yeah, he should be here at any moment."

Lisa

"Why didn't you tell me that he was coming? I would have changed my clothes."

Charles looks at Lisa's attire. She is wearing khaki shorts, and a purple top. He then looks at Bin, Eddie, and Orchid who are also wearing casual attire.

Charles

"You guys look fine. I just found out that he was coming in. It was last minute. This works out perfectly. You guys are visiting from Olympia. It's a good look."

Lisa

"That's good. But I am glad that I get to see you. What are the plans for tomorrow?"

Charles looks at his watch.

"Honestly, I have to fly to Europa later this evening. Just for the day. We have some United World matters to handle."

Lisa

"Charles, I didn't come here to be on a retreat. Especially with a guy that I was going to hire and his happy door man. I wanted to be with you."

Charles

"Lisa, I understand. I apologize. I really didn't realize that you were coming this week, and my schedule is hectic. These are the repercussions of having this type of responsibility. I will make it up to you. I promise."

Lisa and Charles continue to talk to one another. Bin and Eddie have been looking at a few chemicals in the A28 Aqua lab.

Eddie

"Now, the reverse hyperoxic that sits in that mineral is critical."

Bin

"Eddie, I never knew you were this smart."

Eddie

"Yup, the only reason I am a doorman is because I got laid off."

The lab is secluded, hidden in the mountains of Paragon. The only way to get to it is via wind tunnel or helicopter. Bin and Eddie are enjoying this since they both are into science and improving humanity.

Eddie continues to look at different types of A28 on the shelves of the lab. They are lined up bottle after bottle. Some are labeled with photos of cars. Some have labels that resemble a human stick figure.

Eddie reaches for a smaller container and notices that's this one has a powdery substance instead of liquid.

Charles notices and tries to catch him.

Charles

"Hey. Hey. Hey! Buddy! No!"

Before Charles can get his attention, Eddie spills some powdery substance on his hand, and it immediately sizzles and bakes into his skin. He screams and holds his wrist to try to ease the pain

Charles

"It's very powerful, and it isn't diluted. Which is a reason why the label says do not touch unless suited."

"What is this? I thought it had to be sparked by water."

Charles

"It is still a chemical at the end of the day."

Charles tends to Eddie's hand and the burn. Lisa and Bin come by to take a look at it. Bill takes notice, but then hears a knock on the door. He opens it and walks out.

Charles

"It's not that bad."

Charles begins to chuckle, as one of his lead scientists, Calvin, hands him a band-aid and wipes to clean the wound.

Charles

"But that burn on your hand is "unique"."

Eddie looks at his burn from the A28. He studies it and notices that it has two dots and a curved line. He then tilts his hand. Only to notice that it's marked like a smiley face hand stamp.

Eddie

"Now that is whack. Now it's going to look like I have been going to the bar every day."

Charles's A28 scientist Calvin speaks up

Calvin

"You're lucky that it didn't go through your bone. A28 is a potent substance - it's shaved right off the inner mountain. Until we dilute the shavings, it's deadly. That's how it can make fuel, because it has so much packed into it. It's just like the seltzer drug that you drop inside a cup of water. That fizz creates a combustible reaction. That is what acts as fuel to converted vehicles."

Calvin was hired by Charles many years ago to lead most of the A28 operation. He is tall, and lean. He can easily be mistaken for a super model.

He continues to clean Eddie's wound. Bill comes back into the room with a secret service agent. He looks at Charles.

Bill

"Sir, President Grover is on location."

Charles excuses himself form everybody. Bin and Lisa look at him as he walks out, as they both would like to meet the President. Eddie didn't even look up, as he is still zoned in on Calvin. Talking about "A28."

Charles gets escorted through the Lab with Bill and one of President Grover's secret service agents. Charles and Jacob see each other from a distance. Charles can see that Jacob only has a small amount of security detail with him. Charles was expecting a convoy of them, but it is only a team of five. Three of them armed with enough ammo to last them days.

Charles knows that Jacob's visit warrants business which is a big reason why he invited him to the A28 lab, just to show that he is being open with him. Charles is kind of nervous about the President being around. It was last minute and the media hasn't even gotten a hold of it. But at the same time, it works pretty well because they don't have to worry about too many politics about Jacob visiting.

Charles walks up to Jake and shakes his hand. They greet each other for a moment, and Charles tells Jacob and his detail to follow him and Bill in.

Charles begins to show the Olympian President around the barracks of the A28 site.

Jacob

"So this is the site, huh? A lot smaller than what I expected. Feels like there's nothing but a mountain out here."

Charles

"I haven't started production. It's also the last place where folks will expect A28 to be."

Jacob

"Do you think it's secure?"

Charles

"It is, but even if it wasn't, A28 is like an advanced warship. If you don't know how to use it, it won't work. Or you're going to mess something up. Especially trying to rush it into production."

Jacob

"Make sure it's secure. Once you guys become recognized, you will have many attempted breaches. Bad guys won't care about the negative aspects about it. They just care about what it can do. Along with how much money that it can make them."

Gary is alongside Jacob. For some reason, he hasn't said anything. He is sweating and has been complaining that he doesn't feel well ever since they landed. As Charles and Jacob talk to each other as they enter the inner laboratory. Gary interrupts the two.

Gary

"Jake, I think I am going to head back. I am not feeling very well."

Jacob

"Okay. I shouldn't be long."

Gary

"No, I think I should go. I may head straight to Europa, so I can rest on the plane."

Jacob looks at Charles.

"Okay. Do you think that one of your guys can give him a lift? To the airport at the least?"

Charles

"Yes."

Jacob

"Shit, Gary. I hope you feel better. I thought you wanted to see this chemical, after that long haul."

Gary

"No, something isn't right. It could be my diabetes. My insulin is in the aircraft."

Jacob

"I didn't even know you had diabetes. Make sure that you get some rest, and whatever you need. I am going to need you at the summit tomorrow. I would give you the jet, but we have already pulled too many strings just being here."

Gary

"I will be fine."

Charles grabs Gary's shoulder.

Charles

"Follow those guys, they will helicopter you back to the airport. It's up to you, but I have an aircraft that you can use to take to Europa."

Gary

"No, I can request one from one of our embassies."

Charles

"If you can't get a lift, feel free to take one of ours."

Gary

"Thanks, guys. I will see you tomorrow. My apologies for my early exit."

Jacob

"Gary, take care of yourself, bud."

As Gary walks off with a few of the Aqua lab security agents, Charles and Jacob walk towards the building. Once they reach the door, the system requests a fingerprint to gain access. Charles pushes his finger inside the slot, and the doors open. The same sequence occurs three more times with the final door requesting a ten digit code. The sliding doors open, and they walk into a private office.

Inside the small office lounge, Jacob and Charles talk. Charles hands Jacob a tube of A28. It is a split tube with grayish liquid on one side, and a powdery substance on the other.

Jacob looks at the bottle, spinning it with his fingers.

"So this is the first thing that you give me when I come here unannounced?"

Charles

"We might as well cut to the chase."

Jacob, still looking at the A28 tube.

"Once this UW bill passes, what's your next move?"

Charles

"I have a few things up my sleeve. You couldn't wait to see me at the UW? It's only tomorrow."

Grover

"Your sleeve. You don't trust me yet? We've known each other for years. What's going on with A28?"

Charles

"Grover, we have been through this before. If you guys start to talk to me with some morals, then we can do business, but I'm not giving up confidential information. If I do, then there will be plots to blow me away."

Grover

"Just like that F22 pilot that blew away a few weeks ago."

Charles closes his eyes, and looks back up to Jacob.

Charles

"Why was he in our airspace?"

Grover

"Who's airspace? That air is just as free as air is to breathe. I don't see a name on it."

Charles

"He's currently an Olympian pilot. Flying undercover in our fighter squadron. He wasn't here on a joint mission or with the Olympian unit. He was disguised as a Paragon citizen. So it sounds like you have some talking to do."

Grover

"All I know is that one of our men went down. Over here in Paragon. It wasn't reported."

Charles

"What do you want? What?"

Grover

"Would I like a piece of that powerful piece of salt that you have growing? Hell yes! But I have more important things to handle. I'm in my first term as the President of Olympia and I have a country that I am losing. I will NOT be the one to have the failure under my belt! You have accepted business from many of our best engineers, blue collar workers, heck, you even got a lot of our street cleaners. I need my people back, at least some of them. I have guys that are ready to blow Paragon into shambles. I haven't let them, and I won't. Nonetheless, I will think out of general respect, that you will understand my standpoint and pay me back somehow. I issued and pushed for those bills you needed, so you could have extended joint forces and manufacture products over here.

"I need to know what is the deal with A28. We need to find a way for it to work for the Olympians. I need to get my country back into a powerful state. All we have now is debt and a cloud of unhappiness. I want to change that."

The room gets quiet. The two men gun each other's face down, like they are in an eye staring competition. It's a tough decision for Charles. He doesn't know whom he can trust.

Grover has been an Olympian all of his life. His group ignited many wars. Not necessarily over negative measures; but more so for profit. Not only for profit of foreign commodities, but profit for control. Members of these parties made profit from war scenarios, ranging from fuel supply, defense products, technology, all the way to the contract to be the supplier for food for the troops.

These contracts typically last for 10 years. Even if a half of a dollar is made per pound of food. Supplying hundreds of pounds of bananas every day equates to a hefty profit. The same goes for water, seasoning, and other items that one would rarely think would profit certain Olympians. All while the majority of other Olympians suffer from the effects of the economy. This includes the middle and lower class.

Grover was always different from his Republic party. Although it took him some time to come out of the conditioning which surrounded him, he began to see the light. Most of his tests and trials began with heavy protest with many folks from the lower communities of Olympia. Jacob wasn't an advocate of food stamps by any means, but to earn the vote from millions of the lower class and urban neighborhoods, he had to physically show that he cared.

Unlike any President, Jacob had a three-month project in process where he would set up a mini-headquarters inside one of the worst cities of Olympia. Though he was heavily secured, as any politician running for president would be. Jacob still interacted with the urban community, did several blind rides along with government authorities, and witnessed the murders, the blood, the drugs, the corruption, and some of the self-degrading tendencies that many of these struggling communities had. He noticed that there was a bigger problem with these gang-provoked communities, because the kids were being born into a war zone.

After first handily witnessing this, Jacob realized that for most of these inner city issues is "what you know, is what you know". He saw many of these children were in situations where if something isn't done to end the cycle of destructive behavior, then that person would be sucked into the same kind of situation as his or her parents were in. For example, whether they were arrested or had a child at the wrong time in life. Not to say that that child isn't a blessing, but it can hinder him or her from seeking higher education, which also hinders the community from positively progressing.

These facts give Charles the faith in Jacob, only because he knows that Jacob doesn't perform publicity stunts, and truly does care about the people.

Jacob

"Chuck, if I don't know what A28 is, then you may expect things to get ugly. Very ugly. You know how things can get when that occurs."

Charles takes no threat to it as he knows how Olympia operates when they want something. Although Paragon is a small nation, they still have a high amount of power, not only within themselves but nations that Charles has relations with. Even so, war isn't beneficial to the new country and one deadly blast can knock Charles' whole plan into nothing.

Jacob

"They will strike you before that UW resolution is signed. They are talking about it, and something needs to happen. You have to bend a little bit for me."

Charles grimaces

"So you mean to tell me that I have to give you guys something that I have been holding onto for years, I mean, years? If I had never mentioned it, then it would not have been a problem. However, now that it exists, all of a sudden another countries merit their share of it?"

Charles's euro voice raises a bit.

"That's not a question! That's some rhetorical crap! My grandfather sought help from you guys when we were bombed years ago. You guys played him like a rag doll. Did nothing. But when the time came, he opened the doors to give you militant land during Kawaity War for you guys."

Jacob

"I understand what you're saying, but you need to let that go. Times have changed, Charles. Now, A28 is yours - yes. But remember. You still have millions of Olympians here supporting this country. We haven't mandated them to come back…"

Charles

"You can't."

Jacob

"Look. Bob Polan's dad was a part of the tree administration. He will take whatever he wants. It's in his blood."

Charles

"What do you want to do? I smell the bombs coming in anyway."

Jacob

"Show me A28, all its capabilities. I need to see it, we need leverage. I want my vote to matter to the UW. I want you to be accepted; I want to support your acceptance. But you have to work with me.

"You have to let me see this and its potential. You have to create the correct partners, Charles. You are one amazing man, but you can't do this on your own."

Charles pauses and leans back

Jacob

"We have to do this together. Everybody is against me also. I need you just as much as you need me."

Charles pulls his phone out and calls Orchid.

Charles

"Tell Tommy we are heading out. To the …"

He looks at Jacob

Charles

"What size shoe do you wear? 11?"

Jacob

"Twelve."

Charles

"We need a size 12 gym shoe."

Charles looks at Jacob

Charles

"Okay. I will show you something, and then we have to get on to Europa. You can bring two of your agents."

Ready?

A day after showing President Grover the ins and outs of A28, and the secret to the production, Charles and Jacob arrive in Europa. Separately.

Charles has been visiting the country frequently. It's the location of the main offices of the United Worlds. The UW recognizes each member country and promotes and handles much correspondence in efforts to maintain a balanced level of ethics. They deal with peace and security, social and economic cooperation, and judicial freedoms and democracy. Without this group, many parts of the world would consistently be in turmoil. Nonetheless, the UW gathers regularly to make sure that the involved countries are properly communicating with each other, and they assist with any issues amongst them that they may have. From large to small.

Charles has just landed in one of his private aircraft with a team of seven. They include four advisors, two security guards (one being Bill), and himself. Charles needs his protection for the most part when he travels internationally. He isn't necessarily renowned, but there are political radicals who follow each and everything that goes on with politics, and some would do anything to get their hands on him. Many aren't satisfied with Charles's policies, his goal to add another country to the world, and his successfulness. Every now and then, a few who think that since Charles is a black leader, then he is the Antichrist, speak up. They hold up crossed finger signs to him, and expect him to melt.

One year, an anonymous person sent Charles a gift once he landed in Europa. When Charles opened it, he received a hard glimpse of an actual eye of an elephant. It wasn't a joyful present. They believe that it came from a hunter who didn't like the fact that Charles donates money to protect animals and selected habitats. Ever since, Charles has had to keep eyes in the back of his head. Therefore, he has to retain an advanced security detail unit, though he doesn't like it. The U.W. has also mandated for him to have a detail, along with his advisement. It's an awkward feeling for him, as he is a very private guy, but the take off of Paragon has made him into a social icon; especially with his humanitarian dues, philanthropic investments, and moral donations.

Charles arrives at the house of his long time friend, Er Who Choi. Bill walks in with him, and clears the rest of Charles's team so they can head to the hotel.

Choi is the former leader of the United Worlds. He resigned a few years back, so he can concentrate on his family. He is originally from Jing Jon, which is the capital of Asiana. He and Charles have an excellent relationship which dates back to when Choi and the UW needed Charles's land as a central hub for allied forces. Charles came through for Choi. Along with that agreement, the two have a very strong business relationship stemming from the days when Choi used to be the CEO of one of the primary Asiana electronic companies, named SEE.

Charles is meeting with Choi, to discuss his business plan that he intends to implement for the long term with Paragon. It is a requirement, not only for the country but the acceptance of entry into the UW. Choi's home is miraculous; it sits high in the mountains and is surrounded by nothing but valleys and greenery. The panels on the roof show that the home is solar powered. The turquoise water that sits under the moat is a highlight for any guest. The tropical fish and stingrays display protection and beauty at the same time.

Charles meets Choi at the moat. The two begin to talk about the upcoming process and their current situations.

Choi

"I see you're doing well; no need to ask. So to get to the point. I am keenly excited, but am also eager to see these documents that you and your team have prepared."

Charles

"Why is that?"

Choi

"Charles, countries have done it, but Paragon has been literally been created from scratch. It's - it's - it's different, Charles. Many people don't know what to do with the addition of A28 to society. And we are only speaking industrially. Imagine what they are going to say, when they find out what it does to people biologically. This is going to change the world. Look at us. I love life, but damn. I feel as I am 40 years old. Messing around with that A28, I'm getting younger by the day. You are also.

Anyway, no need to drift. Paragon reminds me of Emirate, and how they flourished though they still had capital before their empire. You and your father had nothing but a long stretch of land.

Charles enjoys Choi's Asiana accent and how he takes his time when he speaks. It enhances Choi's wisdom. Even when he stutters.

Choi

This is big. We have to be careful in implementing this. I'm not going to avoid talking about the difficult tasks. I know it is sensitive to talk about the 28 project, but we have to. You have a key that will change the world; that's where our issue rises. Politically, at least. These guys are sharks.

How far have you come with the past five and the next fifteen?

Charles

It's complete. Just waiting on a few things

The past five and the next fifteen means the past five years and the next fifteen years of analysis. Paragon has to prove to be financially sustainable to be recognized as an official country. They also have to produce a set amount of trade annually; thus the other nations will benefit from the new addition of the "World."

Choi

"You did bring it today, right?"

Charles

"Your home isn't the place to show up empty-handed."

Choi

"You'd be surprised. I am human too. I think."

Charles

"How has the committee been receiving it all?" ("All," meaning, the status of approval).

Choi looks up at Charles.

Choi

"Charles, some things in life just need to be found out on our own."

He puts his hand on Charles's back. Although he is on the committee and is Charles's good friend, he is forbidden to speak to him about specifics that are handled behind the scenes. He also won't make things easy for Charles.

As they walk down the hallway into Choi's illustrious home, the marble floors glisten as they walk in. Dinner has been prepared. Er Choi's wife, Ruth, is an amazing cook, and she loves Charles. She has prepared a meal for the two, an Asian stew. She has a very squeaky voice, although her looks don't match it.

Ruth (rushing up to Charles)

"My favorite snugg'ems! How you been? Don't mind me for not hugging you, I don't want to get that nice shirt damaged."

Ruth grabs Charles's shirt.

Ruth

"------ Wait; what color is that? Pastel? Yes, this pastel colored shirt. I don't want to get it dirty."

Charles (his accent's stronger when in Europa)

"Yes, ma'am. A stain won't be ideal. How about you? Whatever you have smells delicious."

Ruth

"Aw, Chuck, it's just another day. I'm waiting on you to make history. Take a guess what you smell."

Charles (leaning in, sniffing his nose - weird ingredients)

"I smell some parsley. A bit of basil. Smells like some potatoes. And. Umm. I can't put my nose on the main course."

Ruth

"Oh, Chuck, who knows the ingredients and not the main course? Only you. You are such a smart man."

Charles

"No, that was just an assumption because I see all the ingredients sitting on the counter."

He winks at her, and she smacks her lips in response.

Choi

"You almost had her. I believed you for a second. I was like "How did hell did he know the ingredients?" But then again. He did create a freaking country. So what can't he do."

They all chuckle.

Ruth

"No. He's just being Chuck. Good ole Chuck. In fact. Charles it's Baked Pork."

Charles raises his eyebrows and tilts his head.

Ruth

"I'm kidding, sweetie. I know you how you feel about pork and that dark meat. You'd kill me."

Charles (looking at Choi)

"Did you put something in her drink?"

Choi

"Don't put me in this."

Ruth finishes off the last parts of the small hand tossed salads for the men, with a small amount of fresh mozzarella on the top. She is a fabulous cook, which gives Charles even more of a reason to visit Choi. He eats well and they get to discuss various business plans, and other current things that are going on in each other's lives. Charles maintains the relationship, just as he keeps his brand new motor vehicles maintained.

Charles is a very young 44-year-old man with one child, Abe. Choi and Ruth are both in their early 60s, and they have 6 children who are close to the same age as Charles. Ten years ago, it was very hard for them to look at Charles, since he was only 30-years-old, but he had the soul of a man who has lived for 70 years.

Choi gave Charles many wise words, and Charles absorbed them. Choi began to take Charles under his wing, and help him understand the economics of the world. When Charles was younger, he was eager to use some of the money that he received from the government and even some pre-investments for A28; to buy sports teams and other desirable items. Nevertheless, Choi put all that to a halt, and had him focus on building an economy. An empire.

While sitting at the table. Charles thinks back to the year 2014.

In Paragon, Charles and Choi are sitting down, snacking on cheese and crackers at a table right next to a mammal sanctuary which was built on the east side of Paragon, just off the coast of the ocean. In a tank 20 feet away there are dolphin biologists who are nursing a porpoise calf back to health. The site is blue with a tan-colored pool edge. Palm trees surrounding the area and the ocean in the backdrop.

Choi

"What gives Paragon the advantage over other cities, states, or shall I say, countries?"

Charles

"Choi, I'm not trying to compete, I'm just trying to make this thing work. The central goal is letting accounts add up. Have the proper infrastructure for this wave of people who are coming into the land. This is not simple. I never imagined having to create homeland protection, investigative units, lawmakers, biologist, auditors, thousands of auto mechanic - Water Specialists. You name it, we need it. I just, I just want to make this thing work."

Choi

"Then there is your answer."

Expecting a different response from Choi. Charles is puzzled. He leans back looking at Choi while they both sit at the mammal rehab sanctuary. Charles gives him a confused look that a six-year-old would give in advanced trigonometry class.

A small splash of salt water from the dolphin calf hits Charles and Choi on their heads, as it just jumped in its tank. Some of the water lands on Choi's cracker as he eats it, looking cool as usual with his sunglasses, polo shirt, and sports watch on his wrist.

Choi chews on a soggy cracker.

"The extra salt from that water tastes good."

Charles

"You know there's dolphin piss in that water?"

Choi

"Ehhh, I'm sure I've unknowingly eaten a lot worse. Remember, some of my cousins eat snake hearts for protein. So this is nothing."

He chews the cracker. Charles gives him a disgusted look.

Choi

"Charles, why haven't you released or sold that darn mineral yet?"

Charles

"Because we don't really know how it works. We have many more tests to run the ins and outs of safety and production. Why release it and not know the true effect that it can have? Why? You got another buyer?"

Choi

"No. My point is that, in ANY endeavor that you have ever done. The words "just get it" done has never come out of your mouth."

Choi pauses

"Now, you may take your time on things, sometimes too long. But you strive for greatness. Partially, I think that you are ignorant to what's in store for this land."

Charles gets defensive.

"I'm not ignorant about anything pertaining to the Paragon project. I know-"

Choi interrupts

"Don't take it the wrong way, Chuck. My point being is that you are ignorant."

Choi closes his eyes as he says the word again, knowing that Charles isn't taking it well.

Choi continues.

"That you are ignorant to the fact that you will be the first living – well, I'm sure there are a few. But you are the first living person in this era to have started a country from scratch. With life, we can undo things. Now, once you do something that has a direct effect on millions of people, and an indirect but even greater effect on billions of cosmopolitans, it is very hard to take back. Sometimes you can't take it back."

Charles looks at Choi in deep thought. Wanting to take his advice, but not wanting to. But he knows the value of Choi's wisdom.

Choi

"An internet site, you can change. A car defect, you can change. A plane crash, it's horrible, but you learn from it. A computer virus, you can fix. But the way people live their day-to-day lives, even one mistake can ruin and affect them all for years to come."

Charles opens his mouth to speak, but Choi slightly raises his hand off the table. Charles remains mute.

Choi

"Young Charles, you're going to make mistakes. You're going to make mistakes. You're - going - to - make ---- mistakes. However, you do not want to start off with a mistake. You do not want to rush this process of bringing people over here, and a new nation into world, and making it a mistake. Many are waiting to BANK off of YOUR mistake. Particularly with A28. A rushed mistake will make this beautiful land go unseen. Only few will hear about how beautiful it WAS. You want them to know how beautiful it IS.

"You cannot or shall I impose that I will NOT let you build a model for this new country that is based on another model of current states, cities, or countries. You can benchmark, but you need your own model. You need to

248

pick up on what others are doing, where others have
messed up, and where they are currently messing up. You
need to know your enemies, and keep close to them. You
need to make this new world, such an amazing place that
you can't, and won't be, brought down. You have the tools,
you have the relationships, and you have a product that will
change the world. Do it right. Strategize. Take your time.
You are young, son."

Choi points at Charles

Choi

"That's comical, because that's what your dad used to tell
me. I laughed him off, but now that my brain is almost a
hundred years old, I know what he meant.

"He saved this for you, son. He wanted you to take
advantage of the technology that the world offers. He saw
the recessions coming. He witnessed the greedy take, until
there was nothing to be taken anymore. He watched hatred,
and he knew. He also watched you. You were a builder, son.
You and those, those, those, ummm…"

Charles chuckles

"Legos."

Choi

"Right, how can I forget that name? Those Legos. Son,
you used to build anything with those. Literally anything.
Most importantly, you took your time, never rushing. In
school, and during your pre-engineering courses, your dad
used to laugh because you would freak out when you would
be behind schedule for your design assignments. Even if
your assignment was late, the teacher was always astonished
by your work. He didn't care about a deadline with you
because he was intrigued how much time you put into your
work, and you were only 9 years old. Little did you know, he
really didn't mind, because he always wanted to save the
best for last. Just like this Paragon project...will it be the
last? Who knows? That's God's call. You will make the best,
and it will be the best.

"Unfortunately a few years of planning is nowhere near
enough. You need more time. Don't be anxious. Nobody is
going to take your idea, invade, or evolve a better place
than what you have planned. They are too busy trying to

win a game when there is no game to be played. Being fitted in with the unfitted."

It's as if Choi is speaking the words of his father. Since Choi was great friends with Charles Sr., he knows how Charles thinks. Choi also knew that Charles Sr. waited for the proper time for Paragon to be a powerful nation.

There was a time, right before Charles Sr. passed away. Young Charles was in the midst of accepting people in Paragon to be a part of different trades to keep the country alive. This ranged from construction workers, plumbers, data clerks, grocery store workers, logistics specialists etc., to ensure the efficient movement of goods, trade, and people. Charles began to hire consultants from different parts of the world to help him get what he needed done. He had business models that different governments used throughout the world, and everything was set in stone. Paragon's world campaign was being prepared with the media. There were a few major companies that were a part of it, and a good number of financial backers present.

Choi continues the discussion

> Choi

"Right now is not the time. You need more time."

> Charles

"But- "

> Choi (Chinese)

"You are not ready. There's nothing sweet about world politics. It gets ugly. Deadly."

> Charles

"What am I supposed to do, Choi? I have flown around the world. I have sat face to face with many influential people, organizations, charities, and have discussed operational plans with over 100 companies to have Paragon supported! How can you tell me that this isn't the time! I have been around the world, sacrificed all of my time into this for the past 8 years, and you expect me to not pursue this. This may be my only shot."

> Choi spreads cheese onto a brown cracker.

"I never said don't pursue this. It just isn't the time."

Choi's patience is why he was the leader of the United Worlds. He can listen to almost any hostile conversation, keep his cool, and remain reserved. Throughout this whole conversation, he has drilled Charles on what he needs to do, brought back very deep moments of the past with Charles, and helped him understand even more his purpose for being here, and the legacy that not only his father left for him, but the legacy that he roughly paved for him. Yet he still left plenty of work for Charles to do.

Charles is emotional, confused, scared. He has been around the world pitching Paragon to various consultants, contract organizations, associations, film companies so they can publish documentaries on the country's territories so more people can be aware of its presence. He has recruited many of the best industrialists, researchers, electricians, lawmakers, welders, plumbing specialists, all the way to beauticians, to be a part of Paragon. There have been near billions of dollars put into the past few years to get Paragon known by millions of people. But in Choi's eyes it's nothing.

It's very hard for Charles to disagree with Choi. He knows that Choi has infinite wisdom and has made very solid decisions throughout all of his business deals, government organizations, life, and even with Charles's father. On another note, Charles knows his plan for Paragon, and he still believes that the time is now.

Charles

"Choi, it has been eight years and counting of hard work, research, and development. I want to see this place grow."

Choi

"Then continue to water the grass. Don't drench it. It will grow. Trust me."

Charles

"How long are you thinking?"

Choi

"Hmmmm. For the everyday man, it will never grow. For the grand business magnate and visionary, maybe 50 years. For you, I say another decade."

Charles gives Choi the blank look while 10 years is all that is jogging through Charles's mind. It's circling. He can't believe it. Though he has to because if anybody knows Charles, Choi does.

Choi

"So you want to do this before you get any grey hairs?"

Charles

"Buddy, I won't be getting any grey hairs for a while. For all, A28 has resolved that a bit. I see it has been slowing your age process down also."

Choi

"I can say that you are right. Eventually I will have to go on hiatus, otherwise folks will start wondering why me and Ruth aren't aging."

Charles's mind begins to race. Although he is patient, he doesn't want to wait any longer to make Paragon an official country. He wonders if he will be alive by then? Will the world change? Will he be able to bank off of the failing governments of the world? Will the people completely reinstate their faith in the governments, presidents, major corporations, after the corrupted trust has faded?

Right now is the perfect time to offer a new life to many people. To start the proper transition for millions as 8% of the Olympians are unemployed. This equates to almost 30 million people. Paragon can use a few million of them, and there are many more who wouldn't mind taking the risk to live life on another side of the world; the new world. But, it will all have to wait.

Choi

"It's still your choice. Heck, I'm just another guy."

Choi turns his head and looks back at the dolphin calf as it interacts with its trainer in the beautiful aqua colored pool.

Choi

"So what did you do about the proposal that Water World offered? That became a big deal in Olympia."

Charles

"I passed. We found another route to go. It was costly, but worth it and the end of the day."

Choi

"Did it effect the development of the amusement parks?"

Charles

"No, but they didn't give me the deal that we were
looking for. But what the heck, I didn't pay for the land. So
as long as they come here safely and amuse people, I will be
satisfied. They still weren't too happy about the denial of
the marine parks. Though, nothing will be perfect, and I
may not be right by saying this. I feel the life of a bear or a
lion in captivity is different from a whale's."

Charles looks out into the ocean off the coast.

Charles

"A whale is built to travel the world. They live in a body
of water, which is a hundred's times larger than the land
where humans live. In captivity they are just put into a large
pool for the rest of its life. Only for people watch them do
circus tricks in a tank. Are you eye-to-eye with me?"

Choi

"I'm glad that I'm not on that board. If they pulled my
track record up, they will see that I signed a multitude of
those whales over to "rehab". I never looked at it that way.
It's almost like eating a burger. It's so good. Goodness, it's
the inside of a cow that had a life. We don't think about
many things when it comes to animals."

They both look out into the ocean.

Charles

"The final deal wasn't as sweet. They had the entire
plan ready. It wasn't going to be too far from where we are
sitting right now."

Charles points out to the coast. You can see the pinkish /
orange horizon with the light blue waves rippling.

Charles

"It was outstanding and breathtaking. The water was
going to be pumped directly from the ocean; the backdrop
was going to be fascinating. There were plans for the tank
to overlook the edge and straight to the water just as if it
were the ocean. Then my environmentalist, Andy, had a
video created for me."

Charles laughs to himself. A butler pours cold water into
both of their glasses.

Choi (lifting his hand)

"Hey, sir. You got lemonade?"

Butler

"Yes, indeed." Pink, strawberry, or regular?

Choi

"Surprise me. I trust you."

He looks back at Charles. Gets back to the conversation.

Choi

"He made a video? Is Andy the one that?"

Charles (looking down with a smirk)

"Yup, Andy the one put the snake heart in your martini."

Choi (with a serious look)

"That damn kid."

Charles

"Hey, you picked on him."

Choi

"Still doesn't mean he can put that in my drink. What if I was allergic?"

Charles

"Nah, you weren't. You told him that snake hearts are healthy. Don't you eat them anyway?"

Choi

"You have to be braced for the heart! Charles, I thought it was an olive."

The two men share grins. Charles knows that Choi picked on the wrong guy, and Andy caught him slipping. Choi had called Andy "Jungle Boy" in front a group of influential people. Choi didn't know Andy's hardcore personality.

Charles

"Anyhow, when Andy showed us the video when the Water World executives were here to view the final contract. I looked at it, and I saw me in a glass room. It was like I was in a zoo, but worse. The room was about 20 feet by 20 feet, your typical master bedroom. I had a bathroom in there, and he even made it luxurious.

"So he did a time lapse of me living in this glass room. I believe I had him turn the video off around the 5 year mark. He created the whole video to last my marketed lifespan. Which was only about 20 years.

"In that video, while Andy had a million people walking around my window, I was locked into the room. Then, I was instructed to dance because I thought that's what life was about. I thought that's how I was supposed to eat; to get my food. It was a weird video. Only something that Andy would make. But it changed my whole perspective. You should have seen Mr. Web's eyes when Andy played it during their proposal. He was grim-faced and red.

Choi

"I think I heard about that one. Didn't know it was over here though. That Andy…"

Choi shakes his head

Choi

"Well, Charles, I think you've got it. Just give it a bit more time."

Charles

"I asked him why my life was so short in the video. He said it was because I couldn't get the proper exercise, and my brain couldn't handle captivity mentally. That's the life of an Orca. They can live up to ninety years in the wild. In captivity, they get lucky to get twenty. Some may make it to forty."

Charles chuckles as he plays with his wine glass.

Charles

"That guy is a character."

Choi is looking at Charles, thinking deeply. Not just about the story and how amusing it is, but the team that Charles has put together. How Charles only has to delegate just a bit. Since the people who are on Charles's team are all emotionally in tune with what they love. Choi respects Andy because he knows that he disrespected Andy in front of many people. Andy retaliated confidentially, and made it quite humorous. It was also courageous since Choi was the lead of the U.W at the time.

As Charles continues to explain things, Choi begins to realize that Charles is making things make sense, but also improving humanity. Not just with people, but with nature. Although the zoos in Paragon are not as "entertaining" as zoos in traditional countries, Charles is allowing people to see "wild in the wild."

Charles

"With our Orca Whale plan, some whales are captive because they are truly in rehab. Our whales will never lose a sense of home. Their enclosures are in the ocean. They are barricaded, but they are given much space to live in. There will never be a perfect world, but making it a better one doesn't hurt. To try, at least."

The flashback is over. Back to Choi and Ruth's Kitchen

Ruth

"Charles, what is that grey on your face? It isn't Halloween, is it?"

Charles

"Yeah, I never thought it would really come in."

Ruth

"Choi? Did you make him go grey too early?"

Choi (sarcastic)

"I was jealous. One, I don't grow facial hair, and the small amount of hair that I have left on my head, I was losing. Hey, now he blends in with everybody."

Charles

"How is everything going over there anyway? Choi, I love the food, but I didn't make this pit stop for nothing. I have many things on the plate. I've given you your answers as usual. Now gimme a few."

Choi

"I haven't been in direct talks with everybody, but let's let Ruth get upstairs before we discuss it more deeply."

13

In Case of Emergency

The AX-1 squadron has been preparing for Operation Red Ice for the past 2 years. Only a few of the team have had combat experience with other countries before coming to Paragon's unit. This is their first time in a combat scenario as a unit.

Abe, Telda, Rory, and Terry Love are the chosen flight crew to go. Dell, Tex, and a few other members of service also join to support of AX-1's ramp, technical, and maintenance duties. Chris is also with the crew, as a reserve. Carter is still being questioned in Paragon.

The guys are amped, though they have already run into a few altercations. Some of the Olympian guys are rather jealous of the Paragon unit. Mainly because they are the only squadron in the world to operate the F-22 and F-35 aircraft. Furthermore, their planes have some modifications. Paragon's unit is also very diverse, as most of the guys are of a darker skin color which isn't traditional at most Red Ice Gatherings. Besides Abe, Telda, and Jason, Rory and Terry Love are clearly black and Abe looks very particularly biracial if not middle eastern. There are many cultures here from Israelia, Egyptia, Asiana, and Emirate. Paragon is also the new kids on the block. It is still is a bit different for some of the privileged pilots in Olympia. Abe, Rory, and Terry Love stick out like chocolate chips in cookie dough. Although there are 3 other colored pilots in the whole challenge, it still leaves them as the minority.

AX-1 did well on their first two missions. Nobody has failed. Terry Love has been very impressive. He has been speaking with many different groups and understanding different maneuvers of the aircraft. He has also been very reserved after Abe and Jason have in a way taken him under their wing. Today is the final day of the Red Ice, and it is a joint mission with Olympia. Abe and the guys are rather excited. But there are a few guys on the Olympia side who have been giving Abe and Rory conflict throughout the whole competition. There have been moments when the radar control weren't responding to them when they needed some assistance. They haven't been receiving the proper fueling to their aircraft. When raising their hands during briefings, the Olympian instructors try to act as if they aren't smart. When AX-1 walked in, base personnel directed Abe and Rory to the custodian room. When Abe insisted to them that he was a pilot, the receptionist ignored him and told him to "get a life".

That didn't sit well, but Captain Smitten warned them that they would receive some friction. However, they need to do their best and bust their asses to show other countries what AX-1 is about. Which will make another nation think twice about invading Paragon.

As the squadron is getting ready to take off, they are going through their checks. Abe is pumped but relaxed. He is talking to radar to make sure that they are in proper communication and on the right frequency. He hasn't received his mission briefing yet. As this last one is a surprise, because it is meant to keep the guys on their toes and be totally unexpected. Just as any standard scramble, the Alarms sound.

Alert Echo, Alert Echo: Paragon

The Olympians and the men of Paragon hustle to their aircraft. Abe climbs his ladder, Jason follows. Terry Love runs to his airplane. With his large biceps popping out of his flight suit, one can see his young strength. Rory follows. Telda follows, her steps are shorter than everybody else's but she holds her own. She lifts into her aircraft and straps her face mask on.

The ideal time for loading into a scramble into an unoccupied aircraft is to be 3 minutes. AX-1 got it done in 90 seconds. Abe and the guys are already on the taxiway, halfway powered up. Waiting for their mission. A lot of their preparedness has to do with the upgraded systems that Paragon has in their F-22's. The data is inserted immediately when an alert is dispatched. This includes the weather, positioning of all aircraft within a set radius, and other factors.

Abe

"Radar. This is squid. Who. What. When. Where? We don't need to understand why."

Radar

"Alpha X-rays, you have unidentified stealth contacts approaching an Olympian Cargo C-17. They are in heavy subsonic and are closing in onto the aircraft."

Abe

"How far is the Cargo Aircraft away from us?"

Radar

"Two hundred miles, Sir."

Abe

"Roger. Squid requesting sequential take off. Three birds with me - we are elephant walking. Immediate 10,000 then to 30,000. Clearance over that river at our 7 o'clock. Is it salt or fresh?"

Radar

"AX-1 you guys don't have the location of the target yet."

Jason

"Radar. They are due southwest. We got a lock on them. We're taking off upon emergency clearance. Stay away from any windows in the tower because we will be going subsonic immediately."

Radar

"You will burn too much fuel if you do that, sir."

Rory (looking at his GPS in the cockpit)

"Aye bro, don't worry about our fuel. Worry about yours. Squid, the water is fresh. It doesn't have an outlet to an ocean and is trapped by mountains. The pH level is just around 7 so that's damn good for our intake."

A few of the Olympians who are coordinating the mission don't like the way the AX1 Squadron are talking to them. They think that they are too confident to be new guys.

Radar

"I didn't clear you guys yet! The joint force isn't even taxing up yet! You're supposed to wait!"

Rory

"You didn't say that shit when you guys left us last night. You also have an aircraft that's in potential distress. We have no time to wait for another crew."

Last night, the Olympians made the guys from Paragon find their own ride home. They were told to meet up at 18:00 military time and the AX1 squadron got there at 17:40. The coach bus that takes the pilots to the hotel never showed up.

Rory

"We're rolling."

The guys in the control room look. Amongst all of them, a voice that Abe recognizes very well comes over the radio frequency.

Captain Title

"I hope you know that you guys were ALL rejects."

Abe, thinks back to his young days as a pilot. All the racist and degrading things that Captain Title told him when he was Abe's commander in Olympia.

Abe

"Wow, Captain. That's professional of you."

Telda

"Abe, focus!"

Telda knows how Abe feels about Captain Title

Abe

"Radar, so we are en route. What's the issue with our target? Are they carrying anything sensitive? Any souls on board?"

Radar Commander

"You have six souls on board, and the cargo aircraft is carrying a radioactive fluid which fills our nukes. That plane cannot blow up, Squid. If it does, it can wipe out the whole western region of Olympia."

Abe

"Why hasn't it been diverted? Where are its escorts?"
Captain Title jumps on the radio.

Captain Title

"Its escorts have been shot down. They were F-16's. We believe that they were shot down by stealth aircraft that chased them down."

Abe

"That makes no sense."

Captain Title (choking up)

"Don't question me! They averted the shipment."

Abe

"First. You're not my commander, but one thing a commander knows is that an escorted wingman never leaves the side of his job. This sounds like a baloney mission, but we got this. Requesting 40,000 we need to be lighter."

Captain Title is pissed, Abe called his bluff. Some of the guys in the control room are quiet. One even asks why is he trying to set them up, but he quiets them immediately.

Captain Title

"Forty thousand is approved. You need to watch your fuel."

Abe

"Captain Title. You failed me when I went in the reserve training 6 years ago. Don't try to coach me now. It figures why you're on this mission."

Abe thinks about all the slurs that Captain Title said to him. How he risked his life many times for him, only to be backstabbed. Captain Title is a person who grew up with a one-track mind. He is a closet racist, and most of the troops can see it. Many of the pilots don't say anything to him about it. Some have even requested to go to the Navy and fly because Captain Title wouldn't allow a minority to freely fly any aircraft. His daughter is a big conservative who is on the networks. He nearly lost his job when it went public that she got on a commercial airliner and saw a black female pilot in the captain seat. When she saw her she yelled to everybody on the airplane that they need to get off of the plane because a black pilot is flying it, and the fact that she was a woman made it impossible. She blamed it on affirmative action and that the airline was forced to give her the job. She happened to be one of the leaders in the air force.

Abe

"I hope your daughter isn't on this plane because I think you would kill your own self if she found out that a few colored pilots saved her. Is that Affirmative?"

Captain is quiet but he is furious. He has a low military cut, with all of his credentials on his camouflage uniform. A few guys in the command are pissed, and others are laughing. One black guy who handles some of the notes almost closes out his computer. But his white counterpart puts his hand on his hand and says

"No, this needs to happen".

Abe

"Captain Title. Now you got me started. You had your men leave us behind last night in a country that we don't live in? Initially I thought it was an accident, but I had a clue that you were behind this. Speaking of you guys. Where are the Olympians? Are they behind us?"

Radar

"They're..."

Rory interrupts the radar.

"Abe, Their fleet was "shot" down supposedly. Intel already sent it to me. We are on this mission alone."

Abe

"Damn Captain. You give us a mission that is impossible. There is a nuclear shipment over a city with enemy fighters closing in at over mach three? Then you sit your boys down, and make it seem like..."

Telda interrupts on a private frequency.

"Abe. SHUT UP!"

Abe doesn't say another word.

Jason

"She's right, Abe. Let's focus before your brain gets hot. Enemies are 300 miles out. They are slowing up though. It looks like they want to engage. They could be refueling also. We only have a few minutes."

Abe

"Do we all have 28 packs on us?"

Packs are the secret call for A28. The whole unit responds with a quick Roger.

Abe

"We need to go supersonic, dip into that water, lift our levers down, and pull up as much water as we can. It's lining up perfectly. So let's roll up. I'll talk to radar."

As they all begin to thunder their engines .The aircraft begin to zoom at lightning speed. The pilots are all sweaty. Terry Love is trying to hold his own quietly. Although he has never been this fast. Along with dealing with the pressure of failing at the mission.

Jason

"Guys, we will have to descend rapidly until 200 feet. Thrust level, and hold the planes as close to the river as possible. The vacuums pull the water up at about fifteen gallons a second. The river is only ten miles long. So we need to hold back under 150 knots as long as we can. If you go into a stall, thrust your engines to keep above. Then maximize your power to burst out of there. We will be there in 2 minutes. So let's go!"

As they do it, it is a beautiful sight. Abe receives clearances from radar. They expected them to have to refuel airborne, but if they refueled it would only have given them a few minutes to reach the aircraft. With A28, since they are around water it gives them a chance to hover above the water at 200 miles per hour and take right back off with a full tank. They will just have to drop the A28 package into the slot by their arm in the aircraft. Then it will dissolve, turning all the water into a thick combustible fuel.

Captain Title

"What the hell are they doing?"

Radar Controller

"I don't know sir. They requested to go under 100 feet. Above the water. I just figured that they wanted to fly low."

Captain Title

"They need to refuel though. They are going to crash."

Radar Controller 2 (intrudes)

"Sir, I think they are refueling."

The second controller points his finger to his screen and the 3D imagery shows the aircraft over the river in between the mountains. It shows the planes are separated by a few feet. Just enough so they don't get in each other's way. The levers are sucking the water into the planes. Now they have another few thousand miles to fly.

Once that is done. Abe and the AX1 squadron put the planes back into full thrust. Terry Love and Rory are sent to the east and west. Telda stays low, and Abe and Jason stay central so they can see what's going on with the aircraft. Also, they want to be as close to any missile as possible in case one is shot and they can shoot it down. Although this is a drill, this is a realistic scenario that they need to pass to get their squadron approved. It will also play a significant role in the acceptance of the United Worlds. Which Charles is meeting with at the same time.

As the men approach the aircraft, they can see on the radar that two similar aircraft to theirs are nearby. Abe instructs Rory to flank off to the left. Terry flanks off to the right and rolls behind them. Before Abe knows one of the AX pilots are about to engage. The voice comes over their headsets

Radar

"AX-1 - You have downed one."

Terry Love

"Squid, looks like the laser got one already."

Terry Love knocks one of the planes out with his first try. Now Rory has to get his missile locked on the other one.

Rory

"Squid, I got eyes on the other one. I don't know what he is carrying, but I have to be weary."

Rory does a barrel roll, attempting to get behind the aircraft.

Rory

"We are 1 mile apart. He knows I'm here. He's dodging."

Terry Love

"Rory, in eight seconds. Drop off!"

Rory

"For what? I'm behind him."

Terry Love

"Just do it. Drop off and stall out! Trust me! I'm 15,000. I'm going to supersonic up. He can't go too far or too fast. He will go empty."

Rory

"Alright, Love."

Terry hits his throttle with his left hand. He is showing his maturity over the past few days, and maybe something that he learned while talking to other nations about particular situations. He dives his airplane down as he sees Rory slowly drop off. The two warriors are acting as team.

Captain Title

"What the hell are they doing? How much time is left?"

Radar Controller

"Sir, they are 20 minutes ahead of schedule. They caught the enemy fighters before they even got into missile range of the target cargo plane."

Captain Title

"I'll be damned!"

Terry Love speeds up, his nose begins to bleed because he is using the energy and force of the plane to catch up to the other one. As he gains his maximum speed of about 1,600 knots, he releases his missile. On the digital screen in the coordination room the screen turns green.

ENEMY SECURED: ENEMY SECURED.

Radar

"Paragon AX-1 unit Lead by Squid, Your mission is completed. The enemy is down and the target is secured. Come back to base, boys. That's a record. Good job, fellows."

As Terry Love, Telda, and Rory celebrate as they hear the good news on the frequency. Abe and Jason have another situation on their hands a few miles away. They notice that the Cargo Plane that the Olympia was using is not being responsive to Abe rocking his wings once the mission is complete. It's something that pilots do to acknowledge each other.

Abe switches to the frequency that the Olympian pilots are on and talks to the pilots.

Abe

"Olympia Heavy. Do you copy?"

Olympia Cargo Pilot

"I........... Do...........cooppyyyyyy... You........ You.... Got......aaaaaaa....gooooooodd .... Shootttt..."

Abe

"Jason, you hear that?"

Jason

"Yeah, maybe it's the radio."

Abe calls him again.

Abe

"Olympia Heavy. Do you copy me rocking my wings?"

Abe rocks the plane back and forth. But the Olympia aircraft doesn't. They just stay flying.

Olympia Heavy Pilot

"I... Dooooooo. Isn't.... Ittttt. Aaa. Gooooood. Day."

The pilot is speaking slowly.

Jason

"Fuck, he has hypoxia!"

Abe

"I know. Hey, radar. Your heavy pilot is not responsive and I think he has hypoxia."

Radar

"Okay. Hey, Olympia Heavy. Can you land at Foxboro? It's only fifteen miles out."

Abe

"I don't think you want him to land there; it's a bad cross wind right now."

Radar

"Roger... Ummm..."

Abe

"Give me a second."

Captain Title

"Squid, you need to return to base. Your mission is complete."

Abe

"Are you an idiot? I'm not leaving him."

Captain Title

"He is not your ally?"

Abe

"Well, unofficially he is. These guys are about to go unconscious. Radar, I'm going to go inverted and try to get him to pull down to 7,000. Are we clear?"

Radar

"Roger… But my captain said that you are ordered come back."

Abe

"I will take that hit. I'm won't let these guys die. They are barely responsive and are rapidly losing it. They are going to fly until their fuel is out."

Abe speeds the jet to the front of the aircraft. He turns it upside down and stays level with them.

Abe

"Jason, how am I looking?"

Jason

"We are going into the wind. So crank them up a bit. Plus pitch us down a little bit."

Abe pitches the plane down, but it goes the wrong way, almost clipping the other plane. They are cockpit window to cockpit window. The fighter jet is right in front of the mega cargo aircraft. The pilot thinks that Abe is fooling around.

Cargo Pilot

"Whatttttt issssssss he doing?"

From the view of the Cargo Cockpit they can see that Abe is pointing up in direction that they need to drop behind a certain number of feet in order to get back into full consciousness. Otherwise if they continue to fly, they will possibly pass out until they die, which will be a smooth death. But the plane will continue to fly until they run out of fuel.

Abe

"Radar, how long have they been flying? Have they refueled?"

The guys in the radar room are talking to each other to get the reports and the amount of fuel that the plan holds.

Abe

"We would pump a bit of our A28 water in there, but your planes aren't fitted for them."

Radar

"Squid, they only have about 100 miles of fuel left."

Abe takes a deep breath. Realizing that they only have a few more minutes until they large aircraft runs out of fuel. They aren't responding to any of his actions. They think he is kidding.

Abe

"We are flying into a headwind. We are going west. They are zooming this thing too. This fuel is going to go any minute now. And they aren't responding."

Abe begins to point upward

Jason

"Abe, make sure they understand that your pointing down."

Since they are inverted, Abe needs to be sure to point his finger in the right place, as he wasn't before.

Abe

"Shit, my fault."

As the time moves by, it's getting closer to the time that the pilots need to catch themselves. A few more minutes of hypoxia they will go unconscious.

Captain Tile

"AX1 you guys need to report back to base. Your mission is over. We will be fine."

Jason

"That's a negative Captain. We aren't going to leave them here alone. Your guys have hypoxia! Do you get it!"

Captain Title

"That's an order...my men don't need your help!"

The men in the radar room are silent as they realize that their captain is not thinking rationally.

Captain Title

"We will get the proper personnel for this. Retract AX1."

Abe (ignoring the captain)

"All right Jason, we need to release some flares. 3. 2 1. I'm going to go horizontal so none get into their turbines."

Abe shoots the fireworks looking flares out of the bottom of the aircraft. They are usually used as defense, but in this case, he is trying to get the attention of the pilots who are thinking with half of their brain. After a few attempts it doesn't work. Abe looks to the left and sees his wing mates flying near by

Abe

"Telda, Love, and Rory you guys can head back."

Rory

"Are you sure?"

Abe

"That's affirmative. Go back. We got this. Jason, we are going to have to get close."

The airplane is down to lower levels of fuel. Abe only has a few more minutes, and they both are approaching the city. Abe is trying everything that he can do to tell the pilots that they are suffering from hypoxia.

Abe

"C-1. Can you copy me?"

Cargo Pilot

"Sirrrr weee dooo. Whatsss gooinnnngg on?"

His voice is slurry, and deep, it sounds like it has been chopped and screwed.

Abe

"You need to drop. I'm not sure that you understand what's going on."

Jason

"Abe, he doesn't understand. Just give him numbers. That will register."

Abe

"Olympia Cargo One. Immediately drop to 12,000."

Cargo One

"Footer what? Wee are heaadeddd to base right?"

The pilots still don't understand what is really going on.

Jason

"Fuck, we are getting closer to the city area. We can't have that aircraft crash into any skyscrapers."

Abe

"Cargo one. You need to respond ASAP."

Abe turns his plane swiftly towards them.

Jason

"Do they have an Anti Missile on them?"

Abe

"Not sure. Radar, did you copy that?"

Radar

"Sir that is affirmative. It is an automatic missile avoidance system. The plane will drop immediately or turn against any missile on radar."

The red lights inside the cockpit of the Cargo jet begin to go off. The pilots are almost passed out and aren't aware of what is occurring.

Abe

"Jason, we got to get them down. What you got?"

Jason

"Well, we can throw off the systems GPS. That will probably take them off course, especially since they are on autopilot."

Abe

"We have to do something. We can't let them go out this way, and we have a matter of seconds."

Jason

"Let's just be safe and try to talk to them over the frequency."

Abe

"Cargo one, you have hypoxia sir. You need to reduce altitude immediately. You have hypoxia, not me. Not anybody else. You have hypoxia. Decrease altitude."

The pilot finally gets the hint. Problem is, it is too late. The plane is flying on fuel reserves.

Cargo Pilot

"Rooooogggggggeeeeeerrrr Deeecreeeassiinnng.."

As they decrease, the minutes tick down and Abe stays to the left of their airplane.

Abe

"Cargo, how is your fuel looking?"

The pilot's voices slowly start to sound normal again.

Cargo Pilot

"Wee are beloww our fuel reserve. Weee won't make it."

Abe

"Just keep decreasing altitude."

Jason looks at his GPS monitors, for empty areas. Most are mountains, but they have to get over the cliffs. If they can make it over the cliff, then they have a good chance of landing in a desert area although it will be a crash landing.

Jason

"Radar, Cargo one needs to turn 017. They are not going to make it. This is going to be a crash landing."

Radar

"Cargo one, did you copy?"

Cargo Pilot

"That's affirm… How, How, How long have we been out of it?"

Radar

"For a while now. How many miles to empty?"

Cargo Pilot

"We're rolling on fumes now. If we can get over that mountain we should be okay."

Jason

"Radar, it is a C17 so they should be able to reverse in the dirt."

Radar

"Copy. The issue is, if they lose power they can't reverse, and the only alternate runway that I have for them is 80 miles west."

Cargo Pilot

"Yeah, we can't go that way. Were just gonna have to test our luck."

Abe

"No, it isn't luck. You're skilled; you're going to do this."

The word lucky isn't in Abe's vocabulary. It's something that he got from Charles. Normally this Cargo aircraft can land on any dirt fields in short conditions. But, difficulties occur when fuel is lost, which means they will lose power. In turn, they will lose all hydraulics of the aircraft and they won't have control. It can be a pilot's nightmare.

Cargo Pilot

"Command we are extreme mayday now. We are gliding, and over this mountain, there is not enough stretch of land. Permission to aim and ditch, we have our chutes on. We are planning to open the bay so we can jump out."

The radar controller gets permission from Captain Title. He approves. As the pilots aim the plane so it can clear the mountains. They all begin to suit up w their parachutes.

Jason

"Cargo one, don't let that back bay down too fast. It will increase your drag and slow you down. You won't make it. Have the right timing, sir."

Cargo Pilot

"Roger."

In the radar room everybody is silent. A situation like this shouldn't happen during a training exercise. If the crew doesn't get out of the aircraft in time, they will be doomed. Nonetheless, they also have to get the plane over the mountain. Jumping too soon, will give them a hard time being rescued, and they can glide right into the mountain and be killed.

272

As three of the aircrafts four engines go out, the plane begins to glide. The pilot has to try to keep the plane manually level, but this is hard without full power. He pulls the flaps in, so it can maintain its speed. The whole crew of four is rushing to put their parachute vest on.

Cargo Plane Captain

"Guys, I'm going to set the back down. You guys go! I have to keep this leveled."

The second cargo pilot responds.

Cargo Pilot 2

"No, Jesse, just come on."

Cargo Pilot Captain

"Just go to the back, as Crew Chief that's an order. Save your life first."

As the Captain tries to control the plane, he lifts the back of the cargo bay open. The crew members look at him. They don't want to leave him, but they also know that somebody needs to control the aircraft to keep them leveled while jumping.

The airmen jump and soar into the sky. Some of them look up to see if Jesse, the captain is going to eventually jump. As they glide in the air, they notice that the plane gets over the mountains, which gives them hope that Jesse can jump out.

Jesse lets go of the yoke of the aircraft, hoping to gee out before it is too late. He runs to the side of the cargo bay of the aircraft and grabs a parachute. He heads towards the back of the plane, which is still open. Before he is able to reach the back on the plane, he can feel gravity pulling him back to the front. He knows the plane is nosediving. This in turn pulls him down with it, and against gravity, he can't make it out.

The pilots who jumped out wait to see if Jesse's parachute is going to show up. It doesn't. All they see is the cargo aircraft slowly rumble into an explosion. Right into the sand. The flames can be felt, but it is not worse than the inner pain that the men receive from witnessing it. They hold on to their parachutes and try to hover near the plane. They avoid getting too close, as it will result in a burned parachute. Once they land, Abe notices that one of the guys looks up and finds Abe. He then takes his dog tag off, and throws it near the blaze and angles his chute another way. They are distraught. Abe and Jason see it, and it is bad. The radar room knows also, as the radar circle of "Olympian Cargo One" disappears off of the monitor. It is bittersweet as three men were saved, but one won't be going home. His memories will be going home, because there is a good chance that he was evaporated immediately.

Abe and Jason look down, and stay above the cargo one personnel. Until they talk to radar and find out that they are okay.

Abe

"Red Ice Radar. It looks like you got three that came out. How many were on board?"

Radar

"Four, sir."

Abe

"I don't have a visual on four, only three."

Radar

"Yes, sir. We are aware. We believe the captain was inside."

Abe takes a deep breath.

Abe

"We're going to stay with them until you guys get rescue out here."

Radar

"You don't have to sir, but if you do that is very loyal of you. Thanks for your efforts to help."

Abe

"Isn't this why we train together? We are two different countries, but we fly in the same world. We are still one. Well, we should be."

Captain Title walks out of the room.

Abe and Jason circle above the three men as they sit in the dirt. Abe can see them walking towards the plane once they landed with their parachutes, but they are still very far. He looks at them, Telda comes over the frequency.

Telda

"Squid, you okay?"

Abe

"Yeah, just deep. Question is, are you guys okay?"

Telda

"Okay, we are pulling back to base now. You want me to come…"

Abe (interrupts)

"Babe, just handle the guys and do whatever paperwork that they need. O'Donnell should be down there waiting. Have maintenance check the A28 levers and fuel systems. We don't want just any water sitting overnight."

Telda stops for a second as she realizes Abe has called her babe over the radio. Nobody else paid attention to it, but she did. She also liked it, as usual. This time she accepted it. She has grown even more close to Abe. In return, she is the first over frequency to ask Abe if he was okay. She informs AX1's mission control what occurred and they congratulate them on a good job done, as they were nearly flawless on all of their missions. Despite Captain Title trying to mix it up and give them the impossible.

As the rescue helicopter pulls up towards the Cargo Plane crew, Abe and Jason hustle back to base. They land and begin to taxi, only to see a strange sight. Terry Love, Rory, and Telda are all standing next to a group of Military Soldiers, who are in front of their planes.

Abe

"Jason, what's going on over there? Some kind of ceremony for the incident? Respect exchange?"

Jason takes his visor off and looks. Memories of his pays Olympia Air Force days come back. He knows exactly what's going on.

Jason

"No. No. No."

Abe

"No. No. No. What?"

They look as they pull closer, and see that the guys in Olympia military uniforms are guarding Paragon's F22's. You can see Rory trying to push one of the guards, in attempt to get to his airplane.

Abe pulls up as he is guided in by the Marshall with the orange sticks and lifts up the cockpit window. He hears Rory talking to them.

Rory

"I need to get my log sheet. It fell off of my leg."

Five Olympian Military Officials are standing boldly in front of Paragon's aircraft with M16 Machine Guns held across their chest.

Olympian Military Official

"Sir, you can take it up with your Commander. I'm just doing my job."

Rory

"So what? You step in front of my Aircraft with a big gun. I don't give a fuck about that gun..."

Rory begins pushing through the guard and tries to get in the airplane.

Rory (Pushing through as guards push back)

"If you gonna shoot me then shoot me, punk! I got my shit in there."

Abe and Jason jump out of the plane, only to find two more officers in from of him with the same guns, and same uniforms.

Military Officer

"Sir, leave your items on the ground, right here. That's an order."

Jason looks at the young military officer.

Jason (reaching into his pocket)

"Who the fuck are you?"

The guys draw their guns to Jason's head. Jason puts his hands up...

Jason

"Really? You guys are not doing this right now? We just saved a few of your men? What is this about? The crash?"

Military Officer

"Sir, I'm just doing my job. But you need to either remain still, or walk away from the aircraft under my escort."

Jason

"Your escort? Son, I have been in Olympia's force for..."

The soldier puts his gun up to Jason's lips. Jason cuts his eyes to the side. He can see Rory being restrained. Abe is keeping his cool. Telda is being walked into the hangar area. Abe sees her and tries to call her name. The officer stops him from talking.

Military Officers

"You guys are making this harder than what it is?"

Abe

"I'm not making shit harder; I don't know what this is."

Captain Title walks behind Abe and pushes him in the back, almost making him fall.

Captain Title

"Abe Dalton. Abe Dalton. The son of Charles and umm I forgot her name. Remind me."

Abe gives him a cold look in his eye, as he knows that he is talking about his mother.

Captain Title

"You guys think you're gonna come here and show your fancy pants, huh? Well, you guys broke some rules."

Captain Title's voice can be intimidating to many.

Abe

"What, by saving your men?"

Captain Title

"Look BOY... Those men saved themselves."

Abe's head squints and turns sideways.

Abe

"We risked our asses for them, and this bullshit mission. I don't know what you got against me. I've moved across the world, and you still have an issue with me. What do you want?!"

Captain Title whispers in Abe's ear.

Captain Title

"Tell your daddy to stop playing with commodities."

He punches Abe. It's not a soft one either as he is a strong man, though he's is in early fifties. He says the word boy as if he is from the South. His southern accent comes out.

He gives Abe a smack to the face. Abe can't defend himself as he is being held by the Olympian guard. His lip is bleeding...

Captain Title

"You're under our soil now, and you ain't flying out of here either, Boy." `

Jason (intervenes)

"What are you talking about?"

Captain Title looks over at Jason and lasers his deceiving eyes at him.

Captain Title

"Oh, the traitor wants to start talking now huh? ... Oh, you're gonna be talking later for sure."

Title looks at his other officers.

Captain Title

"Take him to the hole. These boys are behind enemy lines. Red Ice officially ended two hours ago. They shouldn't be in Olympian territory."

Jason knows what the hole is. Though many are different, he knows that it means that Title wants to seek some information from him, more than likely about Paragon. Abe, Rory, and Terry Love are now all handcuffed, and the AX1 F-22's are being pushed back into a hangar with the doors closing behind them. The men are clueless to what is going on. Jason knows Title; he knows that he is not too fond of Charles Dalton. He also knows that he has racist spirit in his blood. Jason being the same race as Captain Title feels like he has the right to pull this out of Title.

Jason, as he is led away.

"Captain. You start to see much change in the world, and you lose your mind? If you stop taking that mineral you won't have to suffer with seeing diversity. You were born during slavery. Get the picture, it's over. It's a new life."

Many of the Olympian forces look as Jason is being walked away. They wonder what he is talking about. They think he is delusional, because he is talking about Captain Title being born in the early 1900's. But they know that isn't possible because that will make him over a hundred years old when he is clearly in his fifties.

Captain Title stares at Jason, and walks away. Abe is also escorted away and stays quiet. He also looks at Captain Title and spits the blood that is accumulating from his lip onto the ground, into his direction. Abe knows he needs to be quiet because being loud will get him into trouble and his crew will base most of their emotions from his actions. He looks over at Terry Love, he has tears in his eyes, and his hands are behind his back. Abe shakes his head at him, telling him to stay quiet. Abe looks over at Telda, who is now on the ground being handcuffed.

The rest of the AX1 squadron are also tied by their legs, inside Olympian military wagons.

As they are being escorted off in military vehicles into a private part of the base. AX1 realizes that they are the only crew still there. During the Red Ice Operation there were over 60 fighter jets from over 10 different countries on the base. Now, it is just the Olympian fighters and Paragon's fighters. The moment is calm. The thrill of their achievement of the day was marked off by a death. Not one of their team members, but of their ally. Followed by unforeseen military arrests and custody for no actual reasoning. Other Olympian units look on as they drive past in vehicles. Abe's head rests on the window. It's a moment of embarrassment. However, the looks on many of Olympian Airmen's eyes are more so of wonder. As if they don't know what is going on.

Abe plays one of Captain O'Donnell's quotes in his mind

Captain O'Donnell

*Squid, be smart, and be smarter. Stay alive -
LOYALTY ALWAYS WINS WHEN IT IS AWARDED.
Especially to a person who hasn't gotten much of it.*

Abe keeps his mouth shut, and speaks to his wing-mates with his eyes. Mostly relaxed, but the look more says, "It's going to be okay." Even though he has no clue what they are in store for. He is the leader, and leaders don't just lead through the cool moments.

14

Trust

Unaware of the terrible events occurring at Operation Red Ice, Charles is still talking to Choi. This is the month of the U.W approval, but Charles is wondering why Choi, his mentor, is holding back on what's really going on.

Charles

"Choi, Van Luke is your best friend. There should be no reason why you can't explain, or give me some kind of info towards this approval."

Rob Van Luke is the current leader of the United Worlds. He took over after Choi stepped down to focus on his family. Van Luke is from Austral, which is on the southernmost hemisphere of the earth. About six hours east of Paragon.

Choi softly sets his rose gold tableware down. Wipes his hands with his towel. He looks up at Ruth. She knows this look. Ruth also knows a bit that goes on with Choi, Paragon, and the United Worlds. Although she doesn't know everything, as many talks are sensitive. Nonetheless, most of the time confidential info is the wife's business anyway. Wives somehow become an outlet for their husbands. It also is the same vice versa. Ruth gets up quietly and walks out of the room, as if she doesn't know what's going on.

Choi begins to speak.

Choi

"It's a tough call, Charles. The worlds emotionally love Paragon, but many of the backers want to get their hands on the A28. They don't want the country to be allied until you give them a portion of the revenues. Olympia doesn't like it. The Middle East and Asiana are in between. Though the majority wants to vote you in. Olympia has significant influence on many of them. Not only because of whom they are, but the stock markets and financial systems watch their every move. Voting you in can result in a lower amount of leverage for them. You know they don't want that."

Charles

"Choi, I give their people opportunity. They have money from government contracts. Heck, they even get some of the profits of business that is conducted in Paragon."

Choi

"Understood, but A28 is not theirs. It's not their money touching their hands. The value proposition to their little secret society, especially after their recession, is to have a product in their hands. That is without being the middleman. At the end of the day, everyone wants to have a piece of the pie, and will stop at nothing to get it. I'm assuming you know what some countries will do to get what they want."

Charles

"So what are you saying?"

Choi

"If you don't hand over a good number of A28 soon, you can be in some trouble. Getting accepted into the U.W will be the least of your worries."

Charles

"I spoke to Grover about it yesterday. He's ready for it. We have worked something out, between me and him."

Choi

"You should know this by now. He doesn't call the shots. He is just the lead man. The face of the state. It's the guys with the money. The relationships. Those guys, along with the House and Congress are who control the World. The president is just one man Charles, not the front of the operation. His administration can have power, but it's not just him. Word is that many Olympians aren't too fond of Paragon. Nor with Jacob Grover. So you already have two strikes against you."

Charles is sitting back, tapping his fingers on Choi's table. He notices that the table has water in it, and it bubbles up to keep the plates warm while you eat. However, the water is only on the inside of the table. Choi invented it; he had too many issues with people burning their elbows. It's not the best feeling.

Choi

"They say you have nuclear activity going on. What's that about? Defense?"

Charles

"I think everybody has nuclear weapons in the world. They are the last ones to fuss about nukes in the world. I have none. I have something better than that, just not deadly. Just no nukes."

They lock eyes, as Charles takes a small bite. He looks at Choi.

Charles

"Not yet at least."

Choi

"None?"

Charles

"None...."

Choi

"What's with the Olympian pilot going down, unreported?"

Choi knows almost everything, even if Charles doesn't tell him.

Charles

"We didn't know that he was an Olympian pilot. I thought that it was my son who was blown up in that incident. We were doing silo testing for the A28 camp site and the plane came out of nowhere. The silos sense heat and fly under radar. We were not notified. A plane did get hit. But the pilot ejected. We thought he was dead, and nobody ever said or knew who it was. A month later we found him in our swamps camouflaged in moss and other chemical compounds."

Choi

"They aren't taking that lightly."

Charles

"Choi, they don't take anything I do lightly."

A moment goes by.

Charles

"You have to knock this out for me, Choi. It's been 9 years, and I won't wait 10 more. I can wait, but I won't."

Choi

"Just watch your back. The panel meets tomorrow. I won't be in there, but watch for who is there and who isn't. You are right there. You are very close."

Choi

"The next few days you may need to lay low."

When Charles looks to respond, they hear a knock on the door.

Charles

"Oh, that must be President Grover."

Choi

"Oh. Why is he here?"

Charles

"I figured that I'd surprise you."

Choi

"Chuck! I would have changed my clothes. My goodness. You can't just bring the President of Olympia over unannounced. I hope his security doesn't have to come in and strip my house down."

Choi leaves the table and calls Ruth downstairs. As he walks towards the front of his home, he wipes his hands clean, then opens the door.

Five masked men with guns walk into the kitchen and draw their guns. They wear tactical suits, as if they are an organized military unit.

Masked Man

"Back up, shut your mouth. If you scream, you die."

He puts his assault rifle up to Choi's forehead. Choi is stunned. He begins to walk backwards. With the gun backs up with the man's gun at his head, he falls down over shoes that are on the door. Ruth comes down.

Ruth

"Hon, is everything? Oh my!"

She freezes as another one of the tactical guys points the gun at her and tells her to get down using hand signals. Charles hears the noise, and he comes out of the kitchen.

Masked Man One

"Get down now."

He touches the radio on his ear.

Masked Man One

"Lead 1 has been found, in my arms. It's Dalton."

The masked man grabs Charles and zip ties his hands and his feet.

All that is heard are footsteps and men talking on radios. Charles, Choi, and Ruth are all on the ground tied up, with duct tape on their mouth. One of the masked men walks past and talks over his ear radio.

Masked Man Two

"All is clear. Bring him in."

Not knowing what to expect, Charles looks at Choi, but they can't speak to each other. They can hear the men who are talking get closer and the footsteps get closer. The voice registers in all of their ears. They know who it is. It's President Grover.

Jacob (walks in with agents)

"You know that flight wasn't as long from Paragon as I thought. In fact, it was rather smooth, well besides Gary getting ill."

Grover walks in the door, only to see Charles, Choi, and Ruth on the floor. He looks at Charles's eyes with a deep stare. By the time he can say a word, one of the masked men gives Jacob a quick shock to the back with a taser, sending him to the ground.

Once they get Jacob down and have him tied, they all take their masks off. The first man is a guy that Charles has recognized in Paragon. The second is unknown. The third is Gary. The fourth man is the assistant to Bob Polan, the Olympian Secretary of Defense.

Charles is tied. President Grover is face down on the living room area rug. He is shaking and shivering to the after effects of having the instant volts going through his system.

Gary

"Steve, is Hostile A secure?"

Steve

"Yes, sir. AX-1 are grounded and won't be going anywhere soon. We plan to drop them in the Pacifica Ocean in about 30 minutes."

Gary walks over and puts his foot on Charles's back.

Gary

"Do you have Little Dalton? We need him, because Daddy loves his little boy doesn't he?"

He bends down towards Charles, and tickles with his ear

Gary (whispers in his ear)

"You should have handed A28 over. All we wanted was a piece of it! You greedy son of a..."

Charles tries to respond, but his words are trapped since his mouth is taped. Gary kicks him in the stomach. This is not what one would expect from Jacob's nerdy chubby advisor.

Gary

"What did you say?"

Gary looks around and walks over to the television monitor, cuts it on. He looks at the remote and flicks the channels until he can find a news station. He finds one. He turns the volume up just enough for everybody to hear.

Gary (looking at Charles)

"You said you have nuclear bombs, right?"

Gary points at the TV and Charles looks, but he can barely see.

Gary points to one of the guards.

"Get Dalton up, so he can see this."

The guard lifts Charles up roughly and puts his back to Choi's wall. The TV screen shows Olympian news clips showcasing Paragon and then thermal imagery of mountains in Paragon with cars moving around. On the bottom it says,

"Nuclear Weapons in Paragon. Security is on High Alert. Secretary of Defense Notified".

Chills run down Charles's spine, as he the news anchor delivers the news.

Gary (looking at Charles)

"And this is the icing on the cake."

He pulls out his Phone and dials a number.

Gary

"Hi, this is Gary Dusette. -- Yes, that's me. President Grover's advisor. ---- We have a situation. The President secretly went to Paragon. We have four agents who have died trying to save him. He isn't answering his calls. I am not sure what's going on, but too much is happening. I think he went to confront Charles Dalton face to face about the nuclear situation. I'm guessing it didn't go well. Nobody can find him."

Gary pauses as the Olympia Authorities speak to him

Gary

"I am fine. I am in Europa at the moment. I was waiting on Jacob at my hotel, but he never showed up. Then I got a call from his security detail on what occurred in Paragon."

Gary hangs up the phone. Looks at Charles, then glances at Ruth and Choi. He tells his guards to get them up as well.

Gary

"You know, communication is very important these days. Now watch how fast those few words get on the air. It's like a rumor spreading in high school. Remember those days?"

Right when Gary finishes his sentence the news breaks.

News Reporter

"We have breaking News. President Grover is believed to be under threat in Paragon. It is not confirmed, but a source has stated to us that his personal advisor has just called in. More to come soon."

The world is shocked, especially the citizens of Olympia. They are all glued to their television as they have no clue what is going on, with the possibility of their President being assassinated. In turn, the nation that was mentioned to assassinate Grover may have nuclear weapons. People are on social networks talking about it. The next wave of news come on the TV screen.

"Olympia Fighter Jets en route to Paragon."

Charles looks at Choi and Ruth and realize that the worst thing that can happen is about to happen. Paragon and its people are about to be under attack.

Gary

"Fast, huh? Let me show you something cooler than that."

Gary picks up the phone and dials another number. He puts it on speaker phone. He calls a Paragon Communications Official named Katie.

Katie picks up the phone,

"Hey, Gary, what's going on? Did you guys make it to Europa? I hope you're feeling better also."

Gary

"Oh yeah, we did. How is everything there?"

Katie

"It's, well, just another day in paradise. Did that insulin that we gave you help?"

Katie helped Gary get to Europa, her office also made sure that he got his insulin.

Gary

"You got that right, but listen. Are there any issues going on over there? Any media crises on the internet, on television?"

Katie

"Ummm, not to my knowledge, but I can look."

Gary

"Please do."

Gary begins to pace as he waits for Katie to check. She browses a few TV stations and internet sites.

Katie

"Nope, nothing much. Today is a slow day; it is "Take your kids to work day." My daughter is right here, would you like to speak to her?"

Gary hangs up the phone. Katie, thinking that he is still one the phone grabs her daughters hand so she can talk to the President's advisor. Her daughter grabs the phone.

Katie's Daughter

"Hello."

She gets no response.

Katie's Daughter

"Mommy, nobody is on the phone."

Katie grabs the phone and checks if Gary is still on the line. She realizes that he isn't. He is on the phone with Gil.

Gary

"Go on with the operation. Let's do this right."

Gil

"Commencement."

Gil, sitting in a private room with multiple screens on the walls, presses a button on her laptop. Katie is trying to dial Gary back, thinking that she lost connection. Then there is a loud bang on the walls, the windows erupt with flames and sheared glass.

In Choi's house, Gary looks at Charles, making sure that he hears everything. Charles begins to move around, but he can't do anything as he is helpless. Katie is blown away from her seat, her daughter's face is covered with flames from the bomb. The solar glass rips the interior of the office building. The glass seeps into their eyes, and skin. By the time they feel it, they are dead. Along with the other workers in the office. Others notice the bomb that has just hit one of Paragon's top corporate buildings, which is also one of the central headquarters for the management of the country. Red alerts are going out; the automatic sprinklers are going off. Paragon is being attacked.

More bombs hit the strip of downtown buildings, hitting them one by one, hitting the streets. People with pod vehicles are knocked around from the impact of the bombs.

Paragon's Air Force is notified about the bombing through their alert system. Since AX-1 is in Olympia for Red Ice, the reserve unit - BX-1 will have to take force. Since Olympia has a joint base they should be able to assist in case of emergency. The pilots are running to their aircraft. They begin to start up to defend their land. As the units get strapped in most of the airmen look around. They notice that there aren't any Olympia aircraft on the ground, as there are always at least two fighter jets. By the time the reserve unit can get the planes on to the taxiway, fighter jets and helicopters come in and blow them away. It's a fury; a raging invasion. Bodies are everywhere; steel parts, glass, and smoke fill the once beautiful jet strip. Paragon's main air force base is destroyed. All Paragon owned aircraft, are all on fire.

Gary

"Boom. Now watch this."

Another news headline shows up on the television screen.

Missiles strike Paragon.

Charles begins to squirm and attempt to get out as he watches his country get bombed. The land that was nothing at one point. Until he put his ambition and sacrifice into it. Gary gives another kick to Charles's ribs. The nightmare is alive. Paragon is under siege. Skyscrapers are being shot at, the towers, vertical farms. Cows and other animals are in the street piece by piece. Limb by limb, after falling forty stories.

Gary

"Chuck, what kind of leader does a truce without a true alliance? Guess you have to learn the hard way, Rookie."

Gary's black tactical team keep their eyes on Jacob, Choi, Ruth, and Charles. Jacob begins to wake up and slowly start moving. He looks up; sees Gary and doesn't know what to think. He sees the TV screen and the reporter announcing that the Olympian President is under hostage, last seen in Paragon.

Gary

"Jake the Snake. How many people get to watch their own death? You watched your wife Cindy's, so this shouldn't be as bad."

An evil side has come out of Gary. He's fuming, his words are endless. Charles and Choi look up at him from the floor. Even more surprised at what they just heard about Jacob's deceased spouse, Cindy.

Gary

"You really think I was cut out to be a damn assistant!"

Gary kicks the side of Jacob's face, creating a large gash on his cheek.

Gary

"You're lucky I'm giving you the privilege to enjoy this. I should have ended your life an hour ago."

Paragon as a whole is a mess. The reserve fighter unit can't get a plane off the ground, since the air strip has been bombed. The AX-1 squadron is immobilized in Olympia. The nearby neighbors (Emirate) can do nothing, because most of them are allies with Olympia.

While all the chaos is going on in Choi's house, Andy, Bin, Lisa, and Anthony are attempting to evacuate a building that was struck by an air missile. It's the same building that they have been staying at during their visit.

Andy

"Hurry up! Just get in!"

Andy pulls them to an elevator, that is shaped like a pod. It's everybody, Lisa, Tommy, Andy, Eddie, Bin, and Anthony. All of them barely fitting inside of the elevator pod.

Bin

"Where are we going? I'm not getting in there."

Andy

"Just get in, or else your going be cremated in there."

Anthony, not having time to risk any lives, uses his long and strong arms to pull Bin inside the elevator.

Once everybody is in, Andy presses a orange button on the elevator. On the screen display "Safe Haven" pops up. He puts his key-code in.

Computerized Female Voice

"Begin unlock sequence to safe haven. Please get secured."

Andy

"Hurry up guys, put your feet on the floor marks! Keep your back to the wall!"

They all look down and see the yellow marks on the floor, which are shaped like the sole of a shoe. Anthony has to bend down, since he is so tall. The elevator pod drops swiftly. Shoulder harnesses come from the inside of the walls and strap them in. The elevator pod drops like a roller coaster. Not an easy feeling. As they go, they realize that the building is in bad shape. The pod gets stuck. It reverses on its own then pushes, it reverses again on its own then it pushes again. It's jammed with a piece of metal that was shifted from the impact of the bomb. They can't move. The escape pod tries a few more times. They can hear it slamming into the metal, breaking the pieces in its way. As the pods titanium frame slams hard onto the track it finally breaks through. It was built to only stop when it reaches its designated point. All while reaching speeds of over 100 miles per hour.

Andy

"I hope nothing is collapsed on the way!"

Bin

"Where are we going?"

Andy screams over the winds from outside the pod.

Andy

"The Safe Haven! It's a bunker in case of situations like this!"

Tommy, Lisa, Bin, Eddie, and Anthony are all in shock. In Paradise, enjoying the world's newest country. This is the last place they expected for a bombing to occur. They got comfortable. They were enjoying the sights, and now they are fuming in a pod going to a secret bunker. As they slow down, and the pod raises upright, they look out the mini window. They can see that they are in a forest area, but they also see a large dark cloud. Which are the buildings that once used to be a sight to see. They see airplanes circling around, like hawks searching for prey.

Looking miles away from a catastrophe, they would probably still be in the middle of it. If it weren't for Andy, who just happened to be with them in the main tower, they would probably be dead. Andy was giving them a tour of the facilities, since this was only their third day in the territory.

When Andy heard the bomb, he directed them all to one of Charles's personal Escape Pod. One goes to his home. One goes out into a tunnel in the ocean, and the other is the one that got them to the Safe Haven in minutes, as it is powered by wind and water going over a hundred miles an hour.

They arrive at the Safe Haven Bunker. The escape pod lifts into a secure station, where there are another 30 or so pods parked. They are exactly alike. Andy sees this and feels some kind of relief, as this means that many of the leaders were able to get into their escape pods so they could get to the Safe Haven which is an emergency bunker and battle headquarters, built exclusively for situations like this. The escape pod door opens and Andy leads the way, with Tommy following in the back. This time he is armed and has a serious look to his face. The two security guards who were with them are not there anymore, as they went to get lunch before the disaster struck.

Andy has his lab coat on, and he sees many military people and others in street clothes walking around swiftly. Jim, the head of the military unit, walks to Andy. He grabs Andy shoulder.

Jim

"Hey, glad you made it. Have you spoken to Charles yet? He's nowhere to be found."

Andy

"No, but he is in Europa. I believe with Grover."

Jim

"Yeah, I heard. Heard some shit about him having Grover hostage here. He's not even in the damn country."

Andy

"I know. What's going on? What is this entire ruckus?"

Jim begins to walk, Andy follows. Anthony and everybody else also follow behind. Lisa is scared. Bin is amazed at the Safe Haven. Eddie is relaxed and just hopes everybody is okay. Anthony is reaching out helping others, although many of them are looking at him twice because they recognize him as the world's best basketball player even though it is a crisis.

Jim

"Andy, it's Olympia. They got us. They have blocked off our network. They are claiming we have nuclear of some kind and some other bullshit about Charles having Grover hostage."

Andy

"That's bull crap! Where is your crew?"

Jim gives him a blank look. He doesn't respond. He can't respond.

Andy

"Where are our fighters? Where is our defense?"

A support worker comes up to Jim and gives him papers. Jim puts his glasses on to read the papers. Once he is done he responds to Andy's question.

Jim

"Our reserve unit, BX-1 got taken out before the first strike. I even had three guys in the sky. But I don't have any contact with them either. AX-1 is gone. Captain O'Donnell is in the command room, trying to get our neighbors to help. But none of them want to create any bad blood with Olympia, plus help can take days. So it's just us right now."

Jim is calm. Andy looks at him, being hot tempered, Andy reacts.

Andy

"Then what are you doing? We should be counter attacking with something. You know this is a setup."

Jim

"Stay in your lane! I know what I'm doing! I have lost 55 men in a matter of seconds and most of my troops in every sector have guns to their head. Enjoy the safety, or else take your ass out there in the war zone! Olympia has taken over our country. There is no defense. Our helicopter units are all unarmed and secured by Olympia authorities, same goes with our ground troops and police."

Andy

"Jim, call Emirate, Asiana, they are our friends."

Jim

"We have no friends! Olympia was based with us. They slept with us, and now they are fucking us. Our friends, or allies, aren't going to go up against them! You really think they want to ignite a conflict with that country? Olympia may be falling economically but they are still one of the most powerful, if not the most powerful armed force in the world! It's not that simple, Andy! Right now at this point we are screwed! Our teammate has screwed us! President Grover came in unannounced and Charles is with him. The news worldwide is broadcasting this crap."

Andy

"Jim. I'm stepping back. You were the admiral of the Navy during one of the longest wars in recent history. I'll stick with my animals, and stay in my lane. We either do something, or we just give up here!"

Andy walks away. Jim is looking at the monitors on the wall. He is scanning the destruction of Paragon, how Olympia is slowly moving troops in. They have helicopters surrounding all of Paragon's Sector Bases. None of the Paragon military guys in there were killed, but they are stuck. If any one of them moves out, the whole base will be destroyed by one of the helicopters that are on rotation. If it wasn't for the Safe Haven that can hold around 10,000 people, more people would have been in control by Olympia's force, or be somewhere getting shot by the Olympian troops.

Jim's experience is to remain patient and calm, just as Captain O'Donnell.

Jim continues to gaze over the mounted screens, and analyzes what's going on. There hasn't been any large strikes in the past hour, but he knows that there will be another wave. Especially since he knows Olympia is only attacking because of A28, and they won't kill everybody because they want to know where it is. They could possibly have enough intelligence to figure it out, but deep inside Jim knows they don't know. There are only a few people who know where it truly sits. A person needs more than a geo location to get to it. There are also a high number of pass codes, just to get through the tunnels. Unless a person has Charles' fingerprint, they will need to have particular overrides, and it takes more than one person to get that done. As the fierce look appears stronger in Jim's eyes, he realizes that he needs to be prepared for the worst.

He leans over to one of the support staff sitting at a computer, and gives them an order. Once Jim leans up, an announcement goes over the system.

Announcement

"Nick Du, report to Bravo 2."

Bravo 2 is the area that Jim is standing in the bunker. It's the main command room. There are three areas in the bunker. One being the main area, where there is medical staff, food and drink for citizens and Paragon troops. Two is the command center where Jim is now in. This area is where about 40 support folks are in control of communication in the bunker. Three is the warehouse where many necessary items are stored.

Seconds later, Nick Du walks up. He has brown hair, a button down shirt on, and a laptop in his hand.

Nick Du.

"Sir..."

Jim

"Nick, what is the status of the windmills? That project ready to go yet?"

The wind mills are the silos that shoot missiles; the ones that almost killed Abe, and hit Carter.

Nick

"Well, technically, yes, bureaucratically, no..."

Nick is one of Jim's Defense Engineers. He is very book smart, and is aware of everything that is going on with many of the defense systems of Paragon.

Jim

"Bureaucracy is over. Warm them up. Wait for me for engagement."

Nick

"Yes, sir. Will strike on command."

Jim is very settled when it comes to striking. Making it worse is when he has to strike his original homeland. So, he put his back against the wall.

Jim has one of the support workers turn on the monitor toward the silos which look like a windmill field. They surround the bunker, as it looks like it can be a farm. They also surround every military site in each sector. They power up. As they begin to move. The cameras show how the Olympia soldiers are looking at them, but totally are unaware that they launch missiles.

Jim sees Judy Ruiz, the defense lead for Paragon heading in his direction.

Jim

"Judy… Come here."

She walks over. With a sad look on her face and papers in her hand.

Jim

"Put those down."

Judy

"These are plans for counter strikes."

Jim

"Judy, put them down."

She puts the papers down.

Jim

"We are the last resort. We have no air strike. I'm going to try hold off. Who knows, maybe they will fall back once they realize they can't find the A28 or Grover. But if something happens, I'm executing. I don't know where our people will go from then, but that is the last resort."

Judy looks at Jim and seems like she isn't too happy with that response.

Before she can respond, a support worker calls Jim nearby.

Support

"Sir, we have a large aircraft on low approach heading right to us. They are here. It looks like it could possibly be a bomber. I can't pinpoint the type, because we haven't calibrated our systems to detect plane types yet. But it is definitely an Olympian aircraft. I can tell by the codes that it is sending to the radar."

Jim sinks. If that bomber drops bombs onto the Safe Haven everybody will die inside, and Paragon will lose their last powerful line of defense. That will leave Jim no choice but to release the missiles; knowing that that will make things worse. It will cause more Paragonian deaths. Olympia will react with heavier fire because even though they are in Paragon territory, they don't take retaliation well. If that happens, the Secretaries of Defense, Rob Polan will bring more troops over. The media will put it all over the news networks. It's a catch twenty-two.

While Jim is wondering what is going on. Lex, the battle coordinator for AX-1, walks in and goes straight to Jim.

Lex

"Chief... Chief..."

Jim turns around. Surprised to see her, as he thought she was on base.

Lex

"Chief, you have to be braced for what I am about to tell you."

I can **smell** a setup...

Waking up from his nap in the attic of Choi's house, Bill stretches his arms and gets out of the bed which he usually sleeps in. Ruth got the large bed exclusively for Bill, since he and Charles visit often. Wearing all black, he walks out of the bedroom to use the bathroom. Only to hear a person calling his name from the first floor.

Corrupt Tactical Guy

"Bill, is that you?"

Bill (voice still groggy from his nap)

"Yeah, who's that?"

Once Bill gets to the bathroom, the door opens. Bill looks in and see's one of Gary's corrupt guards, sitting on the toilet. He looks up at Bill. He tries to pull his pants up and get up but before he can reach for the gun that is sitting on the sink of the bathroom, Bill grabs it and points it to him. Bill shakes his head.

Bill

"Don't move. I'll shoot a portion of your brain off, and make sure you still survive. I'll turn you into a super vegetable."

This is the tactical side of Bill.

As the guard sits on the toilet with his hands up, he looks at Bill and notices at the tattoo on his arm. It is as sign of his Olympia military unit, a head of a Golden Eagle. The guard looks again.

Bill

"Take your shit, but don't move. Now tell me what the heck is going on? And how the hell do your guys downstairs know my name?"

The guard doesn't say anything to him. Bill moves the gun, as if he is going to shoot him. It startles the guard. Bill looks to his right and down the stairs of Choi's House. He can see that something strange is going on. He pulls his phone out of his pocket, checks the time, and holds the side button on it for five-seconds. He puts it back in his pocket.

Bill

"You better say something because if not, I'm just gonna kill you. If I don't, and somebody comes up here to bust a cap in my ass. I'm make sure that I bust one in yours. I'll make sure I put a bullet in that shit you're hovering over. You will be self-fertilized."

Once Bill's country voice stops, the toilet flushes.

Bill

"What the fuck. I said don't move."

Guard

"I didn't; it was the washer. I mean it's an auto flush."

As the toilet flushes, Bill can still hear something moving. He doesn't know what it is initially, but looking at the guard's reactions he realizes that it is one of those butt cleaners that nice hotels have, a bidet. The guards reaction seems awkward and uncomfortable because Bill is standing there holding a gun. All while he is doing the "number two".

Bill

"It feels good doesn't it? That bidet is cold at first, ain't it. I hate that part."

The guard is still quiet, surprised that Bill is making humor of the situation. Bill sees a decorative pillow on one of the chairs in Choi's hallway. He grabs it and puts it on top of the gun.

Bill

"Look, this gun isn't loud anyway. But, you better stop bullshitting and get to talking."

Guard (nervously)

"Downstairs. Downstairs. They... They..."

The guard still doesn't say what's going on. However, now the dryer portion of the cleaner begins to blow and dry his ass. The sounds are subtle, just like a hairdryer.

Bill

"Tell me, dammit!"

Bill puts the pillow on top of the gun, the guard squints again and tightens up. The guard is frightened.

Boup. The water drops

A turd comes out of his system. The guard is embarrassed. Not a situation that he ever dreamed of being in. Perspiration is building up on his forehead.

Boup. The water drops again.

Bill (crinkling his nose)

"I'll be damned..... You Nasty Muther Fucker. You are scared shitless."

Another drop of water occurs.

Bill

"Man, you ain't shit... I hope you enjoy it. Because you're about to die like you are on the throne..."

Bill looks to the right hallway, and sees that the guard set his machine gun down, along with a food dish.

Bill

"You're a dumb person. You got comfortable? Then you ate some of the man's food. After you invaded his house?"

Bill still keeps his distance.

Bill

"We gonna do this two ways. You're gonna tell me what's going on? And you may make it out of here alive, or you're not gonna tell me, and hope one of your boys downstairs. Who has my Chuck hostage, come up here and kill me. Which one is it? I'm not a damn fool. You quiet ass."

The guard looks down, realizing that Bill is Charles's main body guard.

Bill

"Well, I tried."

Bill holds the pillow over his gun to silence it. Walks up to the guard and shoots him in head. One of the guards downstairs shouts upstairs.

Guard

"Damn, Bill. You fuckin stink."

Grabbing the towel that's hanging on the wall, Bill catches the guy as he falls over. Bill makes sure that he's dead and lays him down softly, so he doesn't make any more sounds.

Bill looks around, takes a deep breath as he is rather heavy set. He sees the guard's mask, mobile phone, and cloth shooting gloves. Bill picks the gloves up.

Bill

"This boy was a trip. Shit..."

Bill looks back down at his dead body, which is laid out with his hand in an awkward position.

Bill (talking to the dead guard)

"You unprepared dumb ass. You dumb SHIT..."

Still looking at the dead guard.

Bill

"You didn't even think about being in a rich man's home. You idiot, Rich folks don't use no toilet paper in they house these days. They got ass cleaners. You should have kept your gloves on...... You shoulda learned from O.J."

Bill puts the gloves on, the mask and already wearing black so he blends in with the rest of Gary's tactical team. He looks at the toilet as it hasn't flushed a second time yet and he reaches in for a turd. He picks it up out of the water. He is now holding it. It's about 4 inches long, and light brown.

Bill (holding his nose with left hand)

"Whew! Good thing it's not loose. Boy must have been eating some good food."

He takes a few small steps outside to the hallway. Not too far so he can't be seen. Bill then throws the turd over the hallway rails. The shit splats right on top of a case on the floor. The perfect spot, as it will go unseen.

Bill

"That should do the job."

Bill walks away. Pulls one of the gloves off, walks back in the bathroom, and picks the guard up

Bill (as he sits him on the toilet)

"Alrighty, O.J, Let me move your stank ass up before you get too stiff."

Bill lifts the dead guard on the toilet, and positions him so he is balanced. Bill steps back to make sure the guard is positioned properly. He adjusts him a bit to left so he doesn't fall over. Bill is as humorous as he is dangerous; he grabs the pillow used to silence the gun and sets it behind the guard's head. To finish it off, he takes the glove that he used to toss the shit turd and places it in the guard's left hand...

Bill looks at the body.

Bill (his country accent)

"Lordy. Please forgive me fa all my sins. But that shalt have been done. He was evil."

He slowly walks back into the attic. Sits down on the mattress, and pulls the cartridge out of the guard's pistol and analyzes it. He begins to take it apart. He then pulls a gun out of his left lower leg, then a small one out of his pocket. Inside his jacket he has two other guns in his suspenders and a nighttime worth of ammo. He then gets up and goes into the duffle bag that he brings whenever he goes out in public with Charles. He opens it.

Bill

"Hey, Babies."

Inside, there are three small machine guns, a small missile launcher, a taser, and a flame-torch in case he needs to burn something or evidence.

After he loads all of his guns and makes sure that they are safe, he looks at his watch.

Bill

"Damn, I didn't think it would take this long."

Bill leans back on the bed, and begins to count down to himself.

Bill

"4, 3, 2, 1...ummm 4, 3, 2, and 1..."

He gets back up, sitting on the bed in anticipation. Looks at his watch.

Bill

"What the fuck, man."

What the heck is that **smell?**

Downstairs one of the guards realizes that there is an odor. All the men notice, as does Gary. Gary looks at one of the other guards, then at Charles. On the television, the news is showing the damage that has been done with Paragon, and that Grover hasn't been found yet. It also says that Charles Dalton is on the run. Gary looks down at both of them.

Gary (covering his nose)

"Did one of you guys shit yourself? I know you're scared, but my goodness..."

Another guard joins in.

Masked Guard 2

"Seriously, you guys smell like crap. Damn!"

Masked Guard 1

"No, guys. It is Bill. He's upstairs unloading one."

Masked Guard 3

"I told that guy he shouldn't have eaten so much."

Suddenly, guard 3 gets a bullet through the side of head.

Guard 2 is shot with another through the temple

Guard 1 is shot in the back of his neck.

Three bullets flew though the windows and the three guards downstairs sniped. They all fall to the floor. The glass has clean holes in them, but it happened so fast that the men fell to the ground simultaneously. Charles, Jacob, Choi and Ruth look up. Four more quick shots ring outside. Gary is frantic. He's expecting the other guards to help and return fire, but no fire is returned. He knows there is one more Guard upstairs, and he yells.

Gary

"Bill! Bill! We have shots fire outside!"

Gary leans down and drags Grover towards the stairwell so he can try to run up for better safety as he knows something is going down.

As Gary pulls, Jacob slowly wakes up from the taser shock. He looks up to Gary.

Jacob whispers,

"I trusted you."

Gary looks back down at him, still dragging him and walks closer to the steps.

Bill

"Gary, did you call me?"

Gary (still dragging Jacob, back turned)

"Yes, Bill. Bill. They are coming after us. Who gave them our location?"

Bill puts his gun to the back of Gary's head.

Bill

"Checks and Balances. Put him down before I blow your head off too."

Gary has no clue what's going on, but he knows the familiar voice. Bill grabs Gary's hands, and zip ties them together, and lets Gary fall on his back. He looks up at Bill who is standing right over him. Gary's eyes get big.

Gary innocently

"Bill. Yes, Bill. We've been held hostage. I knew you were up stairs. Thanks God!"

Bill

"Shut up. Don't thank God. You really think I'm going to buy your bull?"

Bill looks up at the shit turd that sits on the case next to a photo of Choi and Ruth. He finishes his sentence.

Bill

"Shit. You really think I'm going to buy your bull shit."

Bill steps over him and walks over to Charles. He rips off the tape that is across his mouth. Bill leans down and looks at him. Charles looks bad. He has been tied up for hours and he is exhausted from being in a confined position. Bill also looks at Grover, but doesn't untie him. As he only knows that he can trust Charles. He walks over to Jacob and takes the tape off the mouth.

Bill

"What is going on?"

Jacob (deep breath)

"I don't know. I came in, and they just…"

The doors bust open from both sides of the house. A group of British Seals swarm Choi's mansion.

British Seal

"Don't move! Hands Up!"

Bill puts his hands up.

British Seal

"Don't move!"

They cautiously walk up to Bill. The other seals move around the house. There are about fifteen of them.

British Seal

"We are in and have one secured. We have three code blues, and five alive, four code blues outside. No need for immediate medical. We should be secure in a few seconds."

Bill

"There's another code blue upstairs."

The seal looks at Bill and doesn't respond. They are not taking anybody for trust. Right now, all of them are an enemy. They tie Bill up, tie Charles back up, and untie Grover.

Bill looks as they untie Grover.

Bill

"I'm the one that called ya'll folks. Untie me too."

The seal looks at him, and doesn't trust him.

Bill

"Look, dammit! The alerter is in my right pocket. Why you think I'm not dead. I wasn't gonna bring my ass downstairs. By the way. Inside you got four blues, and five alive, you're not gonna kill me. You really do have a blue on the toilet though."

The seals look at each other. One comes down stairs and takes his mask off. He has blonde hair, and looks like he should be a model. He presses the radio on his ear.

Blonde British Seal

"We got a total of eight blues and five alive. President Grover is secure, he amongst that five that are alive."

Bill

"Look, I called you guys for Charles. I didn't even know Grover was here."

The British's seal looks over at Charles and ignores Bill. As his Job is not to trust anybody but rescue the president due to all the news that is going on. As Jacob gets unzipped he verifies Charles's identity to the troops, as he is still weak from being tased.

British Seal

"Dalton is secure too. It doesn't look like he was holding Grover. I got two suspects and three others who were previously zip tied. 1 female, and 3 males including Dalton."

Bill is surprised, but he understands the situation. He was the only one that wasn't tied, and for all that the seals know, Bill could have been the organizer of the whole setup. The seals ignore him and continue to monitor the scene. Once all is secure, the team shake each other's hands. The helicopters land, a few medics come in and tend to Jacob. They begin to lead him away from the site on a stretcher. Before they leave, Jacob raises his hand, telling the medics to stop. Once they do he points his finger. They call the blonde hair seal over, and he speaks with the President.

Once they are done talking the seal turns around and unzips Bill, Charles, Ruth, and Choi. Gary is in the corner trying to explain that he is the advisor to the President, but they already knew his issue because they were watching him walk around as Jacob and Charles were on the ground before sniping the rest of Gary's corrupt guards. The seals strap Gary's legs up, put a black sheet over his head and walk him out.

As the scene is secured, everybody walks out. Outside is a swarm of police sirens, bright lights, cameras, and helicopters that are hovering over Choi's rooftop home. Charles gets attended to by medics; Ruth is crying while

explaining what occurred. Olympia Secret Service Agents
are talking. They have Gary in the back seat of a black
SUV with agents who are holding large machine guns.
There are about six helicopters on Choi's large lawn. It's a
somber sight. Charles can see the TV from the distance and
can make out words scrolled on the screen.

President Grover Alive. Found by British Seals in Europa.
Details to Come. Dalton not a suspect.

Charles isn't the only to see. Back in Paragon, A few
Olympia troops get to see this message as well. Confusion is
in the air worldwide, all while Paragon is still being
bombed.

What?

Back in Paragon, Olympia strikes have slowed down, but
they are still out continuing. Despite Grover being saved,
Paragonians are still being harassed. Paragon police are
being held at gunpoint. The hover vehicles are not in the
sky. The city is almost motionless, besides the Olympian
military vehicles and helicopters.

Looking at the screen, Charles is depressed at the footage of
the bombing in Paragon. The whole air force has been
knocked out and all of his military bases in each sector have
been taken control by a brigade of soldiers, all of whom are
Olympian. Charles calls Jim. Still standing next to Lex, he
holds her conversation and picks up the phone

Jim (on phone grabbing his neck)

"Charles, it's bad. I'm in the safe haven. But they have
control of every sector. Our base has been wiped out. The
whole BX squadron is dead. It's just a matter of time before
they find out where we are."

Charles

"I see. Where is Abe?"

Jim

"I have no clue. AX was in Olympia the last time I spoke
to them. For now, we have plenty of citizens in here, and
they are slowly getting killed by these Olympian troops."

Charles

"I'm with Grover now, he is rectifying that as we speak.
He didn't approve of this nonsense. Are there any other
axis or allies?"

Jim

"No, to me they all look Olympian. Something isn't right. They are trying too hard to get their hands on A28."

Charles

"Jim, you have the green light from me. Let me know if you need anything."

Charles slams the phone down, and looks at Jacob. They are in a private room in military headquarters in Europa.

Jacob

"Charles, I'm sorry. I…"

Charles

"No, I don't want a sorry. Do something about this. You see this screen! You see it!"

He points at the screen showing the news which is showing the bombs in Paragon, and talking about how the Air Force base has been bombed and breached.

Jacob picks up his phone, makes a phone call to a a military general in Olympia.

Jacob

"Lewis, as commander and chief, I order you to cease all military operations in Paragon and all troops should immediately retreat to their bases. That's an order."

Lewis okays it and Jacob hangs up the phone.

Charles

"I need to go. I need to go! My people need me! We built all of that!"

Jacob

"Chuck, you can't go. Not right now. It's too hostile."

Charles

"Too hostile? Too hostile! Those are people who I have requested to live there are dying!"

The door knocks. Choi walks in. He grabs Charles and puts his head on his head. Charles is in tears. He is watching his country get bombed, minute by minute.

Back in the Safe Haven. Jim is still trying to find his strategy to counter any further attacks. Many of the people who live in Paragon have been sent there through an underground tunnel which leads to the bunker. The main area is open, not yet done but it is filled with food, crops, and showers. It was built exactly for this situation. Bin, Eddie, Lisa, and even Anthony are helping the people come in, some are bloody, and some are almost naked. Anthony sees a woman crying in a corner, bringing him to a different reality from his amazing basketball career.

Paragon Citizen

"I didn't come here for this. I just came for work; I just came to visit my son."

Anthony looks at the people in the eyes. Many of them know who he is, but he isn't a factor at the moment, as many folks can't find family members, are bloody, and just confused about the sudden attack.

Jim walks back into the command center, and looks at his workers. He walks to the radar room. They have their eyes on a brigade of aircraft inbound from Olympia, and that bomber-looking aircraft which is heading directly for the Safe Haven.

Jim

"That plane is still heading this way. Along with a dozen others not too far from it."

Command Worker

"Yes, sir, and they aren't helicopters. Their altitude indicates that they are above 30,000. If they comes lower than 15,000 we will come into immediate contact with him. But he could be..."

Jim (looks at the screen)

"They are sending damn near the whole fleet."

Judy Ruiz walks up. She sees what is going on also. She stands behind Jim. Not really knowing what to do. Although she leads the defense, she isn't used to live combat situations.

Jim

"Guys, we have aircraft inbound for us, and about 500 northwest is a brigade of them. We need to be ready for this."

Command Worker

"Sir, we haven't tested the silo wind mills. But they are our last line of defense."

Jim waits a second.

Jim

"Let's get them going then."

This means that the silos will crank up and shoot any aircraft down that comes within a certain amount of space between them. They put the radar on the big screen. They can see the dots on the screen as they get closer to them. One of the smart guys in the room comes in. His name is Moto, he is very dark-skinned, has thick hair, and is simply smart. He can do calculus and read a newspaper at the same time. He has a goofy grin that makes him unique. In the most troubled situations, he grimaces, he never looks pressured, almost as if everything is a game to him.

Moto

"Capt. Good day, I'm here at your request?"

Jim

"Yes, can you get those silos working? Also, can you pull up the satellite imagery, it's down. I want to see what kind of plane that is flying inbound."

Moto walks up to one of the computers and begins to work really fast. His eyed are glued to the screen and he is typing rapidly. Hitting the enter button hard, he gets the silos running, really fast. Outside they begin to slowly turn, as they look like they are producing power, but they are really radars that detect any movement, and once they shoot, they kill.

The large airplane is getting closer. Parts of Paragon are being bombed, more so the parts near A28; they have no active aircraft in the sky. As the plane approaches the command center is quiet, as they are expected to be bombed at anytime. It comes closer, and closer. Then, over the radio, a voice taps into the speakers in the command room.

Jim is very settled when it comes to striking. It makes it worse when he has to strike is original homeland. But he is backed against the wall.

Jim has one of the support workers turn on the monitor toward the Silos which look like a windmill field. They surround the bunker, as it looks like it can be a farm. They also surround every military site in each sector. They power up. As they begin to move. The cameras show how the Olympia soldiers are looking at them, but totally are unaware that they launch missiles.

Jim

"Get those silos ready. Cut the alarms on for everybody to brace. We are the last line for this country! Moto, get cut the lasers on!"

Lex walks back to Jim as the fear and energy sits in the room.

Lex

"Sir, I know you were just on the phone with Dalton, but I need to speak to you. It's about AX1."

Jim takes another deep breath, because he doesn't want to hear the death confirmation. She pulls her phone out. Jim takes a deep breath.

Lex

"Capt. I've talked to…"

Before she can say his name the announcement comes over the loud speaker.

Over the speaker.

"Paragon Safe Haven. This is Squid Initials Alpha Delta. Do you copy?"

The base all looks up and wonders what is going on, as the only people who can be on a loud speaker is a Pilot who is on the emergency frequency.

Jim walks to the one controller, who controls all the air traffic, and takes his microphone from him.

Jim puts his ear towards the PA speaker.

"Alpha Delta, say again and identify."

Pilot

"Captain, this is Charlie Deltas legacy in a C-17 heavy. We're fourteen miles out on the right base for Safe Haven 27. See you soon. We're home."

16

All the goons come out to play

The command room is ignited. It's the last voice that Jim expected.

Abe

"Don't want our communication to bring any attention. Sir, we are only here because of the loyalty, patience, and me letting this damn captain's ego go. That you and Captain O'Donnell can't stand."

Jim puts his head down, and rests his forearms on the desk. His squadron leader is back. His mind is blown.

Jim

"Squid, Son. Roger. We will see and brief you soon. How many are on board?"

Abe

"Thirty plus. O'Donnell and Smitten are on board also."

This is typical Abe, focused on the mission but not the small details. It gives Jim just enough. Not only is the entire AX-1 squadron on its way back. His two deputies are alive also. It's a feeling of relief and protection

Abe

"This Olympian ship is friendly, so don't let those silos over there loose on us. I've already had my fair scare once. This isn't going to be my last destination. I can only cheat death so many times."

The command room is alive again. Their shocked hearts are back to beating. Although Jim still wants to think everything through. Knowing that his whole unit wasn't killed brings some warmth to him. Although Abe gets no special treatment, Jim looks forward to informing Charles and telling him that his son is alive. He also thinks about losing twenty of his BX-1 squadron in the missile strike at the joint base. Those thoughts have to go to the side right now. He has a land to defend.

Abe comes back onto the loud speaker.

Abe

"Safe Haven. Squid here. We are closing in. We can't get a visual on the runway. Looks like a farm. Are we near the proper coordinates?"

One of the support techs raises his hand to Jim, and acknowledges that he is about to hit the button to release the runway. Jim approves with a slow nod.

The tech support presses the red button along with a few passwords.

Out in the plantation fields near the bunker. Elevator cables begin to roll back and rotate. Slowly, the grass which looked like a farm, rolls back like carpet, and the black runway begins to show. The numbers on it show the number 27. The white markings are pure. Abe and his Olympian copilot are surprised.

Abe

"I see it now…… I haven't had a chance to practice on this runway."

As Abe and the Olympian copilot are fascinated about what they see. They are also focused as this is a short runway made for smaller airplanes. When the carpet comes off of the runway, it slides into the shaft on the far end.

The traffic controller on the frequency speaks.

Controller

"Squid heavy, you are clear ---- to ---- land. Safe Haven 27."

As the plane comes on the approach on the outside runway, people are all out there looking. The rover trucks are driving on the runway to inspect that it is clear for any plane landing. It doesn't resemble the farm that it once was. Though there are still cows out there, it can be noticed that they are strictly a decoy, and they probably live the good life. Since they aren't used to be a burger someday, nor having their boobs milked all day and all night.

The C17 aircraft gets closer. Its four engines and steel grey coloring make it a graceful giant. The red beacon light blinks on top of it, with the red on the left wing, and green on the right wing. It's a good sighting for the air wing and the folks which are there for support. Especially knowing that it is their own AX1.

Lisa, Bin, Eddie, and Anthony are all looking as well. Bin may be the only one with a clue what is going on because he understands defense systems. However, he has never seen any live action, maybe just a missile test or two. The three may not know everything that is going on, but they realize that there is now some sense of hope.

Lisa and the others are in the command room watching as the men prepare for the aircraft to land. The runway is short. It's only 3,000 feet, just enough for a small aircraft to land on in exemplary weather. The C17 is made for short landings, but this is a plane that can carry seven large vehicles, and about 100 men. It's not small by any-means, and the pilots are not scared of any challenge. Especially Abe.

Abe and the Olympian pilot are focused with their eye displays on, and seats harnesses belted in. The rest of the crew else are buckled in on the side of the airplane in case of an impact.

Abe

"Guys. Brace. We got to touchdown right when that asphalt starts. This may not be smooth."

As the plane lands, it hits the ground right when the runway begins. Skilled pilots they are but that's only the beginning. The nose wheel of the large beast hits the ground very hard, smoke from the wheels surround the impact. Once Abe feels the plane touch, he hits the brakes softly; not too hard so he doesn't make the plane go against the physics. He thinks about the last time that he flew this aircraft. Many years ago, when Captain Title gave him a tally of racial slurs after a successful emergency landing. Abe shakes his head to omit the thought from his brain, as he needs every bit of focus to stop the cargo plane before the runway ends. Otherwise a mass casualty can occur.

Abe hits the reverse thrusters on the engines. Turning them around pulling the plane backwards as it goes 140 knots, then down to 100, 80, 40, and 20. The cargo plane barely comes to a complete stop and they have about 500 feet of runway still available. Before it stops, it begins to go backwards, a capability that most planes don't have. Usually they are pushed back by a tug. Nevertheless, the C17, although it was made in the nineties, is made to land almost anywhere.

As Abe reverses the plane down the runway, as if it was erasing its tracks. The Olympian copilot speaks to the control room and verifies where he needs to go.

Traffic Controller

"Go to the midpoint of the runway. Stop and shut down your engines. You're big, so you need to move back just a bit. Then watch some magic happen."

Olympian Pilot

"Roger."

They tell him to stop, and he stops then shuts down the engines. Abe doesn't know what's going on, Lisa is watching in awe. Hearing the communication over the speakers. She knows Abe's voice.

Once Abe stops the aircraft, they tell him to relax. Once this occurs, something unexpected happens. Abe and the copilot look out and realize that they are being lowered. Most of the runway is being lifted down, into the bunker area of the Safe Haven. Only this is the warehouse, but not just any warehouse. As Abe unbuckles, he and the other guys are ready to get out of the plane after the long fifteen hour ride from Olympia. After three refuels and being tied up for a quarter of the trip, he's ready to get out. He also knows that it's time to handle business. Especially after seeing fire and dismantled buildings during his final approach into Paragon.

The world in the warehouse in the bunker opens up to all the men. It has a blue hue over it, light bulbs light up the entire place. What amazes Abe, is that they just landed and they are now underground with the same aircraft. Then, as he gets out he looks to the left, and sees a line of birds. There's about 20 lined up, and ready to go. Jim walks up to Abe, and salutes him...

Jim hugs Abe and checks his pupils with a flashlight.

I was told you guys were put in a chamber.

Abe is unzipping the top of his flight suit. His gold dog tags on his neck glow.

"Capt., we will talk about that. Captain Smitten and Captain O'Donell need a medic. They are fine but they were gassed badly back in Olympia. What needs to be done..."

Jim looks to the left. Abe does also.

Abe

"Whose are those?"

Abe looks at the aircraft as they patiently wait to be put to work, and do what they do best.

Jim

The F-35's? They are ours. A little transition, but the same systems. You ready to get out there? We have no BX1. You get a little rest on the way here?

Jim grabs Abe's face, pulls his flashlight out again and checks his pupils to see how he is looking. They lock eyes and they both know they question that Abe has... Then Abe's phone rings. It's Chris.

He picks up the phone and answers it. He has a few words with Chris, and finally gets off the phone.

Abe

"Capt. Chris is in Emirate. We are ready to go in. We have one F-22 over there. It is the last 22. He parachuted out along with Channing. Send him up. He should be the first in the sky."

Jim

"Fine, there are around twenty Olympian fighters and drones up there, and about fifteen helicopters."

Abe

"All Olympia?"

Jim

"I believe so. From what I know Grover called them off though."

Abe

"Even if he did, it won't matter. Most of them are from some corrupt bullshit. I think most of the Olympian fighters backed off on our way in. The ones who are still in the air are a part of some corrupt mission to get A28. We can talk about the politics later. We got things to blow back into their place."

1 7

Daymares

In a hidden location of sector C, Gil is analyzing the call between Chris and Lex. She has no clue of what's going on; she hasn't talked to Gary, who was the main contact for the mission. She is trying to remain defensive, to make sure they don't lose their leverage in the takeover. She is also jumbling the emotions of being a part of the idea that Colin planned to have Abe and the whole AX1 team dropped in the middle of the ocean.

To make matters worse, she wanted to change the plan up a little bit. Acting off her emotions for Abe being with Telda and knowing that he has feelings for her fueled her to continue with the mission. All she can think about is the kisses, the moments, and the passion that Abe and Telda had in the cockpit. It turns her stomach and ignites fury because of how he did it. How he ended the date with her, so he could go be with Telda. It left Gil with many memories. Along with memories that never happened.

Thoughts of Telda and Abe having promiscuous moments at Operation Red Ice cross her mind. She thinks about Abe and Telda going out on the strip on a evening to spend time with each other. Although they were really studying various maneuvers, tactics, and enhancing their craft so that they could be the top pilots at Operation Red Ice. They were also in different rooms.

Even so, she has the disturbing thoughts, daymares of her lover. She thinks of Telda enjoying Abe's yank. While Abe holds her long braid in a hotel room after a day of flying. He penetrates her deeper. Gil places herself in the room with them, traveling deeper into her own imagination. Gil is watching; looking at Telda. Face to face, as Telda opens her mouth. Enjoying the pleasure of her top gun, Abe. Gil watches; listening to Telda scream. She then looks up Abe, and he looks up at her like she is a ghost, like a woman that he never met. More so like a woman he once trusted.

Gils imagination continues. She sees Abe grab Telda's tight waist. Back and forth, back and forth. Abe, grabbing her nipples from under her, biting down Telda's back, feeling her spine, working her nerves. All while he is still looking at Gil.

Still in a room of imagination, Gil begins to feels the guilt about spying on Abe. He looks up and gives her a look. She has lied to him all his life. She spied on him. She released his father's secrets and had plans to crush his father's vision. Even after several nights that they had together, she still went through with it. Abe takes his frustration out on his dream girl. Telda feels it. She feels the pressure. Telda looks up at Gil with devious eyes. Her and Abe's eyes lock in on Gil. Abe shoots his missile just off of Telda's back. It shoots too far...

Boom. The first time Gil feels Abe's ability to create life.

She wipes the guilt off her face.

He apologizes.

> Abe

> "Sorry, Catherine."

He calls her by her birth name for the first time, but he still stares at Gil. Because that's who he knows. He never met Catherine.

Still in her daymare. Gil gets jealous, because Telda is gorgeous. Telda is honest with him. Telda loves him. Telda is fit. She knows Abe. She connects with him emotionally. Telda fears him. Which ignites her engine and lubricates it. He stimulates her mind even when she pushes him away.

Gil hates the fact that Telda knows Abe more than her, even after spying on him for the past 10 years.

Telda enjoys Abe's drive. His cockiness for the things he deserves to be cocky in. His determination in what he does. She knows facts about Abe's mom because she has spent endless hours studying with him. Charles also enjoys Telda.

These disturbing thoughts have returned to Gil ever since Telda's birthday. They made it easy for her to use her job to knock her frustrations out, along with Colin. As he cares about nothing but making his multimillion dollar commission on securing A28. So, in her mind, she tells herself that it doesn't matter anymore, because Abe is dead to her anyway. Gil's payday is a few moments away. Once the central unit of Paragon is destroyed and the military is demobilized, Gil's group in Olympia will unofficially be in charge of Paragon. That is, as long as the plan goes the right way. In her mind, the money can erase the guilt. The guilt of knowing about Grover's assassination attempt. The guilt of wiping innocent people and kids away in Paragon. The guilt of destroying Charles Dalton's dreams. Finally, the guilt of making sure that Abe was dropped in the middle of the ocean will also be erased.

Gil calls Colin on the phone

Gil

"They have a fighter on the ground in Emirate. Just be advised."

Colin

"Who is it?"

Gil

"A newbie named Chris. I never met him. I ran his info. He is from Olympia. Just moved here."

Colin

"Keep an eye out on him. If he goes up, he's going to get fried. We are planning one more bombing. So hold tight. We are almost done. Grover has been taken down a few hours ago. I think we will be in the White House next month once the vice president takes over. Two for us, none for them...Right?"

A few seconds go by. Gil doesn't respond.

Colin

"Cat, you there?"

A few more seconds go by.

Colin

"I mean, Gil..."

He looks at his phone to make sure that he didn't lose signal.

Gil's jaws drop. She looks at her TV monitor. It's footage of President Grover being airlifted from Choi's house in Olympia. On the bottom it says:

President Grover Rescued. Charles Dalton is not the suspect.

In fine print it states:

President Grover was held custody for eight hours, by an undisclosed party. Grover did not approve of the bombing in Paragon; one of his advisors is in custody. Seven other personnel reported dead during the rescue by British seals. Among them, Son of GELT CEO Herb Kinzel, the Assistant to the Secretary of Defense, and ex CIA director Bill Browning. Others have not been identified. Deaths are unofficial: Bombs over Paragon are still being ignited. No response from Sec. of Defense, Bob Polan or the Olympian Vice President.

Colin

"Gil. What's the problem. I hear that you're still on the phone."

Gil

"Colin, we may need to abort. Grover is not dead."

Colin

"The fuck do you mean he isn't dead? No way."

Gil isn't the only one that is shocked about the news of Grover. Foxwire still hasn't reported anything. They are still focusing on Dalton being the suspect and why Paragon should be bombed. The world is quiet. Charles' mom is quiet, but she is still glad to hear about Charles being alive. The Olympians are confused. They don't know what is going on. Paragon was bombed due to nuclear threats. Along with having President Grover under hostage and Dalton was the one who was accused.

The world is happy, but they are also stilled. The conspiracy theorists have been flooding the internet. Especially the ones who are against the government and think that everything is a setup. This time, they may be right.

Gil is lost, she returns to thinking about Abe. She thinks about him laying next to her, always being honest with her and never lying to her, not leading her on. He never truly attempted to have sex with her, because he respected her. He loved her as a friend, a person who he grew up with, and a person who was there when his mother died in the bombings. He probably didn't want a relationship with her, but he could have lied and lead her on. He never had sex with her because he knew it would lead to something more; something he just didn't want with her. The asshole that Abe sometimes presents, is nowhere near the man that he is.

She eludes the positive thoughts about Abe and snaps back into action.

Gil

"Colin, we need to go get a hold of A28 they won't touch us if we have it. That's all we can do!"

Colin turns to his last resort which is to get the A28 location, and formula. He looks at the scientist that he has hostage in a lab near the mountain that the A28 lab sits in.

Colin

"If they don't give those codes up to the building, there will be more lives taken. Gil, continue with your mission. I will call you back."

Colin looks up and holds a gun to the head of one of the scientists who is in control of the A28 program.

Colin

"You see this? You're gonna die anyway. In about 20 minutes, that brigade of aircraft you see on the screen is going to wipe away this entire country. Then it won't be nothing but a piece of shit that started to come out of Charles Dalton's ass. Now, give me the pathway, codes, and key cards."

As Colin tries to get the final codes from the scientist, someone knocks on the door. One of Colin's men opens it. It's Gabe.

Gabe

"Look what we have here."

He looks at Colin.

Gabe

"Good job, son. How are we looking?"

Colin

"Looks like we are going to have to rush our way in. These idiots won't give us the codes to open up the mountain gates that surround the facility and Grover isn't dead. One of your GELT Employees was in here also."

Gabe

"I'm aware of Grover. What worker are you talking about?"

Colin (brings a photo up)

"Lisa Gasquew and I don't know who the other guys are."

Gabe

"Knock this place to shambles. Grover can't stop us. We are already here and Paragon doesn't have a military. This land is ours. Finders keepers."

Colin speaks over his earpiece.

Colin

"Knock them out. One by one! It's time."

Seconds later, a troop who is next to the mountain where A28 sits leans down, aims and fires a missile into a barrier gate. It is spread on the news that another rocket was sent in. Colin looks at the scientist, and tells his fighter jets to shoot.

Lex

"Captain, A28 Sector is about to be breached. We have been hit again we need to get AX1 in the sky soon!"

Charles sees this on the monitor. He is pissed and has to be restrained.

Fighting Fair

Chris and Channing, just landed by parachute near the Emirate Air Force base.

Their feet fall on the ground and they begin to run towards the base. They look grimy and tired. They show their ID's to the Emirate guards who look at them, as they know that Paragon is going through war-like moments. Once access is granted, they jog into the hangar and are informed that Chris's F22 is waiting for him out on the tarmac. The canopy is open. It has a green glow, and is ready for battle. Chris gets in first, and then Channing hops in the back. He loads up and guns the engines without hesitation. He calls the Paragon base.

Chris

"Safe Haven, this is Warmblood and Chanham. We are ready for lift whenever needed."

Lex

"Warmblood, you are clear. Be advised, hostiles are firing in the mountain area."

Chris

"Roger. Going up an immediate 20,000 feet. Any AX rolling up anytime soon?"

Lex

"That's affirmative."

Chris.

"Lex, is there an avoidance aircraft up there? I see some sort of heavy I'm going to take it out. I think they think that nothing is in the sky and we are supposed to have been dead."

While this is happening, the President's message gets around to the troops in Olympia. Slowly the men are looking at their mobile phones, and beginning to wonder to each other why they were sent over there? The President is okay, he wasn't really held hostage. The people in the rooms assisting Colin and Gil look at them like they are crazy. They recognize that this is a corrupt mission. Especially when they see on the news that many people including the VP are taken into custody.

Olympia Command comes over the frequency

"All troop personnel, including aircraft, break off immediately. Orders from the Commander in Chief."

Colin is furious. Gil is confused, and so is Gabe. They are watching before anybody makes a move. Colin puts his gun in the air.

Colin

"Anybody that gets up and believes this nonsense is dead."

Olympia Support

"Sir, the systems are all locked. Even if we wanted to, there is nothing that can be done."

Gil over hears some Olympia fighter pilots talking over the radio. She looks up at what's going on. Colin looks up at the monitor also, in the submarine that he is in.

Olympia Fighter Pilot

"Command, Paragon just knocked down one of our joint fighters. I don't think he wanted to engage, but the joint fighter wouldn't cease."

Colin

"What the fuck is going on?"

Colin looks at one of the air force command officers. The officer is confused also. It has been a neutral zone ever since the last strike that Colin has conducted. Most of the bombings have occurred because he has some of Charles' officials under hostage and every few hours that they don't surrender the codes for A28, Colin bombs them.

In the middle, Colin gets even more firing news. He is told that the support units who are with him are waiting on Grover's request. Colin looks at them, speechless, as he has to carry on with the takeover.

Colin

"Look, we don't have time to focus on gibberish with what's going on. Stay focused, don't you see we are being attacked. Who knows if they President is really alive?"

The men look at Colin and get back to work. Colin looks at one of his drone operators.

Colin

"Tim. Burn these fuckers up."

Tim is an Olympian drone operator

Tim

"Sir, the President is found. We were told to cease until we find out what's going on. I am a member of the Olympian military. Not your company!"

Colin

"Have we heard from him yet? Don't listen to any crap! Before we get bombed away, you see we just lost six choppers. You can't trust this country! We aren't from here! Hit 'em! I want every building bombed down, Dalton is somewhere in there and we are going to get him!"

Tim doesn't follow Colin's orders.

Colin shoots him in the head. He then puts a gun up to another drone controller, and makes him take down more Paragon targets. The drone operator unwillingly activates his drone. The unmanned machine is high up in the sky, and begins to lower a few of its missiles. The operator informs his mission command that he is about to send one into action. He sends one missile out, and it hits a building in Sector A.

Colin gets on the phone.

Colin

"We need those codes quickly. We are in a deep shit hole. If they don't give them to you, shoot them one by one, slowly."

Colin looks back at the group in the room that he is in.

Colin

"I don't see any fire. You better unload them, because they are coming for you!"

As Colin's group begins to scan their radars, they see many planes. Most of them the joint force drones, they then locate Chris's plane. They try to put a missile lock on it. Before they can make a move, Boom, one plane hit. Boom, another Olympian plane hit.

Chris is zooming. He is coming from the backend of Paragon where Sector D is located. With the gunners on his aircraft he knocks out 6 helicopters that are surrounding Sector D, freeing up Paragon troops. By doing this, it provides the Paragon troops leverage to fight back against the Olympia troops who are making sure they don't leave the camps.

Chris looks out of his window and sees a few Olympian troops running along the fences of the base. He flies low, lines them up with his guns, and lets the bullets fly. Some troops get hit in the back, some get hit in the leg, but the tremendously sized bullets do enough damage to the Olympian bodies that the Paragon troops realize they have help. Paragon troops can now take their base back over. After 45 seconds there, Chris zooms back into the sky so he can stay out of scope.

Chris

"Lex, I'm not stealth now, but I can knock out more of these choppers before they even see me. I want to hold off on my last five big boys for the right time. I got six packs of A28. So, there should be no reason why I can't go supersonic."

Lex

"Roger, stay out of B and A. The further you stay out, the least detectable you are. We have many people in those locations. Free up our guys. Remain cautious."

Jim looks as he realizes that they now have a hope with one of their own out there. Chris is new to the unit, but his fearlessness is showing.

As Chris and Channing pass over Sector C, Paragon citizens can now see that something is going on, not knowing if it is another country. They begin to feel a sense of protection.

Chris heads for the next fighter jet.

Chris

"Unidentified Aircraft, please, identify yourself."

The aircraft doesn't respond.

Channing from the back

"Unidentified Aircraft, please identify yourself."

Chris and Channing zoom in with their scope as they are close to the plane. As they do, their plane does a loop and comes up behind them.

Channing

"Roll left."

Chris rolls the plane to the left, only to see a missile fly buy.

Chris

"Good catch! Where is he?"

Channing

"Your 7 o'clock."

Chris, thrust levers the aircraft to make a full stop in the air. The other plane pulls ahead of him. Chris guns him down. As the plane is hit, they can see that nobody has ejected, and it is a complete stall which means it isn't moving. It's a drone.

Chris

"Whew! That's two down, many more to go."

Channing

"Chris, we got five on us."

Channing is scared. She has never been in combat. The only reason why she jumped with Chris is because she was the only one who wasn't a pilot that knew how to parachute to get the F-22 from Emirate.

Chris

"Where did they come from? Who are these guys!"

Chris is flanking from the aircraft, they are shooting at him. He rolls. Does a quick roll with the plane, and catches one on his radar with his missile. He hits him, but there are four more after him. Chris realizes that they aren't Olympian, they are the drones without any flags on them.

The AX1 guys hear the trouble that Chris and Channing are in over the radio. They begin to get ready to assist.

Telda

"Guys, we got to get out of here. Chris is swarmed."

Jim

"You think he can handle it?"

Lex

"I don't think that is the question. The question is, is AX1 ready. He's moving in, supersonic. This will be the perfect time for our guys to get out there."

Jim stays still.

Lex

"Captain, let's go. Let's get our country back."

Jim nods to her. Fifteen-seconds later, the red lights and horns go off in the warehouse. Abe, Telda, Rory, Jason, and Terry Love are all sitting in their cockpits ready to go, making their final adjustments their systems. They are smart warriors. Transitioning to a different airplane without any hesitation. All of their eyes are locked into the computers in the cockpit, they aren't even thinking about a war. They are just thinking about getting in the sky and doing what they love to do.

Abe

"Guys, it looks like we're given the green. Well, the red light. Let's lace 'em up!"

They all look around. The service men are all ready to go. They are lined up on the platform. Bin, Eddie, and Lisa are all watching. Lisa is watching Abe the whole time. Even though she can't see in the cockpit completely, Abe can see her, and he has noticed her many times looking at him. The command room is about 100 feet away from the glass windows that separate it from the warehouse where all the aircraft are positioned.

Jim runs to the pilots and looks at them. He jumps up to Terry Love's aircraft. He taps him on the head, and then looks into his rear seat. He realizes that Terry doesn't have a navigator in his plane. Not that he needs one; he knows that Terry is new. Telda and Rory fly by themselves. Abe flies with Jason, not because he needs one, but more so for backup because of his aggressive flying. O'Donnell walks away from Terry's aircraft, and gives one of the flight operations personal orders. He then walks over to Telda's plane, and kisses her on the cheek.

Rory has eyes of a lion at the moment. He has a small amount of sweat on his head as he inserts his weight into the flight system, so the plane is aware. Jim grabs his shoulder, and then walks away. Finally, he walks up to Abe's plane. He gives him no words, just eyes locked in on him.

Abe puts his helmet on, and Jim gives him the proper words.

Jim

"I'm proud of you, son. Lead em! Your dad made it out. Now it's your turn. His life is in your hands now. He built this! Now you get it back! I know you have been working with O'Donnell and Smitten, and they aren't here. This is why you're the commander of your unit. You got them this far, now go further."

Abe lets his cockpit glass top down and gives Jim the "X" with his arms. Jim is old school and was always strictly for the salute. This time he responds to with the "X" and zooms in on his eyes. Looking at Abe longer than he did everybody else. He hasn't stopped looking yet. Partly, because he knows that he is the leader's son, but he also knows that Abe is the leader right now. Jim has known Abe since he was a baby. It's interesting for him to look at him as a war hero. This is the time for Abe to take back the country that his dad built, and the few that he semi-trusted blew away.

Abe comes over the radio

"AX, this is squid. Do you all copy?"

Telda, Rory, Jason, and Terry copy. Then one more voice comes on, it's a female. It's Tam, she is in the back of Terry Loves' plane.

Tam

"Squid, this is spirit. I'll be navigating Rabbit, under commands."

This throws the crew off briefly as they never flew with Tam. She was also one of the BX1 squadron members who happened to be offsite when everything occurred. She, Chris, and five other members of the squadron are the only BX1 members left.

Abe

"Command, we are ready."

All the pilots lift their cockpit canopies down, and they all get the go ahead from the marshals with the orange sticks. The platform that the planes are on begins to lift up. This is quite new to most of the pilots, although some of them have had a small amount of Naval training. Everybody in the bunker is looking at them, as the planes begin to heat up.

Command

"Crank them up. Both engines. We got all the water in the ocean to refuel, so don't mind losing any fuel right now."

Terry's plane turns on, next Telda's, then Abe and Rory's. It is time for battle. As they get closer to the top of the bunker's roof, it begins to slide open, and they can see the sun begin to creep in. Abe looks down to take one last glance at everybody, he nods at them, and then looks around. He sees Eddie and Lisa waving. Eddie finishes, but Lisa is still looking at him. It makes him wonder, but he lets it be, as he has bigger things to worry about.

Command comes over the radio

"AX, you guys are all clear for takeoff. No obstructions are on the radar, but stay visual. It seems like one of your BX guys is out there taking guys out. He is in a F-22. The sky is ours."

Abe

"Roger, any idea on how many heads we got against us?"

Command

"It's looking like 14."

Chris comes over the frequency.

Chris

"AX, I'm heading for the AWACS. Most of these aircraft are 22's, which mean they can get to you, but you can't get to them. For some reason I can detect them. If I can knock out their avoidance system, we will gain advantage."

Chris is flying one of the Olympia / Paragon Joint Force Aircrafts. A big slip up in Colin and Gil's plans. Especially since his aircraft isn't identified as an enemy to them.

Abe

"Roger, thanks, Chris. Hold tight, we are en route."

The engines blaze up. The grass-looking carpet rolls off of the runway, showing green-type asphalt for camouflage. The smoke-grey airplanes take off.

Abe

"Radar, we are out."

Side by side and two at a time, they begin to take off. Abe is off the runway. Telda is next to him. Rory is next to Terry.

The AX squad is airborne. Jim looks at them on the camera, excitement sits, but his belly has quick pains, because the inner nervousness hits. Bin, Eddie, Tommy, and Lisa look. Anthony is sitting down, as he is tired, but also surprised that he is in a war-zone. The site is chilling, but amazing. Four jets that the crew didn't even know that they had taking off to defend against some of the best fighter pilots in the world.

Abe takes off.

Abe

"All right, guys, same shit, different day. Slightly different plane, but I like these a little better anyway."

Rory

"Oh yeah. They are lighter. Too bad we aren't stealth."

Abe

"Stealth won't matter soon and it looks like we will find that out, in about two minutes."

Abe is referring to Chris, who is working his way towards the AWACS aircraft where Olympia has their mission command to detect enemy aircraft. As Chris heads toward the aircraft, he notices an enemy aircraft tailing him. Chris, having been trained by Captain O'Donnell, knows that there is never just one aircraft lingering around, and he knows there has to be two or three especially with so many in the area. He speeds his aircraft up. On his radar he sees the AWACS system, and he knows that he needs to take it out. As he heads closer, fleeing away from the Olympia fighters who have him in sight on his radar, Lex is heard on the radio.

Lex

"Chris, there is a good chance that they can hear us. We need you to abort AWACS. We got something else for that. You got two on your tail, handle them for now."

Gil hears Lex over the frequency as she is hacked in. She now knows for sure that Chris is in the sky, and that he is a part of the Paragon flight squadron. She calls Colin to let him know, she also verifies the bad news to him. She is still in her secret barracks. Colin picks up.

Gil gets on the phone

"That's a Paragon fighter that shot two of our drones down. They are up to something. I think it's the kid, Chris."

Colin

"No shit, and is it really true that Grover isn't dead?"

Gil

"He isn't dead. The Vice President isn't taking phone calls either. I advise you to discard any ties to him directly. I think we are on our own."

Colin

"Well, it looks like the middlemen are now the front men. A28 is all mine."

As they speak, Gil overhears a voice on the frequency which she is hacked into.

Abe

"Lex, I got two in sight, I believe they are trailing Chris. I'm engaging."

Lex

"Engage away, Abe. Gun 'em down. Save your missiles."

Gil hears Abe's voice and her heart drops. Her world is split in between good and bad. She also knows that she and Colin are in a tight bind. The mission leaders for the whole invasion; Bob Polan, Gary, and the Olympian Vice President are now in custody. However, this mission must go on. They are in too deep to stop now. They have fighter jets in the sky, Olympian troops with the thoughts of Paragon having nuclear weapons, and that their President has been taken hostage. Telda's voice enters the conversation.

Telda

"Squid, I'm going westbound."

Abe roars his plane, pushing against the wind, in between the clouds. He sees one Olympian fighter jet. It's a hard decision, but easy as he witnesses what they have done to his country. Because they are all on the same radio frequency, Abe speaks to the fighter pilot.

Abe

"To all aircraft who are out here, you have two options. Surrender and understand that you have been a part of some government bullshit. That means that every order that you have taken has been lead by some corrupt fucks that only care about themselves. Or you can continue to firefight us, for your pleasure. You are in our airspace. Now I advice for you guys to fall back, or we will engage."

Olympian pilots hear this, and folks in the mission room hear this as well. They are confused, and a few others are still eager to push for the mission. Gil hears this, and realizes that she and Colin are in deep trouble. They must save face and act like they have no clue to what's going on. The look of confusion sets on their faces. Some look at each other. Other men who are on the ground pull out their phones and look at the news again, that President Grover has been found. The tactical units who have been involved with searching for Grover stop in their steps, and realize that they are in search for nobody. Gil steps out of her secret location, as if she has to take a phone call. Camouflaging her guilt, at what she has done, she walks very fast to her car, and gets in, speeds off. As she drives, she sees smoke in the air. Buildings with holes in them. She notices that they are all still standing, without any doubt in her mind she knew that Abe's father made sure they were built to withstand much impact.

Abe

"Again, all fighters and all aircraft in the sky, you are in Paragon airspace. You have done more than enough damage. You need to land. Check your phones, check your command post. Your President is alive and we have no nuclear threats. This is AX1, the aerial command of Paragon. If you copy, you will decrease your altitude and immediately land just south of the Bay. It's an alternate runway, since our base has been bombed to nothing."

The fighter pilots all look confused.

Olympia Fighter

"Hey Command, is he correct? Is Grover found?"

There is no reply. He asks again, and he gets no response. He responds to Abe.

Olympia Fighter

"AX, Squid this is Pinto, the Olympia F-16 to your right. I have been given no orders, but I will drop as this is your airspace. I am 4,000 feet below you, to your right. With respect."

Abe looks down and observes the Olympian fighter pilot beginning to drop his altitude and banks down. He somewhat feels the friendship and loyalty, but he can't leave his guard down. With his helmet visor, he eyes the aircraft, zooms in and puts a missile lock on him. He softly holds his finger on the red button of his joystick. In case, the fighter makes a quick move.

Olympia Fighter

"Base command. This is Pinto 18.I am dropping out of this. I have been flying around, bombing for the past few hours and have felt no reason to. I won't keep doing this without a proper briefing."

When he begins to descend. Abe looks down and sees something streaking towards that pilot's plane.

Over the radio he hears.

Olympia Fighter Pilot

"Olympus, Olympus! I have a missile inbound. From up…"

Before he can finish. Abe see's the missile strike the Olympian jet. Abe double checks to see if he ignited his, but he didn't. He looks back up, and the aircraft is destroyed.

Abe

"Whoa! What the? Rory did you just shoot this guy down?"

Rory

"No, I am en route to Warmblood and Chanham."

Abe, looks and sees aircraft debris fall from the sky. He thinks of the pilot and how loyal he was to him, to drop. Only to be bombed. Abe's instinct tells him that somebody else is out there, and they aren't friendly.

Miles away from Abe, Chris roars the plane avoiding the two drones following him. A friendly Olympian fighter jet sees that he is in distress.

Olympia Pilot

"Paragon fighter, do you need assistance?"

Chris

"Just get out of the sky. Otherwise you will blend in with these clowns. I don't know if you are after me, or if you are friendly. So please follow my commander's orders."

When the Olympia aircraft drops, he gets blown up. Just like the one Abe witnessed. This makes Chris aware that those two aircraft that Lex informed him of are still out there.

Chris

"Command, I have bandits behind me."

Channing is nervous, in the back seat. Putting all her faith into Chris, the guy who she couldn't stand when he initially joined the Squadron.

Rory

"Warmblood. Hang tight. I'm almost there. In a moment, I need you bank hard right for 20 seconds, then drop."

Chris follows Rory's order. Rory knocks out two of the drones. Boom... Boom!

Rory

"You have a few more drones on you, hang in there for me. Hang in there."

Rory puts his plane into supersonic mode. He sees that there is a swarm of aircraft heading for Chris, coming from all directions

Chris (looking out of the window of the jet)

"They are on me. I can't dodge, and I'm running out of fuel."

Rory

"Drop off."

Chris

"They are on... I got two coming from different..."

Chris's words become shorter. This is his first time in live combat, and probably one of the worst situations that any fighter pilot can be in.

Rory

"Twenty seconds, Chris. Twenty seconds. I'll be there."

Chris's cockpit screens turn red. He pulls his joystick towards him, taking the jet straight into the sky. He dodges one missile, then dodges another. Once he thinks he evades, he notices that his screen is still red, which means he is still locked by another missile. He looks below. Then to the left. He sees the missile inbound. Everything slows down. He tries a maneuver to avoid it, but it hits the tail of the plane. The systems alert him, and Channing feels the impact. The plane is shaking, sounds are buzzing. The computer voice in the plane says

Eject! Eject! Engine Failure! Pull Lever! Pull Lever!

Chris

"Channing, relax. We will be fine."

He knows he needs to calm her down, so they can eject with less fear.

Chris

"Command. Roar. We're hit. No blood, we are ejecting...Thanks, brother. Clear them out for me."

Chris pulls the yellow ejection seat lever. The cockpit canopy raises, and the beautiful glass that sits on top of the fighter jet gets its last moment being attached to the plane. The gases that keep it compressed shoot the roof off. Chris and Channing follow as they get rocketed into the sky. A few seconds later their parachutes release, then they both look down and watch the plane go into the water.

A hundred feet apart, the two float and they can see the warfare going on with the AX unit. Watching that action stops when they feel a vibrating sound coming nearby.

Chris is shouts to Channing. He sees that the Helicopter is going after her. Since he is a bit higher, he cuts his parachute to get more speed. He pulls out his 9 mm pistols that are on the side of the parachute. He draws and aims to the helicopter, leading it as the wind will take the bullets.

In a matter of seconds, he collides with Channing, and immediately wraps his legs around her. He turns her away from the attack helicopter and begins to shoot towards its cockpit. Channing feels every thump from the gunshots of his pistols. She eventually hears his shots slow down, the sounds of the helicopter blades fade away also.

Channing

Is it gone?

Chris

Yup

Channing is frightened and is holding on for dear life. She sees that Chris doesn't have a parachute. She is nervous; as he is wrapped around her. Tightly. Almost to the point where she couldn't breathe. They escaped death again. First, the crew slipped away from death back in Olympia during Red Ice, she knows that there is no way that she can get that chance again. She feels like she got shot, but she doesn't feel any pain. She looks at her body, she feels herself. She is okay. She isn't bleeding.

Face to face with Chris. She looks over his shoulder. He hands are covered in blood. Channing realizes that it's coming from Chris's back. He is staring at her.

Chris

Yup, it's gone.

He blinks and smiles, with a bloody mouth. His guns fall from his hands. Gravity pulls them towards the ocean. He briefly closes his eyes, as if he is upset at himself. He looks back at her.

Chris

"Make sure you tell my mom and brother that I am okay. I'm happy. That was the thrill of a lifetime. It was priceless."

Channing is quiet, she can't believe that he is shot and she isn't. Chris begins to cough. He is chuckling also.

Chris

"I never thought I'd save a gorgeous woman's life before. But, I think I just did."

As he chuckles, Channing feels his legs loosen up from her body. He softly squeezes her shoulders, and she can feel his hands cross her back, making the "X" for AX-1 with his arms. He lets go.

Finally being able to move. Channing looks at his body, as it falls.

She sees the blood running from his eyes. The bloody eye drops resemble tears.

She thinks about helicopter blades as they rotate, with a backwards Olympian Flag on it. Chris's original home. She thinks how he wasn't a threat to him. She can't tear up. All she can do is hold her breath. She is 1000 feet away from shore, and she knows that she has to stay focused. But it's hard. She wants to get Chris's body. But she can't, so she hovers right over him as the beautiful waters of Paragon take him. Soaking its mineral within his skin almost curing the wounds, but he is gone. Drifting away. He was defending the squadron and nation of which he wanted to be a part of, the ones who he sacrificed his all for. He was fighting against the country that he left, not because of hate but because of much tribulation, much sacrifice, and not much return from selfish leaders. He left to send more money back to his family. He wanted to fly, but the income wasn't enough at home. Along with the struggle of earning a pilot slot. He had to take care of his mom, sister, and brother.

Channing reenacts the moment as she saw it all in real time. It happened so fast, she didn't even think he was shot. She processes it all.

Chris shoots towards the helicopter, but gets hit by one bullet in the arm, one in the side, one in the shoulder. All bullets missing her, even after going through his body. The blood begins to exit his body through his nose, then through his ears. However, he blew them up before they headed for her. It is an Olympian owned helicopter but it's not to be a government chopper. It's a privately owned one.

She is crying. She looks down and sees the body of a young man floating on the waves of the Seren Ocean. She radios the news to base.

Channing

"Safe Haven, Warmblood is down. He is blue."

The office gets quiet. Abe gets quiet. Terry Love is quiet. Jim chokes his throat. There newest and youngest pilot, is down. The first one to jump into action.

Jim responds immediately.

"Keep it going, guys. He's your brother. Do it for him."

Jim begins to tear heavily, then wipes them away swiftly before they drop. He has seen death many times around the force - but never takes it well especially with his own men. He begins to backtrack. Thinking about signing off on Chris. About letting him go and experience Red Ice. Wondering if he hadn't signed off on him flying live, would his mom have to take that phone call? He feels the guilt, even though he is very righteous when it comes down to the love of his squadron. Chris' mom crosses Jim's mind when she flew in to visit for mother's day. Now he has to go back to Olympia to see her face to face and deliver the news.

Abe

"Let's stay focused, guys."

Abe zooms his jet. Telda is on the other side of the sector. She's pissed. She sees the helicopters that still are in the sky. She eyes them, and hits them. Abe does the same. Rory is knocking out one of the last planes that are in the sky. The corrupted drones and helicopters are feeling a spectrum of frustration from AX-1. Bullet after bullet. Missile after missile. It took five minutes to knock the corrupt aircraft out the sky.

As they realized that they have wiped everybody out, they begin to cruise. Telda pulls about 2,000 feet behind Abe

Telda

"Abe."

Abe (hitting his canopy window)

"This is not --- real!"

Abe banks his plane and looks down, he sees Chris's body. He sees the coast of Paragon. Burned. Ruined; most of the vertical farms are destroyed. The towers. Pod tracks. The bio luminescent trees are on fire, the small nation is motionless.

Abe

"Do you hear that?"

On the radio but muffled.

Abe and Telda listen and it is a female's voice over the radio, saying "we are going into position into the tower".

Abe

"Safe Haven. Can you have Moto run a scan over the audio of what's going on in one of the towers? We are pulling something in on our radio and it said something about people into position."

Moto does some typing, and looks at Lex back in the control room. He smiles. His big white teeth show when he has to challenge his mind.

Moto

"Looks like this is where most the activity is coming from. There have been sound waves coming from here all day."

Lex

"Can you see any computer transmissions?"

Moto

"Yup, just one-second."

He clicks on the screen, then it opens up. It says, Ethon Mineral.

Moto

"Well, this looks like where many of these orders are being called from. Looks like some Ethon name is attached to some of the transmissions."

Lex

"Squid, it looks like that's where many of the enemy communications is coming from. How many more aircraft do you have to knock down?"

Abe

"I don't see any inbound on my radar or in the area."

Gil, who is in that tower, is targeting aircraft. She can't tell which one Abe, Rory, Terry, and Telda is in. She knows that Abe usually flies in the front, and at the moment she sees the plane. Since the mission failed she decides to get two more shots in from a water launched missile, and the last drone that's not damaged. She fires out for frustration then leaves the room, hoping that the missile hits Telda.

As the missile leaves the water base, Gil leaves. Rory sees it.

Rory

"Abe, you got one coming in, go vertical."

Abe doesn't hear him.

Rory

"Now it is two. I can try to get the first one and where it was initiated from, so they can't launch any more."

Abe dodges one of them.

Abe

"Am I clear?"

Telda

"Abe, Abe! Four o'clock! Four o'clock!"

A missile is headed right for him, and unlike the silo one that Carter intervened, the boom happens. The missile again misses him. He looks up to the right, and he sees Telda flying next to him, serenely. Quiet. She's calm. He sees that she had his back.

Rory is guns down the water-based system which Gil and Colin had installed. He then flies towards the airplane which shot towards Abe.

Rory

"Lex, I'm behind this aircraft that shot the last two. It's an F16 I believe. Its missiles are empty. But he is cruising. Can you zoom in from my eye, and check it out?"

Moto zooms in from Rory's visor cam. It shows the aircraft and shows its tail. Jim looks at it.

Jim

"That's not an Olympia plane. Who's flag is that?"

Lex hands him the paper that Moto printed out earlier. He looks at it, surprisingly. He looks back at the zoomed in screen of the enemy fighter. He pauses the screen and shows Jim.

Jim looks at the screen.

"Ethon? Who the hell is Ethon? And it's a drone. It's radio controlled with no pilot inside."

Moto

"Ethon. Ha! You've never heard of Ethon? One of the most politically powerful private ops company in the world? The signal is showing that it's probably controlled by the tower that we heard, looks like everybody has fled or is fleeing once Roar blasted it."

Jim

"Roar, missile the jet down. Make sure you're over water. There is enough damage done on ground."

Rory missiles the plane down, and it blows up without any defense.

Rory

"This is something, man. Drones, though?"

Jim

"Is all clear out there?"

Rory

From what it seems. I see Squid, Zeld, and Love. Chris went down. Is somebody out to get Channing out of the Seren?

Lex

"Yes, coastal guard got her and Warmblood by the shore. Roar, we have a few more unidentified helicopters left in Sector C. We need you and Love to get them. Shoot them down without any hesitation."

Rory

"Roger, en route. Abe, Telda you okay?"

He looks at them, and notices that they are moving slowly.

Abe

"Affirm. Go handle them, bud."

Rory banks the plane and joins Terry and Tam to engage in the helicopter removal. Abe is still flying next to Telda, after she just saved his life by intercepting an inbound and undetectable missile.

Abe

"Thanks, Telda. That was a close one."

She doesn't respond. He is taking that she is mad at him.

Abe

"Telda…"

A few more seconds go by. She still doesn't respond. His stomach begins to drop.

Abe

"Telda… Do you copy me?"

Jason speaks up.

Jason

"Pull next to her."

Abe closes in on Telda's aircraft since she isn't responding on the radio. As he pulls up she turns her helmet, takes her air mask off, and looks to the floor of her plane. She's bending over as if she is tending to something. Abe rocks his plane side to side to get her attention.

Abe

"Telda! I understand the Punker Level is high but Copy me!"

Telda is crying

"One-second..."

Her voice has never sounded so nervous, and Abe has never heard her voice crackled. Even when she made mistakes or was lagging behind the men in the workouts, Telda has never broken down. In front of Abe at least.

Abe

"Telda, I know Chris is gone. We have to keep our heads up. It looks like the airspace is clear, we're done. Just a few more choppers to get knocked out."

Telda

"It's not that Abe. It's not that."

Without delay Abe increases speed and rolls the jet over the top of Telda, leveling out on her right wing. He sees what the issue is. It's smoke coming from the front side of the jet. The plane is flyable, but not for long, however, the problem lies within Telda as she is hit, and is losing small amounts of blood by the second.

The moment freezes. Abe's heart begins to burn. He looks to the left and she looks to the right. He lifts his visor up to meet her eyes. Though they are fifteen feet apart he inches closer as he can see the fear in Telda's eyes. They only have so much time before the plane possibly explodes. Telda's eyes are bloodshot red from the tears, but still focusing in on Abe; the same eyes that he fell in love with. Her eyes saved his life by noticing the missiles that were heading for him. She took it for him, not knowing if she was going to make it out or not. Death didn't cross her mind when it came down to sacrificing for Abe.

Abe

"Where are you hit?"

Telda

"I don't know, I can't feel my right leg."

Abe

"Put some pressure on it."

Telda tries to squeeze her leg.

"I am. I can't feel it, Abe."

Abe

"Pressure isn't helping? Press hard."

Telda

"No..."

She leans back in her plane, and takes some deep breaths.
She is in shock at what she sees. When she looks down
again she can see the metal going through her leg from the
plane, where the missile grazed. If her plane was five feet
higher or moving a bit slower it probably would have struck
her body and she would be dead, or the plane could have
been blown up.

Abe

"Try your toes."

Telda (frustrated at Abe's stupidity)

"Dammit, Abe - I told you I can't feel my legs!"

She's holding her thigh. Now that her body isn't in as much
shock, touching her lower leg is too painful. The missile has
wedged her foot into the aircraft along with her calf.
There's a good chance that she can be stuck, which won't
be as bad if she could land. The struck plane is beginning
to show that the impact has affected the plane - soon it will
be non-flyable. She will have to eject - taking the chance of
ripping her leg off, as she gets rocketed out of the canopy of
the plane.

Abe

"You got your tourniquet?"

She is quiet, doesn't respond.

Abe

"Telda. Your tourniquet?"

Telda

"NO! I'm not doing that. I'd rather take this son of a bitch out kamikaze style. Just go, Abe, just go!"

She increases the power of her plane. Abe pulls closer to her, slowing her down.

Abe (calmly)

"Stop. Stop. You're already smoking. You have to eject."

Telda (crying holding her legs)

"No! I'm not doing that."

The plane is beginning to dissemble.

Abe

"Telda, it's an order. You have less than two minutes to eject out of that plane. You need to get your tourney on your leg, then eject quickly. I am not going to live life without you. Nor am I going to live life watching you go away, especially if I can help!"

Telda

"Why Abe? Just go! Just go! I won't survive out there. My leg's gone Abe...No... Just go..."

Abe

"I'm not leaving your side. If you go, I go! I'm in this with you....forever... Take my order. Turn it, eject, and we will wrap as we parachute down. Otherwise, you're dead, and I may be dead too."

She gives him a frightened look. Tears flowing down her face. Everything rushes through her head; the fact that she may not survive the rest of this mission, even if she does survive. Flying is her life. She may not have her leg afterwards. She may not even live after she ejects because of her current lack of blood. If she ejects, her leg may rip off. She is a pretty girl but without a leg, she knows her life won't be the same.

Telda

"Why Abe? I won't be the same. None of this will matter. None. Just go."

Abe

"Look. We, me, and you have 90 seconds. Now it's 60. Your bird is going down soon. At least give me a chance at that pretty face, I won't allow for this to be the last memory of you, especially when you're in my hands."

The blood is starting to rush down Telda's leg, and her leg is beginning to swell up. She grabs her tourniquet, which is a tie tool that is used when a bad injury has occurred, and to save the leg. More importantly, it cuts the blood supply off. Reducing the risk of her dying from blood loss.

Telda clamps on the loose strip of the strap with her teeth, as she still has to control the aircraft. With gentle force she grabs her leg, painfully, moves it. She takes a peak and all she can see is the leg of her suit soaked in blood, and it's warm which means that it's not stopping. In minutes she can be dead. She looks up at Abe, and then begins to fix the device right below her knee. Scared and in pain she squeezes. She screams.

Her screams ignite the cockpit of fury and trust. She knows the tighter she pulls the more chance for survival but every turn she makes is a cut to the leg. As she finishes, she puts her hand on the window for support and Abe can see the blood that is coming off of her gloves, staining the window. Everybody at the command center is listening. Gil hears it also, since she is tapped into their communications

Abe

"Let's do this thing. Before we go. Set these coordinates in your cockpit."

He calls back to the command room

Abe

"Radar, were gonna need a medic. Just off the coast. We are both ejecting. Zelda and Squid."

"Telda How much fuel you got?"

Telda

"Five hundred pounds."

Abe

"Perfect. Put these in. You ready?"

She nods.

Abe

"270 for 25. Then turn 300. Airspeed 600."

She puts her numbers on the green and black ID system. Putting the plane in autopilot.

Telda (Crying)

"Done."

Abe

"Okay, you ready, soldier? Hold on for me. Your leg will make it, trust me."

Telda

"Yes..."

Abe

"Let's do it...."

Telda ejects first, then Abe. The planes begin to fly on autopilot, even with the canopy open. They take off in the direction which they overrode them to do. Abe parachutes. Once he gets closer to Telda; he wraps his legs around her. They look up and realize they have a helicopter on their way to them. Just like Chris and Channing.

Terry Love comes by and guns it down, with the guns on his jet. He circles over the two, keeping an eye on them until a medic helicopter can get to Telda.

Terry

"Lex, I'm staying afloat over here. I believe all other hostiles have been engaged and are down. But they keep coming out of nowhere, so I will just keep an eye out on these two."

Terry reminds himself that Tam is in the back of his jet. He doesn't even know how she looks. All he knows is that she is a woman, and she has been navigating him well.

Terry

"I mean we will. We as in, Tam and I."

Abe leans in towards Telda. He cuts his parachute so they don't get tangled. He clips his shoulder straps to hers, and reaches for her leg. He grabs her tourniquet, putting his fingers in her blood. Digging into the wounds, but patching it up with a piece of his sleeve that ripped off. Telda is crying. She is scared. She worries won't be able to land correctly once they reach the ground. Abe continues to tie her leg.

Telda

"Abe, why are you doing this?"

Abe

"I don't think I have to answer that."

She stares at the top of his head. She looks at him as he focuses on making sure her legs are secured in the tourniquet. If he didn't turn her tourniquet more, then she could have lost way too much blood and died. Even after she tied it.

Abe looks up at her

"You know I wasn't gonna let you die? Not if I could help it."

She looks at him, and holds on to him. He hands her two pain pills that are in the pocket of his arm. She chews them. Then she grabs on to him, leans into his chest, and slowly faints in his arms as she is fatigued.

Rory gets on the radio.

Rory

"Lex, all targets are down. It looks like our ground has regained some control of hostiles."

Jim picks up the phone and calls Charles. Charles picks up.

Charles

"Jim."

Jim

"All the targets are down. Abe is fine, although we lost . one airman and three additional aircraft."

Charles

"Forget the planes. Who died?"

Jim picks up a paper.

"Chris, a new guy we just brought in. He was from Olympia. He was shot down by the guys who were trying to get tanks into the A28 field. Not sure how it exactly happened yet."

Charles looks at Jacob. He hears everything; especially the fact that one Olympian born pilot was shot dead by his . own. Jacob feels the pain.

Charles

"Thanks. Can I come back?"

Jim

"Not yet. I say in 48 hours. We have plenty of weeding out to do. We don't know who is who. The city has a lot of cleaning up to do. Just stay there for the next few days so we can secure everything. I must get Emirate to support us until we can figure out a defense system now that our main base is destroyed."

Charles

"Forty eight hours, nothing more than that."

Charles hangs up the phone. He looks at Jacob and a few other folks from his administration who are in the room. Charles looks at them, and then looks back at Jacob. Mutely saying they need to leave. Jacob gives them all a nod, so he and Charles can have privacy. They all walk out. The door closes. Charles holds the phone that he was speaking to Jim on.

Charles

"That kid got killed by the country that he once served in. I know it's not your troops, and he moved, but most of those guys in the Ethon mess were former troops. To make matters worse, they are Olympian. Not good!"

Jacob sits in shame. Wishing the situation was different.

Charles

"And I am the one who has to get approved as a trusted nation?"

Jacob

"Charles. They killed my wife. My kids hate me and won't even come near me. The world has disliked me for years. Whom do I trust? Whom should I trust? I'm the damn President. Look at me. I'm scared to go home. Who has my back?"

Charles

"We got to clean this up. It's not suitable. Not a good look for you either."

Jacob

"Charles, I can't clean this one up. The people deserve to know the truth. My administration planned an invasion on your troops, tried to kill your son. Tried to bury the land you created. We deserve to take the loss on this one. I will help you rebuild it."

Charles

"I don't need any money Jake. That's the least of our-"

Jacob interrupts.

"I'm not talking about money, Charles."

The door knocks. Jacob's assistant walks in.

Barbara Whitaker

"Mr. President, the network is ready for you."

A makeup artist comes in to put makeup on the President.

Jacob leans back.

"No, no. No non-realistic stuff. They need to see me as I am. Why do I need makeup on? I have on sweats. They need to see this gash on my face that Gary left."

Jacob looks like his name can be Jake today. He is wearing grey sweats, which has OLYMPIA on it. He is in a hotel room in Europa. The television production personnel are almost done with adjusting the lighting. They set the microphone on him, and test it. A minute later. He is cued.

"5, 4, 3, 2, 1... Go."

Jacob

"Olympians. This has been one eventful day for me. As President, it is my duty to make sure that the status, the nature, and the respect of this country is within the values of the people and the world. Today, we have dealt with a truly horrific act by some of our own. I have been sorely disappointed. Not by only with what we have inflicted on, but my administration, some corporations, and even some individuals in how they conducted themselves, into trying to simply receive a profit through a takeover of a "revolutionized" country. They are crooks and will pay for their violations.

Charles Dalton did not kidnap me. In fact, we were BOTH held hostage, by some of my most trusted men. We were bound in cuffs for over 8 hours on a floor all while watching the initial bombings of Paragon, without the ability of changing anything. There have been families, friends, and goals that were hindered by this. But there is no exception to the rule with this issue. These non-patriots have all been handled by Paragon, and they are now under complete control by their own authority. I cannot speak on too many specifics now."

As Jacob speaks Olympians are all looking at what has occurred. Many are speechless, waiting to see that what they thought were to be true about a terrorist attack and the president being taken for hostage was all untrue, and setup by the executive board of the country.

Jacob continues,

"I do want you to be informed that all will be safe on your side, and keep the country of Paragon in your prayers. I'm in Europa now, and will be home soon. Olympia is here to unite and make the world a better place. I still believe we are the greatest country, even during this recessing moment. We will bounce back from this and be even stronger. Not just for us, but for all. Take care."

Olympians are waiting for more from Jacob. Lisa, Bin, and Eddie all watch in surprise and reflect on what they had been through. Anthony has witnessed some real warfare that he never would have come across in his life. Featuring another side to life, and why he should truly appreciate his career, even when he loses a game.

18

A new day

Telda is in the hospital, learning how to walk with her prosthetic leg. Abe is in the room reading through his flight manuals to make sure his skills stay sharp. The surgeon who performed on her talks to both of them, while looking at the limb.

Surgeon

"I promise. I have never seen a recovery this fast. Most of the time, the whole leg would have been amputated. Now, whatever solution you used, it almost virtually saved it. If her foot wasn't severed, then we could have probably saved the whole thing."

Abe

"I didn't use anything, Doctor."

The surgeon looks at him, confused.

Surgeon

You did something. Because landing in that water should have infected it at the least. Her leg is almost better then new.

The surgeon thinks for a second.

Surgeon

"Wait. You guys were in the Seren? By the A28 lab, correct?"

Abe shakes his head, yes.

Surgeon

"That explains it."

Abe and Telda let his comment go over their heads. The surgeon writes some notes down on a pad.

Abe

"So how much longer until she can receive the final prosthetic limb?"

Surgeon

"That's up to her. She is a diva, so I am sure she will want a good looking one. For now though, son, just help her get around on it. When she starts to jog with it, then you two can think about a better looking one."

He taps Abe's shoulder. Abe looks at Telda, his love. She sits down on Abe's lap, out of breath from walking with her fake limb. She looks at him. Her eyes are teary, she smiles, then puts her head on his shoulder and begins to cry. Abe feels it. She is happy to be alive, but unhappy with being handicapped.

Over in Olympia. Captain O'Donnell, Smitten, Jim, Channing, and President Grover go to Chris's house, to give his mother all of his final possessions.

Charles is back in Paragon. He touched down for the first time. He has been meeting with families, making sure they get what they need to get back on their feet. He has homes built in rapid time, and puts them into temporary housing. The streets are being cleaned. The bioluminescent plants are being replanted.

More men joined the military after witnessing what happened when the invasion occurred. Charles is bringing in architects and engineers whom he previously worked with to make sure the country gets back on its feet. Lisa, Eddie and Bin have taken the initiative in helping him get the country back. They all go to the SafeHaven where the military have been flying in and out of recently. They all finally get to meet Abe. Bin shakes his hand. Eddie checks him out, but leaves him be. Then Lisa walks up to him, and gives him a big hug, and doesn't let him go. Charles watches. He meets eyes with Abe, and for the first time ever the two men exchange awkward looks.

After the extensive hug with Lisa, Abe figures that he will show them a cool take-off. It makes Charles proud. Not only that his son is a fighter pilot, but the fact that he is defending his father's land because he wants to, and loves doing it. Lisa stands next to Charles and looks at Abe fly further away. She gives Abe the same look that Charles gave him as he took off. Eddie turns his head and looks at both of them, trying to read their minds.

As Abe reaches a couple thousand feet, he begins to cruise around the country. Looking at the landscapes of Paragon, how the people are back on the beach. Cleaning up it. Despite what has happened, he sees people running on the back roads. He flies over the spot where he saw Chris lying in the pool of the ocean with blood on his lips. He thinks about where he saved Telda, more so where she saved him.

It's his airspace.

He does three circles over the water where Chris died, paying his recurring respects. As he flies low, he sees a person jogging with a large Olympian flag on their back. He zooms in with his visor scope. He recognizes his look. It's Colin, taking a jog. Abe knows that he had something to do with Telda getting hit. He throttles the jet, puts his landing needles off to the left of Colin, now Abe is flying very close to the ground. Only a maneuver that Abe will do, he angles the plane just enough, and zooms past Colin.

Abe knew what he was doing. He could have killed him, but he knows that wouldn't have been right, because he is a defender. If he did strike Colin, it would have been a cheap shot. Colin looks down, and doesn't realize that he is cut until he sees a large amount of blood on his right leg. This is the same area where Telda lost her leg. Only difference is, Colin just received a cut; not a missing limb. Colin knows that it's Abe in that cockpit, and Abe can feel Colin's eyes on him. They are villainous, greedy, and corrupt. Which is nothing to the incorruptible man. Abe is the son of Charles, and he is the defender of Paragon, the land of opportunity, equality, and life.

He knows what Colin's true mission is. He knows that Colin didn't care for Telda. Abe just wanted to give him a friendly reminder of how much damage that a tip of an antenna can do, compared to a bomb. It was just a message. Offering Colin the chance to leave. Leave his father's project. To leave Abe's home.

HOME?

Thank You's / *Gratias*

Associate Editors and Plot Enhancement:

Shannon singletary

Evonne turner-Byfield

Final Copy Editor

Cathy morgan

Support / Brain Seeds / Venting

Kenneth wright

Jamie desta

Jay olagbegi

Ahmed madhi

Nikki rocksolid

Vanessa corder

Christina cooper

Jahmal walker

Marc taylor

Otis graves

Christi harbor

Danielle henderson

Erika radley

Nick du

Eric murphy

Nelson walker

Lou akande

Bianca harte

Fred peavy

Sean O'donnell

John stampley

Shaun harvell

Dayna M

Angela marie

Siobhan ford

Myron cousins

Cali rez

And all who I didn't mention

Made in the USA
Lexington, KY
26 September 2014